“So why *didn’t* you get married?”

Jacob raised one eyebrow and continued, “Maybe I’m not the only one concerned about losing someone special. Is that why you got engaged to a man you didn’t really love? No one could blame you after the way your mother and father died.”

Mariah had never slapped a man, b[illegible] was within inches now. Jacob didn’t [illegible]lace questioning her relationship [illegible]nging up her parents.

“Back off,” she ordere[illegible]g Jacob say another [illegible]

The repair of the [illegible] five minutes and she efficiently [illegible]ols in Shadow’s saddlebag.

“We’re done,” she said shortly.

“No ‘we’ about it. You wouldn’t let me help.”

“Don’t push me, Jacob,” she warned. “I may not have liked the city, but I took self-defense classes when I lived there and you wouldn’t enjoy being on the receiving end of what I learned.”

To her utter aggravation, he just laughed.

Dear Reader,

A friend used to speak longingly of the Amish lifestyle, believing it was less complicated and stressful than our fast-paced world. She would often say, "Maybe I'll become Amish someday." I'd smile and think of her sporty red car, passion for movies and lattes, and the ultra modern home she shared with her husband.

Still, the happiest summer of my life was spent in the mountains living in a tent cabin and cooking on a wood stove. I quickly discovered the satisfaction of chopping firewood, living close to nature and taking pleasure in simple entertainments. Yet the adjustments I went through are nothing compared to what I ask of my hero when I send him on a ranch vacation with his rebellious fourteen-year-old daughter.

Imagine a wealthy, city-loving businessman who finds himself sleeping in a tent, riding horses and dealing with a stubborn redhead who isn't the least bit impressed with his money. Mariah is nothing like the gentle wife Jacob lost over ten years before. The only reason he stays is his troubled daughter, whose outrageous behavior has finally gotten her expelled from school. Jacob will try anything to help Kittie and he sees the ranch as a last resort.

I hope you have fun reading about Jacob and Mariah and their families—it was loads of fun writing about them. I also enjoy hearing from readers! Please contact me c/o Harlequin Books, 225 Duncan Mill Road, Don Mills, ON M3B 3K9, Canada.

Wishing you all the best,

Julianna Morris

The Ranch Solution

Julianna Morris

Recycling programs for this product may not exist in your area.

ISBN-13: 978-0-373-71864-1

THE RANCH SOLUTION

This edition published by arrangement with Harlequin Books S.A.

For questions and comments about the quality of this book, please contact us at CustomerService@Harlequin.com.

Printed in U.S.A.

ABOUT THE AUTHOR

Julianna Morris has an offbeat sense of humor that frequently gets her in trouble. She has also been accused of being interested in everything. Her interests range from oceanography and photography to traveling, antiquing, painting, walking on the beach and reading (mysteries and most other fiction and nonfiction). Julianna loves cats of all shapes and sizes. Her family's feline companion is named Merlin, and like his namesake, Merlin is an alchemist—he can transform the house into a disaster in nothing flat. And since he shares the premises with a writer, it's interesting to note that he is particularly fond of knocking books onto the floor.

Books by Julianna Morris

HARLEQUIN SUPERROMANCE

1713—HONOR BOUND

SILHOUETTE ROMANCE

BABY TALK
FAMILY OF THREE
DADDY WOKE UP MARRIED
DR. DAD
THE MARRIAGE STAMPEDE
*CALLIE GET YOUR GROOM
*HANNAH GETS A HUSBAND
*JODIE'S MAIL-ORDER MAN
MEETING MEGAN AGAIN
TICK TOCK GOES THE BABY CLOCK
LAST CHANCE FOR BABY!
**A DATE WITH A BILLIONAIRE
**THE RIGHT TWIN FOR HIM
**THE BACHELOR BOSS
**JUST BETWEEN FRIENDS
**MEET ME UNDER THE MISTLETOE
THE HOMETOWN HERO RETURNS

*Bridal Fever!
**stories of the O'Rourke family

Other titles by this author available in ebook format.

To my talented sister, who is also my best friend.

And to the memory of my parents, two extraordinary people who taught their children to love books and the world around us.

PROLOGUE

"THANK YOU FOR COM—"

The door of the conference room opened, interrupting Jacob O'Donnell's opening remarks to his executive board. His eyes narrowed until he saw it was his assistant. The look on Gretchen's face said it all—his daughter, Kittie, was in trouble. *Again.*

"No injuries," Gretchen whispered in his ear. "Accidental fire. Girls' locker room. But both fire and police departments had to be called."

With effort Jacob kept his expression neutral. Fire. That was worse than anything Kittie had done before, though she'd done plenty. He looked at the men and women seated around the long table. "I apologize, but something urgent has come up that needs my attention."

Right.

Something urgent.

A fourteen-year-old daughter who was single-handedly trying to destroy the civilized world.

Jacob cleared his throat. "So I'll have Cara Michaels take over from here," he continued. "Thank you, Cara."

His vice president of Acquisitions nodded calmly. Of course she was calm—her kids were already grown. She had raised three and lived to tell about it—he didn't have a clue how she'd managed such a feat. As much as he loved his daughter, sometimes he hated being a parent. These days it seemed like a never-ending cycle of worry and self-doubt.

"What's the damage?" he automatically asked Gretchen as the door closed behind them.

His assistant patted his arm. "It isn't that bad—some paper, a wood bench and cabinet, cleanup and new paint. But the principal is hopping mad—I didn't realize his voice could get that high. Mr. Williams shrieked that setting fire to a building rates more than a suspension, no matter how liberal their rules might be. I'm afraid Kittie will be expelled this time—she seems to have exceeded even *his* tolerance."

"Maybe I can pay for a new swimming pool to go with the tennis courts I donated the last time. Money talks," Jacob said with a heavy dose of cynicism.

Gretchen shook her head. "I wouldn't try it. You didn't hear him. I'm lucky my eardrums didn't burst the way he was yelling."

"At least there are only a few weeks left in the school year." Jacob pulled his keys from his pocket.

"Er...why don't you take the limousine?" Gretchen suggested, probably because the last time Kittie was in danger of being expelled, he'd turned too sharply in the parking garage and creased the fender of his Mercedes.

"I'll be fine," he muttered. He didn't like using a chauffeur, preferring to be the one in control.

"Okay, but my car is on the same level as yours, and I'm really fond of that Saturn."

"It's safe. I only hit concrete dividers, not other vehicles," he said, teeth gritted. He didn't want to say something he shouldn't...which unfortunately he'd already done a few times over the past few months. Jacob hurried to the stairs, his head pounding. What a nightmare. Kittie had gone from being a normal high-school freshman at the beginning of the year to a teenager-from-hell at the end.

Was it his fault?

Was it drugs?

The possibility haunted him. Kittie's mother had become

dependent on medication by the time she died. A muscle ticked in Jacob's jaw as he remembered how the pills had made Anna so dazed she'd barely recognized anyone. They had hoped a donor heart would become available in her rare blood type, but she hadn't lived long enough for a transplant.

At Kittie's school, Jacob parked in front of the administration building and went to the principal's office; he'd gone there so often lately he could have made it blindfolded. Kittie sat in her usual chair, arms crossed over her abdomen, looking angry and defiant.

"I didn't try to burn down anything," she announced, her body language screaming that she didn't care whether he believed her or not.

"That's right, she just tried to hide the cigarette she was smoking without putting it out," said a grim Mr. Williams. He was a liberal administrator, but everyone had their limits.

"Smoking?" Jacob asked incredulously. "We've talked about this. I thought you had better sense."

"Like it matters." Kittie sank deeper in her chair. The private school she attended didn't have a uniform, and she'd pushed the envelope on their loose dress code in so many ways that the envelope looked more like a punching bag.

He hadn't put an end to the nonsense because the school psychologist had advised him to let Kittie "express" herself.

Well, hell.

The experts obviously didn't know what they were talking about. Not one of those experts had come up with a decent explanation of what was going on with his daughter, and they certainly hadn't done anything to help make things better.

Jacob listened to twenty minutes of Mr. Williams's ranting about out-of-control teens, silently accepted his daughter's expulsion and endured an "interview" with the police detective who'd investigated the fire. Officer Rizzoli didn't crack a smile the entire conversation, and Jacob's nerves were wound to the breaking point by the time he returned to his

Mercedes with Kittie in tow. She slumped into the passenger seat and scowled at her belly button.

"I'm getting my nose pierced," she declared.

"Over my dead body."

They argued all the way home.

When they finally arrived, Kittie disappeared upstairs into her bedroom; a few seconds later her music roared to life.

God in heaven.

Head pounding, Jacob looked wildly around the living room as if an answer could be found in the furniture. What was he going to do?

Smoking?

Fire in the girls' locker room?

What was next?

Specters of teen pregnancy, STDs and drug overdoses raced through his mind, turning his stomach to ice. He'd tried grounding Kittie, taking away her computer, TV and various other privileges.

There didn't appear to be anything physically wrong with her according to the doctors they'd seen. The counselor he'd consulted seemed baffled, and the only advice she'd had for him was to give it time. His own parents had told him to be patient, that all kids went through a rebellious stage, but he didn't think this was normal rebellion.

Besides, he'd passed the expiration date on his patience; he was now operating on raw nerve.

Jacob headed for his home office. Like the living room, the office provided broad windows, overlooking a panorama of Lake Union. During the day he could sit and watch the seaplanes arrive and depart and the sailboats skim across the water, while at night the surrounding hills glistened with city lights. The stunning view usually pleased him, a reminder that he had succeeded and could afford to give Kittie the best of everything.

Yeah, the best.

At this rate he was going to need the best lawyers to defend her.

Jacob considered pouring himself a drink. Instead, he sat down in front of the computer and typed in the website address his friend Gene had given him. He stared long and hard at the travel-agency home page before clicking the U-2 Ranch link. When Gene and his wife were having trouble with their son, they'd taken him for a ranch vacation in Montana. Since then they'd raved about the U-2, claiming the experience had done wonders for Wes…sort of a boot camp for kids with problems. They'd even taken it in stride that Wes had broken his arm on the trip.

Jacob pressed his thumbs to his aching temples. Was he desperate enough to try something that could put Kittie in harm's way? They'd always lived in the city, and the description of the ranch didn't thrill him—five miles from the nearest town, gravel road into the ranch, guests slept in tents, everyone worked, food served communally, no designer coffee…

He grimaced He was addicted to good coffee, but if it helped Kittie, he'd live without the stuff forever.

Then he read the next part.

No smoking.

No exceptions.

Before he could change his mind, he took out his credit card and started typing.

CHAPTER ONE

"WE'RE ALMOST THERE," Jacob said, glancing at Kittie, garbed entirely in black, including her nail polish and lipstick. He'd decided to deal with her abysmal wardrobe later; getting her out of Seattle had been a big enough struggle.

She blew a bubble with her gum and stared ahead silently.

"You'll be able to ride horses there. You used to enjoy riding. Remember?"

"Whatever."

He gave up and checked the GPS for how much farther they had to go. They'd flown to Billings, Montana, in an O'Donnell International company jet. Upon arrival Jacob had rented a car for the rest of the trip.

Along with losing her MP3 player, Kittie's punishment for smoking and accidentally setting fire to the girls' locker room was having to pay for the damages out of her allowance and composing a written apology to the school. An *acceptable* written apology, since Kittie could easily make an apology sound more like an insult.

Oh, yeah, and she was grounded for life, plus ten years. Jacob had told her if she shaped up during their trip, he might shave a few years from that part of the punishment.

Kittie hadn't even blinked.

Tough love sounded clichéd, but he was desperate. He'd try anything.

Guided by the GPS, Jacob turned onto the U-2 Ranch road and after a mile came over a hill. Laid out in a shallow valley were the ranch buildings and, on the opposite slope, an array of white canvas tents. He winced—he hadn't slept outdoors since he was a boy. A ranch vacation was a far cry from the Caribbean resort where he'd taken Kittie for Easter a year ago.

Jacob pulled to a stop in the parking area. There was plenty of space, likely because the school year hadn't ended for kids who were still attending classes instead of being expelled.

"Hello, there," called a voice as Jacob opened the trunk of their rental. The speaker was a white-haired man who looked older than the hills. But the weathered cowboy had steel in his face; he might be a worthy match for a surly teenager. "I'm Burt Parsons. Welcome to the U-2 Ranch. You must be the O'Donnells."

"Duh," Kittie said sarcastically.

Burt didn't seem surprised. "And you have to be Kittie."

Without a word, she spit her gum to the grass.

Before Jacob could say something about it, Burt gave her a stern look. "We don't allow littering here," he informed her. "Put it in the trash."

Kittie didn't move.

"Pick it up, young lady, unless you'd rather shovel horse manure from the barn."

"Dad."

"Better get the shovel, Burt," Jacob suggested, taking their new sleeping bags from the trunk. It was hard letting someone else discipline Kittie. He had a hunch that tough love might be rougher on him than on his daughter.

Glaring at them both, she picked up the wad of gum and threw it in a barrel marked for trash.

"You folks are later arriving than we expected," Burt said, stepping forward to help with the luggage. He read the baggage tag on Kittie's neon-pink duffel, pushed it into her arms and went ahead of them with an easy stride, carrying the sleeping bags. Jacob followed with his own suitcase.

Kittie trudged next to him with an aggrieved mutter, but as

they passed the largest barn, a young man came out and she stopped dead in her tracks. "Uh, hi," she said, without even a touch of sarcasm or disdain—like his old Kittie.

Jacob stiffened. At first sight the guy appeared to be in his early twenties, but on closer inspection he was clearly younger. Great. That was all his daughter needed—a crush on another messed-up teenager.

The boy checked Kittie up and down. "You're that city kid we've been expecting."

"I'm not a kid, but I am from Seattle. My name is Kittie O'Donnell…uh, that is, I prefer Caitlin. Who are you?" She smiled shyly.

"Reid Weston. You'll scare the horses in that getup," he said.

He walked away and Jacob realized Reid Weston wasn't a troubled teen—he was a cocky, underage cowboy. Kittie's devastated expression showed he'd flattened her ego with a single comment. And what was that bit about Kittie wanting to be called Caitlin? It was the first he'd heard of it.

"Reid and his family own the ranch," Burt explained, as if nothing had happened. "You'll be seeing a lot of them." He motioned them toward the hillside studded with tents.

The tents were utilitarian at best, with mattresses laid out on each side of a canvas partition, along with lanterns, a small bedside table and sturdy army-green footlockers.

"We don't recommend keeping food in here." Burt tossed a sleeping bag onto the mattresses. "We have the usual critters who'll want to share it, but if you do have any snacks, be sure to put them in your locker and fasten it tight. Better yet, store all food in your car."

"Hear that, Kittie?" Jacob asked his daughter. Kittie had a thing for red licorice. He'd bet a thousand bucks she'd filled her duffel bag with the revolting stuff.

She just stuck out her chin.

"The lanterns are rechargeable," Burt went on. "Bring

them to the mess tent in the morning if they need a charge, otherwise you'll be taking care of business in the dark. No candles—it isn't safe. Flashlights are okay if you've got 'em. The bathrooms and laundry and other facilities are in the buildings to the left, and the mess tent is over there." He pointed to a large tent with smoke rising behind it. "Folks are mostly gathered for supper already—we start serving in thirty minutes."

"Thanks, we'll be there."

"No hurry," Burt said. "Take your time and get comfortable. We don't stand on formality." With a short nod, he ambled toward the ranch house.

Jacob shot a look at Kittie. She'd assumed her defiant attitude, apparently having recovered from Reid Weston's snubbing remark.

"I'm not shoveling any horse poop," she announced and disappeared into her side of the tent.

MARIAH WESTON STALKED into the ranch house and slammed the door. She leaned against it and took several deep breaths.

"Problems, dear?" asked her grandmother.

"Nothing a two-by-four making contact with a certain cowboy's privates wouldn't fix. Hurt a guy where he lives and maybe you'll get his attention."

Dr. Elizabeth Grant Weston smiled resignedly. "Lincoln must have broken another heart."

"Yes. We have yet another departing guest who hoped Lincoln had fallen in love with her and wanted to get married. For crying out loud, Linc keeps a supply of condoms in his shirt pocket! It's pretty obvious what his intentions are. Did she really think he was going to change his ways and decide that wearing a wedding ring is better than being a carefree bachelor?"

"It's been known to happen."

"Cowboys don't change—they just get older and stop having luck with the opposite sex."

"Goodness, you're in a mood today."

"Can you blame me? I found Ms. Bingham smoking in one of the barns, so upset she almost set fire to the place."

Elizabeth frowned. "Oh, dear. We don't allow smoking. I wish we could extend the ban to chewing tobacco, but the ranch hands practically mutinied on the no-smoking rule."

"I reminded her about the rules when I grabbed the cigarette and doused the smoldering hay. She apologized and the whole story spilled out in a hysterical swoop. Lucky me. I guess she just needed to tell someone. Linc always breaks things off at the last minute, but the women usually don't take it this hard. Why are people so blind?"

"Patience, dear," her grandmother urged.

Mariah rubbed her aching temples.

Patience wasn't one of her strongest qualities. She did well with animals, not so great with people. Animals were straightforward; their emotions weren't illogical. She felt sorry for Diane Bingham, but she honestly wondered how the woman could have imagined things working out with a cowboy. Diane was a born-and-bred city dweller with a taste for fast cars, sushi bars and nightclubs. She'd come to Montana on a whim and nearly gone crazy with the quiet before getting hot and heavy with Linc.

Linc had grown up on a horse, had never lived in a town with more than five hundred residents, probably thought sushi had something to do with sex and drove a decrepit truck from the 1970s that couldn't reach fifty on a paved road.

The difference between ranchers and cowhands and most people was just too big. You might have a casual vacation affair, but you *never* expected it to become permanent. Mariah had learned that when she was fifteen and discovered that summer promises were too easily shattered...along with hearts.

Elizabeth patted her arm. “I’ll have your grandfather speak with Linc.”

“No, it’s okay, Ms. Bingham admitted Linc didn’t make any promises. But from now on he’s only working with family groups. We’ll keep him so busy that his sorry ass is too tired to do more than crawl into bed.”

“That’s usually where the trouble starts,” Elizabeth said drily.

“Don’t remind me. And they say country dwellers are naive. Is Reid in the office?”

“I think so. I just got home myself.”

Mariah headed to the back of the house, weary though it was only the beginning of the season and she ought to be brimming with energy. Ranching wasn’t easy. There were droughts, floods, lightning storms, disease, harsh winters, ornery cattle, unstable beef prices and a wealth of other problems to juggle. Yet those problems seemed minor compared to managing a bunch of greenhorn visitors and cowboy wranglers.

“Hey, Reid,” she said, stepping into the office. Their parents had converted a storage room into work space when they’d started the ranch vacation business. Originally they’d needed only a phone, a desk and a file cabinet, but the business had changed over the years, as had technology. Now the office was cramped with the newest equipment.

“Hey,” her brother said absently. He was bent over a book, reading intently.

“Studying?”

“Not exactly.” He looked up and pushed back from the old desk. “The travel agency phoned while you were out. Amy is waiting for the computer repair service to arrive, so I cross-checked the reservations that came in this week to be sure they were confirmed.”

“I appreciate your doing that, but I could have taken care

of it later and let her know," Mariah murmured. "Amy works evenings."

Amy Lindstrom was a neighbor and ran her agency from home, largely through the internet. Initially it had stung Mariah to be charged for a job she could have kept handling herself, but Amy had significantly increased the U-2's bookings.

"Yeah, well, you can't do it all. By the way, I saw that new kid you said was coming," Reid said. "She's a real piece of work, and her dad is wearing a fancy suit and tie. I'll bet his clothes cost more than a prize horse and wouldn't last an hour riding fence lines."

"I talked to Burt and he mentioned you'd met the O'Donnells. Just do your best and remember they won't be here forever," Mariah said, the same way she'd told him for years. The thing was, Reid was sixteen going on forty. He didn't appreciate city people wanting a taste of Western living, except those city people were the difference between the U-2 turning a profit or going deeper into debt each year.

The U-2 was a working ranch, owned and operated by the Weston family for six generations. Paying guests worked along with everyone else—not as hard as a ranch hand, and always under the care of a wrangler, but they worked. It was all about the romance of the West and being part of it for a while.

"Sis, they're from *Seattle*." Reid knotted his fists.

Mariah's heart ached, recalling the boy who'd stood by his parents' graves, furious with everyone and everything for taking away his mom and dad. They went through this each summer, the first time guests arrived from Washington State. Their mother and father had died because a vacationing Seattle investment banker was driving too fast and lost control of his car. His blood alcohol level was primarily responsible for the accident, but Reid also blamed the entire state.

"Okay, they're from Seattle," she said, carefully avoiding any mention of their parents. “Don't go near them if it's easier.”

He rolled his eyes. “That kid will want to hang around. I can tell.”

That “kid” was only two years younger than him, but Mariah understood why Reid felt older. Life and death were a daily part of their world.

It *made* you older.

“I've assigned wranglers to the O'Donnells,” she assured him. “You won't have to spend time with them. Anyhow, you have classes and finals coming up. You need the grades to get into a good school, and the ones with pre-vet programs are terribly competitive.”

“I told you, I don't want to go to college and I don't want to be a vet.”

“Even if that's true right now, you might change your mind. We have to talk—”

“There's nothing to talk about.” Reid cut her off. “Don't worry, sis, I'll get the grades.” He went out the door with a mulish expression.

As brother and sister, they were close in many ways, yet a wall rose between them when certain subjects were raised… like the future.

Stomach tight, Mariah went to the desk and saw Reid had been reading one of her books on equine diseases—she would never be a vet now, but that didn't prevent her from staying current on veterinary medicine. As for Reid, though he claimed he wasn't interested in going to veterinary school, she doubted it. He was bright, talented and set to graduate high school a year early the way she had done…and he spent all of his free minutes studying animal care.

Worry and a feeling of helplessness nagged at her. Reid shouldn't have such tough decisions to make at his age, but there didn't seem to be anything she could do to fix it. Maybe if their father hadn't given up after the accident, if he'd tried to survive his own injuries, things might be…

No.

Mariah shook her head guiltily.

She still struggled with the memory of her big, strong dad turning his face to the hospital wall when he learned that his wife of twenty-four years had died instantly in the collision, the light in his eyes vanishing until he was almost unrecognizable. The doctors had thought he would pull through, yet a day later he was gone, too, and she'd been so angry with him for wanting to die more than he wanted to live for the rest of his family. For her and Reid.

Nobody discussed it; after the funeral, Granddad had said that Reid didn't need to hear loose chatter. He was suffering enough. That was fine with her—admitting how she felt was the last thing she'd wanted.

Sighing, Mariah walked down to the mess tent. It didn't make sense to be angry with someone who was dead, and it wasn't as if Sam Weston had committed suicide. He'd just… given up.

"Good afternoon, everyone," she called, forcing a smile.

The cooks waved. The guests, in varying degrees of fatigue from working on the range, waved, as well.

"Oh, my God," said the new bride of one of their annual visitors. She sat, wincing as she made contact with the bench. "My fanny hasn't ever hurt this much. Who'd have known that riding a horse would be so painful?"

Mariah nodded with perfunctory sympathy—it was a complaint she'd heard dozens of times over the summers. "You'll get used to it. We have a dispensary if you want aspirin or liniment."

"It isn't that bad, but I can't believe this is my honeymoon. Whatever happened to rose petals, silk sheets and chocolate-dipped strawberries?"

"If it helps, Chad says you're being a real sport about the whole thing."

The other woman grinned; she was as open and uncomplicated as her groom. "Actually, I'm having a ball. We'll be back every year, but I won't object to an occasional weekend in the Bahamas."

Mariah tried not to laugh…though groaning was a distinct possibility, as well. She'd already moved the newlyweds due to the noise they were making at night. It was fortunate the U-2 didn't have more children visiting at the moment, or some parents would be explaining things they weren't quite prepared to explain.

"Whoa, there's something you don't see every day," Susan said, staring at the rear of the tent.

Mariah turned and saw a tall, well-built man standing next to a sullen teenager. The girl's hair looked as if it had been trimmed by a weed whacker and it was a peculiar shade of streaky black, ending in purple tips. Apparently she was going through a Goth phase because she also wore black from head to toe, including her lipstick. Her T-shirt was ablaze with silver studs in the shape of a skull and raggedly cut to display her midriff…which seemed to have a spiderweb tattooed over it.

A tattoo?

Distaste filled Mariah, but it wasn't for the teenager—it was for the father who'd allowed his daughter to do something so permanent to her body when she was still a child. Echoes of her grandmother's urging to be patient rang in her ears and Mariah squared her shoulders. Fine, she shouldn't make snap judgments. She wasn't doing a stellar job of parenting Reid, either.

Mariah approached the mismatched pair. The man was in his mid-to-late thirties and attractive in an uptight sort of way, with brown hair and eyes. He was intense, focused and had a rock-square jaw. As for the girl, she might be pretty beneath her clothes and I-don't-give-a-damn-what-you-think air. It was hard to be sure. Together they were the most unlikely twosome she'd ever seen going on a ranch vacation.

"Hi, you must be Jacob and Kittie, but Burt Parsons tells me you want to be called Caitlin," she said to the teenager, trying to ignore her bizarre appearance. "I'm Mariah Weston. Welcome to the U-2 Ranch. I hear you've met my brother, Reid."

"Yeah. He says I'll scare the horses," Caitlin said resentfully.

Reid could be right, only it wasn't diplomatic to agree. Mariah sat on the edge of the table. "He helped birth a lot of those horses, so he's very protective. A horse doesn't understand why someone looks or smells different than they're used to, and he worries how new people will affect them."

"Oh." Something flickered in Caitlin's eyes, a blend of powerful emotions that seemed to go beyond normal teen angst. "Birth them…you mean, like, clean the babies up?"

"We do whatever they need. If we're lucky, we mostly get to just watch. It's incredible seeing a horse being born."

Caitlin shifted her feet.

"I can loan you some outfits if you don't have any ranch clothes," Mariah offered. "Things that might be better for working with animals. We keep extras on hand in case they're needed by our guests."

"I don't… Whatever." Caitlin spun and marched from the tent as if the short conversation had exhausted her supply of civility.

Mariah stood, unsure of what to expect from Jacob O'Donnell, though his corporate attire and unbending stance weren't the best signs. Up close she saw lines around his mouth from stress or frequent smiling or both. Right now he wasn't smiling.

"As I was saying, welcome to the ranch," she repeated.

"You may want to borrow suitable clothes yourself to use while you're—"

"I know Kittie can be trying, but your brother could have been friendlier to her," he interrupted. "We're paying good money to be here."

Mariah's temper, frayed by dealing with a distraught guest and a randy ranch hand, threatened to flare again. "My brother feels responsible for the horses—both for their well-being and for our guests' safety. He gave his honest opinion. I'm sorry it upset Caitlin." Reid took on too much responsibility for a boy of sixteen, but it was one of the realities of growing up on a ranch. She wouldn't add to it by asking him to pamper their guests as if they were staying at a fancy resort.

"Your parents should speak to him."

"I'm Reid's legal guardian."

Jacob O'Donnell regarded her narrowly, but she couldn't read anything in his remote gaze. "You're what, twenty at the most? You can't be old enough to take charge of a teenager."

Mariah shrugged. "I'm twenty-seven and I've been his guardian for four years."

"I see. I suppose you have a degree in child psychology to run this kind of place?"

"What kind of place?"

"A place for teenagers with…issues. Like my daughter." The words seemed forced from Jacob O'Donnell's chest. His pride was clearly on the line.

Through the entrance Mariah could see Kittie sitting on a small knob of ground, curled in a defensive posture. "We should talk privately, Mr. O'Donnell."

He followed her with a frown. Mariah headed away from the mess tent and out of sight of Kittie before stopping.

"I think we have a misunderstanding," she said. "This is a working ranch. Guests can remain in their tents if that's what they choose to do, but we don't have activity directors, swimming pools, tennis courts or other entertainments to keep them occupied—basically, none of the luxuries or frills that *some* folks are used to having. Our visitors come to the U-2 to experience ranching. Plain and simple."

"I know it's a working ranch."

"You also seem to think we're a facility for troubled children. We're not, so if you require that, or feel we should put everything aside to wait on you the way they do at an exclusive spa, I'm afraid you'll be disappointed."

A muscle twitched in Jacob's cheek. "I have friends who said it helped bringing their son here."

Mariah hesitated.

Granddad often told her she'd inherited more than her temper and red hair from an Irish ancestress; he claimed she'd gotten Great-Great-Grandmother Eileen's fey instincts, as well. And her instincts were telling her to get rid of Jacob O'Donnell, except she couldn't evict every obnoxious guest—especially guests who'd paid in advance for a six-week stay at the ranch.

"I'm glad your friends had a good visit to the U-2," she said finally. "But if you want things to change for Caitlin, you need to do something about it yourself."

"What is that supposed to mean? I've been going crazy for months trying to do something...*anything* that might work. That's why I'm here. Believe me, a site with such primitive accommodations would be my last choice for a vacation."

Primitive?

Mariah's back went rigid.

He made it sound as if they were making guests dig their own privy holes and bathe in the creek. It had cost a fortune to have commercial restroom and shower facilities built at the ranch—she knew exactly how much, because she'd signed the checks.

"It's too bad the accommodations don't meet with your satisfaction, Mr. O'Donnell. However, they are thoroughly outlined on our website, so they shouldn't have been a surprise," she said coolly. "As for what I mean, you want Caitlin's problems to somehow get resolved at our 'primitive' ranch, and yet you're dressed as if you've just come from a board meeting."

"I *did* come from a board meeting. We left for the airport immediately after it ended."

"I see. That tells me a lot."

She stepped backward as she saw Reid striding toward them, probably guessing this wasn't a normal discussion between her and a guest. Her brother tried to protect her, but she didn't need help. She'd learned to protect herself from pushy, overbearing guys a long time ago. She liked men who didn't think the universe revolved around them. But it was a rare trait—one that Jacob O'Donnell obviously didn't possess.

"I had to make arrangements to cover my business interests while I was gone, but my daughter comes first," Jacob said in a stuffy tone.

"Then act like it. She won't join in if you aren't doing it yourself. This ranch isn't a corporate boardroom. That ten-thousand-dollar watch won't impress a herd of cows, and your custom-made suit isn't the least bit appropriate for the physical work we do here."

"I'm aware of that."

Mariah belatedly reminded herself that working with the U-2's guests was her job. It didn't matter if she disliked them or thought they were pompous jackasses. On the other hand, she had no intention of playing babysitter for a spoiled teenager *or* of letting one of the U-2's wranglers play babysitter. She had enough headaches.

"Well?" he prodded.

"In that case, the sooner you start participating, the better it will be for Caitlin. As I said, we have Levi's and work shirts that you can both borrow. That would be a big move forward."

"We brought our own gear, and if we need more, I'll go into town and buy it. We certainly don't need anyone's loaners." He strode off—bristling with snobbish arrogance—and Mariah had a childish wish he'd slip on a pile of fresh horse manure. *That* would trim him down a few notches.

Reid said something as they crossed paths, but O'Donnell didn't pay attention.

Mariah wrinkled her nose.

City people bothered Reid; men with control issues like Jacob O'Donnell bothered her. The overt wealth, the expectation that everyone should jump at their bidding, the conviction that their money was worth more than anyone else's…she'd met too many men like that when she was waiting tables at an upscale Los Angeles restaurant to earn money for school. She'd quickly found it wasn't wise to accept gifts or excessively large tips from her male customers because of what they thought it would buy them later.

"Why aren't you eating supper?" she said as her brother walked up to her. "Grams isn't cooking because she needed to work at the clinic today."

"I'll eat after a while. What's up with that O'Donnell guy? He's got an attitude you can see from a mile away. I bet he's going to be a pain in the ass." Reid glared in the direction Jacob O'Donnell had gone, though he was no longer in sight.

"He's a worried father. Cut him some slack," she said. It was good advice for her as well, but there was something unusually annoying about Jacob O'Donnell that made it hard to follow.

"I'd be worried, too, if she was my kid."

"Well, she's not. Caitlin is probably just a little mixed-up."

"How mixed-up?"

"I don't know."

Mariah looked toward the U-2 parking area where the O'Donnells' rented Mercedes sat in conspicuous glory, sadly out of place among the usual SUVs and trucks and economy cars. How did they rent a Mercedes in Montana? And why would they rent one to drive to a ranch over dirt and gravel roads? Especially a black Mercedes that showed every speck of dirt.

Burt Parsons had told her about the dust-covered luxury car with a laconic grin. He was the ranch's best wrangler—shrewd, unflappable and great with kids. She'd assigned him to the O'Donnells when she'd realized that Caitlin, age fourteen according to their online registration form, ought to be attending classes. It suggested she'd been suspended or expelled.

Apparently Mariah had guessed right.

Judging from the tightly wound state of her father's nerves, Mariah suspected that Caitlin wouldn't be welcome at her school for a very long time.

CHAPTER TWO

DAMNED OBNOXIOUS...*opinionated...*

Muttering under his breath, Jacob tossed his suitcase onto the mattress in his tent and hunted for a pair of jeans. He hated admitting it, but the Weston woman was right—at the very least he ought to have changed before dinner.

Woman?

Jacob frowned as he pulled his shirt off. Mariah Weston looked younger than she claimed to be, though it was unlikely she'd distorted *that* fact. She didn't seem the type of person he would have expected to encounter running a ranch—more like a Hollywood actress playing a part with her leggy appeal and long red hair. Maybe she was a figurehead, the public image of the business. On the other hand, looks could be deceiving; he still thought that somewhere beneath Kittie's dismal clothes, black lipstick and in-your-face attitude was the great kid she'd always been.

Jacob massaged the back of his neck. Worry and the rush of making arrangements for his unplanned absence from the office had taken their toll. He'd hardly slept since Kittie's latest escapade; he was now operating on autopilot. Even his parents didn't understand. He had been forced to tell them why he was going to be gone for an extended period and could hear his mother saying with indulgent humor, *She's her father's daughter, but you got into plenty of scrapes as a boy and turned out fine.*

Granted, he'd soft-pedaled the incident, but starting a fire was serious, accidental or not. And it wasn't just the smoking; it was all the trouble combined over the past few months. One unholy mess after another.

Naturally the discussion had given his mother an opening, for the hundredth time, to recommend that he find a new mother for Kittie. She couldn't accept that he was never getting married again and certainly not having any more children. Who in their right mind would leap into the prospect of raising another teenager after they'd done it once already? And he had...well, *other* reasons. Reasons he didn't like thinking about.

A chill went through Jacob. It was too hard loving someone, only to lose them. He'd buried his wife and nearly buried his daughter as a toddler due to health problems; he wasn't taking a chance of going through it again. There might be things he couldn't control in his life, but avoiding that particular pain was one that he could.

Yanking his tie loose, Jacob dropped it into the suitcase. The conservative blue silk was another accusation of parental failure. He should have worn the tie that Kittie had given to him for his last birthday, yet he couldn't bring himself to do it—Tweety Bird and Sylvester weren't appropriate corporate attire. It was bad enough that he'd had to call an emergency board meeting on a Sunday morning.

Not that a suit was appropriate ranch attire, either.

The old cowboy had given him fair warning. Burt's urging to "get comfortable" must have meant "change your clothes," but Jacob hadn't been thinking clearly. It wasn't like him. Usually he was methodical, working things out, making sure he made the best decisions and kept everything carefully managed.

Jacob snorted, his irritation rising again.

Mariah Weston had implied he was spoiled when she suggested he wanted to be waited on hand and foot, but there was nothing wrong with enjoying comfort. And he didn't expect to be pampered—he just wanted to receive a reasonable amount of service for the money he was paying.

He rotated his shoulders and leaned on the rolled sleeping bag. Damn, he was tired. That must be why Mariah Weston's criticism had gotten to him. He loved Kittie and he'd busted his ass since Anna's death to make sure their daughter would be safe and secure. Why shouldn't they appreciate and enjoy the benefits?

Stop it, he ordered silently, kneading his throbbing temples.

Anna had been gone for over ten years, yet sometimes he missed her so much it was as if he had an aching, frozen hole in his chest. He knew that things would be different if she was still here. Anna wouldn't have screwed up with Kittie, and they wouldn't have needed to come to Montana, hoping for a miracle.

He'd jumped into the ranch vacation solution out of desperation, not really believing it would work. Yet at the same time, he'd clung to a kernel of hope that the U-2 would do some good. Now he was back to square one and unsure of what to do, though maybe getting Kittie out of her usual environment for several weeks would accomplish something.

In the distance Jacob heard the neighing of horses and other, more unfamiliar sounds. From the opposite direction came the rattle of plates, along with the chatter and laughter of people enjoying themselves. With any luck Kittie's hunger would outweigh her antisocial mood—she was angry with him, not anyone else.

Hell, he hated feeling so out of control.

He ought to have realized the ranch's website didn't say they worked with at-risk children—it was his friend who'd called it a troubled kid's boot camp.

At risk.

That was how Kittie's principal had described her while ranting about the fire. Jacob donated to organizations with programs for at-risk kids, and now his daughter had the same label slapped on her forehead.

Jacob put his arm behind his head and gazed at the sturdy frame of the canvas tent, trying to think of anything but Kittie and how much he wished Anna was still alive. It astonished him that the ranch got so many guests. There were two or three dozen tents on the hill—if they filled to capacity very often, they must make a decent chunk of change each year. Of course, the U-2 had to make their profits during the summer season, since no one would stay out here in the winter.

Someone walked by outside and coughed, and Jacob made a face.

That was another problem with this place…no privacy. If he and Kittie got into one of their frequent shouting matches, everyone on the ranch would know their business.

KITTIE SAT ON a small hump of ground and sniffed.

She wasn't crying—she was probably allergic to Montana. That was why her eyes were burning.

Her dad didn't get it. Nobody did. And it didn't matter anyway, because soon she'd be dead and buried and everybody would forget her.

The same as her mom.

Sniffing again, she picked at her black nail polish. It was stupid anyway. It wasn't as if she had those fake nails that made your hands look cool. The school didn't allow them any longer, not after Bethany Wilcox had stabbed herself at basketball practice last year. Everybody was mad at Bethany for a while after that, but no one stayed mad at the really, *really* popular girls, no matter what they do.

Her dad marched to their tent and Reid's sister returned to the mess tent. Neither of them seemed very happy.

Kittie's stomach rumbled.

The food smelled good, but she couldn't go in there. She might see Reid and he didn't like her, no matter what Mariah said about him protecting the horses. Besides, she wasn't that odd to a horse, was she? Her friends thought she looked totally awesome—why wouldn't a horse agree? They weren't dumb.

Her dad hadn't come back by the time everyone was done eating; he must be really pissed. Well, she was pissed, too. Nobody had asked if *she* wanted to come a gazillion miles from home and what was left of her life. Her dad had said they were going and that was that. So what if she'd set fire to a trash can and it got out of control? Big deal. Not that much got burned, and she didn't mean to do it anyhow.

Someone began playing a harmonica and she heard some dorky singing—"Home on the Range" and junk. Kittie rested her chin on her knees. She didn't want to be a dork like everybody else, even if they were having a good time.

There was a noise and she saw an old man coming toward her.

"Hello, young lady. May I sit down?"

Kittie started to say "Whatever" as usual, then stopped. "Okay."

He sat and put a paper sack between them. She smelled chicken and other stuff. "I brought you supper in case you're hungry," he explained. He opened the sack and took out a foil-covered plate. "Simple outdoor cooking—that's what we specialize in at the U-2. It'll stick to your ribs."

For a second Kittie considered refusing, but her stomach rumbled again. She pulled the foil back on the plate—it was barbecued chicken and beans and coleslaw and corn bread. The corn bread was buttery and drizzled with honey. She ate until she was ready to burst and washed it down with a bottle of cold root beer, which normally she'd say was for babies, but somehow tasted awfully good with the chicken and beans. It was the best food ever.

Mariah came out of the mess tent and glanced in their direction. She was kind of pretty. Dad hadn't hit on her or anything, though he'd definitely checked her out…especially her chest.

Kittie wrinkled her nose.

Her dad acted as if she didn't know about sex, but she was fourteen, not four. She knew all about it. Not that boys would notice her unless she had real boobs.

As if.

"I also put a plate in for your father. I hope he has a taste for medium steak," said the old guy. He had deep creases in his skin and looked, like, *ancient.* "Would you do me a favor and take it to him?"

"Uh, sure."

"Much obliged." He took a piece of straw from his pocket and stuck it between his teeth. "My name is Benjamin Weston, by the way. And my granddaughter says you're Caitlin."

"Mariah is your granddaughter?"

"Yup."

Kittie wiggled her toes. "Um, how does this ranch thing work?"

"It isn't complicated. You'll work with a wrangler and mostly do what he does."

"So you can fix me," she said resentfully.

Benjamin raised an eyebrow. "Do you *need* fixing?"

"My dad thinks so."

"Fathers worry. That's their job. But we just want you to have fun finding out about ranching and what we do round here. That's *our* job."

"Oh," Kittie said, still vaguely suspicious.

The sun was getting low in the sky and she felt tired all at once. It was hard work pretending everything was okay when nothing was okay. Some things were so broken they could never be fixed.

"I gotta go." Kittie picked up the sack with the extra food in it. "Dad must be in our tent phoning Japan or something.

What should I do with that?" She pointed to her empty plate and pop bottle.

"I'll take care of it," he said. "You go ahead."

Kittie didn't know what to expect when she got to the tent, most likely her dad talking business on his cell phone. He worked an awful lot, but she'd bet he was still upset with her. Dreading another argument, she peeked around the partition.

He'd fallen asleep with his legs extended on the ground and his suitcase open on the bed. She tiptoed over, put the food down and tiptoed out. There wasn't any TV and he'd taken away her MP3 player, so she curled up on her mattress and chewed her fingernails as it got dark.

Benjamin and Mariah were nice, and if they weren't going to try to fix her, the ranch wouldn't be so bad.

For a while.

MARIAH ROSE BEFORE DAWN the next morning. A lifetime of getting up to do chores had made it impossible to sleep longer. Her city life at college hadn't changed her; it just made it obvious she didn't fit in there.

"Hi, Grams," she said, walking into the kitchen.

"Hi, dear. Are you in a better mood today?" Elizabeth asked as she mixed a pot on the stove.

"Working on it." Mariah pulled the newspaper away from her grandfather's face and kissed his forehead. "What's new, Granddad?"

He grinned his irrepressible grin and waved the paper. "What do you think of this? It came in yesterday's Pony Express delivery—last year's ball scores!"

"Imagine that."

The family had been getting the *New York Times* as long as the newspaper had been mailing out editions. It wasn't necessary with the internet available, but Granddad said there was no substitute for the smell of newsprint.

He folded the paper and put it on the sideboard. "By the

way, Luke phoned. If you have time, he'll come by later so you can go for a ride together."

Mariah smiled. "I didn't think I'd see him before the barn dance next Saturday. I'll call him. He can come with me when I go out to check on the greenhorns."

Luke Branson was the U-2's closest neighbor, but she'd hardly seen him for weeks, spring being one of the busiest seasons on their respective ranches. It would be better once they were able to get married. Not that they were formally engaged; it was more a mutual understanding for the future.

"When are you two going to set a date?" Grams asked. "I'd like to have great-grandchildren while I'm young enough to chase after them."

"One of these days. Luke understands why I want to wait."

Reid stumbled into the kitchen as Mariah was sipping tea and eating oatmeal. He served himself a bowl and stared at it bleakly. He showed an equal lack of interest in the eggs and whole-grain toast that Grams put on the table. Mariah knew from the light under his door last night that he'd been up late studying. He needed to get more sleep, but it was hypocritical to urge him to get good grades and then interfere with his studies.

"I saw you take food to Caitlin O'Donnell," she said to her grandfather.

"The purple streaks in her hair are a nice touch, but she's death on a stick gussied up in so much black. I'll have to teach her to have fun." Granddad rubbed his palms together and Mariah figured *he* was the one who would enjoy himself the most. Benjamin Weston was a kid at heart.

"You won't have a chance—you aren't the O'Donnells' wrangler," she said edgily. But it wasn't her grandfather who aggravated her; it was the thought of Jacob O'Donnell believing he could dump his daughter's problems on someone else. No one at the U-2 had time to babysit an unruly, privileged teen. "I don't want any of us to get involved. Her father didn't go into details, but apparently she has issues to resolve. We need to let him deal with them."

"Teaching her to have fun won't do any harm."

"For heaven's sake, Reid and Mariah have enough to handle without your interfering, Benjamin," Grams scolded, sitting down with the rest of them.

"Guess you'll have to keep me busy."

Mariah knew they'd clasped hands underneath the table. Above all, Granddad was a romantic. However hectic things might be, late every afternoon he and her grandmother strolled up the shallow valley, arm in arm, as if they were still a courting couple. That was how Mariah wanted things to be with Luke, a closeness that just kept growing.

Elizabeth poured milk into her tea. "What about Caitlin's mom? She should be here if her child is in trouble."

"She wasn't mentioned, but I feel sorry for anyone married to that guy," Mariah said. "I bet they're divorced."

"Mmm, not necessarily. He's quite attractive."

"And rich. Shame on you, Grams," Mariah teased. "What will Granddad think?"

"That I'm a normal, red-blooded woman who can appreciate a hunk from a purely aesthetic point of view."

Granddad chuckled. "And fortunately I'm so handsome I don't have to worry."

Mariah ate her last bite of oatmeal and dropped the spoon in the bowl. It was time to start the day, one she hoped would turn out better than the previous...especially when it came to Jacob O'Donnell. She'd made a resolution to treat him the same as any other guest, no matter how much he annoyed her. The trick would be keeping that resolution.

Reid headed to the barn while Mariah and her grandfather went down to the mess tent where the wranglers were gathered for coffee. She loved seeing Granddad transform from cheerful jokester to tough-but-fair ranch boss. He didn't know a ledger sheet from a gum wrapper, but he understood the practical end of ranching like nobody else. Ben Weston was close to a legend in Montana. She was trying to learn as much as possible from him before he retired.

"Hey, Mariah," whispered a voice as she entered the tent. It was Caitlin O'Donnell.

"Go on," she told her grandfather, who smiled at the teen.

Mariah looked back at Caitlin. "You're up early. Is something wrong?" The first slivers of sunlight were barely visible on the eastern horizon.

"Um, yeah." The agitated girl shifted from one foot to the other. "There's an animal in my dad's side of the tent. A really big animal. I think it's a wolf and he's *snoring.* He must have come in for the steak Mr. Weston gave me. I put the plate by the bed 'cause Dad was already asleep. Omigod, he's dead and it's my fault because I didn't wake him up."

Mariah hesitated.

She fully intended to make Jacob O'Donnell deal with his own daughter, only some things were ranch business, not personal. "I bet it's just Pip."

"Pip?" Caitlin trailed after her.

"Our dog—part Alaskan malamute and part mystery mutt. He's a mooch and a thief, with a snore that raises the rafters, but harmless aside from that."

They crept up to the tent.

"Pip, get out here," Mariah whispered.

Pip's distinctive snore continued unabated.

She gave Caitlin a sideways glance. "Go get some sausages from the cook in the black cowboy hat. Tell him they're for Pip."

The teen took off for the cooking area at a run. Mariah thought her reaction showed how much she loved her dad, though she'd probably deny it. In less than three minutes, Caitlin was back with a bowl of grilled sausages.

"Want a sausage, Pip?" Mariah asked softly.

Pip made a slurping sound. Within two seconds, he appeared through the tent flap, a happy, overgrown goof of a dog.

Caitlin released a tiny shriek and then clapped her palms to her mouth.

"Here you are, you old bandit," Mariah said, setting the bowl in front of the animal. Pip inhaled every scrap. She scratched behind his ears and his tail wagged, merrily unrepentant at being caught where he wasn't allowed. They'd tried to get him to understand that some people were nervous around dogs, but he couldn't be convinced.

Everybody was Pip's friend.

"He woke up because you asked if he wanted sausage?" Caitlin breathed, extending a cautious hand. Pip darted over, delighted to get attention from anyone willing to offer it—men, women, young, old, city dweller or country lover. He was a very democratic canine. "Why didn't you just say so?"

Mariah straightened. "If I tried getting him out any other way, it would wake everyone up."

"Is he the reason we shouldn't keep food in the tents?"

"One of them. We also get mice and ants and squirrels, among other beasties. Go on," she said, motioning toward the mess tent. "You can meet whoever's awake and let your dad get more sleep."

JACOB STARED at the dark roof of the tent as Kittie's and Mariah's voices faded. It was almost like hearing his daughter the way she used to be—normal and well-adjusted.

He stretched. After midnight he'd woken up and checked on Kittie, eaten the corn bread he'd found on a plate of food by the bed and crawled into his sleeping bag. Later the dog woke him up again, but he'd been too exhausted to care. The animal was wearing a collar—what harm could it do?

Reaching over, he switched on the battery lamp. The remains of a steak, beans and coleslaw were scattered across his silk shirt. It seemed symbolic of his relationship with Kittie—an utter disaster.

"Argh." He rubbed his face and got up. Perhaps a shower would clear his mind.

The heated restrooms were clean, serviceable and very basic. There were two buildings, one for men and the second for women. It was so early the place was empty. He felt more human after his shower, though until Kittie showed improvement, he wouldn't feel completely right. It was strange how he could love his child to death and still be driven insane by her.

An idle, guilty thought occurred to him.... Did they have military school for girls? Was that even an option?

Everyone was up and moving by the time he was dressed and back in the tent. The air was chilly and there were good-natured complaints about the cold, teasing accusations that somebody had forgotten to pay the power bill and mad dashes for the restrooms to avoid a wait in line.

"Kittie?" he called, pushing aside the tent flap.

She wasn't there.

Jacob spread his towel on the mattress to dry and headed to the mess tent. Inside there were cowboys drinking coffee, but no sign of Kittie.

"Anything I can do for you, Mr. O'Donnell?" asked Burt Parsons.

"Yes, I'm looking for my daughter."

"She's around. I'll be your wrangler during your stay at the ranch. And that young fellow—" he gestured at a man who was nearly as deeply wrinkled and weathered as Burt himself "—will be coming along today, as well. His name is Ray Cassidy. Nice boy, Ray. You'll like him." Burt sounded quite serious calling Ray a boy. Maybe when a person reached a certain age, everybody else was young by comparison.

"In that case, I want to be sure that my daughter's safety is your top priority," Jacob said.

"Not to worry. We haven't lost anyone yet." Burt ambled off to the serving table, cup in hand.

Resisting the urge to pound the importance of Kittie's safety into everyone, Jacob got his coffee and turned in time to see Mariah Weston arrive. He blew on the black brew as she spoke with the cowboys and cooks. Some of the men focused overly long on her curves, but they were discreet. Their interest was understandable. Her worn jeans were molded faithfully to her bottom and she wore a soft flannel shirt that did nothing to conceal the swell of her breasts.

A stab of awareness hit Jacob. *No.* Mariah was impossible, the complete opposite of the kind of woman who had always appealed to him.

In another few minutes Mariah flipped him a cool look. She wasn't drop-dead gorgeous, but striking with those high cheekbones and vibrant hair. Was she a natural redhead? Her blue eyes and creamy, lightly tanned skin suggested she wasn't, but he was no expert. He preferred blondes anyway.

Anna had been blonde.

Blonde. Beautiful. *Fragile.*

Sighing, Jacob swirled the contents of his enameled metal cup. It wasn't fair. Anna had wanted a baby so much, but she'd died less than three years after having Kittie, and a lot of that time she had been too weak to enjoy her daughter and be a mother.

He pressed his thumbs to his throbbing temples. He'd tried to do right by Kittie and by Anna's memory, and yet he'd failed. Kittie was in trouble and he didn't know what to do for her. If he could only put his finger on what was wrong.

"Good morning, Mr. O'Donnell," Mariah said, yanking him from his thoughts.

"Hello, Miss Weston."

Jacob noticed her gaze flick between his shirt and jeans—probably evaluating how suitable they were for the ranch—and almost asked if he passed muster. His irritation from the previous night returned, but he squashed it down. This was not a moment to be bothered with personality conflicts. By the same token, he wasn't going to apologize for coming from the city and not knowing how to chase cows.

He cleared his throat. "I need to discuss safety issues with you. I'm a businessman, so I know why you require a signed waiver in case of an accident. As a father, though, I can't help being concerned."

A range of emotions flitted across Mariah's face. "A ranch isn't the same as a city park, but I've assigned our most experienced wrangler to you and your daughter for the duration of your visit, and a second one while you're learning the ropes. Caitlin should be fine if she behaves herself. Now, your registration form says you've ridden before...?"

Jacob nodded. "We used to go horseback riding every week," he said absently, still chewing on Mariah's comment *if she behaves herself.* It gave him a nasty sensation in his gut—Kittie never behaved herself these days.

"I'm guessing you rode at a private stable with a riding track."

"It wasn't a ranch. We live in Seattle. But we haven't gone out for several years."

"That won't be a problem. The horses I've chosen for you are older, savvy and unflappable. You ought to be all right on them—they're practically catatonic," Mariah said, a bit too smoothly.

Jacob leaned forward. "I want my daughter to be safe, Miss Weston, not bored. What good will the ranch do her if she's bored?"

Mariah didn't blink. "The U-2 isn't boring, but we do insist that our guests don't stretch their limits too far."

Limits?

That was like waving a red flag at a bull, yet before he could react, she went on, "Vacations here are meant to be fun, not dangerous. My grandmother is a doctor and lives on the ranch. My aunt is also a doctor, and she lives in town behind her clinic. They've mostly treated our guests for aching bums, upset tummies, cuts, scrapes and sprained ankles. Since you haven't ridden recently, I suspect you'll be added to the aching-bum list."

Nonplussed, Jacob opened his mouth…and then closed it. He wasn't sure if he'd been insulted or patronized or if Mariah was simply doing her job by informing him of the ranch's medical support. Taking into account the few amenities the U-2 offered, having two doctors available was a surprise. He just prayed they wouldn't be needed. Kittie had her mother's rare blood type, so he always ensured adequate emergency services were present wherever they traveled. In preparation for this trip, his staff had learned there was a well-equipped clinic in the local town, but they hadn't said a doctor lived on the ranch.

"I'm not sure about that," he said. "Remember those friends I told you about? Their son came home with a cast on his arm. He broke it at the end of his visit here."

Mariah's expression chilled, no doubt from the censure in his tone. Fine, she should know he wasn't accepting her word without question.

"It happens occasionally—usually when people aren't practicing reasonable caution or when parents don't keep tabs on their children, assuming someone *else* will do it for them. That can happen anywhere, even in the city. Anyway," she murmured, swinging her legs over the bench to stand up, "your wranglers will catch up with you after breakfast. We work hard on the U-2, so you might want to make sure Caitlin has a healthy meal before starting out. Have a pleasant day, Mr. O'Donnell."

Jacob glared.

He wanted to call to Mariah's departing back that he worked hard in Seattle as well and *of course* he'd ensure that Kittie had a decent breakfast…except it was pointless. Especially about Kittie. He knew perfectly well he couldn't force his daughter to swallow a bite of food if she didn't want to. And considering the precarious state of their relationship, she'd probably refuse to eat if he said anything about it.

CHAPTER THREE

LATER THAT AFTERNOON Mariah and Luke Branson rode in the direction the wranglers had taken the O'Donnells. She routinely checked on visitors to be sure the greenhorns were doing okay, and today the newest greenhorns were Jacob and Caitlin…not that Jacob O'Donnell would enjoy being described that way.

Her horse tossed his head, playfully testing her control of the bit. Shadow loved to run, the wind racing by, his hooves thundering across the land.

"You're a live wire, aren't you, boy?"

He whinnied and leaped a step. His black coat gleamed warm in the sunlight and his ears were pricked forward, alert to every sound.

"I swear that animal is your best friend. I come in a poor second," Luke complained good-naturedly.

"He's my best *horse* friend," she agreed. She'd raised Shadow from the day he was born, right after her mom and dad's accident. It had helped get her through those bleak, grief-filled days. "But you're my best people friend."

"So is Reid still saying he doesn't want to go to college?" Luke asked with a pleased grin.

"More or less."

"Maybe he's worried how you'll pay for it."

"Could be. It's tight, but we're doing better. The debts are paid and I'm putting money aside. We should be able to swing the expense."

"That's great." His mount sidestepped skittishly. "Stop it, Ghost, or I'll turn you into dog food," he warned the gray-and-white piebald.

Ghost snorted in disbelief.

"I could talk to Reid," Luke offered. "He might open up for me—man-to-man, that sort of thing. Or at least as his future brother-in-law."

"Thanks, but I've pushed enough. He's got finals soon and they have to come first."

"It's your call. Are those the greenhorns you're checking on?" Luke gestured to the south, down a sloping hill.

"Looks like them."

Mariah bent over Shadow's neck and watched the group in the distance. Though she'd still dressed in black that morning, Caitlin had forgone the silver-studded shirt and purple accents in her hair. Other than those small changes, she'd remained pure defiance. The anxious daughter from the predawn morning was nowhere to be found a few hours later. She'd mouthed off to the cowhands, told the cooks they were serving heart attacks on a plate and shown up an hour late to the corral. She wouldn't say where she'd been, but Burt had calmly informed her that if it happened again she'd either sit her rear end in the tent for the day or spend it shoveling out the horse stalls.

Burt was always calm. It made him a terrific wrangler for kids. Things that might give anyone else a stroke made him yawn. She wished she could say the same thing about herself. Having Jacob imply she was lying about the injuries on the ranch had infuriated her. There *had* been a boy who'd broken his arm the prior year…but he'd fallen in Buckeye when his parents stopped to buy postcards on their way to the airport.

Luke controlled another sideways jump from his horse. "This O'Donnell fellow sounds like a real piece of work. I've never heard you gripe so much about a guest."

"He rubs me wrong."

"That's interesting."

She gave Luke a sharp glance. "There's nothing interesting about it. He's difficult, that's all. He actually advised me that my parents should speak to Reid about being friendlier to guests. What nerve. He thinks the world revolves around him and his money. It isn't that I don't care what his daughter is going through, but he has to deal with it, not just throw his checkbook at the problem. On top of that, he said our facilities are primitive. Since when are hot showers and commercial-grade restrooms primitive? If he wanted a resort on the Riviera, he should have *gone* to the Riviera."

"Okay, okay," Luke placated. "I'm not the enemy. I'm on your side. Let's go meet this difficult guest."

Mariah brushed Shadow's flanks with her heels and they cantered toward the others. As they got closer she could see that Jacob O'Donnell and the wranglers were working with a cow—its calf bawling in loud, unhappy tones—while a white-faced Caitlin remained in the saddle, some distance away. Mariah swung to the ground, her focus narrowing. The mother cow had a nasty cut running down her rear haunch. She was in pain, and that would make her more unpredictable than usual.

"It's not too bad, Baby Girl." Burt cursed amiably as he received a kick in the stomach. "But that gentle touch of yours will come in handy, Mariah."

Her mouth curved. At rare moments he still called her Baby Girl, the way he'd done when she was four years old and would sneak into the barn to be with a favorite horse.

"Hey, Burt," Luke greeted the cowhand.

"Howdy. Sorry to mess up your old-fashioned courtin' with old-fashioned work."

Luke chuckled, the cowhands sniggered, and Mariah could have belted all three of them. Luke wasn't courting her. They had an understanding; you didn't have to court somebody you were already going to marry.

The noise from the frightened calf was increasing the mother's agitation, so Mariah nudged it into her sight. "Don't fuss, silly, nobody is hurting your baby."

Both animals quieted.

"I have the first-aid kit," Jacob said when she looked up. He lifted the canvas pack that was a standard piece of equipment on the U-2.

Mariah took the kit. "Thank you. Stay with Caitlin, and we'll take it from here." They couldn't let guests be involved in this kind of situation. It was funny, though. Jacob didn't seem bothered that he might get injured himself at the ranch, just that his daughter be kept safe.

He stuck out his chin. "What about that guy?" he asked as Luke rolled up his sleeves.

"That 'guy' is our neighbor and an old hand at doctoring livestock. Luke Branson, meet Jacob O'Donnell."

The two men gave each other measuring looks, testosterone zinging through the air, and she sighed in disgust. Men were men, regardless of where they'd grown up. She'd have to intervene before they started chest bumping or doing something equally stupid to prove their masculinity.

She cleared her throat. "Mr. O'Donnell, your job here is to reassure your daughter."

"It's Jacob, and I'm going to help. Kittie is fine. I told her to stay well back on her horse."

"She's the color of old paste and needs her father more than we need you getting in our way. You're just delaying treatment for this cow by arguing with me."

"That's right," Luke added, and Mariah dug her elbow into his rib cage. Did he think she couldn't cope with Jacob O'Donnell on her own? She did not need his assistance; he would simply make it worse. He ought to have figured out by now that the Westons took care of their own troubles.

"Please...*Jacob,*" she said. "We have it under control."

He glared darkly and stomped away.

Caring for the cow's cut was messy and unpleasant, but Mariah finished as quickly as she could in order to make it easier on the animal and her calf. Burt untied the cow's legs and she lunged to her feet, restrained from further movement by the lasso around her neck. Range cattle were tough; they could be down to their last ounce of strength and still be dangerous. She wouldn't like being corralled, but the wound was septic and severe enough to warrant a few days back at the ranch.

Mariah dropped another rope over the calf's head. "Caitlin?" she said, motioning to her.

The teenager swallowed. "Is she going to be okay?"

"Yes, you found her before it got too bad. I want you to take the lead. The mother will follow her baby, so go nice and slow."

"I don't…um…don't know the way."

"You don't have to. You're riding Blue—he knows the ranch better than the rest of us. Say 'Home, Blue,' and he'll get us there." She gave Caitlin the end of the rope and focused on Luke. He'd hooked his thumbs in the pockets of his denims and was giving her a quizzical look. "*You* aren't coming with us," she informed him.

"You're mad at me."

"What gives you that idea?"

He laughed and kissed her lightly. "It was easy. I've known you since birth and recognize that expression in your eyes—it's the same one you had when you were seven and hit me with a horseshoe. Am I still invited to the dance on Saturday?"

"You're always invited. You know that."

As he rode off, Mariah climbed onto Shadow. She *was* annoyed, but it wouldn't last long. Luke was a handsome man, with the powerful build of someone who worked hard every day of his life, but she was surrounded by good-looking cowboys and sexy visitors like Jacob O'Donnell. It wasn't Luke's appearance that set him apart—it was the friendship that had survived childish squabbling, years away at school, and her need to concentrate on Reid and repay her school expenses before making a commitment. It didn't matter how much you loved someone. You had to believe in the same things to have a lasting relationship.

When they were ready to leave, Caitlin said "Home, Blue" in a high, squeaky voice. She held the rope in a white-knuckled grip as Blue ambled toward the ranch. He had more common sense than most people, which was why she'd chosen him for Caitlin.

The cow limped forward, attention fixed on her calf. The baby was young, born late in the spring drop, but it wouldn't be orphaned like the other calves they fostered annually.

Jacob jockeyed his horse next to Mariah. "She's scared," he muttered.

"Responsibility is scary, but that isn't a reason not to take any."

"I didn't say it was."

"But?"

His jaw set stubbornly. "She's just a kid and this must feel like life and death to her. It's too much."

"She's leading a calf to the barn, not doing brain surgery," Mariah said drily. "I think she can handle it, but if you're so worried, you could ride *with* her instead of complaining to me about it."

Jacob scowled. "I'm planning to. It's just that you don't know anything about my daughter, so you don't know what she can or can't handle."

"You're right, we don't know her. Which begs the question…why did you think we could do something to help her if you couldn't do it yourself?" Mariah winced as soon as the retort left her mouth. So much for her resolution to treat Jacob like any other guest.

"*Hell.* Are you rude to everyone, or am I special?"

He was special all right…especially irritating.

She couldn't deny that Jacob's lean, masculine intensity pulled at her senses. Physically he was a compelling man; it was his other parts she wasn't so crazy about.

"I'm not trying to be rude," she said evenly. "But it's important for Caitlin's welfare that you don't expect a service we aren't able to deliver. And if I have to push to get the message across, that's what I'll do."

"At least we agree about her safety, but you can't act as if she was raised on a ranch, with the skills and experience you and your brother have acquired from everyday life."

"Kids grow up fast here. There's nothing wrong with that. Everyone has to take chances to learn and really live. We just risk a few more than parents allow their children to in the city."

"That's *so* reassuring," Jacob said sarcastically. "But I'll decide how fast my daughter grows up, if you don't mind."

Mariah bit her lip to keep from saying something else she'd regret. For example, if he was so concerned for Caitlin, why did he spend so many hours working? She'd heard that he had already asked where he could charge the batteries for his smartphone and laptop computer, whether the ranch provided wireless internet and if they had a fax machine for guest use. What did he plan to do, set up an office in the mess tent and run his business while everyone *else* dealt with Caitlin? Surely she needed her father's time more than she needed to ride in a Mercedes or have other expensive frills.

Mariah's dad used to say it took all kinds to get by, but she wasn't as certain. While she appreciated the income Jacob O'Donnell's "kind" brought the ranch, it came at a stiff price. Money was a means to an end for Mariah; it wasn't a priority the way it appeared to be for Jacob.

"By the way," she said finally, "we never put our guests in the middle of a situation as serious as treating a wounded cow, so I know my wranglers didn't ask for your help."

"It seemed the right thing to do, and I wish you hadn't interfered." Jacob's eyes were hard and impassive.

"I interfered, as you put it, because it's *my job.*" She wasn't sure what to make of his statement. Chauvinism? Or was it ego? She'd encountered an excess of male ego over the years—typically from weekend warriors taking risks to prove something to themselves or someone else. Except Jacob didn't seem the weekend-warrior type. "Did you get kicked or hurt before I arrived?"

"Not to speak of." He slapped some dirt and grass from his clothes. "You aren't going to be sued. I signed your waiver-of-responsibility forms, remember?"

"Does everything boil down to money for you?" she asked, her nerves on edge...maybe because she knew that the waiver forms might or might not protect the U-2 in court. And the threat would go up if somebody with Jacob O'Donnell's resources decided to sue them. He could likely purchase a hundred ranches without noticing the change in his bank account.

"There's nothing wrong with money, and it safeguards my daughter."

Mariah watched Caitlin. Despite what he thought, being rich didn't offer guarantees. And while it was natural for parents to worry about their children, Jacob seemed to worry more than most. He must have been frantic about Caitlin's behavior to bring her to Montana. Riding horses and working with range cattle was worlds away from going to a safe, air-conditioned movie theater.

"For what it's worth, I think Caitlin is a good kid at heart," Mariah said awkwardly. "I realize she has problems you're trying to—"

"Problems?" The word burst out of him. "You could say that. Kittie set fire to her school gymnasium last Wednesday."

The impulsive revelation was a shock, yet Mariah couldn't believe the girl who'd panicked thinking a wolf might have eaten her father would deliberately set a fire. Besides, Jacob

O'Donnell might be able to buy his way out of most of Caitlin's mistakes, but arson would surely have landed her in juvenile court.

"How did it happen?"

"It wasn't on purpose. She tried to hide the cigarette she was sneaking without putting it out. Kids are kids—they get in trouble," he said, an aggressive thrust to his chin. "I only told you in case she mentions it and you get the wrong idea."

"I see." Mariah released the breath she'd been holding. Smoking was less worrisome than arson, and she could make inquiries to be sure Jacob was telling her the full story and not the sanitized version. "Does she have any cigarettes with her now?"

"Of course not."

There wasn't any "of course" about it, but Mariah didn't want to antagonize him further by pointing that out.

"I'm going to check on my daughter." Without another word, Jacob urged his horse into a trot. The tension in Caitlin's body increased visibly as he rode up by her.

Mariah gazed at the O'Donnells and the calf and beyond at the tree-studded hills. Thank goodness she didn't have the same problems with her brother as Jacob had with Caitlin.

Setting fire to the school?

Lord.

She began mentally reviewing the locations of the U-2's fire hoses and extinguishers.

AN HOUR AND A HALF LATER, Jacob stepped under a spray of water and rubbed soap on his chest. He was grateful they'd gotten back to the ranch center early—between cows, horses, sweat and dirt, he'd never needed a shower more.

The high window in the concrete shower stall was open and he saw Mariah Weston and her brother standing by the foremost barn. The afternoon sun turned her auburn hair into a dark flame, painting her curves with light and shadow, and he felt another unwelcome flash of attraction. She was so different from Anna it seemed almost disloyal to find her sexually appealing.

Not that he was a monk.

He dated and enjoyed an occasional discreet liaison as long as it was understood he didn't want anything permanent. Lately, though, he'd hardly looked at women, what with Kittie acting out every parent's nightmare. So it didn't make sense that someone as impossible as Mariah was getting to him, even in passing. Hell, if nothing else, the jagged white scar he'd spotted on her left forearm and the half-healed gash on her right palm should be enough to warn him off.

How had she acquired those injuries?

A hundred disturbing possibilities came to mind, each attached to the knowledge that the same things could happen to Kittie. And it would be his fault for bringing her to Montana. Parenting had land mines he couldn't have imagined fifteen years ago when he was debating with Anna whether it was too soon to start a family. He'd wanted to wait until he graduated and was established in his career, but she'd talked him into fatherhood without too much effort…the same way she'd talked him into everything.

Before long Reid went into the barn and Mariah stood there alone. For somebody operating a vacation business that ran on goodwill, she had a strange way of communicating with paying guests. Yet Jacob shifted uneasily. *Strange* wasn't quite the best description; it was more a brutal honesty with a dash of temper. Still, the honesty was from her point of view, and it didn't make her right.

Kids might grow up faster on a ranch than in the city, but he saw no reason for Kittie to grow up faster than she already had—particularly if it meant taking unnecessary gambles with her safety. Adulthood would come soon enough.

He *did* respect the way Mariah had treated the cow. Getting close to a wild, thrashing animal took guts; it had convinced him she was a genuine rancher, not just a figurehead. What Mariah didn't understand was that Kittie had wanted him to help, and failing the request had put a new black mark on his parental report card.

He ducked under the showerhead and scrubbed his hair, aware that working with an outraged cow had also seemed easier than dealing with his own child. What kind of father did *that* make him?

He groaned.

It was so frustrating. One minute Kittie seemed almost like her old self; the next she was at her worst. Nobody else was bothered by her lightning mood swings, and why should they be? She wasn't *their* daughter.

He hadn't been this scared since Anna died.

When Jacob peered through the window again, Mariah was gone. Instead he saw Kittie. She walked to the barn, peeked around carefully and then went inside.

Crap.

He got out and grabbed a towel. Kittie had a crush on Reid Weston, and she'd already disappeared a couple of times—disappearances she hadn't explained. Reid might have snubbed Kittie when they first met, but he was a teenage boy, and Jacob didn't trust teenage boys.

After all, he used to be one himself.

I WISH MOM AND DAD were here.

Reid Weston spread fresh straw in the horse stalls, the familiar refrain going through his mind. If his parents were alive, *they'd* be managing the ranch and Mariah would be a veterinarian. But they weren't and she wasn't. She'd quit school after the accident and returned home.

And nothing had ever been the same again.

He blinked furiously and forked a load of straw into the last stall. Mostly he missed his mom and dad, but it would be nice not to feel guilty that Mariah had left school to take care of him and the ranch. She'd given up her lifelong dream of becoming a vet.

Another twist of guilt hit Reid's midriff. He wanted to be a veterinarian, too. Yet how could he go away to college and leave Mariah in Montana to deal with everything on her own? On top of all the other stuff she took care of, she ran the business end of the ranch by herself, doing what their parents used to do together. And Reid knew that they couldn't afford extra payroll costs, much less school expenses, no matter what Mariah claimed.

He wasn't blind. No one talked about it, but he knew that if it wasn't for the ranch finances and being responsible for him, Mariah and Luke would have already gotten married. Instead, his sister was working herself silly running the vacation business and taking on more and more of the things Granddad handled so he could retire. Never mind that Granddad didn't want to retire.

"Why don't you like me?" asked a voice suddenly from the barn door.

Damn.

It was that city brat. *Kittie*. He'd avoided her for a day, but his luck had run out.

Reid spread the straw more thoroughly than necessary. "I don't dislike you."

"Yeah, right."

"It isn't you I don't like. It's where you…" Reid stopped, realizing how dumb it sounded to say that he didn't like her because a drunk driver from Seattle had killed his folks and that was where she came from. Maybe it *was* dumb. He'd have to give it some thought.

"If it isn't me, then what is it?" Kittie insisted.

"Just take my word, it isn't personal." He hung the pitchfork on the wall and dusted his hands. The kid might not be so odd if her hair wasn't so weird. And he should be polite—it was what his mom and dad would have expected. "I'm going to see that cow you brought in. You can come if you want."

Kittie bobbed her head eagerly. "Mariah says she'll be all right."

"She ought to be. My sister has a knack with hurt animals."

"My dad thinks she's hot," Kittie said matter-of-factly as she tagged along. "I can tell from the way he checked her out yesterday. He thinks I don't notice that stuff, but I do."

Reid didn't break step. O'Donnell wouldn't get anywhere with Mariah—the night before he'd overheard his sister telling Grams that he was an obnoxious jerk who thought his money was better than anyone else's. At any rate, Mariah didn't go for men wanting a vacation fling. Short-timers were a regular feature at the ranch; they could try hitting on her, but they never got out of the gate.

"Are breasts really that important to guys?" Kittie asked.

That stopped Reid in his tracks. He stared at her, nonplussed. "What?"

"I mean, nobody will date me unless I have bigger boobs. Isn't that right?"

She looked so miserable that he was doubly at a loss for words. "Uh…well…uh…different guys like different stuff. We're not all the same."

It was a lame thing to say and Kittie obviously agreed. "Oh, sure. Some guys prefer brains and personality."

Reid could have told her she wasn't doing any better in the brains and personality department, but she'd probably try to scratch his eyes out. He could take her down easily, except Granddad would kick his butt for fighting with a girl and her dad would only make things harder for Mariah.

"You've just got to grow…er…up more," he mumbled, wishing he was on another planet. "You could be like your mom. Do you know when she got…bigger?"

"Not really. She was awful pretty, though, and Dad says I'm like her." Yet Kittie's face became glummer. "I don't know much about my mom 'cept she first got sick in high school. Real sick. They tried to make her better, only it didn't work or stay that way or something." All at once Kittie seemed alarmed. "Please don't tell my dad."

"About what?" Reid couldn't think of anything he'd want to tell Kittie's father, especially about her questions. Honestly, asking how he felt about breasts? The brat didn't have a lick of sense.

"Nothing. N-nothing I said."

"Don't worry, *I won't*."

He headed again for the corral where they'd put the mother and calf. It was in the rear of the far barn where she wouldn't be upset by too much activity. Range cattle had little contact with humans and didn't take kindly to being penned at the best of times. True to form, the mother cow grunted and moved in front of her baby, stamping the ground in warning.

Reid ran a practiced gaze over her and the feed box. Her muzzle was wet, so she'd obviously drunk some water. And a portion of the feed had been eaten. Not bad after getting roped, stitched, dosed and confined.

"How is she?" Kittie rested her arms on the top fence rail, the same as him, but she had to stretch to do it.

"Not bad, considering."

"What would have happened if we never found her?"

Reid thought of the animals they lost each year. Life was hard on the range; he couldn't sugarcoat it. "Could have died. The baby is too young to survive on its own, and the mother's wound was infected. But even if you hadn't located them, someone else would probably have come along."

Footsteps came from behind them and Reid grimaced at the sight of Kittie's father. "Mr. O'Donnell."

"Hello, Reid. I haven't seen much of you since we got here." There was a faint emphasis on the *I* and a hidden query whether another O'Donnell *had* seen him before now.

Reid tipped his hat back. As if he'd be interested in a city runt with an attitude. “Stands to reason—I’ve been busy and I’m not your wrangler.”

“That sounds like something your sister would say.”

“Yup. Some things run in families.”

O’Donnell flicked a look at Kittie, whose attention was no longer on the mother cow and her calf. “I guess.”

“Dad, am I really, truly like Mom?” Kittie asked intently.

A smile softened O’Donnell’s expression. “Really and truly, sweetheart. She was beautiful, the most beautiful woman I’ve ever known.”

“I… Whatever.” Kittie pressed her lips together and turned back to the corral.

“I’ve got work to do,” Reid said, deciding it was time to escape. “Don’t stay long, and don’t get near the mama or her baby. It’ll make them nervous.” With a curt nod to Jacob O’Donnell, he strode away.

All in all, he felt kind of sorry for Kittie. Her dad was rich, so she had plenty of money, but apparently her mom was dead, and he knew exactly how that felt.

Lousy.

CHAPTER FOUR

LATE IN THE EVENING Mariah reviewed and accepted four reservations for July and added them to the chart where she tracked which wrangler was assigned to each group of visitors.

She leaned back in the office chair and rotated her shoulders to loosen her tight muscles. The gray tiger-striped cat on her lap protested the movement before settling down again. Squash was a fine old fellow, preferring long naps these days to terrorizing mice the way he used to when he was younger.

The U-2 was now fully booked for June, mostly booked for July and had more than half their openings taken for August—recent good news on the economic front had bumped their bookings considerably. Regular, middle-class people hesitated to go on vacations when the economy was bad. The ranch didn't get many guests with Jacob O'Donnell's wealth—the whole sleeping-in-a-tent thing generally turned them off.

Hmm.

What should she do about the O'Donnell family?

Jacob was different from their other guests in more ways than just the generous size of his bank account. He wasn't curious about ranching or the stuff that brought most people to Montana, yet he and his daughter were staying for several weeks. The only thing recommending him was the way he sat a horse. It might have been years since he'd ridden, but he seemed at ease in the saddle.

Years...

A wicked grin crossed Mariah's face. She didn't care how

great Jacob O'Donnell was on a horse—he was going to wake up in the morning with the biggest case of sore butt ever. It was inevitable. You didn't ride for the first time in ages and get away unscathed. The interesting part would be whether he pretended it was all right or asked Grams for liniment and aspirin to relieve the aches and pains.

She was betting his pride would win.

"It wasn't nice to tell Mr. O'Donnell that he'd have an aching bum tomorrow," she whispered to the fur ball curled up on her thighs. "Not nice at all."

Squash gazed at Mariah drowsily. He was accustomed to having conversations with her in the middle of the night. She'd adopted him from one of the barn cat's litters when she was thirteen—he'd listened to the highs and lows of her high-school years, sulked when she was away at school and was the confidant she had needed when her parents died. She'd told Squash the things she couldn't tell anybody, even Luke. Squash didn't judge; he just purred and blinked at her.

"I'm usually much nicer to our guests. And I bet now he'll feel that he has to prove something by being an iron man."

Or maybe not.

It probably didn't matter to rich men what "the help" thought of them, and that was what she and her wranglers were to Jacob O'Donnell...the hired hands who were supposed to shut up and obey his commands.

Ha.

A lot of visitors came to the U-2 again and again because they loved the ranch. Some of them had to save awhile for their vacations, but they arrived excited to be there once more. It was why Mariah had begun offering a 10 percent discount for return visits, and she wouldn't let a spoiled entrepreneur with a chip on his shoulder ruin anyone else's trip.

The computer pinged, alerting her that she had an email waiting. She toggled to the message program and saw it was from Luke.

Still mad at me? Up late with a mare dropping a foal. Thinking of you and wondering if you are awake. Love, L.

Mariah smiled and typed a reply.

Not mad. Trying to decide what to do with Jacob O'Donnell and his daughter. He's impossible. At least he didn't go out of his way at dinner to annoy me. M.

Yet she wavered as the cursor hovered over the send button on the computer monitor.... Maybe she shouldn't say anything about Jacob O'Donnell. She deleted the note and started again.

No, not mad anymore. Was it Little Foot having her foal? I'm juggling reservations and the schedule. Got a few days' work for two of your cowhands in the second week of June, if you can spare them. M.

She reread the text and sent it. That was much better. When the U-2 was heavily booked, they hired additional wranglers from neighboring ranches, sometimes the ranchers themselves when things were slow. Ranching had its lean years and the extra income could come in handy. She didn't go to Luke very often, since he was primarily a cow and horse breeder and didn't have the same financial ups and downs as some of the other ranches—he shipped prize-bull semen all over the world and got paid extremely well for it.

Another message came right back.

Yeah, it was Little Foot. You can have Pedro and Tommy in June. They're best with people. Call me if you're not too tired. Love, L.

Mariah lifted the phone and dialed.

"I hope this is an obscene caller," Luke said when he answered.

"I don't have the energy to be obscene."

"Me, either. Little Foot had me worried at the end."

"You should have let me know. I would have come over."

"By the time it seemed there might be a problem, it was too late to get you here." Dull thuds sounded through the line and she figured Luke had pulled off his boots and thrown them across the room. "She's a small mare and it was her first, but Dr. Crandall thought I could handle it. He wasn't able to come when Little Foot went into labor—he was working on a German shepherd that someone brought into the clinic. She was found on the highway. I'll bet some damned fool didn't tie her properly in their truck and she either jumped or was thrown out when they were screaming down the road."

"That's awful." It infuriated Mariah when she saw kids *or* dogs in an open pickup. Luke felt the same—they'd seen it turn out badly too often.

"I guess she was pretty busted up, but Doc thinks she has a chance. Anyhow, it was a really big colt. I don't know where Little Foot was hiding so much baby."

Having assisted at births where the foal seemed impossibly large, Mariah chuckled in sympathy. Most of her experience with animals came from years of ranch life and tagging after the local veterinarian. In college it was often a question of associating technical terms with something she already knew, which enabled her to carry a heavier course load than her fellow students. Back then she'd been in a hurry to get through school so she could take over for Dr. Crandall; now he had to find another vet to buy the practice. Mariah minded Dr. Crandall being unable to retire almost as much as she missed being a veterinarian herself—Doc couldn't keep working forever.

She shifted and Squash dug the tips of his claws into her

skin as a warning to stay put. "Tell me about the new arrival. I remember you bred Little Foot later than usual last year."

"He's exactly what I was hoping for—a chestnut, same as Little Foot, with her sleek, clean lines. Look, I gotta grab a shower and hit the sack. I just wanted to hear your voice before going to bed."

The comment surprised her. It wasn't like Luke to be sentimental.

"Oh, okay. Sleep well."

"You, too."

Mariah hung up and put her cat on the floor so she could do a walk-through in the guest area. She'd intended to get down there earlier—someone else had mentioned the noise from Susan and Chad's tent, saying the newlyweds were "enthusiastic about their honeymooning." It was said with a grin, but Mariah didn't want the situation to escalate again.

Outside, the stars blazed across the sky and she walked in their faint glimmer to the slope opposite the house, Pip at her heels. Things seemed fairly peaceful. Susan and Chad were in a tent set apart from the main group—they were whispering and smothering a laugh as she passed, but it wasn't too loud.

It would be noisier when more kids were visiting the ranch after school got out for summer vacation. Nobody could chatter like two girls making friends.

A guest, Judy Hartner, mumbled "Hi" to Mariah as she stumbled toward the restroom wearing flip-flops and a jacket over her pajamas.

Pip's eyes pricked forward when he saw a light shining from one side of the O'Donnells' tent. She could see the wheels turning in his mind…the hope of another midnight snack. He let out a yip and whined.

"No," she breathed.

She slapped her thigh to get Pip's attention and he followed her to the barn. The cowhands made rounds to check on the animals, but it didn't hurt to check on them herself. Most of the horses were asleep and didn't stir as she switched on the lights and looked into each stall; they were used to familiar people coming in at night. But Shadow peered out the moment he caught her scent.

"Hello, boy."

He nudged her shoulder and she rubbed his velvety black nose. Extending his neck over the stable door, he sniffed her pocket with unerring accuracy.

Mariah laughed. "Okay, okay." She took out the carrot she'd brought from the house and he crunched it down. "You are one pampered pony."

"Pony?" said a voice.

Startled, Mariah spun, her heart pounding. His tail wagging furiously, Pip dashed to greet Jacob. This was the human being who'd provided him, however unwittingly, with a steak dinner. Without much effort, Jacob could be a friend for life, yet he didn't pet Pip or even greet him.

Pip cocked his head, puzzled. "Rrrrffff."

"Just a minute, boy," he murmured. "I'm a little stiff." He bent and gave Pip a slow stroke on his shoulders. The canine wriggled with delight.

Mariah raised her eyebrows. So Jacob *was* acknowledging he hadn't escaped the day unscathed. Of course, he might be sorry he'd said anything in the morning…but he was going to be sorry, period. She knew what happened when you went riding after a long absence.

"I don't suppose your grandmother has a hot tub filled with that liniment you referred to this morning," Jacob said, straightening. "I'd like to spend the rest of the night in it. And maybe tomorrow."

The corner of her mouth twitched—she hadn't expected him to have a sense of humor. "No, but an economy tube is available. I'll unlock the dispensary for you. It doesn't require an M.D. to hand out, though Grams prefers to manage first-aid services herself."

"Don't bother for tonight. I'll survive...barely," he added in a droll tone. "By the way, was your grandmother responsible for laundering my shirt after Pip used it as a doggy bowl? I threw it away, but found it in my tent this evening. My dry cleaner would claim it was impossible to get those grease stains out, and it looks perfect."

"Possibly. Grams has many talents." Mariah motioned at Pip to come to her. Some people didn't like dogs—especially large ones—and there was definitely a lot of Pip to go around. "I was doing a quick patrol and saw your lantern was on. Are you having trouble dropping off after drinking all that coffee, or did Pip wake you up?"

"I drank the coffee for a reason. I'm reading contracts coming up for renewal in November and December."

Contracts?

Naturally. What else?

He'd acted aloof and bored at the informal after-dinner social hour. Activity in the fresh air sent most of their visitors to bed by nine or ten, but first they mingled—singing or chatting or playing games in the mess tent. Jacob hadn't participated; instead, he'd sat in the back, radiating tension, drinking regular coffee instead of decaf.

On the flip side, while Caitlin hadn't been the soul of the party, she had played a game of checkers with Burt and gobbled down two servings of peach cobbler, topped by chocolate cake with ice cream and a glass of milk. Whatever was bothering her, it wasn't her appetite. Since getting to the U-2, she'd eaten the same as any other teenager with a bottomless pit in place of a stomach.

"I see."

She'd tried not to sound critical, but Jacob looked defensive. "I waited until Kittie was asleep before starting. And you're working, too. How long a day does that make for you?"

"Summer is hectic. It's a family business. We all work."

"You have employees. Ever consider delegating?"

Delegating? Mariah pressed her lips together. She didn't need management advice from a city-dwelling, money-obsessed workaholic. Delegation was fine, but everyone on the ranch had duties that kept them busy. As the business manager, she took care of odd tasks such as walking through the U-2's tent town to see if the newlyweds were engaging in noisy sex and disturbing anyone.

"We get by," she said finally.

Shadow nickered softly and nuzzled her neck, a reminder that the U-2 was about more than ledger sheets and keeping score with dollars and cents.

Mariah smiled, and this time Shadow got the apple she'd put in her left pocket. "And it isn't just about the bottom line at the ranch. For example, when Shadow was born, I spent the entire night out here. Drowsed on a pile of hay with his head on my knee. And I'll take that over curling up with a contract any day."

"Don't horses sleep standing up?"

"Nope. That's kind of a myth. They go half-asleep on their feet, a part of their brain remaining alert for approaching danger. It's a survival instinct—that way they can go from a drowsing state to running in nothing flat. But for deep sleep, they have to lie down. It's complicated because lying down too long can also be a problem."

She stroked the stallion's mane. His coat gleamed from the thorough currying she'd given him. Unless she was occupied with an emergency, Mariah groomed Shadow herself, making sure he was clean and comfortable. She did it because she loved him, not because he contributed to the U-2's profits. When you were responsible for animals that depended on you for food and health and comfort, you'd best care about them, or find something else to do.

Mariah glanced at Jacob. He was dressed in the jeans and shirt he'd worn to dinner. Surprisingly, he looked so relaxed and gorgeous in them, no one would ever guess he had arrived at the ranch in a business suit. He'd probably end up sleeping in his clothes if he planned to study paperwork the whole night. Didn't he realize getting rest was important for dealing with Caitlin and her issues?

"Do you *enjoy* reading contracts, Mr. O'Donnell?"

He looked taken aback. "I told you, it's Jacob, and I've never thought about it. Contracts are part of the process. You have your lawyers evaluate them carefully and do it yourself as well if you're the cautious type. *Their* lawyers do the same, and the agreement goes back and forth."

It didn't appeal to Mariah in the slightest. He must spend more on legal fees than the U-2 made in a year, visitors and cattle sales combined.

"These agreements shouldn't be as bad. All parties want to renew, and we've done business with them for a while." Jacob continued, "The paperwork simply needs updating."

Yet he was up at one in the morning, ostensibly on vacation, reading legalese. One thing she could say for Jacob O'Donnell was that she doubted he was underhanded in his business—a man like him couldn't afford to be dishonest.

"By the way, how is the cut on your palm doing?" he asked. "It couldn't have been easy treating a wild cow with an injury."

Mariah frowned, confused. "My palm… *Oh.*"

She flexed her right hand—she'd practically forgotten getting hurt. Aunt Lettie had taken the stitches out yesterday—she'd said it was healing well, just warned her not to do much lifting for another week to avoid reopening the wound.

"I'm fine. I have to wear gloves for work like shoveling out the stables and mending fences until it toughens up, but I usually wear them anyhow. We don't stop for little stuff."

"It doesn't look little." Jacob stepped closer. "How did you get cut if you use gloves for heavy-duty work?"

Realization dawned on Mariah; he was worried the same thing could happen to Caitlin. He didn't have to be concerned.

Unless his daughter was a klutz in the kitchen, there wasn't any danger of a repeat incident. Besides, while the guests took turns helping with meals, they had a rule that no one under the age of eighteen handled the knives.

"I cut it in the outdoor kitchen—our version of the cattle trail chuck wagon. I'm not much at cooking and got distracted slicing potatoes. Reggie, our cook, has now banned me from doing anything except washing dirty dishes, fetching coffeepots and saying hello. He didn't appreciate having to wash up and start over with the spuds."

Surprisingly, Jacob smiled. He was even more attractive when he did that, and Mariah felt guilty for noticing. Yet it really wasn't a big deal—Luke was a terrific guy, but it didn't mean she couldn't take pleasure in the view. She didn't expect *him* to wear blinders if a well-rounded woman crossed his path. It wouldn't be reasonable.

"That's a rough way of getting out of doing something you don't like," Jacob said.

"I don't dislike cooking. I'm just no good at it. My mom gave up…and now *Grams* has given up on me, too." She bumped Pip with her foot. "Let's go, boy."

JACOB HOOKED HIS THUMBS in his jeans pocket and watched Mariah slip out of the barn, the dog at her side.

He wasn't sure why he'd followed Mariah after hearing her walk past his tent on the hill—maybe for someone to talk to or simple curiosity about why she was awake, the same as him. She was an interesting woman, and her affinity with animals was striking. The black horse, goofy-eyed when she was teasing him, was suspicious and stamping the ground now that she'd gone. He'd bet that Pip *or* Shadow would go into fire for her. And she'd even managed to soothe the range cow crazed with fear and anger and pain. Maybe ranchers developed those skills since animals were their bread and butter, yet he suspected Mariah's abilities went beyond average.

Jacob stretched cautiously, trying to relax his muscles. He missed the scents of the city and the faint hum of traffic that penetrated their loft. Seven years ago he'd bought an old commercial building in North Seattle and converted the second floor and parts of the third into a spacious home overlooking Lake Union. There were interesting features left from the original industrial use, but it had the advantages of modern conveniences. He hadn't decided what to do with the remaining space, though he'd created a five-car garage on the ground level.

The ranch, on the other hand, was too quiet to sleep unless he was dead tired the way he had been the previous night.

Jacob stepped out of the barn and closed the door. At the tent he peeked into Kittie's side. He could barely make out his daughter's outline in the dark. She stirred restlessly, muttering, and Jacob's heart ached more than his sore body.

He went into his own side and turned on the battery-powered lamp by the mattress. Gingerly lowering himself, he thumbed through the next contract. He'd arranged to have a courier pick all of them up in a couple of days so his lawyers could go over his notes. They ordinarily communicated via email, but the U-2 didn't see a need to provide wireless internet, so he'd been forced to make other arrangements.

Yet even as Jacob thought about it, a twinge of guilt hit him. The U-2 hadn't claimed to provide internet, any more than they'd claimed to provide designer coffee or hotel rooms with hot baths and daily maid service.

He'd contacted Gretchen that morning to let her know he wasn't available online. She'd checked and discovered his cell phone could be used as a modem on the computer; he just required the accessories and would be back on the Net as soon as they were delivered. It went to show that a top executive assistant was more valuable to him than a dozen vice presidents. Gretchen would be getting a sizable bonus.

Do you enjoy *reading contracts...*

Crossly, Jacob tried to push Mariah's question from his mind. He had read hundreds of contracts over the years, and while some were more tedious than others, the idea of enjoying or not enjoying the task had never occurred to him. It was merely something to be done. Yet, as he stared at the words on the page, he knew it was the most boring aspect of his work. He didn't even sign the majority of the contracts within the company, only the major ones. Of course, executive meetings also weren't his favorite thing, any more than reviewing the reorganization plans some managers regularly submitted instead of really addressing problems they had likely created themselves.

All at once he threw the papers aside and snapped off the light. With the caffeine coursing through his bloodstream, he might not get much rest, but he could try.

REID TOSSED HIS BOOKS into the bed of the pickup. Thursday and Friday were short days at school to let the staff get ready for final exams. What he didn't understand was why they'd bothered having classes in the first place. Everybody goofed off on short days, even the teachers. He had better things to do than listen to Art Blanco cut up or Joey Newton brag about his new dirt bike. And when Mr. Matano began telling stories of his stint in marine boot camp, everybody's eyes glazed over.

"Hey, Reid," said a voice behind him.

It was Laura Shelton and he smiled; Laura was real easy on the eyes. "Hey, Laura."

"The first barn dance is this Saturday, isn't it?"

He almost snorted. A bunch of the girls had asked the same thing, and they all knew darned well when the dances started for the season. The U-2 held weekly barn dances throughout the summer for both their visitors and the local folks. For twenty-four years they'd begun the third Saturday in May and ended the second Saturday in September, unless it snowed.

"Yup, the third Saturday in May, same as usual."

"Does Mariah need help? I could get there early."

"Naw, she's got it covered."

It wasn't the first offer that Reid had gotten, but Mariah had nixed his classmates from coming early. She said the girls flirted with the younger wranglers and they got less done.

"It'd be great if you could bring your chocolate chip-cookies, though," he said when Laura's smile disappeared. "The ones you won a prize for at the county fair."

She brightened. "I'll bake several batches."

He was about to say one batch would be enough seeing as there were always plenty of sweets, but had a hunch she'd be pissed. Girls got a knot in their rope about the strangest things. "Uh…sure. Only don't work too hard. Want a ride home?"

"Oh, *yes.* Thank you."

Reid opened the passenger door the way his dad had taught him and offered a hand. Laura climbed in, a pleasant-smelling mix of curves and long legs. He liked girls. They were bewildering and giggled too much, but as Granddad said, they had compensations.

Before he got into the truck himself, he sent a text on his cell to Mariah and his grandparents. He knew it had been a struggle for them to let him start driving to school, so he tried to let them know any time he expected a delay.

It wasn't far to Laura's house. The Sheltons had a small spread that was closer to town than the U-2 and right off the main road. Her dad ran some cattle, but he also did the farrier work in the area. He called himself a blacksmith, but he didn't do any true blacksmithing. Horseshoes were mostly mass-produced—not like in the Old West—though you still wanted an expert to put shoes on a horse.

Once they arrived, he got out of the truck and waved to Mrs. Shelton as he opened the door again for Laura. She was hanging sheets and towels on the clothesline and waved back.

"How are you, Reid?"

"Fine, ma'am. And you?"

"Couldn't be better. Tell Mariah we're looking forward to the dance on Saturday."

"I'll do that, ma'am. And let Mr. Shelton know the shoeing job he did on Buttons was just fine." He turned to Laura. "See you at school."

"Bye. Thanks for the ride."

"No problem." He tipped his hat to them both and drove home.

When he got there, he could hear Mariah in the office talking. On the way to find out if she wanted him for anything, he stopped by the fridge and found a bowl of fried chicken. It was crisp and spicy, just the way he liked it. He headed to the rear of the house, munching happily on a piece.

"Yes, I know it's confidential," Mariah was assuring someone on the phone. "I simply—"

She stopped, apparently interrupted by the person on the other end of the line.

"I don't *need* the child's name, I already know her name. Uh…can you wait a moment?" Mariah covered the speaker and looked at Reid. "Hi. I see you're eating lunch. Be sure to have potato chips or a hot-fudge sundae to go with it—you know, something healthy."

He swallowed a bite and grinned. "You sound like Grams. If she doesn't want me to eat fried chicken, she shouldn't make it."

"Once a week she indulges us so she can pretend to be an old-fashioned granny. Now go away. Take Buttons for a ride or put your feet up in the hammock and sleep."

"I have time for chores. We have a short day again tomorrow and our finals don't start until next week. Anything special you need me to do?"

Mariah sighed. "You've stayed up late studying for a week. Let the chores go and relax this afternoon. Shoo."

That was nice of Mariah. But he wasn't going to listen to

her, not when she was working her ass off. He collected another piece of chicken and went to change out of his school clothes. No doubt there was a stable with straw and horse manure in need of shoveling.

MARIAH PUT THE RECEIVER to her ear. "I'm sorry for the interruption, Officer Giles. As I was going to explain, I simply want to speak with the police officer who investigated the fire at the Garrison Academy. I'm aware that a minor's record is confidential—I want to discuss the fire itself. That part of the report should be public record, correct?"

"Very well, it was Officer Rizolli who handled that case," the public-affairs liaison told her reluctantly. "I'll transfer you to his desk."

Mariah waited, her patience stretched to the limit. She'd spent an hour trying to reach someone who could talk to her about the incident at Caitlin O'Donnell's school. Honestly, how many times could she be transferred with nothing productive coming of it? And how many times could she explain she wasn't asking for confidential information? Heck, she *knew* who'd started the fire.

"This is Officer Don Rizolli," said a deep voice. "How can I help you?"

"Officer Rizolli..." Mariah rocked forward and wrote down the name. "*Hello.* Did you investigate a fire that occurred at the Garrison Academy in the past two weeks? It's a private, rather exclusive high school in North Seattle, near Ballard, I think."

"I'm familiar with the facility. I was called in by the school authorities after the blaze."

She practically fell off her chair. Could she actually have reached the right person? "I'm relieved to get through to you finally. The young lady who was responsible for the incident is visiting our ranch and I need to know the...the circumstances. Rest assured I'm not asking for information about

Caitlin. Her father tells me it was an accident, but I want to get that from an unbiased source. We've had a dry year in Montana, though fire is always a concern for us."

"I see. What is the name of your ranch?"

"The U-2. If you want to check us out on the internet, our website is *U2RanchVacations.com.* I can hold while you're looking."

She waited, hearing the click of a keyboard in the background. She'd done her share of web surfing before making her calls to Seattle. Caitlin had mentioned to Ray Cassidy that she attended school at Garrison Academy, which turned out to be an outrageously expensive educational institution. Mariah had contacted the academy first, but the principal had not been forthcoming; she hadn't expected him to be—advertising a fire wouldn't encourage student enrollment, no matter what the cause.

"And to whom am I speaking?" queried Officer Rizolli after a few minutes.

"I should have introduced myself. I'm Mariah Weston, the U-2's business manager."

"The owner, too, I presume. According to your online description, the Weston family has owned the ranch for several generations."

"Yes, the U-2 is family owned." Mariah tapped her pencil on a pad of paper. Phone numbers and other notes were scribbled over it, along with the doodles she'd done during her numerous waits on hold.

"Tell me what you need to know, Ms. Weston."

"Mostly what I said…whether or not it was deliberate. Caitlin appears to be a good kid, but I can't allow a budding arsonist to stay at the ranch. Parents can be reluctant to admit problems with their children, and I don't believe her father had planned on telling me about the fire. It just slipped out in a conversation."

"I can give you a general account of the incident," Officer Rizolli said slowly. "The student was sneaking a cigarette in the girls' locker room. She hid it in a trash can when a teacher entered the gymnasium unexpectedly. The paper caught fire, then a wood bench and a cabinet where the towels were stored. Fortunately, there were limited combustibles in the area since the floors are stone-and-glass tile and the lockers are metal."

"You don't have any reservations about the situation?"

"I'm confident it was an accident, Ms. Weston, and so is the fire chief. I also spoke with the school counselor. The student tried to put the flames out with an extinguisher and pulled the fire alarm when she was unsuccessful. Nobody was injured, including the young lady at fault."

The knot in Mariah's stomach began to loosen. She'd never forgotten a frightening drought-stricken summer when she was a child. Dry lightning had set dozens of fires on the ranch and her parents had canceled all the guest reservations to protect both their visitors and the U-2. For two months they'd lived with a silent, uneasy anticipation of something that might happen.

"That's a relief to hear."

"I understand, Ms. Weston. I've dealt with juvenile arson and it isn't pretty. You're wise to be cautious, but I wouldn't worry on this particular count. I…" He hesitated. "I couldn't let the parent or student know how I felt, but I was rather sorry for her. She was truly terrified, though by the time her father arrived, she'd masked it well with belligerence."

Mariah laughed. "Having met Caitlin, I can imagine. She has attitude to spare. I appreciate your speaking with me, Officer."

"We're here to help, Ms. Weston. I'm sorry you had trouble getting through."

Mariah disconnected. In a way it would be easier to have

an excuse to evict the O'Donnells, yet it was good to know she hadn't read Caitlin wrong.

As for Jacob…the jury was still out. He wasn't just a closed book she couldn't fathom; he was an entire library of closed books.

CHAPTER FIVE

ON FRIDAY MORNING Jacob dragged himself from bed and took a walk around the perimeter of the ranch complex to loosen his muscles. It helped, though there was a distinct ache when he sat down with a cup of coffee in the mess tent.

He'd looked in on Kittie, but she was curled up asleep and he had decided not to disturb her. There was time—the wranglers and Benjamin and Mariah Weston were the only ones stirring.

"I understand you asked for more liniment. Grams sent this for you," Mariah said, coming over and handing him a tube. "You must be really sore if you already used up the other."

"It isn't bad, but we had an…uh…*incident* with the stuff Dr. Weston gave me yesterday." He didn't want to explain that Kittie had acted her usual charming self and squirted the contents of the original tube in the trash—at least he figured that was what she had done. He'd given it to her and she'd gone into the restroom for a minute before coming out and giving it back to him, totally flat. She couldn't have applied it in so short a time, so she must have emptied the tube deliberately. His one consolation was that at Kittie's age, the aches and pains didn't last as long.

"That's okay. We have plenty in stock."

"Appreciate it. Didn't your grandmother want to speak with me herself?" Elizabeth Weston had asked a number of questions and checked his blood pressure prior to dispensing the liniment. Whether she did that for everyone, or mostly overworked businessmen with rebellious teenage daughters, was something yet to be discovered.

"She'll catch up with you after breakfast. At the moment she's stitching up a cowhand who got on the wrong side of one of his girlfriends."

"*One* of his girlfriends?"

"That's the problem. Judy was under the impression she was the *only* one. She threw Billy's boots at him…along with everything else she could put her hands on."

Jacob grinned. "Does that happen to him often?"

"They usually stop short of drawing blood, but Judy doesn't take things lying down—she's a very forthright lady. Billy loves her—he just can't keep his jeans zipped. He's lucky she didn't get her shotgun and fill his keister with buckshot."

"I'm sure his keister is grateful for her restraint," Jacob said drily.

The corners of Mariah's lips twitched. "I'm sure it is. Let us know if there's anything else you need."

She walked away as a ranch hand ambled over with a coffeepot and refilled Jacob's cup. He nodded his thanks. The brew wasn't bad for something boiled on an outdoor cookstove and kept warm on a hot plate, though the dregs contained a fair amount of coffee grounds.

It was interesting to observe the early-morning camaraderie in the mess tent between the Westons and their employees. The chatter was comfortable, but when Mariah and her grandfather weren't in the mix, the talk became earthier and the jokes more ribald. The tales of Billy's war wounds from Judy were a particular source of amusement, and when the young man came in with a white bandage on his scalp and an impressive shiner, the ranch hand endured a royal roasting from his fellow wranglers.

"One at a time, boy," advised one of them after several minutes of kidding. "And don't make promises."

"I didn't make promises. I just didn't tell her about the

other girls. I work all over the state. What am I supposed to do when she ain't around?"

"Well, you should ask Judy that. But I'd wear an iron cup, 'cause next time she's gonna aim for your privates."

The wranglers laughed as Billy dropped his cowboy hat on his head and slunk to a table. He was plainly the youngest among them and the least experienced at holding his own.

The teasing ended as the guests began arriving. A lot of them knew each other by name and Jacob shifted uncomfortably, not having made an effort to be sociable.

He was climbing to his feet to rouse Kittie from bed when his daughter showed up wearing her most hideous outfit—a black T-shirt with a leering skull and crossbones in red rhinestones, and black jeans ripped at the knees. The fake spiderweb tattoo she wore over her belly button was visible below the raggedly hacked hem of the knit shirt. It appeared to be fading, but that was the only nice thing he had to say about her entire appearance.

Hell.

Late the previous day he'd driven into the nearest town to buy shirts and jeans that weren't so outrageous, though he'd doubted she would wear them. Apparently he'd been right. Yet despite Reid Weston's comment that her clothes would frighten the livestock, Kittie's assigned mount seemed unfazed by her bizarre taste in apparel. Of course, Blue was a gentlemanly horse that probably wouldn't twitch an ear if Kittie rode him wearing a *Star Wars* costume.

As the majority of the guests were happily eating, Mariah came in and whistled for attention.

"You may be aware we have a barn dance on Saturday nights during the summer," she said.

A ripple of pleasure went through the group and even Kittie looked interested.

"The first one is tomorrow and the barn we use for it has to be swept and gotten ready. I need volunteers to help with the job. It shouldn't take more than two or three hours if there are enough of us, and anyone volunteering gets a slice of triple-layer chocolate-fudge cake afterward."

"You didn't bake the cake, did ya, Mariah?" shouted a cowhand from the back.

She wrinkled her nose. "No, Grams did."

"Then I'm in. I was gonna clean and oil my saddle, but it can wait."

"Count Susan and me in, too," called a man at the front, and Jacob vaguely remembered that he was a newlywed, visiting the ranch for his honeymoon.

Mariah smiled. "Thanks, Chad."

A number of others volunteered as well and Jacob looked at Kittie. This was what Mariah had talked about that first day—getting involved. "We should help," he told her.

Kittie crossed her arms over her stomach. "That's illegal child labor."

The headache he got when Kittie mouthed off began to grow in his temples. "No, it's being part of the group and doing something that needs doing. Ranching isn't just riding horses and eating sack lunches on the range. It's hard work. We have to take our turn with things that aren't as fun, the same as everyone."

"Whatever. You're going to make me do what you want anyhow."

Jacob swallowed a discouraged groan and put his hand up. Mariah seemed startled, but she added them to the list and told everyone they'd start after lunch.

"OKAY, GUYS," Mariah said as she opened a set of double doors to the U-2's biggest barn. "Let's turn this place into a dance floor."

The guests and wranglers who'd volunteered for cleanup duty trooped in with brooms and other supplies. The cavernous space did not appear promising, but Mariah didn't give them a chance to think about it. Come Saturday night, it would look just fine. She flipped on the light fixtures and opened the remaining doors so the breeze would help clear any dust they raised.

With things so busy, Mariah hadn't found time to get the barn ready for the weekly event. Yet the dances were important, both to their guests and to the U-2's neighbors, which included everyone in the nearby town of Buckeye.

Buckeye served the needs of ranches for miles around—it had schools, churches and a variety of businesses. But the one thing it lacked was a nightlife. So the U-2 provided Buckeye's summer nightlife, every Saturday evening. The neighbors brought desserts to the gathering. The U-2 supplied the beverages. And the wranglers took care of the music and called the square dances—between them they had a mean Western band, though they only rehearsed for an hour before each dance started.

While the barn was built in the style of the older U-2 ranch buildings, it was less than twelve years old. Her parents had designed it with the community dances in mind, with multiple sliding doors on each side to make the space open and inviting. Not that it didn't have other uses—from late fall to early spring the "Big Barn" was where they stored gear like the guest tents, mattresses, footlockers and winter feed.

"This wood floor is great," Susan said as she and Chad swept the last corner. "And it looks different than the rest. Did you build over an earlier foundation?"

Mariah was surprised the other woman had noticed, then recalled that Susan was an interior designer. "No, but you have an excellent eye. It's American chestnut and was cut in the 1800s."

"Chestnut?" Susan knelt and ran her fingers across the smooth grain, polished from decades of human and animal use. "It has a wonderful grain. I wonder where I can get a supply—one of my clients is a natural-wood fanatic."

"You probably won't find any except in historic buildings from the plains states or in the East," Mariah said. "My parents spent years locating nineteenth-century barns that were being demolished and buying the usable chestnut planks. Unfortunately, blight hit the American chestnut a long time ago—the roots are alive, but those tall, beautiful trees are gone."

Chad helped his bride to her feet. "What a shame. Can't it be cured?"

"Not unless they've found one in the past few years. My mom and dad stayed current on the research, but I…well, I haven't kept up with it."

Caitlin leaned on the handle of her push broom. "Why use such old stuff?" She'd been sullen since her father had volunteered them, and it was a relief to see her showing an interest in something other than sulking.

"For a lot of reasons," Mariah said. It was hard to explain choices that weren't made for practicality. "We could have saved money using new timber, but it wouldn't have been the same. Think of the feet that have walked on this floor… not only the animals, but the barn raisings and weddings and other celebrations that it's seen. Can you sense the spirit of those people in here, laughing and dancing and being happy?"

Caitlin rolled her eyes. "You mean it's haunted. That's *so* dumb."

The barn wasn't haunted, or Mariah was certain she would have felt the echo of her parents there. It used to be their special place, a tribute to the lost chestnut trees that Dad's Tennessee grandmother had loved from her childhood.

"No, I wouldn't say *haunted,* but I believe people have an energy that rubs off on things," she said. "Good and bad, like a memory. And this barn has wonderful memories. I try to hear them whispering to me when it's quiet."

"What a lovely thought," declared Edna Sallenger, one of their retired visitors. She'd stopped sweeping along with the others and was listening. Edna had come from Hartford, Connecticut, with her husband, a Western fiction fan who'd never been west of the Alleghenies before their U-2 vacation. Now they were debating a move to Montana. They might do it, but Mariah figured they'd go home and decide their roots were too firmly planted in Hartford. It wasn't unusual for one of their visitors to talk about moving to Montana, but most people couldn't change their life so radically.

"Are you folks gonna keep dillydallying or get back to workin'? I got another job for ya if you're done with the sweeping," Burt said gruffly. The aged wrangler gestured to the strings of lights that needed to be tested and hung; the twinkling lights weren't traditional barn-dance decor, but people liked them and they made everything festive.

The guests good-naturedly returned to their chores. All except Caitlin, who'd crouched down and had her palms pressed to the wood floor. There was an odd look on her face, almost as if she was trying to hear the bygone whispers that Mariah had talked about.

"You weren't serious, right?" Jacob said in an undertone, watching his daughter with a frown.

Mariah glanced at him. "What do you mean?"

"Buying old lumber to build a barn…that's a story concocted for the tourists. You can get wood from a lumberyard and beat it up to look ancient. Hell, the designer for my corporate offices went on and on about the popularity of 'distressed' wood. You may think it's harmless and adds to the ambience to tell tall tales, but I don't want my daughter getting fanciful notions that will end up disappointing her."

"It's the truth." Mariah's temper, which had been unaffected by Caitlin's sour mood, quickened. She grabbed Jacob's arm and pulled him outside for privacy. "I don't invent stories for tourists. We're a ranch, not a theme park."

"You're running a business. Why would you spend that kind of money? It's pointless."

"I didn't spend the money, my parents did, but I would have made the same decision. Don't you have any sense of history or continuity?"

His baffled expression showed he didn't, or at least that he'd denied that part of himself for so long he could no longer find it. "Do you honestly think it makes a difference whether your family used hundred-year-old timbers or new ones?" he demanded.

"Yes." Mariah didn't know how to make him understand, but it was more than just choosing the right words. If Jacob didn't understand already, she doubted he ever could. To him the barn was merely a place built of new and ancient timbers. Yet through this place, she felt connected not only to her parents, but also to the men and women who set out in covered wagons and trusted to God and fate that they would discover a safe home in the West.

Jacob rolled his eyes the way Caitlin had done, and Mariah resisted the temptation to point out where his daughter might have learned her attitude.

"That nonsense about 'sensing' spirits and hearing them whisper to you is foolish romanticizing," he said.

"It isn't nonsense. Why does it annoy you so much? Or do you resent someone being able to value something beyond the dollars and cents that it represents just because you can't?"

JACOB OPENED HIS MOUTH to retort, but Mariah turned on her heels and disappeared inside again.

Damn it all. What was the problem with practicality? If anything, he would have expected a Montana rancher to be the ultimate pragmatist.

He glared at the barn and the cheerful discussion drifting through the wide doors. Mariah was wrong—he didn't resent what she'd said; he was simply watching out for his daughter's best interests. If someone wanted to have idiotic fantasies over a ranch building, that was their concern. To think he'd believed that volunteering for cleanup duty would be good for Kittie; instead, she'd gotten a load of mystical crap and another chance to be rude.

Still annoyed, he went in and saw Kittie putting up tables with Burt at the end of the barn near a faucet and a broad, odd-looking sink. He couldn't tell if she was being difficult or cooperative or somewhere in between. So far she hadn't found many ways to wreak havoc on the ranch, but she seemed to like it in Montana and might be holding back. On the other hand, she could be taking a hiatus in order to plot her next act of wholesale chaos.

Mariah stood on a ladder with a string of lights over her shoulder, stretching to catch the cord on hooks fastened to a crossbeam. The last of his irritation fled as he watched. Whatever else he thought of her, she took his breath away with her long, auburn hair and sweet curves.

Even if she wasn't blonde or sophisticated.

The unbidden afterthought made him shift his gaze to the snug fit of Mariah's jeans. It was a sight no red-blooded man could fail to appreciate, regardless of their preferences when it came to women. Luke Branson was a fortunate man if Burt's and Ray Cassidy's jokes about him "courtin'" her were to be taken seriously. Mariah would be a delectable armful for any man willing to consider giving up his freedom; she certainly wasn't the type for a brief affair where both parties knew the rules and didn't expect more.

"It isn't diplomatic to ogle a man's granddaughter in his presence," said a voice at Jacob's elbow.

It was Benjamin Weston. Thankfully, Mariah's grandfather seemed more amused than insulted.

"I didn't realize you were present," Jacob said. He couldn't claim he hadn't been ogling, since it was exactly what he'd been doing. Mariah had a body he could take a lifetime getting to know.

Benjamin's merry eyes grew more solemn. "That girl of

ours is pretty special. She's got a fine man, too. They'll be married in a year or so. Luke Branson lives on the next spread over. I hear you met him the other day."

Whoa. Was the old rancher warning him not to poach in another man's corral? A warning wasn't necessary, but Jacob also suspected Mariah would be displeased about the interference. She seemed determined to take care of herself.

"Yes, I've met Mr. Branson," he murmured.

Kittie marched up to them. "Dad, you're supposed to be working. Jeez, *you're* the one who said we should help," she announced resentfully.

"I'll be there in a moment, Kittie. I'm speaking with Mr. Weston—it isn't polite to interrupt."

She stomped away and Jacob's jaw tightened. Even when Kittie was pleasant to other people, she acted as if she hated him.

He turned to Benjamin. "I apologize for my daughter, but she's right. I should be working."

Jacob joined the group using rags to wipe off wooden folding chairs and small square tables. Cleaning the barn might not have sounded fun when Mariah asked for volunteers, but everyone appeared to be enjoying themselves. Chad, the newlywed, was telling his wife and the others in the group about the dances he'd attended on previous visits to the U-2.

"Gregory is terrific on the banjo. And Burt Parsons plays the fiddle like a maestro," he said, pointing at the wrangler on the far side of the barn. "He reminds me of the song from the Charlie Daniels Band where the devil goes down to Georgia and challenges a kid to a contest, with the winner getting a gold fiddle. Burt would win it, every time."

Susan looked at her new husband in astonishment. "The Charlie Daniels Band? I didn't know you listened to country music."

"Uh…yeah. Occasionally, when I can't get anything else on the…uh…radio," he stuttered.

"I love country."

"You *do?*" Chad gave her a delighted—and relieved—smile. "I thought you just listened to jazz."

"I play Coltrane at the design showroom to create a specific atmosphere, but I'm a Nashville junkie at home. I never said so because I thought *you* didn't like it."

"Oh, sweetheart..."

They kissed and a shred of nostalgia caught Jacob by surprise. He remembered the little disclosures after getting married, the accidental "oh my God" revelations that turned out to be nothing at all. It likely seemed worse when you were younger, as he was when he'd married Anna. Everything loomed so large at that age. Cocky self-assurance only carried you so far, particularly for a middle-class grad student marrying a girl from the wealthy social upper crust.

A pickup truck drove up to the barn and Luke Branson got out.

"Hey, Luke," Mariah called. She gave the coil of lights she was stringing to one of the wranglers and hurried over. "What are you doing here?"

The tall rancher shrugged. They didn't kiss, but he tugged a lock of her hair in a familiar way. "Benjamin mentioned you were setting up for the dance, so I brought the hay bales you like to use as extra seating. You'll need it—folks are really looking forward to tomorrow night."

"I appreciate it, but the U-2 has hay. You're busy. You didn't have to spend the time to come over."

"That doesn't mean I don't want to..." The conversation continued in tones too low to make out and Jacob dragged his attention to the chair he was working on. The hinges were tight from disuse and he jammed his knuckle trying to unfold it.

Damn.

The wounded digit throbbed, but it was the illogical flash of jealousy that bothered him the most. Okay, so he was attracted to Mariah and thought she was attracted to him. That and a couple of bucks might get him a cup of coffee at a roadside café.

A short while later Luke Branson lowered the gate of his truck and began unloading the hay bales. Several wranglers pitched in and soon the bales were distributed along the walls of the barn, leaving the broad center clear for dancing. The bales were a nice country touch, and Jacob frowned. The Westons might be a longtime ranching family, but they'd been entertaining tourists for two-plus decades—some of what they did *must* be calculated for effect. Still, hay bales were inexpensive seating and could be used afterward for feed or bedding.

"Is anybody ready for dessert?" queried Benjamin after another ten minutes. He'd returned with some ranch hands, carrying a chocolate cake big enough to serve an army and two large buckets that proved to be hand-cranked ice-cream freezers.

A chorus of agreement came from the workers and they gathered around, eager to get the reward for their less-than-glamorous task.

"Do you want to lick the paddle?" Mariah asked Kittie. She'd pulled it from one of the canisters and it was adorned with thick globs of vanilla ice cream. "You'll have to eat it quickly—homemade melts faster than ice cream from the store."

"Uh…I never had homemade." The questions were churning visibly in Kittie's face as she hesitated. In particular, how uncool would she look if she accepted, yet how could she turn it down? "O…okay, sure."

She settled at one of the small tables with a plate for the paddle. Next to it was a plate with a thick slab of fudge cake and a mound of strawberry ice cream from the second canister. Jacob shook his head. She was so skinny—where did she put all that food?

Susan and Chad were offered the paddle from the other freezer and they giggled as they ate the treat, taking turns licking it and sharing kisses in between. Their innocent pleasure sent a strange sensation through Jacob. They were obviously an urban couple with upscale careers, yet were having fun with a simple ice-cream paddle, their sophistication falling away like rain off a roof.

Maybe it was from being on a honeymoon or being in love and feeling as if anything was possible.

Jacob pushed the odd thoughts away. He knew the harsh lessons life could teach, and since he would never be going on another honeymoon, he didn't need to worry about the crazy things love could do to a person.

KITTIE LOOKED AROUND, hoping Reid wouldn't come in and see her eating cake…or, especially, licking the ice-cream paddle. Her friends at school said guys didn't want girls who ate a lot of food, so they'd have a sandwich or drink milk before going on a date. Then there was Nana Carolyn, who was always telling her to take petite portions and be ladylike. She loved Nana Carolyn and Grandfather Barrett, but that junk about being a proper lady was boring.

Grandma and Grandpa O'Donnell were more comfortable, and their house wasn't so formal and fancy. The only thing she liked about Nana Carolyn and Grandfather Barrett's house was getting to sleep in her mom's old room. They'd kept it the way it was when she was a teenager.

Kittie's mouth turned down. Sometimes she thought she remembered her mom or could hear her voice, but she was never sure.

Mariah switched on the little lights crisscrossed overhead and everybody clapped. Kittie kept eating since it was dumb to clap, but it did look pretty.

Her dad was across the barn. He was looking at Mariah, probably because they'd had another fight. Kittie scrunched her nose. They sure didn't get along. Of course, he was real good at pissing people off.

Burt plunked a cup of coffee on the table. "You mind?" he asked and sat opposite her without waiting for an answer.

"N-no." But it was weird. She was sure Burt didn't like her. He only seemed to talk to her when she'd done something wrong or when he was saying it was time to learn to clean up after the horses. *That* was what they were supposed to do on Monday morning and it sounded gross. She'd refuse, except she knew that Reid shoveled horse stalls nearly every day, so she'd just have to suck it up and do it.

"Y'er missin' old Blue, aren't you?" Burt said.

Kittie blinked. Cleaning the barn for the dance hadn't been so bad, but she *did* miss the gray horse. There weren't any kids visiting the ranch and things didn't seem so lonely when she was with Blue. He was a really smart horse and already recognized her when she visited him in the barn or corral.

Still…she wouldn't have gotten chocolate cake if they'd gone riding, and this homemade ice cream was the yummiest stuff she'd ever tasted. It was yummier than pepperoni pizza, and she *loved* pepperoni pizza.

"Blue is awful nice. When was he born? Everyone keeps calling him 'old.'"

"Let's see now…" Burt drank some of his coffee. "He was foaled the year after Mariah went to college, so that makes him nine, and horses can live twenty, thirty years if they're took care of. And nobody takes care of horses like the Westons."

Kittie was glad that Blue would be on the ranch a long while, even if she wasn't going to be here to see it.

"Does it matter to horses if you're sad or sick or anything?"

Burt looked at her over the rim of his cup. "I suppose that depends on how you see things. Folks who don't have the heart for 'em think they're nothing but dumb animals, but I know Ringer takes extra care of me on the days my arthritis hurts. I don't trust most people the way I trust Ringer."

"I trust Blue."

"And he trusts you. I can tell. By the by, a girl your age is coming on Sunday with her family," Burt said. "From Brisbane, Australia. They'll be here two or three weeks. It's a long way to Montana from Brisbane, and she won't know the ropes round here."

"Yeah?" Kittie tried to sound casual and hide her excitement. There was the barn dance tomorrow, and she was hope, hope, *hoping* that Reid might want to dance with her. And now a girl from Australia was arriving who may have seen a real koala bear, not just one in a zoo. Better yet, she might want to be friends. "I guess she'll have to learn."

"Guess she will."

In the middle of the barn, a wrangler pulled out his harmonica and another got out his banjo. Soon a bunch of them were playing and Burt tapped his foot in rhythm with a song that Ray Cassidy was singing. The words were sad, about a man whose son had died in a war, but he was going to ride his horse forever, only stopping when the angels called.

Burt seemed faraway when the song was done.

"Did you ever get married, Burt?" she asked when the cowboys started playing something else.

"Nearly did. My sweetheart was a rancher's daughter down by the Big Horn Mountains in Wyoming. She was pretty, too, with hair the color of corn silk."

"What happened?"

"I went to Texas to work so I could save up money and get us a place, but someone told her I got killed in a stampede. She married a man in Cheyenne before finding out it weren't true. Her oldest boy sent a letter when she passed—said she never forgot me…and that we'd meet again in heaven."

Kittie hugged her tummy. "That isn't fair. She should have waited to get married until she knew for sure."

Burt rubbed his jaw and she heard the scratchy rasp from his whisker stubble. "I don't know 'bout that. She did what she had to do. You see, that boy who wrote me…he was mine, and in those days it weren't proper for a girl to have a baby without a husband. I didn't know that Wade was my boy till I got that letter, but his stepdaddy did and loved 'em both, just the same."

"Omigod, you have a son," Kittie said, fascinated.

"Grandkids, too. Wade comes to visit often, and seein' his smile is like seein' my sweetheart's again."

Burt fumbled in his pocket and took out a worn leather wallet. It was thin, without much inside but some pictures. A girl smiled at Kitty from a faded photograph, and a man with Burt's brown eyes laughed at the camera. He said the other photos were of his grandchildren and great-grandchildren.

"Do you see them, too?" she asked.

"Now and then. Wade wants me to retire and come live closer to him and his wife in Cheyenne, but I've been at the U-2 for forty years and I ain't ready to go yet. You make a place yer home, and it's hard to leave."

Kittie sighed, unable to decide if she was sad for Burt or glad that he had a family, even if he'd only known about them for a short while. She got up and collected the ice-cream paddle and plates.

"I'm going to visit Blue. Do you think he's still in the corral?" That morning they'd moved a herd of cows to a new grazing area before coming back at lunch to help with the barn.

Burt nodded. "Yup. I didn't know if we were going out again later, so I left him there. Bring him an apple. They're his favorite. He snorts when you jis got a carrot."

"Uh…thanks," she said.

"Not at all. Us horse folk gotta stick together."

Horse folk.

Burt thought she was horse folk?

Outside the barn, Kittie grinned and broke into a run toward the corral, stopping first at the apple barrel to grab the four biggest apples it held. Horse folk took care of their mounts, and Blue deserved the best.

CHAPTER SIX

"MA'AM, HAVE YOU ever considered paving the road from the highway?" asked the courier as he handed Mariah an electronic clipboard. "It's a long drive into your ranch over gravel, and this is the second time I've been out today."

"Maybe in four or five years." She signed her name, deciding not to tell him that he'd probably be coming to the U-2 regularly while Jacob O'Donnell was staying there. As for paving the road, it might happen when Reid was through college and more pressing needs had been taken care of. In the meantime they'd just keep laying down gravel, which was expensive enough.

"Hmm." He gave her the two packages he held and climbed back into his truck.

Mariah wasn't surprised to see both parcels were for Jacob, and both had been sent by overnight shipping. One, a large envelope from O'Donnell International, was marked urgent. Good grief, the guy had been in Montana for a few days—what could be urgent already?

She thought about getting a wrangler to give Jacob the packages, then decided it would be an act of cowardice. She'd lost her temper...*again*...and it would be uncomfortable talking to him so soon following their argument, but it might teach her to keep her mouth shut. Okay, so he'd cynically assumed the story about the Big Barn was an invention, basically accusing her of telling a lie to turn a buck. It wasn't enough of an excuse to kick him back to Seattle the way he deserved.

Stop, Mariah ordered herself crossly. Just thinking about it annoyed her. They'd had difficult guests in the past, but none of them had frustrated her so much or made her wish she'd refused to let them come to the U-2.

Sighing, she went hunting for Jacob.

She saw Caitlin and Burt in one of the corrals. He was teaching the teenager to groom Blue. Even after several days, the sight of Caitlin in her black clothes was startling, though with the bright red rhinestone skull and crossbones on her T-shirt, the spiked leather collar and belly tattoo were barely noticeable.

Jacob wasn't in his tent or the mess tent, so she checked at the guest "power" station. Sure enough, he was unplugging his phone and plugging in his computer. Three years before, she'd faced up to the fact they *had* to have a spot for visitors to charge their cell phones, camera batteries and other toys. Granddad hadn't liked it, particularly since they'd already built a similar station to recharge the lanterns used in the tents, but he'd finally agreed it was a necessary evil. The alternative was having the guests constantly asking to plug their electronics in at the house or casually appropriating outlets in the barns or elsewhere, causing its own set of problems.

Mariah held out the deliveries. "These were just dropped off for you." She almost added *Mr. O'Donnell,* but knew he might see it as a provocation when he'd told her twice already to call him Jacob.

"Thanks." He tucked the envelope under his arm and looked at the other package for a long moment.

"Is something wrong?"

"It's from my mother-in-law. Do you have a knife I can use? Carolyn used a lot of tape sealing this."

His mother-in-law?

Not *ex*-mother-in-law?

"Sure."

Mariah led him to the nearest barn and unlocked a storage cabinet. The question of in-laws could be sensitive. Five years ago Luke's parents had transferred the ranch into his name and moved to Florida for his mother's health. The Bransons were in their forties when he was born, a gift after they had given up hoping for children. Mariah got along with them, but they'd started pushing for a fall wedding. It wasn't tough to guess the reason—they were anxious for grandchildren. Ranchers around Buckeye tended to marry young and have big families.

Jacob sliced the package open and read the note inside, a curious expression on his face. When he tipped the remaining contents into his hand and cut away the protective bubble wrap, Mariah saw a gold locket on a chain. He clenched his fingers on the necklace so hard that his knuckles went white.

"Put the knife back in the cabinet when you're done. I'll lock it later," Mariah murmured, eager to escape. It was as if she'd stumbled into something that should have remained private.

"Mariah, wait," Jacob called when she was almost to the door.

She turned reluctantly.

"I want to apologize for that crack I made about foolish romanticizing," he said. "But the way you talked about the barn and the spirit of people being there—it hit a sore spot. Kittie tends to have an overactive imagination and I don't want to encourage her."

That sounded like Jacob. He probably thought any imagination was too much. Still, she had the impression he was trying to keep from saying something else to offend her. Apparently he believed in nothing beyond the here and now, or maybe he didn't want to believe in *anything*. She was sorry for him, but mostly she was sorry for Caitlin. Her father was protecting her to the point of smothering her, and yet he discouraged the imagination that could give her soul some freedom.

"I suppose it's never easy knowing what to do with kids," she said awkwardly. "Reid and I used to talk, but lately he's very closemouthed. I don't know if something is wrong, or if it's just a phase, or if I should even worry about it at all."

Jacob slipped the gold locket and the note from his mother-in-law into his pocket. "That's right, you mentioned you were Reid's guardian. I take it your parents are gone?"

"They were…" She swallowed. It shouldn't be so hard to say after four years. "They were broadsided by a drunk driver on their way home from Billings one night. Mom was killed instantly and Dad was critically injured. I got to the hospital in time to see him. The doctors thought he'd make it, but he… he simply gave up when he found out Mom was dead. Reid was twelve and he's still having a rough time dealing with it."

"It can't be any easier for you."

"I'm managing."

Jacob absently rubbed his neck with the hand holding the borrowed knife, nearly causing Mariah heart failure. What if he stabbed himself? She'd hate to see a guest get hurt, but he also might have to spend the night in the Buckeye Medical clinic, leaving *her* temporarily responsible for his daughter.

Gingerly, she took the knife and locked it in the storage cabinet.

"I saw Caitlin and Burt at the corral, combing Blue," she said. "She's very fond of him."

"Which one, Blue or Burt?"

The corner of her mouth twitched. "Blue. I wouldn't know how she feels about Burt. Children connect well with horses—they're sensitive, intelligent animals. What's more, they're usually eager to please."

"Unlike teenagers."

Mariah shook her head at Jacob's droll tone. They had nothing in common, but if he got the pompous stick out from up his butt and let go of his preoccupation with money and the bottom line, he might be tolerable on a short-term basis.

"You used to be a teenager yourself," she pointed out. "And don't tell me you were an angel."

"Far from an angel. I was an expert in getting myself in hot water. For example, there was the weekend I rebuilt the engine on my dad's car when he was away from home on a business trip. I was twelve and already planning to be an engineer, so I redesigned the fuel system. Unfortunately, I bypassed the catalytic converter, in addition to making some other miscalculations."

Mariah whistled. She wasn't a mechanic, but she was pretty sure the catalytic converter was important. "The car didn't start?"

"It never ran again, and the repairs would have cost twice what it was worth. Dad sold it to a junkyard and suggested I go into an engineering specialty that didn't involve cars—he didn't think Detroit was ready for me."

She laughed, yet it wasn't so much what he'd said that touched her as the vision of a much younger version of Jacob O'Donnell making mistakes and being teased by his father. He obviously hadn't grown up with money if his parents had owned a car not worth fixing.

"What area of engineering did you choose, or did you major in something else after totaling your dad's ride?"

"I have a doctorate in aeronautical and astronautical engineering," Jacob said. "I wanted to build planes that were faster and safer than anything ever conceived.... I even flirted with the thought of working for NASA on the space shuttle."

"No cars, then."

"Yeah, that made Dad happy."

They walked outside and he stood watching his daughter in the corral. Caitlin was grooming her father's horse under Burt's supervision, giggling as Blue whinnied and nosed her neck for attention. The horse had quickly grown attached to the rebellious teen, almost as if he knew they'd be riding together for several weeks.

Mariah expected Jacob to say something else about Kittie's safety, but other than his mouth tightening, he didn't react. Maybe he realized it had all been said yesterday when they'd "discussed" his daughter learning how to curry Blue. He'd likely envisioned broken bones in his daughter's feet from getting stepped on, crushed ribs from being thrown against a stable wall or fence and a range of other unlikely injuries. He'd actually called Caitlin's doctor in Seattle to be reassured that her vaccinations were up-to-date after someone told him horses were associated with tetanus.

Mariah couldn't promise that nothing would happen when Caitlin picked up a currycomb and brush, but nobody was suggesting she groom a bucking bronco. The horses used by the U-2 guests were carefully selected for their gentle temperaments.

"So international business mogul is a long way from aeronautical engineering," Mariah said as a distraction. "What happened?"

A spasm of pain crossed Jacob's face. "Anna."

"Anna?" she asked tentatively. She'd speculated that Jacob was divorced, but that was all it was, a guess.

"Kittie's mother."

Without another word he turned and strode back into the barn, leaving more questions than he'd answered.

IN THE QUIET of the barn, Jacob drew a deep breath. Thinking about Anna had erased the lingering imprint of Mariah's touch, but before that it was as if static electricity had brushed his skin. He had no doubt she'd meant it innocently, simply taking the knife to put away safely, yet he'd remained conscious of the sensation for the rest of their conversation.

Disgusted with himself, Jacob pulled the note from Carolyn Barrett from his pocket and read it again.

Dearest Jacob,

Thank you for letting us know where you'll be staying.

I'm sending the antique locket Anna used to wear when she was a girl. You may remember she wore it on her wedding day—it was her "something old." I ran across the necklace in the safe last year and thought we'd give it to Kittie when the time seemed right, but perhaps you'll have a better idea of when that should be.

I wish we knew how to help Kittie, but I'm sure you'll do everything possible to get her through this troubling period. Please tell us if there's something we can do, as well.

You are so very dear to us, Jacob. I don't think we've expressed how grateful we are for the happiness you gave Anna. We wouldn't have made it without you, though I fear we've been too set in our ways to be the best grandparents.

Our warmest love to you both.

Carolyn

Anna had been the light of Carolyn and Richard's lives, but they'd rarely spoken of her since her death. When Jacob had first read the letter, the references to Anna had shaken him. Now something new was bothering him—the note didn't have Carolyn's usual reserve. Was there something he should know? The Barretts weren't elderly, but they also weren't exactly young.

Taking out his phone, he dialed his in-laws' number.

"Hello, this is Jacob O'Donnell," he said when the butler answered. "Are Richard or Carolyn at home?"

"Indeed, sir. I'll let Mr. Barrett know you are waiting on the line."

A short while later, Richard greeted him. They spoke about trivialities for a few minutes before Jacob cleared his throat.

"Richard, I received a package from Carolyn today. Is everything all right? The note didn't sound like her."

"Oh, yes, no need to worry. A friend had a minor stroke on Monday and it was one of life's wake-up calls—a reminder that we should say important things to the people who matter to us. Not that it comes easily—at heart we're just transplanted New Englanders, crusty on the outside and soft as pudding underneath. Carolyn tried to let her pudding side show when she wrote that note to you."

"You're certain that's all it is?" While Jacob had always been fond of his in-laws, he was surprised by the urgency he felt.

"Very certain. We should be around for many more years. You'll be quite tired of us by the time we go."

"We've tolerated you so far."

Richard chuckled and they chatted awhile longer. The conversation was relaxed enough that Jacob was no longer worried by the time he said goodbye. At the best of times the Barretts were difficult to fathom. He didn't think they meant to be inscrutable, but they came from a rarified stratum of old money and strict propriety that was hard to get past. On top of which, there was the New England crustiness his father-in-law liked to joke about.

Before returning to his tent, Jacob collected the second package, which he'd left on a bale of hay. Another contract was in the envelope, along with a memo from Gretchen, giving him a status report and letting him know that a spare battery for his laptop and accessories for his smartphone had been shipped and would be delivered directly to the U-2. Provided his phone had a sufficiently strong signal, he would be able to use it as a modem on his computer.

"Stay in Montana. I get more done when you're away," she'd written at the end of her message. Gretchen might be the only employee in the company who would dare to make a comment like that, but she knew she was indispensable.

And she probably *did* get more done when he wasn't jogging her elbow.

Jacob leafed through the dreary contract; his legal staff had made notes regarding the updates they'd made. He'd look it over after Kittie was asleep. Yet he scowled at the thought of another night reading paperwork and tossed it into the storage trunk by the bed. It would have to wait till tomorrow—tonight he planned to sleep. He was so shy on rest that surely not even the silence would keep him awake.

HOW COULD YOU HAVE *told Jacob O'Donnell about Dad and the hospital?* Mariah scolded herself as she washed pots and pans that evening. The dinner crew hadn't needed help, but scrubbing the heavy cookware was cathartic and she'd needed to burn up the frustration she was feeling. Normally she headed for one of the barns to find a task that would keep her mind and body busy when she felt this way, but Reid and the ranch hands had said the horse stalls were already shoveled out for the day.

Idiot, she added to the litany in her brain.

People on vacation did *not* want to hear anyone else's troubles. They wanted to relax and forget the outside world existed. It was a basic rule she'd followed faithfully—after all, she had Grams and Granddad and Aunt Lettie if she needed someone to talk to or just listen. Then there was Squash, who purred and didn't offer opinions.

And Luke, Mariah amended quickly.

But not Jacob. He was a passing fixture on the ranch. And though he was staying longer than most of their guests, that didn't mean she shouldn't follow her rules with him. Yet so far she'd done a lousy job of dealing with Jacob.

"Hey, take it easy, you're rubbing a hole in my favorite pot," Reggie complained. "You've scrubbed the bottom so thin I can see daylight through it."

"That's utterly *ridic*..." Mariah stopped and swallowed her reply. Honestly, where was her sense of humor? She rinsed the pot and gave it to Reggie. "I think you rescued it in time, but don't tell the cast-iron skillets it's your favorite, or they'll get jealous."

"If you won't tell, I won't. Now scat."

"Scat? Some people think I'm in charge around here."

"Not in my chuck wagon."

Mariah grinned and discarded the rubber gloves she was using. She suspected that old-time chuck-wagon cooks had often gotten away with outrageous behavior—possibly measured by how skilled they were at filling stomachs with tasty food. Reggie would have gotten away with murder. What was more, he took his ever-changing crew of helpers in stride and the guests liked his good-hearted bossiness.

"Why don't you take the night off?" Granddad said quietly as she went into the mess tent where the usual games and music had begun. Some of the chess sets and checkerboards had been around since her father was a boy.

"Me? No, I'm fine. Why is everyone is chasing me away tonight?"

"Because you got a burr under your saddle, and don't tell me different."

Burr under her saddle?

Mariah had heard the turn of phrase a thousand times, yet it reminded her of Jacob O'Donnell's accusations.

"Granddad, do you think we ham it up for the tourists, putting on a show of ranch life that isn't entirely real?"

He regarded her with blank astonishment. "Why would you question such a thing?"

"No reason. That is, not a *good* reason. It was something a guest said today. As a family we don't regularly eat the way Reggie cooks—chili and barbecued steak and fried potatoes and such. Do you know how much sausage and bacon he goes through in a week? Not to mention butter, eggs, cheese and cooking oil. A heart doctor would be horrified."

Granddad snorted. “We don’t eat the way my mama cooked because your grandmother won’t let us. It isn’t everybody who has an M.D. presiding over the home kitchen. Besides, you both insisted that Reggie include vegetarian and other choices for the ‘health conscious.’ And he does, but a whole lot of it goes to the hogs.”

True enough, but the U-2’s guest menu always had a traditional Western theme: lots of meat—especially beef as they were on a cattle ranch—with corn bread and biscuits and beans at every hot meal. Granted, it was also the kind of food they could produce easily in volume, which was why chuck-wagon cooks had fed cowboys that way for generations.

Granddad put his hand on her shoulder. “Mariah, the way I see it, we’re cooking for company. You don’t feed company everyday fare. You feed them what they’ll enjoy. We just have more company than most.”

He was right; it was what their guests expected and enjoyed. Even their so-called health-conscious visitors often ate steak and biscuits and bypassed the healthier dishes.

As for the rest of what went on…they weren’t making up stories or pretending something wasn’t what it was; while they made adjustments for greenhorns, they were definitely a working ranch. The U-2 raised cattle for the market and didn’t pretend otherwise—their herds weren’t just for show the way some guests assumed.

“You know, I think I will take the night off,” she said.

“Excellent. We don’t have to be here all the time. Anyhow, the wranglers can take care of most everything, and if there’s a problem, they know where to find us.”

Mariah wandered toward the Big Barn. She remembered how excited she was when it was being built after years of searching for old chestnut planks. Her parents had originally wanted to build it all out of chestnut, but they weren’t willing to dismantle working barns to do it. And in the end, they’d decided the mixture of new and historic wood worked best.

The sun was low in the western sky and Mariah crouched by the cornerstone, tracing the words on the brass plate affixed to it.

> Dedicated to the past and future. May they be bridged with more laughter than tears.

Laughter and tears.

With a feeling of melancholy chasing her heels, Mariah walked inside and sat by one of the hay bales, using it as a backrest. It was sweetly fragrant, and she wondered how Luke had found the time to bring it over to the U-2. Taking that horse ride together the other day had been an indulgence in such an active season of the year.

Pip padded up and lay by Mariah with a quiet *wumpf.*

"Hello, boy. Did Granddad send you?"

He put his head on her thigh as she stroked him.

She closed her eyes and listened with her heart, more than her ears. Sometimes she *did* seem to hear whispers from the past, yet it wasn't an ancient memory she heard now; it was footsteps crossing the threshold.

"Do you need something, Jacob?" she asked.

"Your back was to the door. How did you know it was me?"

"I'd claim to be fey like my great-great-grandmother, but it would annoy you."

Warmer tendrils of air brushed against her cheek as he got down next to her. "Do you think you're fey?"

Mariah looked at him. "I think the world is more than what we can see and hear and touch, but the truth is that I knew it was you from the way you walk—straight, single-minded, placing your feet firmly."

"I can deal with that."

Jacob fell silent. Though she hated to admit it, somehow he'd gone from being a guest to something more, though she couldn't have defined what that meant. She didn't even want to. The awareness darting through her body was undeniable and she couldn't recall ever feeling the same sharp, intense ache for Luke. That was the most disturbing part of it. What was wrong with her? She was supposed to marry Luke; they'd been planning it for years.

The rays of light from the sun grew longer and the shadows deepened as they sat, each lost in their thoughts.

"Anna was my wife," Jacob said finally, as if just finishing their earlier conversation. "And I worry about Kittie having fanciful beliefs because she used to fantasize about her mother. You see, Anna…Anna died when Kittie was two."

Mariah's stomach tightened; it was hard enough to have your life torn apart as an adult. But for such a young child?

"That must have been awful."

"There aren't any words." Jacob pulled a piece of hay from a bale and rolled it between his fingers. "She was diagnosed with a heart condition too late to do anything about it. A transplant was the only option, but she had a rare blood type, and a donor heart is one of the few things her parents' money couldn't buy. Kittie has the same blood type," he added. "Travel is an issue since she may not be able to get a transfusion if it's needed. You must think I'm crazy to be concerned about that, living out here the way you do."

Mariah shivered. A situation you might philosophically risk for yourself loomed much larger when it was someone you loved. "It isn't crazy. We're lucky to have two doctors in the family for emergencies, but there are many ranches located an hour or more from medical care. It's a trade-off for having this life."

Jacob hiked his eyebrows. "Don't take this the wrong way, but it seems as if you accept a *lot* of trade-offs."

He was right, and one of them was the influx of visitors each summer. Yet in some ways Mariah didn't mind—she'd met people from around the globe. While it would be wonderful to ride fence lines for a day without thinking about the demands of strangers, it was never dull with so many guests at the ranch. And by the time she was truly weary of it, fall arrived and they had peace.

Jacob was actually the first guest she regretted; his presence had become far too personal for comfort.

"We get more than we give up." She was used to people who thought the U-2 was a nice place to visit and the last place they'd want to live, yet the open land was as necessary to her as breathing. *That* was what she had to keep in mind whenever Jacob got to her.

"I can't claim to understand," he murmured. "I grew up in a small town and couldn't wait to get to the city. You might like it—Seattle has an energy that's really exciting."

"Naw, I can't imagine living anywhere but Montana. We have energy here, too—it's called weather and cattle prices. One minute the prices are up, the next they're sliding into the basement."

"Doesn't sound appealing."

"You get used to it. And there's nothing like the sensation that goes through your body when a herd of horses gallops past, their hooves thudding on the ground. Or the beauty of an eagle soaring over the prairie on a summer afternoon, the air currents carrying it higher and higher. I love being connected to the land and knowing its rhythms and moods."

"You must need a poet's soul to live here."

"It can't hurt."

Jacob sighed and took something from his pocket. Though the light was low, Mariah saw a flash of gold and knew it was the locket he'd received in his package. He turned it around as if searching for an answer in it.

"Did life on the ranch—dealing with life and death on a regular basis—make it easier to accept losing your parents?" he asked. "Because even though it's been over ten years, I haven't stopped missing my wife. Especially recently, with all the problems Kittie is having. I keep thinking how different it would be if Anna was here."

Mariah rested her head on the hay. "I doubt anyone stops missing the people they love, no matter where they live."

"I adored Anna from the moment I met her in college," Jacob said slowly. "She was sweet and gentle and it seemed incredible that she'd fall in love with an ex-jock working his way through grad school. I would have done anything for her." He smiled faintly. "Remember that the next time you call me a soulless businessman."

"I never called you a soulless businessman."

"But you thought it, right?"

A smile tugged at Mariah's mouth, as well. "Not quite."

"Ah, diplomacy. I'll have you know that I provide top employee benefits, including health insurance, and I run a green company. It's good business to keep your employees happy and be environmentally responsible."

Good business? Was that his *only* reason for being fair to his employees or having taken measures for O'Donnell International to "go green"? He shouldn't have added that part if he wanted her to see him as more than a soulless businessman.

"And you love your daughter," she said. That, with his devotion to his wife's memory, was his best recommendation. She couldn't count his unparalleled sex appeal, which had nothing to do with likability, just biology.

"More than anything. I know you think I'm overprotective, but what I haven't told you is that Anna's problem was congenital. Two months after she died, Kittie needed surgery to correct the same defect. I don't think she remembers.... I *hope* she doesn't."

Mariah shuddered. It didn't make Jacob more likable, yet it explained why he was so protective of Kittie...*Caitlin,* she reminded herself. She didn't want to fall into bad habits.

"Are you close to Caitlin's maternal grandparents?"

He shrugged. "More or less. The Barretts come from an

exclusive social background—they could have fought the marriage, but instead they welcomed me. We mostly just discuss Kittie and she visits them often. Anna was Richard and Carolyn's only child and I think they'd like to be closer, but it's awkward."

Mariah had a sneaking suspicion that Jacob was too busy building his fortune to be close to anyone, but it wasn't any of her business. Still…

"Do they know about her current problems?"

Jacob nodded. "Some of it. More than my own parents. I don't deny that I've made mistakes raising Kittie. For a couple of years after Anna died, she would have these imaginary conversations with her mom. It was as if she actually thought Anna was there, doing things with her. When Kittie finally realized she *wasn't* there, it was as if her mother had died all over again."

"She didn't lose her belief gradually?"

"No, maybe somebody said something to her. I don't know. Kittie cried for days. That's when I knew it should have been handled another way from the beginning. But she was two when Anna died, and there was the surgery to get through. I was still in shock myself, and I figured if it helped Kittie to imagine seeing her mother…what was the harm? I didn't think she really believed it."

Mariah could hardly comprehend what it must have been like for him to bury the wife he'd loved so deeply, only to see their child undergo major surgery.

"When I was little," she said, "I used to think my great-grandmother came and told me bedtime stories of the tall chestnut trees she'd known in her childhood…about the fall harvest of nuts and the glow of color across the hillsides. I would go to sleep and dream about those trees, walking in thick stands of them, while the autumn leaves drifted down on my face. It wasn't until I was older that I realized she couldn't have told me those stories."

"Is that good or bad?"

"Neither. It just was. Being a teenager is hard. Caitlin may not consciously remember her fantasies, or if she does, they may be a comfort. My great-grandmother died the year before I was born, yet it's as if I know her. Is that so terrible?"

"You aren't on the verge of self-destruction."

"True." Mariah shook herself. What was it about Jacob O'Donnell that unhinged her tongue? She'd told him things she hadn't told anyone, much less Luke or her family. She'd heard that it could be easier confiding in a stranger than in someone you knew, but this was idiotic, since they'd likely be fighting again in five minutes.

"I simply don't get Kittie's clothes and everything," Jacob said. "They're dreadful. You'd never know what a beautiful child she is under that stuff. And the hair dye…? Thank God it isn't permanent, any more than that damned spiderweb on her tummy. At least, I hope it isn't permanent."

"Then it isn't a real tattoo?" Mariah asked, unaccountably relieved. The idea that he'd allowed his fourteen-year-old daughter to get a tattoo had appalled her.

Drat him anyway. She'd feel better about disliking Jacob if she didn't know the complicated reasons he was *absolutely impossible.* But no, getting that necklace must have rattled him enough to say things he wouldn't usually reveal. She certainly hadn't asked him to tell her about his wife or Caitlin's heart surgery. Yet now she knew more about his life, and it wasn't something she could easily dismiss.

"She claims they're temporary applications she got from a costume shop—I hope it's the truth. If I find out someone is giving minors tattoos without parental consent…" The look on his face was chilling. "She also wants to get her nose pierced and I won't agree to that, either. As for the rest of it, the school psychologist said I should let her express herself, so I've tried to keep from saying too much. It's hideous, though. All that black…even her lipstick."

"Some people like the Goth style. I'm sure she thinks it's terrific or she wouldn't be wearing the stuff."

Jacob frowned. "You mean the Visigoths that invaded the Roman Empire? They didn't wear black jeans and T-shirts with leering skulls on them, and why would anyone copy how they dressed in the first place?"

Mariah blinked.

Visigoths?

How out of touch *was* Jacob?

"No, the Goth movement," she said. "You know, the subculture that started back in the eighties. I think it began with the Gothic rock scene, but there probably isn't a single definition of a Goth, and people are adopting aspects of the look without embracing the subculture."

"Oh…right. Goths."

"By the way, where *is* Caitlin?" Mariah sat up, somewhat alarmed. "Are you sure it's safe to leave her alone?"

"She's in the mess tent. Ray offered to teach her chess. I suggested we play cards, but she gave me a drop-dead glare and took Ray up on his offer instead. I went for a walk and saw you come in here. It gets old being the bad guy," he said reflectively. "I love Kittie to distraction, but I decided two things a long time ago—one, I'd never remarry and, two, I'd never have more children. Raising another teenager would take twenty years off my life. I swear, they're a different species altogether."

"Hey." Mariah poked him. "I haven't had my kids yet. Stop scaring me."

"If you think you're scared now, just wait until they're fourteen. You'll be terrified."

Mariah laughed. For all his faults, Jacob did have a fair amount of wit.

CHAPTER SEVEN

KITTIE STOOD IN FRONT of a mirror in the U-2's guest bathroom, twisting back and forth to make sure there wasn't anything out of place on her outfit and that her black lipstick was on straight. She wanted to be perfect for the dance. A lot of people didn't seem to like her skull-and-crossbones T-shirts so she'd picked another top that wasn't as awesome, but *much* better than the junk her dad had gotten when he went shopping a couple of days ago.

Jeez.

He'd bought three pairs of blue jeans that were sort of baggy and four long-sleeved plaid shirts that would make her look like a hillbilly if she was stupid enough to wear them… the kind of hillbilly who stayed a virgin her entire life.

Oh, *puleeeze.*

At the bottom of her duffel bag she'd found a sort-of-okay black T-shirt that had a red snake on the front with funky yellow eyes. She'd redone her nails with fresh black polish, though they were even shorter than they were when she'd first gotten to Montana, and then she had washed and dyed her hair to get rid of the icky blond streaks. Permanent dye would be nice, except sometimes it was fun to make it a different color.

Kittie checked herself in the mirror one last time before heading to the mess tent. Supper was early because of the dance, but she was almost too excited to eat. *Almost.* She got hungry riding and doing fun stuff all day.

"Is that what you're wearing to the dance?" asked her dad, sitting down across from her with his food.

"What of it?"

He seemed annoyed and shrugged. "Nothing."

Reid started to come over and she was glad she'd gotten salad instead of meat and beans. She moved the lettuce around with her fork so he wouldn't see how much blue-cheese dressing and buttered croutons she'd put on it.

"Hi, Reid," she said.

"Oh…hi, Kittie. Mr. O'Donnell, my grandfather wanted you to know a shipping service delivered two more packages from your company. We have them locked in the ranch office for safekeeping. Would you like me to bring them down now?"

"No, I'll go up before the dance."

Reid stuck his thumbs in the loops of his jeans. "I guess that's all right. The office is in the back of the house."

Kittie could have spit. *That* was why Reid had come over? It had nothing to do with her, just deliveries for her dad's dumb company.

"And earlier this morning a courier picked up the package you were shipping to Japan," Reid added. "He said to remind you they don't come out on Sundays."

Her dad let out an exasperated breath. "I know."

Reid nodded to them both and left.

Disgusted, Kittie shoved her salad away and went to get another plate. "I'll have steak and beans and corn bread," she announced at the food table.

"Rare, medium or well-done?" Edna Sallenger held up a pair of tongs and smiled. She *always* smiled and Kittie was sick of it. Nobody was happy all the time.

"Whatever."

"Then I'll give you a medium. That's a good choice if you're undecided." Edna put a steak on the plate. The servers down the table added beans and two squares of corn bread and gave it back.

Kittie loaded the corn bread with butter and honey and poured barbecue sauce on the steak. The teacher who'd taught her class about nutrition last semester would get a sour-apple look on his face if he saw what she'd loaded her plate with, but she didn't care. And what did it matter anyhow?

Defiantly, she sat down and began eating. She didn't care if every cute boy in the whole wide world saw her.

"IS ANYONE THERE?" Jacob called as he walked to the rear of the sprawling ranch house.

From the back he couldn't see the barns or tents or restrooms, just a rising vista of wild land dotted with trees and a thicker stand of cottonwoods. The fenced kitchen garden to the south wasn't even visible. However, extensions had been built on each end of the house, creating a private patio protected on three sides, the fourth side being that incredible view. Dr. Weston was on the patio, working on a quilt set up on a frame.

"Hello," she said, looking up. "I thought I heard someone."

He stepped closer. "You sew, too, Dr. Weston? Baking, sewing, doctoring—you have many talents."

"Sewing is the same principle as stitching up cowboys." She snipped a thread and smoothed a seam.

"How do you find the time for everything?"

"I'm semi-retired. My daughter runs the medical clinic in town, though I go a couple of days a week and for emergencies. And I do my bit on the U-2, fixing up visitors and cowboys. But I've always quilted, no matter how busy I might be. It's an excellent stress reliever. Keeps me centered."

Dr. Weston's clear gaze and the tiny laugh lines around her mouth suggested she didn't need "centering." She must be seventyish, yet she was one of those timeless women you occasionally met, beautiful and ageless. It was incredible to think she'd lost a son and daughter-in-law in a senseless accident and could still radiate peace.

"I'm sorry to disturb you while you're getting 'centered,' but I came for some packages your grandson said had come."

"Oh, yes, knock on that door. Mariah is taking care of a reservation for August before the dance starts. You're attending, aren't you?"

"Of course. And you?"

Her eyes twinkled. "Oh, yes. My husband and I do a mean polka. We'll teach you—it's fun."

Jacob smiled. He would love to hire Dr. Weston for the health clinic in his corporate headquarters. She was the type of doctor who could keep everyone healthy. And if her daughter was anything like her, she might also be a viable recruit. He should check it out. He could offer a generous signing bonus, and who wouldn't grab the chance to leave a flyspeck town in Montana?

Mariah, a voice whispered in his head.

Stop it, he answered crossly.

He knocked on the office door and went inside when Mariah called to come in.

The small space was jammed with office furniture and equipment, including a fax machine. *And a computer hooked up to the internet.* He practically salivated. After a week of being cut off from modern conveniences, the prospect of sitting in a comfortable office chair and getting on the internet was seductive. Maybe the Westons would let him use their facilities for a couple of hours every night after Kittie was asleep. He'd have to find the right moment to propose an arrangement.

"Jacob...hello," Mariah said, spinning around in her chair.

Thoughts of the internet and fax machines vanished from his brain at the sight of her. Instead of her usual jeans and shirt, Mariah wore a blue camisole-style top and skirt that contrasted nicely with her auburn hair and lightly tanned skin. *Fresh and delectable.* The outfit was far from chic, but it suited her and was snug in all the right places.

A fleeting thought went through Jacob's mind—it was a good thing Benjamin Weston wasn't there, because Jacob was definitely ogling the man's granddaughter.

"Is something wrong?" he asked, noticing her distracted expression.

"Not really. A professor from Sweden and a group of his film students are planning a trip to the ranch, but only one of them speaks English. I'm searching for a wrangler who's fluent in Swedish before confirming the reservation."

"Why bother? The English speaker can translate for the rest."

"It works better if the wrangler can communicate directly," she said. "If there's a problem on the range, you don't want to go through a translator to deal with it."

Jacob's attention kept drifting to the taut fit of her camisole top and he struggled to drag his focus to a more appropriate location. "How often do you have non-English-speaking visitors?"

She tapped a pencil on a pad of paper that was covered with scribbled notes and artistic doodles. "Three or four times a summer. It can be interesting. One vacation season we had several master chefs from Italy—they taught Grams and Reggie how to make gnocchi and a fabulous spinach Provençal. Anyway…I assume you're here for your packages." She stood and retrieved two large envelopes from a locked storage cabinet. "I'm afraid you aren't popular with the drivers from the shipping company. They don't enjoy coming here so frequently."

"It would be easier if you put asphalt down over that gravel road," he said absently, reading the address labels on the envelopes.

Mariah shut the cabinet with a bang. "So they've suggested, but ordinarily they come out to the U-2 once or twice a year—not once or twice a *day.* We can't spend thousands of dollars on a road so you can get your deliveries ten minutes earlier."

Her tone was crisp and Jacob's mouth twitched. He was tempted to fan her redhead's temper but decided to resist. It was entertaining to battle with someone so quick-witted and passionate—there weren't many people who talked back to him. He ought to think about whether he'd gotten too autocratic at his company. Being the boss might have its privileges, but he could be missing out on things, too.

"Will they begin refusing to deliver and pick up?"

"Refuse considering the amount of money your company is paying for shipping?" Mariah sounded scandalized. "I doubt it."

"We're paying the standard rate, less our corporate discount."

"That's enough."

"I'll bet the Pony Express cost more and they weren't overnight."

"I wouldn't know," she said drily. "It was before I was born, and they didn't ride through Montana, just across the Oregon–California trail. Um, the dance is starting soon and I still have an email to send. So..."

Jacob recognized a brush-off when he heard it. He stepped outside, tapping his finger on label of the shipping envelopes. They were from the Munich, Germany, division of his company. He frowned; while his visit to Montana wasn't a secret, he preferred that everything go through the Seattle office. Gretchen wouldn't have circulated his temporary address, but the guys in the shipping department could have put it in the computer network to be handy.

He looked around and saw Dr. Weston was no longer stitching her quilt, though it remained on the patio. Curious, he went to examine it closely; even to his untutored eye, the piece was a work of art. It was formed from strips of various fabrics, the overall design created crossing diagonal bands of color that gave the illusion of being woven.

"That's a 'log cabin' quilt," Mariah said from behind him. "It's a traditional pattern, though ones such as the 'wedding ring' or 'basket of scraps' are older. Originally those patterns were made with smaller amounts of milled fabric and a great deal of off-white homespun for the background."

"Why homespun?"

"It was cheaper and could be produced by women at home. The early colonies weren't allowed to build fabric mills, so fabric had to be imported and there were high tariffs on it. Even later it was expensive. And when cheap unbleached muslin became available, it took the place of homespun in the old-time patterns."

"Old-time or not, it's stunning. This is something I would frame and hang in the lobby of my office building in Seattle."

MARIAH HADN'T EXPECTED to hear Jacob admiring the artistry of Gram's craftsmanship. He might remain devoted to his wife's memory, but the man he was today was obviously *not* the grad student who'd fallen deeply in love with the girl of his dreams. The mystery was how he'd gone from adoring husband and prospective aerospace engineer to hard-nosed businessman.

"Did you get your email sent?" Jacob asked.

"Yes."

All she'd had left to do was enter the address and hit the send button, but she'd felt a need to get him out of the U-2's office—and away from her. She was accustomed to tall, powerfully built men, but it was easy to forget Jacob's lean height until they were in close confines. He moved well for a city-dwelling snob. Almost sensually… Mariah clenched her jaw. It was one thing for an engaged woman to think another man was attractive, another to get hot and bothered around him.

"You'd best get going. I hear the music starting down at

the Big Barn." Mariah gestured to the path around the house. Normally they didn't have guests in their backyard since the U-2's office wasn't designed as a reception area. Gram's dispensary was attached to one of the barns, and visitors could ring the bell there in case of emergency, or if something was needed and a ranch employee couldn't be found.

"Trying to get rid of me?" Jacob sent her a knowing grin.

"No, just wondering what mischief Caitlin might have found while you're up here, and she's…somewhere else," Mariah said sweetly.

The humor faded from his face. "Right."

He turned on his heel and strode away, much to her satisfaction. Yet when she headed toward the Big Barn a few minutes later, he caught up and walked with her.

"According to witnesses, my daughter went to the dance with Burt," he explained. "If she's plotting global domination, that's where it's going down."

Luke was already there when they arrived and gave her a determined kiss. "You look wonderful," he whispered against her lips.

"You don't look bad yourself," she said, startled. He usually wasn't demonstrative in front of people.

"Evening, O'Donnell," Luke said over her head.

"Branson."

The men measured each other and bared their teeth in something that might pass as smiles.

Mariah thumped her shoulder into Luke's chest. She hadn't deliberately arrived at the dance with Jacob, something Luke should know without being told. "You don't need introductions, do you?"

"Nope."

They shook hands and she was glad to see they were mature enough not to get into a finger-squeezing contest…at least she hoped they were that mature. She'd met grown men who acted like children with the smallest provocation.

What was more, Mariah knew full well that Luke had a temper, same as Jacob. The big question was, what would set them both off and how much?

It had been an unseasonably warm day for May, but a cooling breeze blew through the multiple open doors on each side of the barn. The public welcome to the dance got under way, the wranglers in the band explaining to the greenhorns about basic square dancing and moves such as the do-si-do and promenade. They enlisted the U-2's neighbors to demonstrate, who then pulled in the greenhorns to practice, with promises that everyone messed up now and then and that it was fun regardless.

Next, Grams and Granddad showed the crowd how to do a basic polka, U-2-style. The band began playing and soon the barn was filled with couples enjoying the fast, lively dance.

"I've waited all winter for this," Luke said and swung Mariah out onto the floor.

Talking was impractical during the vigorous folk dance, along with hanging on to darker feelings, and they were both in a cheerful mood by the time the tune ended.

Mariah was pleased to see the usual group of neighbors in attendance, in addition to a few that didn't often come to community events. She said hello, keeping her greetings low-key so she wouldn't make them self-conscious.

"Can you believe old man Price is here?" Luke asked quietly. "He's the biggest hermit in three counties. Maybe he's hoping to catch a wife who can cook something besides beans."

Mariah laughed. Luther Price was notorious. He had a spread south of Buckeye and the cowboys who worked for him claimed he bought pinto beans by the hundred-pound sack…and little else.

"Maybe he's just lonely."

"Speaking of lonely…" Luke gestured to Caitlin, who was hanging around the refreshment tables, standing out like a sore thumb. The spiderweb tattoo on her stomach wasn't displayed, but her black clothes and dull, black spiky hair were bad enough. "I thought you said her father got new clothes for her. She doesn't look different to me, other than the snake adorning her T-shirt. And I wouldn't call that an improvement."

Mariah sighed. She didn't know who she felt sorrier for—Jacob or Kittie.

"He drove into Buckeye late one afternoon and returned with shopping bags, but that doesn't mean she's willing to wear what he bought. The Buckeye Booteek doesn't carry anything decorated with spiders, skeletons or snakes—they don't even cater to the Harry Potter crowd, much less someone going Goth."

"Yeah, but the men's shop carries a nice selection of hats."

"Hmm, that's right." Mariah stood on tiptoe and tapped the brim of Luke's cream-colored cowboy hat. "I thought this was new. Are you trying to look like one of the good guys?"

He chuckled. "Would it work?"

"Not a chance. By the way, why didn't you bring Moonfire over tonight? I have the stall next to Blue ready for her."

Moonfire was an exceptionally gentle and intelligent mare Luke was donating to a program that worked with autistic children. He'd learned about the project eighteen months ago and had evaluated his horses to find one with the right personality. Moonfire was ideal. She'd foaled twice and had a natural mothering instinct. When things quieted down in the fall, Luke planned to truck the ten-year-old down to California and see the facility she'd be staying at for himself.

It wasn't any surprise to Mariah that horses worked well with special-needs kids; they were responsive and learned quickly. She was going to have their younger visitors ride Moonfire to polish the horse's training. If the mare could tolerate a bunch of eager, underage greenhorns, she'd be terrific with children who had difficulty relating to the rest of the world. Originally she'd thought that Caitlin and Moonfire might be a good match, but in light of the growing bond between the teen and Blue, she was glad the timing hadn't worked out.

"I changed my mind. I'll bring her over tomorrow or the next day," Luke said unconcernedly.

Mariah cocked her head, puzzled. "You've already been here several times this week."

"Don't you want to see me?"

"You know I do, but this is your busiest season. You don't have time to waste coming over here."

"Seeing you isn't a waste." The serious note in his voice made Mariah wince. Sooner or later they'd be married and she had to be more sensitive.

Luke was better at the everyday courtesies—she tended to get so busy with her family and dealing with ranch visitors that she didn't call or email as much as she should. Mariah also knew that she should make an effort to visit the Branson spread more often.

"I appreciate that," she said. "And I'm always glad to see you. I just worry that you're stretching yourself too thin and don't want you doing it on my account."

"I'm a big boy, Mariah. I can decide that kind of thing for myself."

"Okay, okay." She put her hands up in a surrendering gesture. "I'll shut up."

"You?" He winked, yet there was an odd expression in his eyes. "Doubtful."

A set was forming nearby that needed a couple, and she and Luke were coaxed into joining. Mariah was uncomfortable because she generally moved around, visiting with the guests, rather than dancing so much. But Grams and Granddad were here, as well as Aunt Lettie, and they could get folks to join in, same as her.

Caitlin O'Donnell was the guest that Mariah worried most

about, and she kept watching her from the corner of her eye. The teenager danced, *reluctantly,* with her father, though she was more animated when Granddad took her out for a couple of sets. Burt took a break from playing with the band to dance with her, but it was obvious that she'd prefer having partners her own age. The local boys were usually enthusiastic about new girls since guys outnumbered gals at these affairs, but apparently Caitlin and her Goth-look apparel were too peculiar for them.

"I'll dance with her," Luke said softly when he noticed Mariah's attention had shifted again to the troubled teen. "It might get Reid and his pals going."

"Thanks." She kissed his cheek. "You're one in a million."

"Yeah, and don't you forget it."

KITTIE STUDIOUSLY PRETENDED to be interested in the band where Burt and Ray Cassidy were playing, tapping her feet to the music as if it was the only thing that mattered. She'd tried to dress right—what was wrong with everyone? Reid and his friends were ignoring her; it was just *old* guys who'd wanted to dance with her, like her dad and Mr. Weston and Burt. Her dad was standing next to her and had suggested they join another set, but she'd seem pretty pathetic dancing with him five times in a row.

"Miss O'Donnell, would you honor me by being my partner in the next set?" someone said, and she turned. It was Mr. Branson, the one who was sweet on Mariah. He was older, too, but really cute. "The band is taking a break now, but another will start when they're done."

"Okay."

Her father looked at Mariah, who'd come over with Mr. Branson. "Mariah, seeing as I'm losing my partner, would you dance with me?"

Ooh, that was *rad.*

Mr. Branson's face got weird and Mariah looked funny,

too. Her dad and Mr. Branson went stiff and stared at each other even harder than when they'd met on the range.

"How about it, Mariah?" her dad asked again.

"Uh…sure."

Kittie almost giggled. This was the only fun part of the night so far. Grown-ups could sure act strange—and they thought *she* was the one with a problem.

"Why don't we have a piece of cake or a cookie while we're waiting?" Mariah suggested.

The long tables they'd set up when cleaning the barn were covered with white cloths and more desserts than Kittie had ever seen. They had cream pies and nut pies and fruit pies. There were chocolate, vanilla and lemon cakes, and other ones she didn't recognize. Then there were the brownies and cookies…piles and piles of them.

Kittie had reached to take a cookie loaded with chunks of chocolate and pecans when the container was snatched from under her fingers by a girl wearing a yellow dress.

"Reid, these are the cookies I brought," said the girl, holding them out to him, who was standing off to the side. "I baked them just for you."

"Thanks, Laura." He grabbed a handful. "But I think one of the U-2 guests was going to have a cookie, too."

Kittie wanted to drop through the floor. He'd called her *one of the U-2 guests*. As if she was an absolute nobody. It was even worse than when he'd stopped in the mess tent to tell her dad about the packages from his company and had paid no attention to her.

The girl gave Kittie an apologetic look. She was perky and filled-out like the cheerleaders at Garrison Academy in Seattle, with shiny brown hair that fell smoothly down her back. "I'm sorry. Do you want some?"

She offered the oblong pan, but Kittie would have died before taking one. Baked especially for Reid, were they? This *Laura* probably thought he was her personal property.

"I'm having something else."

"Are you sure?" Laura seemed confused, as if she couldn't believe anyone not wanting to eat her precious cookies. "They won the grand prize at the county fair last year."

"I'm sure," Kittie said, thinking she could trip Laura flat on her perfect face if she stuck her foot out in the right place. Not that it was a very nice thing to consider doing, but she didn't feel like being nice these days.

She took a slice of lemon-meringue pie instead and it was yummy—she just hoped Laura hadn't made the pie *and* the cookies.

"Ladies and gentlemen, it's time for our next dance," Ray called as the wranglers went back to their banjos and other musical instruments. "We're going to pick up the pace, so grab your partner and get busy doing an allemande left and a right and left turn."

Mr. Branson smiled at her. "Are you ready, Miss O'Donnell? You said you'd be my partner."

"I'm ready." She threw her paper plate in a trash can and they joined a square of dancers that included her dad and Mariah.

She wasn't very happy, but the others didn't seem too cheerful, either.

AN HOUR LATER Mariah had circulated, danced with Luke and the unattached male guests...and gotten frazzled nerves. Though Caitlin had danced twice with Luke, her father, Burt and Granddad, Reid and his high-school buddies were casually overlooking her. The teen was growing increasingly hurt, but Jacob didn't seem to see it.

She isn't your problem, Mariah reminded herself. Short of Kittie damaging the ranch or doing something reckless that would get her injured, it wasn't her business what the teen did or how she felt.

"Mariah," said the pastor's wife, "the punch tastes odd,

though I drank some earlier and it was fine. Could the juice in it have spoiled so quickly?"

Mariah took the cup from Barbara and sniffed. "It's not spoiled. That's whiskey," she said crisply.

"Whiskey?" Barbara was a teetotaler, so it wasn't surprising she didn't know how it tasted or smelled.

"Yup."

Mariah dumped the contents of the large bowl down the farm sink. It didn't happen often, but a couple of times in the past somebody had tried to be funny by spiking the punch. Having lost her parents because of a drunk driver, she was determined to keep the dance "dry." Nobody was going to leave the U-2 and get in an accident if she could prevent it.

Grams came to help as Mariah assembled the makings for a new batch. "I smell whiskey. Who did it?"

"I hate to speculate." Yet Mariah couldn't stop herself from glancing at Caitlin. The teenager was carefully gazing in a different direction and had assumed an innocent air. It seemed possible that she was responsible or knew who was.

Grams's eyes widened. "Caitlin? Surely not. How would she get alcohol? We don't have any in the house and I haven't seen signs that her father is a midnight tippler. Aside from black coffee, of course."

"Reggie locks up the bourbon whiskey he uses to flavor his barbecue sauce. Other than that, I don't know. But she's upset and I saw her here a few minutes ago. She could have hidden a bottle nearby and slipped it in when no one was looking. That isn't enough to make an accusation, though."

"I'll get Linc to watch and make sure it doesn't happen again."

Mariah lifted the fresh bowl onto the table. "Linc? Good luck. If a woman over eighteen and under fifty is going by, an elephant could spike the punch and he wouldn't see it. He'll be too fixated on her fanny or bustline."

"Someday he'll fall in love and his wandering ways will

come back to bite him, but we can try." Grams crooked a finger at Linc. "Young man, somebody spiked the punch. As far as we are concerned, you are already on probation. Keep an eye on this bowl, and if anyone pours something into it that shouldn't be there, I'm holding you personally responsible."

"Yes, ma'am."

"I'm serious, Linc."

"I know, ma'am."

Mariah hurried to where Luke was standing—it made her nervous to see him near Jacob and Caitlin. The two men were worse than stallions, stamping and pawing the ground to warn the others of their general male superiority.

Luke raised his eyebrows inquiringly when she got close and she leaned forward to whisper in his ear, "Somebody dumped whiskey in the punch."

"That could liven up a party."

"Stop it." She rapped his ribs lightly with her knuckles.

Caitlin? he mouthed silently.

Got me, she mouthed back.

While she suspected the youngster, she didn't have any proof. It was the sort of teen prank she might have once pulled herself if she hadn't always felt so protective of the ranch. Even so, her high-school years had been more carefree than Reid's. Her parents had confidently told her she could study what she wanted and not to worry about how they would pay for it. She was trying to get the same message across to Reid, but with less success.

"How about another dance, Caitlin?" Luke asked.

Mariah squeezed his hand. He was truly one of the good guys. Dancing with a sullen, morose kid couldn't be appealing, yet he was doing it, nonetheless.

Caitlin appeared ready to accept the invitation, then Reid walked by with Laura Shelton holding his arm. He'd danced with several of the girls from high school, but Laura more than any other, and she looked smugly satisfied.

"I don't want to dance with *anyone.* Square dancing is stupid. It's totally for losers," Caitlin said loudly. It was one of those quirky moments when the music from the band ended as she was winding into her speech, and her words echoed through the barn. A number of the U-2 guests and neighbors turned toward them curiously.

Jacob's eyes darkened with anger. "Kittie—"

"I hate you all." She stormed across the dance floor and out the far doors.

"Damn it," Jacob muttered. He took a step forward and Mariah caught his sleeve. *"What?"*

She'd rather not get involved, but she had to be fair. "*Think* before you confront her," she said in a low, urgent tone. "Cool down first. It's understandable that Caitlin is upset. The other girls have been invited to dance by the boys their own age, but she has been left out. Believe me, at fourteen it doesn't matter how often you dance with your father—it isn't the same."

Comprehension dawned on Jacob's face, along with conflicted sympathy. Mariah didn't know whether to feel sorry for him or kick him for the sake of all adolescent girls struggling to become adults. And it had to be worse for Caitlin, with no mother and an overprotective father who didn't want her to grow up.

"What if she tries saddling Blue and running away?"

Belatedly, Mariah released his arm. "She can try getting a saddle on him, but Blue won't leave the corral unless we tell him it's okay."

"And you think that it's normal she got upset?"

"I don't know about normal, but I would have felt the same in her shoes."

Some of the tension eased from Jacob's face. "Fine. I'll talk to her tomorrow."

"Good. Now, why don't you just go grab a cup of coffee—I'm sure you're planning to work after the dance. Reggie made regular for you."

He looked at her darkly but stomped toward the beverage table.

Luke put his hands on Mariah's shoulders. "*Regular* coffee? Isn't he wired enough without the caffeine?"

"I'm pretty sure he mainlines the stuff. He drinks coffee all evening, and you know how strong Reggie makes it."

"I might do the same if Caitlin was my daughter. Is that what we have to look forward to as parents?" Luke said in mock dismay.

Mariah laughed. "You never know."

"God have mercy."

By mutual accord they walked outside of the barn for some fresh air and he tugged her against him. "This is nice," he murmured, kissing her upraised face.

It *was* nice, but Mariah couldn't relax, unable to stop picturing Caitlin's hurt, angry expression in her mind.

Why was growing up so hard?

Reid was having just as much trouble in a different way, and she hated knowing he wasn't free to feel as if the future was spread out in front of him with unlimited possibilities. That was how it should be at his age. She wanted to fix what was wrong, but she couldn't get Reid to talk to her any more than Jacob was able to get his daughter to open up to him.

Darn it anyhow. She shouldn't have interfered between Caitlin and her father—what did she know about raising kids? And Jacob *was* trying to connect with Caitlin, though he didn't seem to have a clue how to do it. No one could claim the angst-ridden teenager was easy to deal with.

"Hey, what's up?" Luke asked after a moment.

Mariah shook herself. "Nothing."

"Come on, I know you better than that. Is it Reid? Whatever it is, let me help."

He always wanted to help, yet the ranch and Reid were her responsibilities. It wasn't fair to unload them onto someone else.

She kissed him again. "It's nothing. Tell me more about Little Foot's new colt."

A flash of emotion crossed his face, gone so fast she couldn't guess what it meant, but then he shrugged. "He's thriving, and Little Foot is proving to be a fine mother. I've decided to name him Light Foot since he has his mama's easy step."

"I'd love to see him. Maybe I could come over on Monday or Tuesday."

Luke held her tighter. "That would be great."

CHAPTER EIGHT

EARLY SUNDAY JACOB PULLED out his smartphone and typed *Goth* into the internet search function. Mariah had mentioned Kittie adopting a Goth look, and he'd had no idea what she meant.

Describing them as a subculture wasn't much help.

He browsed the top informational hits, his eyes widening. Kittie's clothes and makeup *were* similar to the pictures and descriptions of modern-day Goths. How had Mariah known about them? He hadn't known and he lived in the city, not the back roads of Montana. Of course, it was becoming uncomfortably clear that he hadn't noticed very much outside of his company these past few years.

At the mess tent he found Burt telling Kittie how cowboys took care of their tack—tack being the equipment that went on a horse—and how to properly saddle a horse. Jacob expected Kittie to furiously declare that she already knew it all, but she listened solemnly and ended by asking if Burt would give her a lesson after breakfast.

On the other hand, she gave *him* a cool glance that could have frozen a polar bear. It reminded Jacob of what he'd told Mariah—he was tired of being the bad guy. But that was parenting, sometimes having to say no more often than saying yes. Hell, with his bank account and investment portfolio, he could say yes more often than some parents, and he was *still* the bad guy.

"When does the family from Australia get here?" Kittie asked Burt.

"Well, now, they said they'd get in around five. They're takin' a drive through several states and were spending the night in Rapid City over there in South Dakota."

"Okay. Well, I'm going to get my camera to take some pictures of Blue."

Kittie left, seemingly oblivious to the stares of their fellow vacationers who'd witnessed her outburst at the dance. Or maybe the stares were Jacob's imagination. But with most of the U-2 guests finishing their breakfasts, he decided to talk to Kittie where there were fewer listening ears. It would be crazy later in the morning, since departing guests would be busy packing their belongings and loading up their cars.

"We need to discuss last night," he said when Kittie emerged from their tent with the digital camera he'd given her at Christmas.

Her mouth set stubbornly.

"I'm sorry the local boys didn't ask you to dance, but…well, next time you could ask them."

"I'd rather die. It's all your fault. You didn't tell me there'd be a barn dance," she said accusingly. "You didn't want me to bring the right stuff so I'd fit in and the guys would like me."

"*What?* That's absurd."

She set her mouth mulishly and glared.

"Kittie, I went into that town…Buck-something…and got you appropriate Western outfits, which you refuse to wear. And you know very well that I don't even like those black clothes. You have perfectly nice outfits at home that you could have brought here instead."

Without another word, she pushed past him toward the corral, and Jacob would have laughed if he wasn't so frustrated. Her accusations were comical considering how defensive she was about the Halloween outfits she'd been wearing all year. Goth or not, she looked horrible in them.

From across the compound, he saw Mariah coming out of the barn they'd used for the dance. As she came closer, he saw she was carrying a bottle, making him remember something *else* he'd intended to speak with Kittie about—basically, did she spike the punch at the party? Few people had tasted the whiskey-laced fruit beverage prior to it being discovered, but the story had rapidly filtered through the partygoers, with varying degrees of amusement. And his daughter was the prime suspect after her rude performance.

The prank might have been more effective if the culprit had picked something like vodka, being a less dominant flavor... which made Jacob suspect Kittie even more. He doubted she knew one type of liquor from another. Dumping booze in a punch bowl might not be as serious as smoking and setting fire to the school, but he couldn't afford to dismiss it.

Jacob caught up with Mariah before she reached the ranch house. "I hear somebody spiked the punch last night," he said. "Are you checking for fingerprints on the evidence?"

"Nope. Just headed for the recycle barrel."

"You have recycling in Montana?"

"You'd be surprised at what we have here...though we do have to haul glass to Rapid City in South Dakota." She glanced at the whiskey bottle she held and back at him. "No one saw Caitlin do anything, Jacob. It could have been anybody at the party."

"We both know it was Kittie."

"Not necessarily. Somebody may have figured that Ki... *Caitlin* would be blamed and decided to pull a joke and let her take the rap. The winters are long in Montana and folks can kick up their heels when it's over."

That might all be true, but Jacob had a gut feeling that Hurricane Kittie had struck again.

"Anyway," Mariah continued, "it was relatively harmless as practical jokes go. I wouldn't tolerate an employee doing it at a family dance, but it isn't as if the guests were going to get drunk on a pint of whiskey diluted by two gallons of fruit punch. That's a Hollywood invention."

"And exactly where Kittie could have gotten the idea."

Mariah frowned. "I realize it would be hard to switch the name you use for Kittie, but didn't she say she prefers Caitlin?"

"She said that because of Reid and wanting to sound more grown-up. She's always been Kittie to me—it's what Anna called her."

"I see."

A truck towing a horse trailer came over the hill on the road from the highway.

Mariah waved as Luke Branson got out. "Excuse me," she said and hurried back down to meet him.

Jacob's eyes narrowed as Mariah and the tall rancher kissed briefly. There was a subtle nuance to the embrace, with Mariah a half step behind Branson. Less eager, perhaps? Or was he reading something into it that wasn't there?

And why did he care in the first place?

The rancher apparently made a joke about the empty bottle she carried, taking it to examine, then tossing it into the bed of the pickup. He put his arm around her waist and they walked to the gate of the horse trailer. After a few minutes, Mariah led a silvery-gray horse down a ramp.

Guests leaving the mess tent soon surrounded them, and the animal stood quietly amid the commotion. Kittie was in the front of the group and Jacob joined the admiring crowd, hoping his daughter would be polite and not make another scene.

"What a beauty," an older woman declared.

"This is Moonfire," Mariah said. "Mr. Branson is giving her to a program in California that works with special-needs children. We're going to polish her training at the U-2."

Kittie appeared fascinated. She let Moonfire sniff her fingers before rubbing the horse's nose. "Can I ride her?"

"Sure."

"But I want to keep Blue for when we go out on the range," Kittie said quickly.

Mariah nodded. "I understand. You'll stay assigned to Blue, but we need volunteers, particularly kids, to ride Moonfire around the corral and the ranch buildings to get her used to having different riders."

"I can do that."

"Great. She'll be settling in today, but you can have a turn tomorrow."

THAT AFTERNOON Reid let his horse, Buttons, race across the rolling grassland, wanting to outrun how he felt.

He and Mariah had almost gotten into an argument after lunch, with her wanting to talk about college. He'd left before she could say much. He didn't want to talk; he knew what he had to do and it was dumb believing anything else was possible. He would sign up for college courses over the internet instead of going away to school. Not that he could become a veterinarian or anything with online classes, but it would be good to know more about business and accounting.

A little later Reid pulled up on the reins and rode Buttons along the crest of a low hill. The air was balmy and the cattle in the distance seemed to be appreciating both the warmth and grazing on the lush grass. He was far enough away that they paid no heed to his presence, though it wouldn't take much to spook them.

He understood animal behavior, partly from being in a ranching family and partly from all the reading he did. But Mariah understood it instinctively. She had a way with animals that left everyone else in the dust. Heck, she just seemed to *know* what they were thinking and what was wrong with them. It was one of the reasons the ranch hands respected her, especially the older guys. They'd been around and seen it all, and yet she could do things with cows and horses they couldn't dream of doing.

I'll never be that good, Reid thought. It was just as well he wasn't going to veterinary college. He could learn every scientific theory in existence and still not measure up to Mariah. But he could be a good rancher and run the vacation business his folks had started.

Yet another guilty thought niggled at Reid and he squirmed.

Kittie O'Donnell.

Jeez, *why* had he ignored Kittie at the U-2's weekly gathering? She'd looked peculiar, but he could have at least danced with her. If he had, his buddies might have danced with her, too. Mariah tried to make sure their guests enjoyed themselves; if he was going to operate the ranch someday, he had to do better, be more responsible. She wouldn't ever feel free to marry Luke if she had to keep taking care of everything herself.

As for Kittie…she was an odd duck. He liked her okay, only it was hard paying attention to a loudmouthed, troublemaking squirt when Laura and the other girls were around. But he should have done it anyhow. After all, Mariah was being nice to Kittie's father, despite him being a stuck-up jerk. She'd even danced with Mr. O'Donnell, which sure hadn't made Luke happy.

Reid fingered Buttons's reins. "Come on, boy, let's get back to the ranch," he muttered, turning the horse.

He put Buttons in the corral; with any luck he'd have time for another ride later. A lot of their guests left for home on Sundays, so it was usually quiet following the flurry of departures. Meals were served, the pastor came out and did an open-air service, and the usual chores caring for the horses and other livestock were handled, but otherwise there wasn't as much to do.

He knew that Burt had taken Kittie and her father riding,

but Blue and Strider, the chestnut that Mr. O'Donnell had been assigned, were already curried and back in their stalls.

"Hiya, Blue," Reid said, going in and running his hands across the horse's withers and shoulders. Kittie had begun grooming Blue herself and he wanted to be sure she was doing it right. To his surprise, the animal was immaculate, without a speck of dirt anywhere. He lifted Blue's feet and found them just as clean. "Looks like you've been done proper, old boy."

Blue snorted softly.

"Burt showed me how to do it. You don't have to check up on me," Kittie declared out of thin air, startling him.

Reid cursed under his breath. Peering over Blue's neck, he saw Kittie sitting in the hay in the shadowed corner of the stall. How had he missed spotting her there? Was it all the black she wore? Crabby, one of the barn cats, looked up from his nest in her lap and let out an irritable meow.

Was that really *Crabby?*

He stared. Crabby had earned his name by being antisocial with people, though when it came to horses, he was as mellow as maple sugar. He had a special friendship with Blue and slept curled up next to him. A lazy snooze in the middle of the day was the kind of thing he'd resent having interrupted, so it was strange to see him cozied up with Blue *and* Kittie.

"I always keep an eye out. It's nothing personal," he said. "We take good care of our horses. They rarely get sick because we groom them every day and make sure the stables are clean and dry." And it didn't hurt that Mariah was there, seeming to know when something wasn't quite right.

"Yeah, guess I have to learn how to shovel horse poop, too."

She got up and hugged Blue before sliding out the stall door. Crabby left, as well, tail arched high, stopping at the threshold to hiss at Reid. It was typical of the black-and-white feline.

"Hey, Kittie, wait," Reid called, racing after her. "I…uh…

thought I should apol…um, say I'm sorry about last night. I should have been…" His voice trailed off miserably.

"NEVER MIND," Kittie said awkwardly, wishing Reid wouldn't say anything else. She'd rather forget the dance entirely.

"Do you want to go feed the orphan calves?" he asked, checking his watch.

She bobbed her head eagerly, unable to hide her excitement. "Yeah, sure. That'd be awesome."

"Let's go, then."

He led her to the east rear barn where they kept the babies. One of the ranch hands got there at the same time.

"We'll do this feeding," Reid said.

"Much obliged. I'll return to my nap. Can't beat a warm Sunday afternoon for a nap under a cottonwood tree." And with that the man ambled away.

The calves began bawling, crowding the walls of their pens, as Reid took out the supplies. He showed her how to mix the milk replacer, and together they filled the bottles and fastened the nipples on the tops. Each calf would get two bottles, four pints each. Kittie had once visited a friend while she was babysitting her baby brother, and this routine was kinda like that, except these bottles were huge and they were in a barn. And cows didn't have stinky diapers to change.

Mariah and her dad came while they were still working, but Kittie pretended he wasn't there. She felt funny about the way she'd blown up at him earlier. It wasn't his fault for the way things had turned out at the barn dance, only she couldn't see why the boys in Montana disliked her so much, even if she didn't have real boobs yet.

She tugged at her black T-shirt with its skull outlined in silver studs and looked at the black nail polish she'd put on for the dance. None of the other girls had worn black polish or black lipstick. If her clothes were the problem, she needed to get something else to wear.

Maybe Mariah could help her.

Kittie looked at Reid's sister. Well, Mariah *might* help if Dad would stop pissing her off every five minutes.

"Can I go in with the calves?"

Reid tightened the top on the last bottle and gave it to her. "Sure, they won't hurt you. These are the smallest ones, less than two weeks old." He let her into one of the pens and two of the calves pushed against her, bawling louder. The third stayed separate. It mooed too, but much more softly, and had a sad face.

"Here you go, you little guys." Reid hopped over the gate instead of going through it. He had a bottle in each hand and the ones fussing at Kittie darted to him.

Kittie went to the third calf and held out her bottle. "Aren't you hungry, baby?"

"That one isn't doing as well as we like," Mariah said from the next pen as she fed two of the bigger calves. "The extra attention is good for her. Cows are very social, but she's the youngest, so she may not have made friends yet."

Kittie sighed. *She* didn't fit in, either, at least not with the pretty cowgirls that Reid liked better than her. She sat on the hay to make herself look smaller and held the bottle out again. "Here, baby," she said.

The calf extended its neck and grabbed the nipple, sucking slowly at first, then with growing enthusiasm. Kittie giggled; she didn't even care about the milky formula dripping on her jeans from the calf's muzzle. She'd have to change her clothes, but the U-2 had washing machines for them to use, so it wasn't a big deal.

It was weird. She hadn't wanted to come to Montana, but it was really nice on the ranch and she didn't have to think so much about everything that was wrong in her life. She could think of other stuff…like Reid.

Was a first kiss too much to ask? It might be her very last chance to get kissed at all….

When the bottle was empty, the baby let out a complaint, almost as loud as the other two calves in the pen had sounded.

"Here's her second one." Reid gave her another bottle. The two calves he was feeding were already nearly finished.

This time the calf came close and Kittie laughed as it drank. "You're pretty, little one," she whispered.

"We feed them twice a day," Mariah said. "You're welcome to help. You're going to be at the U-2 for several more weeks, so you'll be able to see them grow a bit. These older ones will be weaned off the milk replacer before long."

Kittie gulped. "Are they *all* orphans?"

"Actually, most of them aren't," Mariah explained. "Some were rejected by their mothers—we're not always sure why that happens. And others we've decided to raise by hand because the mama cow doesn't have enough milk."

That was sad, too, but not as sad as being orphaned.

"I'll help whenever you want. Can I name this one Emily?" Kittie patted the calf that was nodding sleepily but still sucking on the milk replacer in the bottle.

"Sure. Emily likes you, so you should be the one to feed her when you come by."

"ANIMALS RESPOND TO CAITLIN. Has she ever had a pet?" Mariah asked quietly.

"What…?" Jacob said, distracted by the sight of his daughter with the calf. In spite of her black clothes and unnaturally dark hair, she seemed so normal, giggling as she fed the animal. And, while she'd behaved as if he was invisible, at least she hadn't been rude to Reid or his sister.

"A pet," Mariah repeated. "A cat or a dog, or even a hamster or rabbit."

He dragged his gaze from Kittie. "No, nothing like that."

"I see."

"We're busy and they don't fit into our lives," he added, though he shouldn't need to defend himself. Lots of children didn't have pets. Yet a part of him wondered... He'd grown up with a faithful golden retriever who'd gone with him everywhere. Sparks had slept on the end of his bed, was fed scraps from the dinner table and cheerfully fetched foul balls at impromptu baseball games. Friendship took different shapes. *He'd* had a younger sister and brother and Sparks to keep him company, but Kittie was an only child.

Hell, he could second-guess himself forever.

And, in all honesty, having enough time to feed and care for a pet wasn't the reason his daughter didn't have one. Cats and dogs carried germs and he'd refused to consider getting any for years after her heart surgery, though the doctor had said a few months would be more than sufficient time for Kittie to completely heal and be out of harm's way. But it had developed into a pattern that was hard to break.

"I suppose you had a dozen pets growing up," he murmured.

Mariah tossed an empty bottle onto the hay outside the pen and got another. "I don't know about dozens, but this is a ranch and we're surrounded by animals. We have our favorites, like Pip. I also adopted one of the barn cats years ago. Squash has been my pal ever since. He's old now and doesn't chase around the way he used to, but he's my buddy."

"Squash? That's an interesting name."

She grinned. "He was ten weeks old when I brought him up to the house. Barn cats have a wild streak that can make it difficult adapting to indoor living, but he instantly recognized the advantages. He got underfoot so often demanding affection that my dad said he was going to get squashed."

"So everyone called him Squash."

"Yup."

"And then there's Shadow."

"He's my horse. No one else rides him. He foaled right after..." A spasm of pain crossed her face.

"After what?" Jacob prompted.

"Er…soon after I quit school."

"Surely not high school."

Mariah shook her head. "Grams wouldn't have put up with that. No, I was in veterinary school." She rolled her shoulders, probably as a signal to move on from their present topic of conversation. "I'll start sterilizing the nursing bottles and nipples for the next feeding. I'm sure Caitlin would rather nurse the calves than get dishpan hands."

She walked away to collect the empties while Jacob digested her small bombshell. She'd planned to be a veterinarian? He'd assumed she had grown up on the U-2 and never left. It shouldn't be a surprise that she'd gone away to school with both her grandmother and aunt being doctors—the Westons plainly respected education—but why had she quit? He thought furiously, putting together the bits of information he'd learned about her over the past week, and he realized that Mariah must have left college following her parents' deaths.

They'd both made tough choices. He'd given up engineering for a career that would enable him to take care of Kittie and repay the money that his in-laws had put out for his wife's and daughter's medical care; she'd given up a veterinary career so she could look after her brother and the family ranch. He admired her for it. Few of the women he'd dated since Anna's death would give up anything they wanted, whatever the need.

Damn.

In spite of Mariah's sharp edges, which he seemed destined to bump against, she was intriguing…and desirable. He found himself watching her, finding ways to begin a conversation, however much they clashed. When he was searching for his daughter, *she* was the one he'd gone to, asking if she'd seen Kittie. Mariah had a good idea of everything going on at the ranch, so she was a logical source if he were looking for someone, but was that mostly an excuse?

Stop, he ordered sternly.

Mariah might be a tempting combination of feminine curves, but she was attached to a man from her own world. Moreover, she was a risk taker whose plans included marriage and babies one day. She was the last woman who should appeal to him, and he *definitely* couldn't see Mariah moving to Seattle, even if he did change his mind about what he wanted for the future. Mariah's opinion of the city was akin to his opinion of the country—sleeping in a tent and working outside wasn't as tedious as he'd expected, but people could tolerate most things for a while.

"Hello, everyone," hailed a man's voice, and Jacob almost laughed.

Luke Branson.

Of course. He must have a sixth sense for when someone was appreciating Mariah's…assets.

Mariah was across the barn washing bottles at the sink and she turned around with an astonished expression. "Luke? You were over this morning. What's wrong?"

"Nothing." He shot Jacob a quick look before kissing her forehead. "Just checking on Moonfire and seeing how she's settling in."

"Regretting the decision to give her away? You don't have to, you know."

"Nope. She'll be great with the kids. But I was also wondering if you'd be able to arrange your schedule and go with me when I drive her to California in the fall."

Mariah dried her fingers and appeared to be picking her words carefully. "I think that would be great, only I can't give you an answer right now. But there's plenty of time before you leave. You didn't have to ask me tonight."

"Sure, but I also thought I'd invite myself to dinner."

"YOU'RE ALWAYS WELCOME." Mariah knew that Luke wasn't trying to make her feel guilty—especially since he was aware that she couldn't cook an edible meal to save her life—but she felt bad. With his parents living in Florida, he usually ate alone, and he wouldn't be eating alone if they were already married.

"Besides," Luke continued in a low tone, meant only for her, "I want to see more of my fiancée. You're getting so caught up in the O'Donnells' problems, I'd like to be sure you're thinking of me, as well."

There was a possessive quality in his voice and Mariah blinked.

"I'm not caught up in their problems. Mostly I'm trying to keep Jacob O'Donnell from shoving those problems back onto us," she breathed. "And *of course* I'm thinking about you. I just don't want you getting overworked."

"We've had this discussion. I'm fine. Now, let's finish washing those bottles." He unbuttoned his cuffs and rolled up his sleeves.

She didn't object to him helping; but he'd acted so odd the past few days she hardly knew what to say. Was he getting tired of waiting for her to set a wedding date? After her parents' accident, it had been comforting to have Luke there, as solid and unchanging as the hills of Montana, but she might have taken him for granted.

Jacob O'Donnell would *never* allow himself to be taken for granted.

The idle thought shocked Mariah—*was* she overly involved with Jacob and his daughter the way Luke had suggested? And not just with Caitlin's problems, but with Jacob and the way he compelled her senses?

"Mariah, do you know if the new girl is here yet?" Caitlin came over and asked as the bottles were stowed for the next feeding.

"They weren't earlier, but we can't hear anyone arriving when we're back this far," she said. "We still have to give the calves their solid feed, but you could run to the mess tent and check."

"You can all go. I'll finish the feeding," Reid called across the barn, already opening the bin where they kept the creep pellets.

Luke slung his arm over Mariah's shoulders as they headed for the mess tent. Caitlin came as well, but she appeared torn between wanting to stay to help Reid and meeting the new visitors.

It was late enough that dinner was being prepared. The scent of chili, barbecuing meat and baking corn bread wafted through the air, along with laughter and conversation. Yet it was quieter than usual, since the majority of their new guests were scheduled to come on Monday and Tuesday. Paying guests rarely stayed more than a week or two, so in the peak vacation season it was an endless revolving door at the U-2.

Caitlin raced ahead of them into the large tent. A girl her age was talking to Burt.

Burt waved. "Here she is now. Shayla, this is Kittie O'Donnell…sometimes known as Caitlin."

"G'day, Kittie," Shayla said in a broad Australian accent. "I'm from Brisbane. I guess you're an old hand here."

"Hi. I'm from Seattle. Do you…uh…want to go meet my horse? His name is Blue and he's awesome. And I can show you other stuff around the ranch before we eat. If you want."

"Mum, Dad, is that okay?" Shayla asked a man and woman standing nearby.

They both smiled at Caitlin. And, more importantly, they didn't seem the least offended by her attire.

"Sure. Go on, then," agreed Shayla's father.

The two girls left as Mariah shook hands with the couple. "Welcome to the U-2, Mr. and Mrs. McFee. I'm Mariah Weston, the U-2's business manager. This is Luke Branson, one of our neighbors, and Jacob O'Donnell, Caitlin's father," she said, introducing the two men.

"Pleased to meet you, but we'll have none of that 'Mr. and Mrs.' nonsense. It's Bill and Gladys. We're not formal."

"All right, Bill. Have you seen your tent?"

"We did that. A sight more comfortable than we thought it would be, too."

"I'm glad to hear it." Mariah couldn't resist a peek at Jacob; his face was cool and noncommittal. The U-2 didn't pretend to provide luxurious accommodations, but you could stand up in the tents and there were thick mattresses to sleep on instead of hard, canvas-covered ground. The rest of the ranch's facilities weren't bad, either, no matter how he felt about them.

Luke tugged her away and they walked up to the ranch house to sit on the porch swing. She wanted to relax, yet her mind wouldn't let her.

She went back to worrying about her reactions to Jacob. Though largely negative, were they more intense than what she felt for Luke? But she loved Luke, didn't she? They were the perfect couple.

A future with Luke was surely far better than falling for a man who didn't want to get married again or have more children…a guy who spent half the night on his computer after the other vacationers had gone to bed. She had little in common with Jacob beyond them both having quick tempers and enjoying Grams's artistry with patchwork quilts. Sure, they both worked hard, but the ranch wasn't just a profitable business for her; it was a way of life.

"This is nice," she said finally.

"Except you don't think you should be sitting while everyone else is working. Right?"

"Maybe. A little."

It was true…and not true.

Mariah's brain kept chewing over how much Jacob O'Donnell had occupied her thoughts since getting to Montana. It wasn't reassuring, and what did it mean for her future with Luke?

CHAPTER NINE

THE MOON SHONE brightly through the bedroom window and Mariah rolled away from the light. It was the first time in a month she'd gotten to bed before midnight, and now she couldn't sleep.

Luke had stayed for several hours. They'd eaten dinner, visited Moonfire in her stal, and generally avoided any subject more serious than whether vanilla or chocolate was the more popular flavor of ice cream. It shouldn't be so hard to talk about important things with someone she loved, but she wasn't doing well with anyone in her family, much less Luke.

Blast.

She punched at her pillow, only to hear Squash's bad-tempered *marrooow* at the movement. Squash had moved to a corner of the mattress after she'd rolled over for the third time, probably figuring it was safer than being next to her. Now, thoroughly disgruntled, he jumped to the floor, likely headed for his bowl, since food was the cure for most of his feline ills.

Turning over again, Mariah stared at the ceiling. She hadn't examined her feelings for a long while—as far as she'd been concerned, it was simply a question of when things at the U-2 would settle down enough that she could marry Luke.

Now she wasn't so sure.

Did she love him the way a woman should love a man she was going to marry? He was her best friend. They'd practically grown up together and knew each other so well they could almost read each other's minds. Or she'd thought so, until he began acting strangely.

She couldn't remember…was Luke possessive *before* Jacob showed up with his daughter?

Mariah got up and restlessly wandered into the living room. The house was large, intended to accommodate a family made up of multiple Weston generations. Native stone formed the fireplaces, harking back to a period when heat was provided by wood and not a modern furnace. The kitchen and bathrooms hadn't gotten updated since she was a kid, but they were big and solidly built. And the hardwood floors were worn to a smooth, rich patina from steady use and a hundred and ten years of cleanings.

The old ranch home wouldn't meet Jacob's standards, but it was unlikely that anything in Montana would measure up for him.

She peered through the curtains and saw a light shining in one of the tents on the hill—no doubt the O'Donnells' tent, though she couldn't be certain. The fact that she'd checked was infuriating. Jacob wasn't as bad as she'd originally thought, but it didn't make him a friend or potential lover.

Letting out a disgusted groan, she sank onto the couch. She'd been attracted to a variety of guys since she had begun noticing the differences between boys and girls and had gotten her heart broken big-time when she was fifteen. That was when she'd made a personal rule not to get involved with visitors, realizing the disparity between ranchers and cowhands and everyone else was too great for a serious relationship.

But she had to admit that she'd never been attracted to someone as much as Jacob O'Donnell. He was a pain in the ass, yet he had grabbed her attention from the day he'd arrived. Except for brief flashes of humor, he was mostly annoying, yet the way he talked about his wife was compelling. He had loved Anna without reservation, the way he loved Caitlin.

Was seeing that kind of devotion the reason she was questioning her commitment to Luke? Her parents had been willing to do anything for each other and she'd believed she felt that way about Luke, but now it wasn't so clear. Did "anything" mean throwing caution to the wind and marrying him despite the responsibilities she'd inherited? He would have welcomed her brother—once he'd even suggested they get married and live at the U-2 until Reid was eighteen or went away to college.

But no, she'd wanted to wait. She hadn't thought it was right to burden Luke, though he clearly hadn't seen it as a burden. How often did she tell herself that the Westons took care of their own problems? But "Westons" meant family, and the man she loved was family, right?

And now she had Jacob O'Donnell confusing everything.

Mariah rubbed her face and tried to put Jacob out of her mind. She'd told Luke she would visit his new foal this week. Maybe it would be easier to talk things over at his place, away from the U-2's hustle and bustle—then she'd see how crazy it was to question her feelings for him.

A sound came from the opposite side of the room and she looked up to see her grandmother. A silvery braid of hair hung over Elizabeth Weston's shoulder and she wore a pale sage-green silk dressing gown. Silk dressing gowns were impractical on the ranch, particularly during the winter, but Granddad had been buying them for her as long as Mariah could remember.

"Did I wake you, Grams?"

"No, apparently insomnia is making the rounds tonight. I got up so I wouldn't disturb Benjamin. What has you awake?"

"Just…stuff."

"Stuff? That's descriptive."

Mariah shrugged. She couldn't reveal her doubts about marrying Luke. If she was going to break up with him, it was only right that he hear it first. Yet even the thought took her breath away—she'd expected to marry him for most of her adult life.

"How about you?"

Grams sat in her rocking chair. "Nothing really."

Mariah tucked her legs beneath her and didn't challenge the "nothing." Then she realized it was past midnight—today was her father's birthday. Grams was probably thinking of her son and giving birth to him when she was a medical intern. It must have been rough, falling in love with a rancher while still attending school and having a long-distance marriage until she finished getting accredited. Grams had been a brilliant student but had given up a surgical career for a family practice in Buckeye.

"When did Granddad start buying you silk dressing gowns?" Mariah asked idly.

Grams chuckled. "It began with a movie. Do you remember that little theater we used to have in Buckeye? The one they tore down when you were five?"

"Barely. It was in an old World War II–era Quonset hut."

"That's right. They didn't have air-conditioning, just a water cooler, so in summer they had to show movies in the evening when it wasn't as warm. And the films were years or decades old—current theatrical releases were too expensive."

A warm, nostalgic feeling went through Mariah. "Yeah, that's where I saw *The Wizard of Oz*."

"Well, soon after your aunt Lettie was born, we went to see *Murder on the Orient Express*. I felt frumpy, overweight and groggy from being up with a newborn baby, and then onto the screen walks Lauren Bacall and Jacqueline Bisset, slim and impossibly glamorous in those beautiful period costumes. I could have strangled them on the spot."

Mariah searched her memory of the classic Agatha Christie mystery film. "Bisset played a countess, and Bacall's character turned out to be her mother, a famous stage actress."

"Yes. They looked so amazing and elegant that I sulked the entire movie."

"You?" Mariah sat up, dumbfounded. Grams didn't sulk—she was far too direct.

"It was a touch of postpartum depression. Regardless, when the countess informed Poirot that her dressing gown was apricot silk, I sniffed and said that she couldn't possibly be a mother, because mothers didn't get to wear silk. Next thing you know, your grandfather had gotten me a half-dozen silk negligees. I think he called every department store in Los Angeles until he found a salesperson he could sweet-talk into helping him."

"That sounds like Granddad. He doesn't know fashion, but he'd break his neck to make you happy."

Grams rocked back in the chair, smiling at the fond memory. "He has his moments. I never told him that silk and baby spit-up didn't mix well."

"No more than silk and horse manure."

"Yes. And it's nice to have something so frivolously feminine in such a male-dominated atmosphere. It's you and me out here with a whole bunch of men."

"True." Mariah bent over the end of the couch to throw a scrap of paper into the wastebasket. She frowned. A manila folder was inside and she fished it out—inside were the college applications that she'd given Reid a couple of days before, along with information on various university campuses. She'd downloaded the material from the internet, thinking the sooner he began working on his applications, the better.

"What is that, dear?"

"Oh…just something that got thrown out by mistake."

But Mariah knew it wasn't a mistake. If she truly thought Reid didn't want to go to college, that would be one thing, but she wasn't convinced. And even if he *didn't* want to go, why not apply to the schools he liked anyway in case he changed his mind?

"I'm going to warm some milk to help us sleep," Grams said.

They chatted about plans for the next barn dance as the milk heated. The scent of vanilla and cinnamon rose from Mariah's cup as she carried it to her bedroom and saw Squash curled up on the bed once more. His eyes closed to narrow slits as she sat beside him, sipping the creamy concoction. She was reminded of Caitlin, who'd never had a pet, though she plainly loved animals. What sort of life did the teen have, encased in her father's protective cocoon? Mariah felt sorry for her. Visiting the ranch must be the most fun she'd had in years. Caitlin needed…

Damn, Mariah mouthed silently. She had to stop worrying about the O'Donnells' problems.

She flipped through the applications that she'd fished out of the garbage. Except for some slight wrinkles from being tossed in the trash, the papers weren't creased. She would bet that Reid hadn't even bothered to look at them. Sighing, she put her cup on the bedside table and turned off the light.

She'd have to get through to Reid somehow—she just had no idea *how.*

THE NEXT MORNING Kittie tapped tentatively on the wall of Shayla's side of her family's tent. They'd agreed to get up early to feed the orphan calves, but Shayla had said she might not wake up and to come get her—apparently her sleep was messed up because of the traveling her family had been doing.

"Shayla," she whispered.

"Crikey," Shayla muttered on the other side of the canvas. "Coming." She stumbled out a few minutes later, yawning and fastening her jacket.

"Did I wake up your mom and dad?" Kittie asked worriedly as they walked toward the back barns. She wanted the McFees to like her. They seemed like awesome parents. Shayla had told her that when she'd gotten sick the previous year, her mom and dad had homeschooled her while she got better. But they weren't weird about it or anything, and they'd taken her on a long vacation before she started regular classes again.

"Naw, Dad could sleep at a football game, and Mum is using her Kindle. She has some books she's reading on holiday."

Kittie liked to read, too…or at least she *used* to like it before finding her mom's diary. Now she wasn't so sure. You found things out when you read stuff. Bad things.

"Uh…is it really winter in Australia right now?" she said as a distraction. "And Christmas is in summer? That seems upside down."

"Things seem upside down to me here. But in Brisbane it doesn't get that cold, even in winter. You can go diving or surfing all year—Kittie, you have to come stay with us and I'll teach you how to surf. Someday I'm going to try out a beach in Africa that I heard about from some surfies."

Surfing?

Yeah, right, Kittie thought crossly. Only if her dad got amnesia. He'd never let her go surfing. What she couldn't figure out was why he'd let her come to Montana and ride horses. If it was the cigarette and accidentally burning up a trash can, she was kind of glad all that happened now. But she couldn't imagine what she'd have to do to get on a surfboard…probably paint a mustache on the Statue of Liberty.

They got to the barn that housed the orphan calves, yet Kittie hesitated when she saw two ranch hands she didn't know very well. They were mixing the milk replacer and debating their favorite brand of saddle soap for cleaning leather. After a moment they stopped and smiled when they noticed her and Shayla.

"Hello. May we help?" Kittie asked in her most polite voice. "Reid showed me what to do yesterday, and Mariah said it was okay. She wants me to feed the littlest calf. I named her Emily."

"Mariah let us know. We usually don't have guests work the first feeding of the day—it's too early for town folks—but you're most welcome," said the ranch hand in charge. Kittie knew his name was Hector, and even if he didn't seem as old as Burt, he was still pretty old. "Go on and visit the calves. We'll bring the bottles when they're ready."

"This one is Emily," Kittie said to Shayla, climbing into the pen and pointing to the calf in the far corner. "She isn't doing as good and needs extra attention. She's shy."

"These beggars aren't." Shayla laughed as the two other calves crowded around her, bawling. "I've gone horseback riding before, but I haven't seen a cow close-up. They're real corkers."

Kittie petted Emily. "You've never gone to a ranch? Someone said that Australia raises a bunch of cows in the outback." She didn't say the "someone" had been her dad *or* that he'd told Ray Cassidy he was surprised anyone would come from Australia to spend a few weeks in Montana when there were spots like New York and San Francisco for them to see.

"Mum is afraid of dingoes," Shayla explained, "so there isn't a flipping chance of us visiting the outback."

Kittie had heard of dingoes—they were a kind of wild dog—but she only had a vague idea of the "outback" from geography class. Mostly her teacher had shown them pictures of koala bears and the Great Barrier Reef when teaching about Australia.

"Here you go," said one of the ranch hands, giving them a basket with six of the filled bottles.

Giggling, Shayla fed the two noisy calves, balancing the bottles on each arm, and Kittie sat with Emily. The anxious look was still in the calf's big, soft eyes, but she drank almost two full bottles of milk replacement and fell asleep afterward.

"Nice job," Hector said approvingly. "Nobody else has gotten that much into her. At this rate it won't take her long to catch up."

A thrill went through Kittie...and a nervous shiver. *She* was the only one who could get Emily to eat enough and it was an important responsibility. She would have to get up early every morning and see if Burt would take them back to the ranch in time for the afternoon feeding.

It took a while for all of the calves to get their milk, and afterward Hector showed her and Shayla how much hay, grain and specially made calf creep pellets to give them. "Not too much at once," he said. "It needs to be fresh. And later we'll let 'em into the paddock where they can eat grass."

When they were done and the calves were settled, Kittie stayed for the cleanup. "You can leave if you want," she told Shayla. "Breakfast is starting soon."

"I'll stay. Do you think they'll let us go out together? Last night our jackaroo said Mum and Dad and me are supposed to ride fences, whatever that means."

"Jackaroo?"

"Station hand. You know, the bloke who's showing us how to be real American cowboys."

"Oh, your wrangler." Kittie put a batch of washed bottles in their racks. "We rode fences our first day, too. It means you're checking the fences for damage and also checking the stock—looking for cows out on the range, making sure that any you find are okay. We found one that needed doctoring and had to bring it back here. Mariah and Burt and Ray fixed it up. But I can't go with you today." She wrinkled her nose. "We've got stable duty this morning. I have to learn how to shovel hay and manure out of the horse stalls."

"Gaw." Shayla made a face. "That's bloody awful."

"I know. It's going to be so gross."

"Can't you pretend to have a sick tummy?"

Kittie shook her head. "I better not. My dad is mad at me for some stuff, and that'll make him madder. He doesn't believe anything I tell him."

Between the four of them, they got everything washed up

fast, ready for the next feeding. Breakfast was being served in the mess tent when they arrived and they got their food together.

Kittie felt funny that she'd pretended to be upset about cleaning the stables. While she didn't *want* to shovel poop, it was part of taking care of the horses, and she had to take her turn along with everybody else.

TUESDAY EVENING MARIAH DROVE to the Branson spread after dinner. She'd visited often over the years, usually riding her horse across country. Now she didn't know if she'd ever be on Luke's ranch again; would he be so angry he'd tell her to get off and stay off?

She had hoped for a bolt of lightning to make her come to her senses, but nothing happened. Nevertheless, she and Luke needed to talk…a talk that was long overdue.

One of Luke's ranch hands waved as she swung into the compound. "Señorita Weston," he exclaimed, racing to open the truck door for her. "Señor Branson said you might come tonight to see our Light Foot."

"Hey, Pedro. How are you?"

"Good, very good. I'll get Señor Branson."

Mariah waited by the truck, looking around at the place she once thought would be her home. The Bransons had nearly as many barns and outbuildings as the U-2, including a bunkhouse, though being both a cow and horse breeder, Luke had more fenced paddocks. What he *didn't* have were the commercial restrooms and other facilities the U-2 provided for the greenhorns.

"You did come." It was Luke. He gave her a slow smile and kissed her cheek. "Come see my prize baby. Other than my cowhands and Doc Crandall, you'll be the first."

As they approached the paddock, Little Foot ran around the perimeter. Her colt ran with her, a smaller version of his light-stepping dam.

"Luke, he's wonderful."

"Yup, I'm pleased with him." Luke leaned on the fence and watched the two horses. The colt was a perfectly proportioned Morgan and was already displaying an alert, friendly disposition. Little Foot stopped and grazed in the lush grass, while Light Foot scampered up to nurse, his tail swishing happily.

"They're such incredible animals," Mariah murmured.

Luke didn't say anything for a moment, then gave her a sideways glance. "I know you didn't come to admire Light Foot. Just say it, Mariah."

She swallowed. "I don't know how."

"Straight-out is usually the best."

Mariah massaged the base of her neck. She'd barely slept since Sunday and continued to fight with herself over what she ought to do.

"The thing is, I need time to decide what's right for the future. I can't bear the thought of hurting you, but getting married for the wrong reasons would be worse. And whenever we talk about our plans, I feel..." She shrugged.

"Trapped?"

"No." She gave him an appalled look. "I'm just not sure of anything. It sounds crazy, but I've been on autopilot since Mom and Dad's accident. And I think I've tried to make everything keep fitting into old places...places that no longer exist."

Light Foot had stopped nursing and come to the fence, staring curiously at them. Mariah put out her fingers and let him smell them before stroking his neck. His mother promptly trotted over to stand nearby. She only trusted the man who'd hand-raised her.

"I didn't change, Mariah. I'm the same as ever."

"But I've changed, and I don't even know how..."

Luke was silent for several minutes, then released a heavy sigh. "I can't say I'm surprised. You've been distracted and distant the past year, but especially lately."

"Is that why you started coming to the U-2 so often?"

"I suppose. A last-ditch effort to hold on to you. I wasn't being fair, but it's difficult to be fair when you really want something."

"No, it's my fault," she said miserably. "You must be furious."

A sad, faintly humorous smile curved Luke's mouth. "Don't go Joan of Arc on me, Mariah. I could have forced the issue. It was my decision as much as yours."

"You're my best friend."

"Except that isn't enough…for either one of us." He stroked her cheek with the tip of his finger. "I love you, but if I'm not what you want, time isn't going to make a lick of difference—you've *had* time."

"I'm so sorry."

"So am I." He gave her a quick, hard kiss and pushed her back to her truck, closing the door behind her after she hopped into the cab. "Call if you need me for something," he said, slapping the door and stepping away.

Mariah drove off the Branson spread and pulled to the side of the road, trying to stop from shaking. If only Luke had gotten angry, yelled at her, accused her of leading him on… *anything.* He could be as unreasonable and argumentative as any other person—they'd had some terrific battles in the past—but instead he'd been understanding. And honest. She'd asked for time, but he'd known their engagement had to end.

She blinked rapidly to keep from crying. She didn't have any business crying—it was Luke who'd gotten hurt. He'd wasted years waiting for her. And now she didn't even know if they could salvage their friendship.

TWO DAYS LATER Mariah went to Billings for supplies, welcoming the solitude of the long drive and the absence of her family's curiosity. She hadn't told anyone about her talk with Luke, but they'd sensed something had happened.

The shopping took hours. A grocery supplier delivered goods like cornmeal, flour and beans, and the rest of their needs were purchased every Thursday in Billings. Mariah alternated trips with the wranglers.

The list included Reggie's special items for the kitchen and required a number of stops. At her request he'd checked the bourbon whiskey he kept to flavor his barbecue sauce—the punch had indeed been spiked with the same brand—but none was missing from the locked cabinet where it was stored. She decided to get a new padlock to be safe. Fortunately most people who knew about the incident seemed to think it was funny.

It was late in the afternoon when Mariah got back. She honked and the ranch hands within earshot showed up to unload the truck and sort out the contents.

"Burt, what are you doing here?" she queried, surprised to see him in the group.

He gave her a level look. "Waitin' for you to get here. Mr. O'Donnell let Kittie go out with Shayla McFee and her folks."

"What?"

"They left before I knew about it. O'Donnell said afterward that he had a problem with his company to handle."

Her lips tightened. Visitors often made friends and wanted to work together—the wranglers used their judgment when a request was received. It was *Jacob's* judgment that bothered her. She'd made it clear that he was to cope with Caitlin and her issues himself—not push them onto others.

"Where is he?"

Burt shrugged. "Don't know. Didn't see him at lunch, but that fancy car is sittin' out there, so he's not in Buckeye." His eyes glinted and she could see he was genuinely annoyed, which was rare for Burt. He was usually tolerant of greenhorns and the mistakes they could make.

As quickly as possible, Mariah excused herself and went looking for Jacob. He wasn't in his tent or around the barns or other guest areas, and the horse she'd assigned him was drowsing in the corral. Gritting her teeth, she went up to the house, wondering if Reid was home from school and might know something. Grams and Granddad weren't available—Grams worked at the Buckeye Medical clinic on Thursdays, and Granddad had driven to the Big Horn Mountains to visit a childhood friend who'd broken his leg.

Broken leg… There was a sobering prospect. Maybe Jacob had gone for a walk and was lost or had gotten injured. If he didn't show up soon, they'd have to send wranglers out to look for him. Wouldn't it be ironic if Mr. Overprotective Father had to be rescued himself?

Faint sounds came from the ranch office and she headed that direction, expecting to find Reid, but instead walked in on Jacob. He was multitasking, furiously typing on her computer while talking on the phone. On top of that, everything had gotten shoved about to make room for his laptop.

"What are you doing?" she demanded.

He held up his arm in an imperious you'll-have-to wait gesture. "That isn't acceptable," he said into the receiver. "This isn't the first incident of this kind, and I want to know what you'll do to remedy the situation. You're getting one more chance because we've been allied for years. That's it."

Mariah wanted to rip the cord from the wall but didn't since it would take a week for the local phone company to repair. Her temper rose as Jacob continued talking, and reached the boiling point when she found a faxed reservation request in the recycle trash can. Irate, she leaned across him and hit the flash button on the phone, knowing from experience it would disconnect the line.

"What the…?" Jacob slammed the receiver down and glared. "I was in the middle of something important."

She waved the fax in his face. "You threw away a reservation. What makes you think your business is more important than anyone else's?"

He glanced at the sheet of paper. "Sorry, it must have gotten in with the other trash by accident, but that was no reason to disconnect my call."

"An accident? Oh, well, that makes it all right," Mariah said sarcastically. "For your information, this is *my* office, not yours."

She stepped forward, only to catch the toe of her boot on a stack of books he'd piled on the floor. Jacob caught her before she landed on his laptop, and for a shocked moment, they stared into each other's eyes. His gaze traced her lips, focused on them with a hunger she recognized…and shared. Perhaps being with him wasn't such an implausible idea. They could try to see if they…

No.

She squirmed free. "I can't believe anyone on the U-2 gave you permission to come in here and take over. This is our home, not a public space. Our visitors have always respected our privacy until *you* got here."

"I didn't have permission," he admitted. "No one was here. But I didn't go into the house. I stayed in the office. An issue cropped up with my company and I had to take care of it. I run a global business and can't let a deal just fall apart. There's a lot of money at stake."

"My, my, aren't you special?" Mariah clenched her fists. "You would have done better arguing that people's livelihoods could have gotten hurt, instead of your wallet. But you aren't personally concerned for your employees, are you? They're only figures on a payroll."

"That's not true. I take care of my staff."

"Because it's good business. You said so yourself. And what about your cell phone? That Bluetooth device is embedded in your ear. You could have used *it* to make your calls."

"I'm using the cell as a modem for my laptop."

"Then why are you using *my* computer?"

"I needed both." He looked slightly abashed, but nowhere

near as repentant as he ought to be. "We have dual computer monitors at my company, where you can look at two documents or emails side by side. It's a much more efficient way of working."

Mariah let out a shriek. "*This isn't your company* and your bottom line isn't any more critical than ours."

"Look, it was only one reservation and I'm sure I would have found it. I planned to clear up after myself."

"You really don't have a clue, do you?" she said, torn between fury and pure astonishment that he could be so blind. "Ranching isn't predictable. Our vacation business supports ranchers for fifty miles around by providing jobs and income to get them through the lean periods. Our business relies heavily on word of mouth, *so we don't screw up reservations.* We cannot afford to."

He snorted. "Judging by your daily rate, you're doing fine. Granted, I pay much more when I visit the Caribbean, but then I'm staying at a luxury Caribbean resort, not a tent."

"That again? You're a businessman. You should have figured something out by now—like how much it costs to run the U-2. For one thing, we have to hire half as many ranch hands as we have paying guests. Then there's insurance, food and other bills on top of that. But hey, I have an idea how to increase our bottom line—we'll tell everyone to bring their own toilet paper and coffee. Think of how many gallons we would have saved on you already."

Jacob frowned and Mariah couldn't tell if he was irritated or actually thinking about what she'd said.

"I'll pay more for the inconvenience."

Obviously, *not* thinking about what she'd told him.

"How can you claim you want to help Caitlin when you consistently put work and profit first?" she challenged. "For Pete's sake, you have couriers coming to the ranch every day, delivering and picking up parcels related to your company. You're up late at night, working and making calls, so you're sleep deprived when you do spend time with her. What message does it send when all you think about is business?"

"My daughter—"

"Is out riding her horse and moving cattle with people you met less than a week ago," Mariah interrupted. "You let her go with them because you wanted to work on a business deal. I'm sure she appreciates coming so low on your list of priorities."

CHAPTER TEN

"DON'T BE RIDICULOUS. Kittie is the most important thing in the world to me," Jacob snapped. He stood, expecting Mariah to step backward, but she crossed her arms over her stomach and glared without moving an inch.

"You have a strange way of showing it."

"We've already *had* this argument."

"And I'm sure we'll have it again if you pull anything else like disrupting our office."

His jaw hardened. Okay, he shouldn't have used the U-2's office without permission, but he'd learned something interesting from his hours working there. He lifted Mariah's scratch pad, covered with numbers and names, and thrust it under her nose.

"Speaking of 'pulling' something, I see you contacted Kittie's school and some other places in Seattle. Officer Rizzoli, for example. I trust he reminded you that information regarding a minor can't be disclosed."

Mariah shrugged and took the pad from him. "I wasn't pulling anything. I was simply verifying that your version of the fire was accurate. You honestly don't get it, do you? We're responsible for our visitors and over two thousand animals. For everyone's sake I *had* to be sure Caitlin wasn't guilty of arson. If you had a shred of understanding you'd see that anybody would have done the same, but you're so arrogant you think you're the exception to every rule."

Jacob's anger cooled as quickly as it had flared. Mariah

had a point—not about him being arrogant, but about her responsibilities. He would have checked up on Kittie, too, if their situations were reversed.

"So, what did the school and police say? I assume they corroborated what I told you."

"Nothing personal. Garrison Academy wouldn't answer any questions. The police department was discreet, but Officer Rizolli confirmed it was an accident. He said 'the student' tried to put out the fire and pulled the alarm when she was unsuccessful. It would have been nice if you'd told me *that* part of the story—I wouldn't have worried as much."

Kittie had tried to put out the fire?

Jacob didn't recall being told that, either, and a chill went through him, because fighting a fire was dangerous. He attempted to keep his expression neutral, thinking of the afternoon he'd been summoned to the school and the adrenaline shooting through his system—the anger and fear that Kittie was spinning so far out of control that he'd never get her back. The principal had ranted, practically spitting with outrage, and Rizolli had lectured with crisp precision. Yet neither of them had revealed that she'd called the fire department or tried to extinguish the blaze.

You could have asked...

The internal voice was annoying…and right. He *could* have asked more questions instead of trying to get his daughter off school property as fast as possible. And just as annoying was the realization that Mariah probably would have insisted on knowing every detail. As a matter of fact, if he'd listened to Mariah better, he wouldn't have asked Kittie if she had spiked the punch at the barn dance on Saturday night.

The memory made him wince.

Mariah might have suspected Kittie, but she'd warned him there wasn't any evidence and that it could have been anyone. Yet without proof and just the burden of her history to hold against her, he'd confronted Kittie when they were out riding on Monday.

He could have incinerated a steak on the scathing look she'd given him.

"Sorry," Jacob muttered. "Now, if you'll excuse me, Kittie and her new friend should be returning soon. I want to be there when they ride in."

He powered down his laptop and gathered the remainder of his belongings. But it wasn't until he was halfway to his tent that he remembered he hadn't left money to cover the phone calls he'd made to Seattle and overseas. And other tasks remained undone as well, though he'd intended to put everything back where he'd found it.

Hell. He'd really blown things, both with Mariah and Kittie. In retrospect, he knew the issue with his company hadn't been that serious, but he'd used it as an excuse to avoid his daughter and the hatred she seemed to have for him. At least the past few days had passed without any outbursts from her. Though Kittie had ignored *him,* she'd acted reasonably polite and cooperative with everyone else.

Deciding to give Mariah a chance to calm down before returning to the office, he stopped by the mess tent. "Hey, Burt," Jacob said when he saw the wrangler.

"Did you get your business settled, Mr. O'Donnell?" Burt's tone was unusually formal and it didn't take any intuition to know he was upset, as well.

Great.

Kittie was making friends, and he was driving them away.

"Partially. About this morning, I realize I should have spoken with you before letting Kittie go with Shayla and her family."

"We had work to do, Mr. O'Donnell. A ranch don't run itself." Without another word, he put his coffee cup on a tray and stomped away.

Jacob grimaced. The day was just getting better and better, and the ache in his groin wasn't helping.

Hellfire, he couldn't deny wanting Mariah, and having her land on his lap had made it a hundred times worse. It wasn't just work and caffeine keeping him awake at night—it was a grinding need that wouldn't go away. She wasn't the most beautiful woman he'd ever met, but there was something about her that compelled him physically.

Compared to the women he usually dated, she was exotic. Perhaps that was the appeal.

The mess tent, though it supplied coffee eighteen hours a day, was suddenly unappealing, and Jacob wished he could go riding. Odd, after spending a week and a half in the open air, it had felt tedious being shut up in a room in front of a computer screen. But he realized that a ride was out of the question; he needed to wait for Kittie.

He went outside and watched. Ten minutes later Kittie and the McFees rode over the hill. They were laughing, along with their wrangler, and they dismounted by the foremost barn, chattering away as if they'd known each other forever. It was a relief to see his daughter bonding with the wholesome Aussie teen, despite the differences in their backgrounds. Kittie had friends in Seattle, but for all he knew they were part of her problem.

"You should get ready for dinner now. The bathrooms can get awfully busy when everyone comes back," Kittie said to the McFees. "I'll groom the horses before feeding the baby calves." She sounded as if she'd always lived on a ranch and was accustomed to handling the list of chores.

"I'll go with you," Shayla said.

"Thanks, ladies," Bill told them heartily. "It was a ripper day, but I'm looking forward to a seat that doesn't keep rocking."

Kittie's bright smile faded when Jacob came closer. She

scowled at him and turned away deliberately. "Come on, Shayla, I'll show you what to do."

The two girls and the wrangler took the horses into the barn. Jacob sighed, discouraged. They'd obviously had fun, but it hadn't changed his daughter's attitude toward him.

Was Mariah right—did Kittie believe she came second to his work? Could that be what she was so angry about?

It was a sobering thought. He'd gone into business to provide for his daughter and repay the money he had borrowed from his in-laws, yet even after achieving both goals he'd continued to spend a significant amount of time at the office. Running his own company had been more challenging and satisfying than he'd expected after giving up a career in engineering. It *had* consumed him. He might have even subconsciously dismissed the U-2 as a business because it was so small in comparison.

Mariah's furious declaration that the U-2 helped support ranches for miles around still rang in his ears. It really mattered to her, and he could now see how critical the ranch might be to the local economy. What was more, he hadn't taken the operating costs into account when considering their rates—all he'd seen were the canvas tents and communal restrooms.

Yet even more disconcerting was seeing himself from Mariah's point of view…the obsessed businessman, with no high goals aside from making money.

He hadn't always been that way. Once he'd had dreams and ideals he couldn't wait to make come true.

"I CANNOT BELIEVE he did that," Mariah stormed as she put everything away in the office. She located another fax, one adding to a prior message about food allergies, under the books Jacob had piled on the floor and slapped it on the desk for review.

The majority of their reservations were handled over the

internet, but some people didn't use the Net or didn't trust putting personal information online, so they preferred fax or phone. No doubt Jacob had also tied up the phone line so nobody could have gotten through to the answering machine while he conducted his *important* business. The local phone company kept promising to invest in the technology for electronic voice mail, but in the meantime, everybody around Buckeye was using more old-fashioned ways of recording messages.

"I should have locked the house when I went to the clinic, but it didn't occur to me that someone would come in here," Grams said with a frown. As a doctor, she was fierce on confidentiality. "You know, I was starting to like Mr. O'Donnell. I'm very disappointed in him."

Mariah was disappointed in Jacob, too, for a variety of reasons. Maybe she was naive, but a pretty nice class of people usually came to the U-2 for their vacations...people who wouldn't dream of intruding the way he had.

The phone rang and Mariah picked it up. It was Amy from the travel agency; she'd spoken with a couple of travelers who'd tried to reach the ranch directly. Nothing pressing, just guests double-checking their reservations. As she hung up, Mariah realized that Grams had stepped out to the patio and was talking to someone in low tones.

She continued tidying and checking to be sure nothing else had gotten lost. The space was small, but it worked well if everything was kept in its proper place. She'd considered using one of the larger rooms in the house, but this was the office her parents had set up when they'd started the ranch vacation business. And it had exterior access for the rare occasions a visitor came up to the house.

"Mariah?"

It was Jacob, standing at the open door.

"What?"

"I forgot to leave money to pay for my calls. Several were

overseas and they'll be expensive." He gave her an envelope. "This should cover it, but if not, you can bill me when you receive the charges from the phone company."

"Whatever." She threw it into the petty-cash box.

"I know you're still angry…"

Mariah gave him a withering look.

"But I want to apologize. I didn't properly before, and I am sorry."

He seemed sincere, and it was remotely possible that her temper had gotten the best of her.

It wasn't easy to stay calm these days. Her life had gotten radically turned upside down that week, and Jacob's presence wasn't making it easier to handle.

Aside from his daughter, the man didn't seem concerned about other people in the least, and he certainly didn't have an interest in the land or animals. He was probably a decent employer, but not because his employees were individuals with needs and lives of their own—it was just good business. But for her, ranching was a way of life that the Westons had chosen for generations, and their neighbors and cowhands were like extended family. How could she be so unsettled by someone who didn't care about the things that mattered most to her, much less understand why they were important?

As for that brief instant when she'd tripped and he'd caught her… Mariah swallowed. However much she tried to ignore it, the heat between them crackled with an intensity she'd never felt.

"Fine. You've apologized," she said. "I thought you wanted to see Caitlin when she got back."

"I saw her. She went to groom Blue."

Mariah lifted an eyebrow at his dour tone, though she didn't know if it was because Caitlin had reacted poorly to him or the reminder that his daughter was combing and brushing an animal that outweighed her by a thousand pounds.

"Burt says she's very thorough. He thinks the responsibility has been good for her," Mariah couldn't resist adding, though it might be the same as throwing a lighted match on gasoline.

Jacob made an exasperated sound. "I'm no longer uptight about her working with the horses. Well…not much."

"Glad to hear it. Well, you'd better head over for dinner. Mr. and Mrs. Cardoza are assigned to help with the meal tonight and they're cooking a specialty from their restaurant in San Diego."

"Aren't you coming?"

"Believe it or not, we have a kitchen here at the house, with a stove and everything. I usually don't eat a full meal at the mess tent." She didn't add that when Grams worked at the clinic in Buckeye, they usually *did* eat with the guests.

"But you don't cook."

Mariah was surprised he'd remembered. Of course, he hadn't built a global company by being forgetful.

"I may be down later, but Grams always stocks food in the fridge. Now, if you don't mind, I have things to do."

GIGGLING, KITTIE AND SHAYLA raced to the showers once they were done with their chores. The McFees' wrangler had made sure they were currying the horses properly, and now that she understood how important grooming was to Blue's health, Kittie didn't mind that the ranch hands regularly checked to make sure she was doing everything right. Besides, it was like gym class—you didn't get perfect at something without practicing and having someone teach you. As for Emily, she was doing really well; the wranglers said she was gaining weight and getting playful with the other cows. And she ran over as soon as she saw Kittie, crying and wanting attention.

Almost everyone had gone to the mess tent, so they didn't have company in the bathroom. Kittie dried off and shimmied into clean jeans and a T-shirt, trying not to look at herself in the mirror. She'd never done laundry in Seattle and the things she'd washed at the ranch had come out of the machine blotchy. She couldn't wait to talk to Mariah about helping her get new clothes. She sure wasn't going to the dance if she had to wear one of her faded shirts or the crap her dad had bought.

Shayla tucked her top into her jeans. "Ready?"

"Uh-huh. Let's go. I'm starving."

"Me, too."

At the mess tent, they got into line at the food table and Kittie's stomach rumbled as she sniffed the delicious smells. The U-2 always served steak and barbecued chicken with beans and all, but they also had special dishes every night, and some for people who didn't eat meat. Today the special dish was enchiladas with carne adovada and rice, covered with tons of melted cheddar. Her mouth watered.

"Do you like spicy food?" asked Mr. Cardoza as he served Shayla. "We made it mild, but you can use the fresh salsa if you want it hotter."

"Yes, sir," Shayla assured him. "I like it spicy."

"Me, too," Kittie chimed in and stuck her plate out. Their different housekeepers had cooked various kinds of foods, but Kittie *loooved* cheese, so Mexican and Italian were her favorites. She sat with the McFees and dug into the food; everything tasted yummier in Montana.

A few minutes later Mariah arrived and looked pissed when she saw Kittie's dad.

Kittie's heart fell.

Jeez. Why couldn't he stop making Mariah mad?

"You seem to be off your tucker," said Mrs. McFee. "Are you all right?"

Kittie remembered Shayla saying that *tucker* was *food* in Australia. "No, I'm fine." She began eating again, though it didn't taste quite as yummy.

Mariah left as dessert was being put out and Kittie followed her outside. It might already be too late to ask. The next dance was in two days and Mariah always had lots to do.

"Uh...Mariah," she called, running after her.

Mariah turned around. "Yes?"

"I wanted to...er...see if you would..." Kittie bit her lip. "That is, I don't think the boys here like my clothes. I thought...well, I *hoped* that if you weren't too mad at my dad, you might take me to buy some outfits that Montana guys prefer so I can be a real cowgirl. Before the dance on Saturday, if you have time. Just us, not my dad."

Mariah didn't say anything at first, then she nodded. "I'd be happy to, but I'll have to get your father's permission."

"Can you just say we're going shopping?" Kittie asked anxiously. "Not the junk about guys in Montana. Dad won't let me date or anything. He wants me to die a virgin."

"Oh." Mariah rubbed her mouth. "Sure, I can do that."

"Thanks, Mariah! I need new things anyhow—the clothes I brought got ruined when I washed them. See?" She tugged on her faded black T-shirt. "At home the housekeeper does the laundry, so I don't know how to do it right. I put something in that was supposed to get things extra clean, but they came out this way and smell like a swimming pool."

"It must have been bleach for whites. When you do it again, try cold water and something that says 'color-safe bleach.'"

"Okay."

Kittie could have asked Shayla or Mrs. McFee what to do with the laundry, but she thought she'd sound dumb or bigheaded, since most people didn't have housekeepers. Besides, Kittie figured Mariah was used to people not knowing how to do stuff on the ranch.

Mariah waved toward the mess tent. "Shall we see if your father will give his permission?"

"Are you sure it isn't too much trouble? I mean, I know you got a lot to do."

A funny expression crossed Mariah's face, but she shook her head. "No, it's not too much trouble."

MARIAH TRIED TO STAY composed as she returned to the mess tent with Caitlin. She hadn't been able to turn down the teenager's request. In Caitlin's shoes she wouldn't have gone to her father for help with clothes, either—no one could have accused Sam Weston of being a fashionista.

The cleanup crew was working on the dishes in the outdoor kitchen, and everybody else was settling into their evening activities—games, singing and friendly chit-chat over coffee and dessert. A number of the wranglers hung around the mess tent rather than going to the bunkhouse, so it tended to stay cheerfully noisy until hard work and fresh air caught up with visitors and employees alike.

Jacob sat to one side as usual, looking vaguely out of place, the ubiquitous cup of coffee in his hand. His cell phone Bluetooth device wasn't in his ear—it was likely burning a hole in his pocket.

"I'm gonna wait with Shayla," Caitlin said hurriedly. "Maybe he'll let me go if it's just you asking."

She bolted away and Mariah wrinkled her nose. Caitlin being there probably wouldn't make any difference. Jacob was so protective he might not allow *anyone* to take his daughter into town regardless.

"Caitlin wanted a favor, so I need to speak with you," she said as she approached Jacob.

He tensed. "What favor?"

"We should take a walk and discuss it," Mariah suggested, conscious of the teenager's hopeful gaze from the opposite side of the tent. She'd hate to disappoint Caitlin, but the decision was entirely up to Jacob and she didn't want to get into an argument with him in front of everybody.

"Sure."

Outside she went up the shallow valley to the open country

beyond. The setting sun cast a golden light across the landscape and there wasn't a cloud in the sky, though Mariah still wished for some rain. It wasn't a bad drought year yet, but she preferred the grass to be greener this early in the season so they didn't have to worry as much about fire.

"This is nice," Jacob said approvingly when she stopped.

"Oh...yes." With a start, Mariah saw that she'd taken him to her favorite spot in Montana—the crest of a small hill, topped by a single tall ponderosa pine. From there she could sit and look at the land for miles in every direction.

"It's hard to imagine," he murmured finally.

"Imagine what?"

"That buffalo used to roam by the millions on the Great Plains. As a kid I was fascinated when we visited Yellowstone National Park and saw one. They looked so primitive, as if they could have strolled off a cave painting. And huge—the ranger said a charging buffalo could bash in the side of our car."

"They're amazing," Mariah agreed. It was strange that they were both intrigued by the massive animals.

She sat down cross-legged and breathed in the wild scents of grass and flowers and the cool breeze. Jacob dropped down next her, too close for comfort.

A hundred and forty years ago, Mariah's ancestors left the security of their homes in the East and drove covered wagons into the northern territories. Catherine Heider Weston was expecting her first child, and her husband had treated her with unusual care; instead of walking by the wagon like so many wives and daughters, she rode in a cushioned chair. And a month after arriving on the land where Mariah now sat, Catherine safely gave birth to a son who was christened Matthew Thomas.

More children were born and baptized. A cemetery was consecrated. The original ranch house burned and was rebuilt. The second one burned as well, years later, and the family stubbornly built again. You had to be stubborn to survive on the land; it didn't let you be anything else.

The sun had dropped lower and color streaked up from the horizon—the land was so broad and wide that the sky felt bigger. She could breathe in a place like this. It wasn't loud with cars and televisions and people blasting their stereos. She'd practically gone crazy in college when a neighbor played music endlessly, the *thump, thump, thump* of the bass rubbing like itching powder on her senses.

What was wrong with silence—were people afraid of being alone with their thoughts?

Yet it wasn't silent, even here.

The breeze ruffled the grass, and birds called through the evening air. And there was Jacob beside her; Mariah was aware of each tiny sound he made, from the intake of his breath to the rustle of his clothing.

"Were there buffalo in the area when your family came here?" Jacob asked.

The question startled Mariah. It was almost as if he'd read her mind about the past.

"A few. But the bison herds were mostly wiped out by the time Catherine and Timothy Weston homesteaded here in the 1870s. Catherine was a wagon maker's daughter. They both died on the ranch in their nineties."

Jacob plucked a blade of grass and twisted it in his fingers. "Have you ever looked into stocking bison on the U-2? I understand there's a market for buffalo meat."

"Maybe someday. I like the idea of keeping a breeding herd, since they were nearly driven extinct by hunters, though not as a commercial venture." Mariah shifted. "Anyway, Jacob, the favor that Caitlin wanted…she had some difficulty with her clothes when she washed them. Bleach got in and now they're discolored. She'd like me to take her into Buckeye to do some shopping." It was part of the truth, but she kept the teenager's other comments private.

"I already bought her clothes in town. She refuses to wear them."

"You know kids—they like to pick their own gear. I don't mind taking her, but I told her we'd need your consent."

Resignation filled his face. "She doesn't want me to go."

"Uh, well, it's kind of a feminine thing, shopping for clothes. My dad was terrific, but he would have been useless in a women's clothing store. You don't have to worry—the Buckeye Booteek doesn't stock anything risqué. We don't get enough tourists wanting to buy that sort of thing, being off the main highway."

Jacob moved restlessly. "What if I take you both into town and stay in the car while you shop?"

What if I tell you to go jump yourself? Mariah thought crossly. If he didn't trust her to drive his kid five miles, he should just say so.

"I don't think that's what she had in mind."

"I wouldn't be in the store with you, and that way I could simply come in and pay for everything when you were done. It would be less complicated dealing with the bill."

"But she'd still feel as if you were keeping an eye on her. If that's what you want to do, then *you* tell Caitlin. Have fun."

Mariah got up and started back to the ranch center without waiting to see if he followed. Jacob couldn't get lost; the lights and peaks of the buildings were visible from their vantage point.

"Hey," he said and grabbed her arm and swung her around. "I blew it again, didn't I? I'm sorry. It must have sounded as if I don't think you're a safe driver."

"I don't object to you being concerned. I object to you making up excuses," she hissed. The imprint of his hand on her skin sent a hot sensation straight to her abdomen. Damn. She'd heard that heightened emotion led to heightened sexual response; it must be true. He'd ticked her off more than once today.

"I'm sorry. It *is* hard for me to let Kittie go with someone I don't know that well," he said. "Or anyone, for that matter. How about a compromise? Take the Mercedes—it's one of those models that are built like a tank—and I'll work with Burt while you're gone."

Mariah counted to five, trying to get hold of her temper. "All right, but she's hoping to fit in a bit more around here, like a cowgirl, and it would be easier to do that in my truck. Mercedes aren't seen around these parts too often—they smack of city snobs without country sense."

A muscle twitched in Jacob's jaw. "Then take your truck."

He remained silent, and when they entered the mess tent, he immediately went to get a cup of coffee. Mariah was certain that one of these days he was going to have a heart attack from all the stress and caffeine and long work hours. If he was bucking to leave his daughter an orphan, he was going about it the right way.

Caitlin looked across the room hopefully and Mariah gave her a thumbs-up gesture. The teen got so excited she actually jumped up and gave her father a hug before running over. "When can we go?" she asked eagerly.

"I'll let you know—most likely tomorrow afternoon. I can arrange the work schedule so you eat lunch here, rather than out on the range."

"*Awesome.* And I can feed Emily when we're done?"

"Absolutely. She needs you."

Mariah avoided Jacob's gaze as she left the mess tent again. Local fashions hadn't changed much since she was a teenager herself, and she was sure they could find something at the Buckeye Booteek that would make Kittie appear more appealing to boys her age.

Dad doesn't want me to date or anything. He wants me to die a virgin.

The memory of Caitlin's disgusted announcement made Mariah grin despite her churning thoughts. She was almost looking forward to the outing, and it wasn't just because it annoyed Jacob—she'd feel for any girl without a mother, especially one with an overprotective, out-of-touch father.

CHAPTER ELEVEN

"Is it total Dorksville?" Caitlin asked, twirling to look at herself from every angle in the clothing store's mirror. She was trying on sundresses, and the latest one was pale pink.

"No, but it would be better if your hair was its original color," Mariah said honestly.

That morning Jacob had shown Mariah a picture of Caitlin from the previous year. She'd had long, light blond hair and a sweet, eager smile—no wonder Jacob was worried about what had happened to his little girl.

Caitlin's expression became hostile and she stuck out her chin. "What about my hair?"

"I can tell from your skin tone that it isn't natural, and because it gets lighter and darker," Mariah said carefully. "Maybe you should try one of these outfits with bolder colors and geometric patterns. They might fit more with black hair and lipstick."

"But they aren't like what the other girls were wearing at the dance."

She was right, the local girls her age had all worn soft, pretty outfits with floral patterns, the U-2's weekly summer barn dance being one of their few opportunities to get gussied up outside of church. But Mariah was concerned that Caitlin would be even more conspicuous if she wore a feminine sundress with her Goth-style makeup, hair and jewelry. And at the moment the teen had decided she wanted to fit in rather than be a maverick. Whether or not she was willing to do what was needed *to* fit in was the question.

Caitlin turned to the mirror and fingered the roughly cut locks around her forehead. "What if I wash the black out? It's temporary and I have to dye it every couple of days for it to look good anyhow. It's gross when it gets like this."

"That would work. If you want we can trim the ends and use combs to draw it back from your face to make your eyes seem bigger."

"Awesome." Caitlin brightened. "And I could get sandals and new lipstick and all."

"Right." Mariah searched through the dresses on the rack and pulled out another. "Try this," she said.

It was cadet-blue with small red-and-white flowers, and she suspected it would complement Caitlin's natural coloring more than the washed-out pastels she'd been considering. So far they'd picked out a number of T-shirts and blouses, a stack of stonewashed blue jeans, several skirts and two pairs of cowboy boots that Caitlin couldn't choose between. There wasn't a black top or leering skull in the lot, but Mariah didn't pretend it was due to her persuasive skills—the Booteek simply didn't have any in stock.

Jacob had provided his credit card to use with a letter of authorization, and Mariah was uncomfortably aware of its presence in her wallet. When she'd asked for Caitlin's spending limit, he had looked at her blankly. "Whatever she wants," he'd finally answered.

"Ooh, I like this one," Caitlin said, spinning in front of the mirror. She was wearing the blue sundress and it looked good, even with her streaky hair.

Mariah hid a smile and selected two more dresses for consideration. Caitlin put them on the pile, then impulsively ran across the store when she spotted a cowboy hat that appealed to her.

"Nice youngster," commented Chloe Gardiner, owner of the Buckeye Booteek.

The Booteek specialized in Western wear, and it was the only shopping option for clothing unless they drove into Billings. Chloe's husband ran the men's side of the store, which went by the not-so-inspired name of Buckeye Menswear. The Booteek had earned its moniker when gales of laughter rose at Chloe's original choice—the Buckeye Fashion Boutique. The residents had gone around saying "boooooteeeeek" in such an exaggerated way that after a month Chloe surrendered and got the sign repainted.

"She don't have no clothes sense, though," added Bertha, her mother. "Glad you're helpin' out."

"Caitlin has her own unique style," Mariah murmured, glancing at the teenager to be sure she was out of earshot. Though she didn't think Caitlin's Goth preferences were becoming to her, they were a question of choice.

Bertha shrugged and her daughter chuckled. Chloe was a live-and-let-live sort, though she undoubtedly made a few comments about her neighbors behind closed doors. Gossip was an indoor sport in Buckeye—it didn't take long for everybody to know your business. Once word of Mariah's broken engagement got out, it would spread like wildfire through the community. There would be endless speculation as to why and they might even connect Jacob O'Donnell to the news. Jacob and Luke hadn't exactly been subtle at the barn dance, the way they'd snorted and maneuvered around each other.

Mariah's stomach tightened.

She hadn't broken things off with Luke because of Jacob, but the role he'd played made her uneasy. It would be horrid if Luke thought she had gotten cozy with another man while they were still making plans for the future. He'd claimed to see a change in her over the past year, and she supposed her restlessness, the feeling that something wasn't quite right, might have started that long ago. Having someone like Jacob at the ranch could have just brought everything to the surface much faster.

"What do you think?" Caitlin excitedly tottered toward them in absurdly high gold sandals with ribbon straps that wrapped around her ankles.

Whoa.

Mariah tried not to cringe. "Uh…they're pretty, but it would be hard to square-dance in them," she replied, conscious of Chloe's hopeful gaze. The store owner had gotten a deal on the glitzy footwear a decade before and done everything short of standing on her head to sell them. Unfortunately, they were the sort of thing you wore to a nightclub in New York, not to anything in Buckeye, so Chloe was left with two dozen pairs of useless stock.

"I didn't think of that. Can you take a look and tell me what might be okay for dancing?" Caitlin wobbled back to the modest selection of shoes in the center of the store.

Mariah followed and found a pair of white sandals in the right size. They were attractive and well made, and would go with any of the outfits Caitlin had chosen. And more importantly, they wouldn't result in a broken ankle from her falling off a four-inch spike heel.

"Here, try these," she said.

Caitlin approved the sandals and picked out two more pairs in other colors. Additional items were selected, including makeup and hair-care products, which might be necessary with all the dye jobs she'd given herself. With luck it would come clean in a couple of washings and wouldn't be too damaged.

The Buckeye Booteek didn't charge exorbitant prices, yet Mariah whistled when Chloe gave her the total. It was more than she spent on clothing over the course of several years—she hoped Jacob had meant it when he'd said Caitlin could get whatever she wanted. Still, a couple of designer outfits would likely cost more than Caitlin's entire ranch wardrobe, so maybe he wouldn't blink when he saw the bill. Well, except for the cowgirl hat Caitlin had wanted—that might cause Jacob to blink. A top-of-the-line hat cost a small fortune, and the Buckeye Booteek carried the best.

It was midafternoon when they returned to the U-2 and unloaded everything into the O'Donnells' tent. Caitlin would probably have taken longer selecting her new clothes if not for Emily. Caitlin hadn't missed a feeding for the orphan calves since she'd begun working with them, and she wasn't about to now. She was hoping to meet Shayla at the calf barn if the McFees got back in time from moving cattle to new pastureland.

"Thank you, thank you, *thank you,*" Caitlin said, throwing her arms around Mariah.

Mariah hugged her back. "I'm glad you found things you like. Why don't you come up to the house tomorrow after you're done with Emily's second feeding, and we'll work on your hair?"

The teen nodded happily. "Okay."

Mariah watched her running to the far barn; she remembered being that age and feeling the need to run everywhere.

She'd enjoyed the shopping trip, though it was a reminder that having broken up with Luke, it might be years before she had children of her own. Single cowboys were plentiful at the U-2, but they weren't the most promising husband material. Of course, neither was Jacob, and it wasn't just because they had nothing in common—he didn't want to get married again or have more kids. He hadn't said why, but she guessed it was mostly due to Caitlin's surgery and what he'd gone through with his wife. Ironically, Jacob's devotion to Anna's memory was one of the most attractive things about him.

It suggested he could be more than a cash register if he wanted to be.

LATE SATURDAY AFTERNOON Kittie crammed her clothes and other gear for the dance into three shopping bags and dashed up to the ranch house. She was too excited to eat dinner; all she could think about was whether Reid and the other boys would pay more attention to her. Anyway, there'd be snacks and desserts to eat at the dance if she got hungry.

She had her new cowgirl hat smashed on her head, not wanting anyone to see her hair yet. It was blond again, and it looked funny to her after being black or another color for so long. She hadn't even let Shayla see it.

Her dad had asked to see her new clothes, but she'd just shown him the hat. It was a genuine Stetson cowgirl hat, made of creamy fur felt. A band of braided leather adorned the base of the crown, and the wide brim would shade her eyes when she was out riding. She'd told him he should to go into Buckeye and find one for himself, along with cowboy boots—she'd even offered to help him pick them out. *Talking* to her dad was sure better than being mad and fighting with him.

"Good evening, little lady," said Mr. Weston when he opened the door. "Are you going to save me a dance tonight?"

"Uh, sure."

"Excellent. Mariah mentioned you were coming up here to get ready, so go down that hall, third door on the right."

Kittie decided it was the greatest house ever, old and rambling, with two cats curled up on opposite ends of the couch and Pip padding down the hallway behind her. It wasn't like their loft in Seattle. It was warm and comfy with lots of old wood and color, not bamboo and glass and chrome.

Pip nosed her palm and she leaned over to hug him. Shayla was scared of Pip because he was huge and his eyes were so dark in his white face, but Kittie thought he was splendid. Mariah had called him part mystery mutt, but Burt had said the part that wasn't a mystery was the type of dog they used in Alaska to pull sleds in the snow, which made Pip superstrong.

Kittie went through the door where Mr. Weston had told her to go, and her fingers tightened on the handles of her shopping bags. The room was real pretty. Light came in from two long windows, and the bed was covered with a quilt that had a single big star on it made of tiny blue and white diamonds. Everything was simple, but there was a bureau where you could sit in front of three mirrors, and she saw a really old silver hairbrush and mirror sitting on a silver tray. They were like the ones Nana Carolyn kept in her bedroom—the ones she claimed had once belonged to Kittie's great-great-grandmother.

"You're right on time," Mariah said, breezing in.

She was already dressed for the dance in a white eyelet sundress and Kittie sighed with envy. *Mariah* didn't have to worry about a flat chest. Reid had said that different guys liked different things, and maybe he was right—the newlyweds who'd left earlier in the week could be proof. Susan didn't have big breasts, and Chad seemed to think she was terrific. But a girl had to have *something* under her shirt.

"How is Emily doing?" Mariah asked.

"She butted one of the other calves when it tried to get her bottle."

"That means she's sticking up for herself. Good job, Kittie," she said. "Now, let's see if that black dye washed out."

Reluctantly, Kittie took off her cowboy hat. "I bet it looks dopey."

Mariah shook her head. "Not at all. It has a curl without the heavy dye and it's a lovely color, Caitlin. Black is fine, too, but blonde goes with your new clothes."

It was nice the way Mariah remembered to say *Caitlin*—Kittie *did* sound like a kid's name.

"Do you want me to trim it, or would you prefer keeping it the same?" Mariah asked.

Kittie gulped. She might as well change some things and see if the guys in Montana liked it. "Trim it, I guess. Just not too short."

"Okay." Mariah opened a drawer in the bureau and took out a worn leather case. "This is a barber's kit—we cut our own hair on the U-2. I won't take very much off, just enough to make the ends even."

She combed and snipped and then Kittie used the bathroom to put on one of her new dresses and a pair of sandals. "I forgot to get panty hose," she said, coming out with her lip down. She'd never worn nylons, but the popular girls at school always did.

"Cowgirls hardly ever wear panty hose," Mariah said firmly.

Kittie felt better. "Oh, okay, then. Can you…uh…show me how cowgirls do their makeup?"

"Sure." Mariah didn't actually apply the makeup. She just gave directions, saying the trick was to only use a little. Then she demonstrated how Kittie could hold her hair back with the decorative hair combs they'd bought.

"Awesome." Kittie turned and twisted, trying to see herself from every angle. With Mariah's help, she looked older and prettier. Was that what having a mom was like…having someone who took you shopping and showed you how to do stuff?

A yucky feeling went through Kittie's tummy, except it wasn't because of Mariah.

Both her mother and her biological grandmother on her mom's side had died really young from having bad hearts, but nobody else knew she'd found out that Nana Carolyn was Grandfather Barret's *second* wife. She'd read it all in her mom's diary. Kittie touched a finger to her chest where there was a faint visible scar. And she had the same bad heart. Supposedly it was fixed now, only her dad wouldn't talk about it. She knew that they'd tried to fix her mom, too, yet she died anyway.

Kittie wasn't stupid. If she was okay, why wouldn't he let her do ordinary things like other kids? Coming to the ranch was the most fun she'd had in forever. And why wouldn't her dad talk about what had happened if she was really fixed?

Then there was the *other* stuff that her mom had written in her diary…stuff Kittie's dad didn't know.

Someone tapped on the door, making her jump. She didn't feel guilty exactly, but it was awful to think about…and it made her mad. It wasn't fair getting born sick.

"Hello, you two," called Mrs. Weston. "It's after seven and the dance is starting."

"Thanks for the heads-up, Grams. We'll be there in a minute." Mariah smiled at Kittie. "Are you ready to face all those people?"

Kittie checked her reflection again in the mirror. She *thought* she looked like the other girls from the last dance—the pretty cowgirls that Reid had danced with. Well, she looked a *little* like them. He'd danced a lot with Laura, with her perky boobs and smile.

"How do I look?"

"As if you could have grown up in Montana."

"Honest, truly?"

"Honest, truly. But you know, it really isn't where you grow up—it's where you feel at home. I lived in California for over six years and I was completely out of place, while you grew up in the city but seem totally comfortable here."

"Montana *feels* like home," Kittie said, and it was true. She didn't want to ever leave, though most of her friends were in Seattle. But she had new friends now, like Blue and Emily and Burt. Shayla wasn't staying at the U-2 as long as she was, but they were going to write to each other using email after she left.

"Then let's go show those cowboys what you've got."

JACOB PACED BACK and forth along a side door of the Big Barn, trying to keep an eye out for Mariah and his daughter without being obvious. Surely Kittie couldn't have gotten too outrageous with the clothing available in Buckeye. They seemed to focus on casual wear, and Mariah would have kept Kittie from getting anything shocking anyway.

You mean the way you *kept Kittie from wearing skulls and spiderweb tattoos,* an inner voice jeered. *Her own father. She isn't Kittie's mother—how much influence could she have?*

Shut up, he ordered.

The fact that Kittie had asked Mariah for help was huge. She'd been so belligerent about her clothes and appearance that even a small shift toward her old self, behaving the way she used to, would be a relief. With that comforting thought in mind, his jaw dropped when Mariah and Kittie appeared. His daughter's hair was blond, she wore a pretty dress, and a mere hint of conventional makeup highlighted her face—she was utterly beautiful. She also looked older, something that didn't please him quite as much.

Jacob went to invite his daughter to dance with him, only to have a teenage boy beat him to it.

"I'd love to," Kittie said, smiling brilliantly. She took the boy's hand and they joined a square that was forming with couples their age, including her friend, Shayla.

"Right-o, Kittie," Shayla said, giving her a thumbs-up.

Jacob turned to Mariah, practically speechless. "She's..."

"Is *awesome* the word you're searching for?"

Awesome, one of Kittie's favorite words—it was right up there with *whatever* and *gross.*

"I suppose you're going to dance with Branson," he said.

"Not right now." Her expression was strained and Jacob wondered if she'd had a fight with the rancher. It was possible. Mariah seemed to treat her intended husband more as an easygoing pal than a lover, and it was plain that Luke Branson wanted a whole lot more.

"This square needs a fourth couple," called Burt from the platform where the Western band performed. He gestured to a spot in the middle of the dancers.

"Shall we?" Jacob said.

Mariah nodded after a brief hesitation and a few minutes later walked rapidly away when the set ended.

The next hour was torture. Jacob could hardly get near his

daughter; the boys who'd ignored her the week before were buzzing around her like bees that had discovered a field of flowers. She danced and smiled and flirted, and the only thing preventing him from going ballistic was Mariah's cool stare, challenging him to let Kittie enjoy herself. She might be onto something. While Kittie resembled her mother, he was now well aware that she'd inherited *his* stubbornness. What was more, they had actually managed a few civil conversations since her shopping trip, and he didn't want her to stop making progress out of mulish pride.

Then there was Mariah…

The easy camaraderie between her and Luke Branson was missing. They were polite to each other, but there were no kisses or private exchanges like they'd shared previously whenever Jacob had seen them together. Were those signs of an "amicable" breakup?

His pulse quickened at the prospect—he would never have interfered in their relationship, but if it was over anyway…

Mariah was pale when she slipped out of the barn, and Jacob couldn't resist going after her. He was physically drawn to Mariah, but she also made him think about the man he used to be, before his wife's illness and death.

What had happened to his idealism? His sense of fun and adventure? Or the guts to love without reservation? What had happened to the man that Anna had married…and would she still love the person he'd become?

He was afraid the answer might be no, but how could he go back and find the part of himself that he'd lost? Even his reasons for following Mariah weren't altruistic—he desired her, but he wasn't looking for happily ever after. He hadn't changed his mind about not getting married again—there was too damned much possibility of getting hurt.

Once he would have thought an affair with a woman living so far away was ideal, but now he realized it was risky, as well. You couldn't prevent yourself from developing feelings for someone, and what would it be like to start caring for a woman living in Montana, while he was in Seattle? It was probably why he'd instinctively gone out with a certain kind of woman since Anna's death...the kind who didn't inspire profound attachments. *Superficial and self-absorbed,* his conscience added annoyingly.

"Hey," he said when he found Mariah by one of the paddocks, gazing at the horses in the moonlight.

"What do you want, Jacob?" she demanded. "You gave me permission to take Caitlin shopping, and her dress is perfectly respectable for a girl her age. Sooner or later you'll have to accept that she's no longer a child."

"Whoa, I was just checking to see if you were all right. I noticed things were different between you and Branson."

Mariah didn't say anything for a moment and he detected everything from irritation to regret in her face.

"I'M FINE, and Luke Branson is none of your concern," Mariah lied. She hadn't anticipated how difficult it would be to interact with Luke in front of everyone now that their relationship had changed. She'd needed a quiet moment to gather her thoughts, but it obviously wasn't going to happen. You'd think that on a ranch the size of the U-2 she'd be able to get some privacy.

"You aren't fine." Jacob stepped nearer. "Your family keeps watching you and they're plainly worried. Haven't you told them that you've broken up with him, or is it a secret?"

Great. Grams and the others had been casting puzzled glances at her the whole evening and it seemed that even a guest recognized that things had changed between her and Luke. Except Jacob was no longer just a guest, and that was infuriating.

"It isn't a secret. I just haven't told anybody. And it's none of your business."

"It is if I want to do this."

Mariah gasped as he caught her close in a deep, soul-searing kiss. The thin cotton of her skirt and top was little defense against the bulge in his pants or the hard length of his body from thigh to shoulder. She would have put a well-placed knee in his groin, but she couldn't remember the last time she'd felt so much...pure sensation.

Jacob slid his hand under the hem of her camisole blouse and splayed his fingers across her bare skin. Streamers of edgy heat shot through her abdomen and for an instant all she could think of was wanting more.

Reality abruptly set in and Mariah pulled away, staring at him in shock. She'd promised...she had absolutely *promised* herself that she'd never let an outsider get to her again, and Jacob had done it with ridiculous ease.

Without a word she spun and hurried back to the Big Barn.

"DO-SI-DO AND ALLEMANDE right," called the wrangler in rhythm to the music.

Reid wasn't dancing the set. He kept looking at Kittie, barely recognizing her duded-up in a dress, without a smidgen of black in sight. He liked girls with long hair, but he had to admit that her short, blond curls were cute. His buddies thought so, too. He hadn't even needed to say something to them or dance with Kittie himself to get them going.

As a matter of fact, now that she didn't look so awful, getting a minute with her might be tough the way the other guys were jostling for her attention.

"Reid, aren't we going to have some dessert?" Laura asked, tugging at his arm.

"Uh...oh, sure."

She snuggled closer to him. "I brought more of the chocolate-chip cookies you like, and I also baked a chocolate-pecan-nut pie. You'd better get a piece before it's all gone."

"I don't care much for nut pie," he said without thinking.

Laura blinked a bunch. "I would have brought something else if I'd known."

"Uh…I'm sure other people will like it."

"But I didn't bake it for them."

Crud. She was all weepy-looking and upset. Why were girls so illogical? A guy didn't have to like everything they baked, did he?

"Uh, I'll go ahead and try some anyway, seeing as you made it."

She hugged him. "That's sweet of you, Reid. I made homemade whipped cream for the pie, too—I'm sure you'll love it."

The pie was too sugary, along with the whipped cream, but Reid pretended that it was the best he'd ever eaten. Laura didn't have any; she just nibbled pieces of cut-up fruit from a tray. It was dumb; he knew she ate dessert.

Reid turned to watch the dancers again. He couldn't believe he *wanted* to dance with Kittie. Art Blanco was her partner in the current set—he was probably bragging about his dirt bike as he do-si-doed around her. Art was a town kid. His dad owned one of the gas stations in Buckeye, so he didn't have any use for horses. And because Kittie had gone horse crazy since getting to Montana, he couldn't imagine they had anything to talk about.

"Huh?" he murmured, realizing Laura had said something.

"I asked if you'd like more pie." But she wasn't looking at him—she was glaring across the barn at Kittie.

"No, I had a big dinner."

She cuddled up to him again and Reid frowned. Laura had been acting as if he was her personal property the entire evening—they might have dated occasionally, but that was all. She wasn't his girlfriend or anything.

"Excuse me," he said as the music ended, pulling free and heading toward Kittie.

"Reid, where are you *going?*" Laura sounded furious, but he kept walking. Kittie was laughing at something Art had said. He had to move fast, or one of his buddies would beat him to it.

"Evening, Kittie. May I have the next dance?"

She smiled shyly. "I'd love to."

The cowboy callers kept up a fast pace, but Reid was familiar with the moves and spotted his sister coming into the barn as he swung Kittie around for the third time.

Mariah appeared uptight. Was it because of Luke? They'd barely spoken all evening, and he knew something had gone wrong between them.

A couple of minutes later, Jacob O'Donnell came in from the same door Mariah had used and Reid nearly missed a step. They were deliberately not looking at each other.... Was it possible they'd gone outside together?

Surely not. His sister was too smart to get involved with one of the guests. She was the one who'd warned *him* that vacation romances usually didn't work out and that they were much tougher on the person left behind.

Granddad came over as the dance was ending and asked Kittie to be his partner for the upcoming polka.

"I thought she'd dance it with me," Reid said quickly.

Kittie seemed surprised. "Oh, I'd like to. How about the dance after that, Mr. Weston?"

"Dee-lighted. I'll just find my wife and do the polka with her." He winked and trotted off to where Grams was putting out more cups for the punch.

The music started and Reid put his hand on Kittie's waist. "Ready?"

"Ready."

JACOB DIDN'T CONSIDER working on his contracts or the computer once the U-2 had settled into quiet that night. He switched off the lantern and lay on the mattress, staring into the dark. He'd been with women since Anna's death—casual, easygoing lovers. Sex was something pleasant he'd pursued when his body demanded it, but a single kiss with Mariah had taken his breath away, leaving him in so much need it was hard to walk afterward.

He would have sworn it was impossible that another woman could affect him as deeply as Anna had. Yet here he was losing sleep over a stubborn redhead with a lifestyle that not only conflicted with his, but was permanently planted in another state. Two weeks ago he would have written off that lifestyle.... Now he was beginning to see why it was important to Mariah.

Jacob punched his pillow. Getting close to her was hazardous to his peace of mind as well as his body. She was making him examine his choices for the past twelve years and he wasn't sure he liked what he saw. He had always believed family was his first priority, yet he might have lost sight of that. He'd built his business so he would have the resources to protect Kittie, but he maight have missed out on her childhood in the process.

He'd told himself that *now* he had the money to properly care for Kittie and repay his in-laws. But while he might have kept his daughter from physical harm, she was still in trouble.

CHAPTER TWELVE

JACOB'S DILEMMA WASN'T RESOLVED come morning, but he hadn't expected it to be. There was nothing easy about parenting *or* relations between men and women. The way things were going, Kittie would probably ask Mariah to adopt her so she could stay in Montana. Mariah might even agree…and then get a shotgun to run him off the place.

Mariah was talking to one of the wranglers when he got to the mess tent. He stopped in front of them and waited.

"Yes, Jacob?" she asked finally, her face expressionless.

"I wondered if you'd like to eat breakfast with me."

Though he was the one who'd posed the question, a part of him was astonished. He was setting himself up for the kind of situation he usually avoided—an opportunity to discuss the "morning after." In this case, not the morning after sex, but the morning after a hot kiss.

"Thank you. However, I ate with my family earlier," Mariah replied with a pleasant smile. She all but added "sir" or "Mr. O'Donnell" to the response. "As you know, we don't assign heavy work on Sundays, but Burt said he'd be happy to take you and Caitlin out on the horses. You can move one of the herds to fresh pasture or simply ride. Just let him know. Or, if you'd prefer, you can relax today—it's your choice."

She nodded and went to talk with Reggie while Jacob digested the fact that she was definitely *not* interested in talking to him. Normally he would have been relieved, but things with Mariah were far from normal.

So he followed and stood at her elbow.

"Is there something else you need?" she said after a moment, her body language screaming *Back off.* The barriers she'd thrown up were clear...and a challenge he had trouble resisting.

"Why don't we walk down to the calf barn and see how Kittie is doing with Emily?"

"I have work to take care of, but go ahead, by all means."

"Anything I can do to help out?"

Her eyes narrowed. "Thanks, I can handle it."

This time she left the mess tent altogether.

"Breakfast, Mr. Weston?" asked a woman at the nearby serving table. She was one of the newer guests, and Jacob searched his memory for her name.

"Uh...thanks, Delores, but I'm waiting until my daughter gets here," he said. "And call me Jacob. This isn't the place for formality."

"Okay, Jacob."

He filled a blue enamel cup with coffee and sat at a table, waiting for Kittie to return from the calf barn. It had surprised him to see his daughter taking her responsibility for the orphan calves so seriously. Of course, baby animals were appealing and visitors often showed up at the afternoon feeding, but Kittie had proved extremely faithful, and she even got up every morning to do the early feeding. He would have to consider getting her a cat or dog once they got back to Seattle.

He glanced at the serving table where Delores and her husband were working. They were a friendly, gregarious couple, like so many of the people who visited the U-2. He *ought* to have known her name without a second thought, and it made him uncomfortable. More than once Mariah had implied he didn't care enough about people, and while it had offended him, maybe it was partially true.

Shayla and Kittie bounced in twenty minutes later. They were chattering and giggling as if they'd known each other for a lifetime instead of a week. Shayla whispered something to Kittie, who looked in his direction and whispered something back.

His daughter picked up a coffeepot and walked over. "Do you need a refill, Dad?"

He was immediately wary—she wanted something or had committed an act of wholesale destruction.

"Sure. Thanks."

Kittie topped off his cup. "Shayla and her parents are going for a drive this morning to see a historic site mentioned in a Western biography that Mrs. McFee is reading."

"Oh. That's nice." Jacob hoped she wouldn't want to go with the other family.

"Anyhow, I thought it would be a good…that is, I thought that Mariah might be willing to go on a picnic with us. If it's okay with you, and all. Since we're not really doing anything else."

A grim amusement swept through Jacob. Mariah was pretending nothing had happened between them, but if she agreed to a picnic, she'd have to talk to him, if only to be polite in front of Kittie.

"That's a great idea," he said. "Mariah told me we can do as we please—it's sort of a day off. I can ask Reggie for three sack lunches and see if he'll throw in something extra. Provided Mariah's able to go. If not, it can be just the two of us with Burt."

Kittie threw her arms around his neck and gave him a smacking kiss. "Awesome. I'll talk to Mariah after breakfast."

Warmth crept through Jacob's chest. *That* was his little girl, happy and impulsive, wearing her new cowgirl clothes and hat. He didn't know if she was here for good or temporarily visiting, but he was elated to see her again.

IDIOT, MARIAH FUMED silently as she leaned against a fence and watched the Sallengers saying goodbye to their wrangler.

She should have gone with her first instinct last night and put a knee in Jacob's groin. *That* would have hurt him where he lived; he might be a business mogul, but he was still a man.

With a sigh, Mariah headed for their departing visitors and chatted with them for a few minutes.

"We'll be back," Edna promised. "As neighbors. We talked and decided to spend summer and fall in Montana, and winters in Connecticut so we can see more of the grandchildren. We're hoping they'll come here for vacations."

"I'm not sure what homes are available in Buckeye," Mariah warned. "You should check it out before you get too committed."

"We may build our own place outside of town if we can't find a small ranch," Carl explained. "The local real-estate office says there's a stack of current listings. We want enough space for five or six horses and will board them during the winter. We've already spoken to Mr. Branson and he's willing to help us out with boarding if we can't find anyone else."

Apparently they were serious, though they'd modified their plans. It made more sense, yet Mariah found it hard to believe the urbanites would last in Buckeye. She loved her hometown, but it was a long way from, well, *everything.* Their home, Hartford, Connecticut, was the state capital and teemed with activity. Several months was a long time for people accustomed to the amenities that cities offered.

"Mr. Branson is a fine horseman," Mariah said, her throat tight. It had been depressing to see Luke again and have things so awkward between them. They'd always been so at ease with each other.

"Mariah?" called a voice. It was Caitlin and she was running toward them.

"We'll go and let you get to work," Edna said, giving Mariah a hug. "After all, we'll be seeing you soon, *neighbor.*"

Mariah turned to Caitlin as she got there, breathless. "Hey, what's the rush?"

"I just wanted to…that is, I'd really love it if you'd go on a picnic with us today. Maybe we could go for a ride and eat… you know, out on the range. Dad said yes."

Oh, God. The hopeful look on the teenager's face was inescapable. She was dressed in a pair of jeans and a shirt they'd gotten at the Booteek, though she'd taken Mariah's advice to break her boots in slowly and was wearing the athletic shoes she'd brought from Seattle.

"Pleeeeze," Caitlin begged. "It'd be so fun and Dad said it's a day off from work if we want."

"Sure," Mariah agreed reluctantly.

She knew the teen would be hurt if she refused, particularly after their shopping trip, but it was the enthused *dad said* that had gotten to her. Caitlin's relationship with her father seemed to be getting better, and Mariah didn't want to do anything that might upset the delicate balance.

"Tell you what," she said, "I'll see if Reid has plans and can come with us. Let's meet by the main corral in a couple of hours. It's warm today, so you might want to wear your swimsuit under your clothes in case we stop at the swimming hole to cool off."

"*Awesome.* I'll tell my dad. He was going to ask Reggie for sack lunches—we'll need another if Reid is coming."

She dashed off and Mariah's annoyance with herself gave way to irritation with Jacob. He'd tried to corner her that morning and was probably snickering about this latest development. While she appreciated his sense of humor, she didn't enjoy that it came at her expense. At least having Reid along might buffer the situation.

Mariah found her brother grooming the horses that the Sallengers had taken out for a ride before leaving.

"What's up, sis?"

"Are you interested in a picnic with Caitlin and her father? You don't have to go with us, but it would be nice if you'd want to—it's difficult with Mr. O'Donnell right now and it would help having you along."

"Yeah?" Her brother finished wiping the last horse with a soft cloth. "Why is it difficult?"

"He's demanding and we don't get along—I really blew up at him for taking over the U-2's office the other day." It was only some of the truth, but Reid didn't need to know the grisly details. "So how about it? Kittie asked me to go and I couldn't turn her down."

He shrugged. "I don't mind. She's not bad once you get to know her."

Not bad? A stellar recommendation, certain to infuriate any female unlucky enough to hear it.

"I wouldn't put it that way to her," Mariah advised.

"Don't worry, I'm not an idiot."

No, you're smart, just not around girls, she thought wryly. Reid's IQ was in the gifted range; his social IQ was still developing. He'd made Laura Shelton so angry at the dance he was lucky his classmate hadn't sunk a pitchfork into his foot.

"Good. We're meeting at the big corral at ten-thirty. I'll see you then."

THREE-AND-A-HALF HOURS later, Jacob leaned against a cottonwood tree, munching one of Reggie's triple-chocolate brownies. They weren't a gourmet dessert, but he couldn't think of anything he'd ever eaten that he'd liked more.

Reggie had fixed a delicious picnic. Instead of sandwiches, he'd provided slices of ham and cold fried chicken and all the trimmings. They'd eaten until they were stuffed.

The sun was clear and warm, though a cooling breeze swept their shaded picnic spot. There weren't any buildings in sight, and some of the tension in his shoulders eased. Mariah had claimed there were compensations for her ranching world, and he was seeing more and more of them.

"I wish we'd get some rain," Mariah said, frowning faintly.

"Bite your tongue," Jacob ordered. "I prefer it this way. Besides, Kittie and I are sleeping in tents, not a house."

"The tents are waterproof and it's a dry year. Rain would green everything up. In the two weeks you've been here, we should have had at least one or two showers."

"Is drought that much of an issue in Montana?" he asked.

She exchanged glances with Reid. "It can be. And since we usually have rain in the late spring and early summer, we worry when it's dry."

Reid yawned. "Kittie, let's take advantage of the warm weather. There's a swimming hole nearby—we could ride over and cool off. Is that all right with you, Mr. Weston?"

Jacob bolted straight up, instant denial on his lips only to see Kittie's excitement and Mariah's averted gaze. She'd told him that he would have to deal with his daughter's problems himself, though she hadn't been shy about offering her opinion. No doubt she'd disagree with him this time as well if he denied Kittie some fun.

"Uh…you don't have your swimsuit," he said, stalling.

"Do, too. Mariah told me to wear it under my clothes."

"Maybe we could all go," he suggested.

Kittie glared. "You don't trust me."

His reluctance wasn't a question of trust…exactly. Protecting her was an instinct he couldn't escape. "It isn't that, but you just ate a meal and could get stomach cramps."

"Ha."

"The swimming hole is mostly a curve in the creek," Reid assured him. "It's shallow. You can float in the water, but it's no more than hip deep since we haven't had any rain for several weeks."

"See, Dad?" Kittie insisted.

Reid Weston was a reliable young man, and while Jacob wasn't sold on Mariah's less restrictive views on child rearing, swimming in a shallow creek was relatively harmless compared to other things that Kittie could be doing.

"I guess it's all right, then. Go ahead, and we'll see you at the ranch."

The teenagers rode off and Jacob let out a heavy breath as he looked at Mariah. "I suppose you want to go back now."

"Actually, I was considering riding fence lines. Granddad and Grams are seeing the departing guests off, and we're not expecting anyone new until tomorrow. Might as well take advantage."

Together they packed the remains of their meal into small coolers and tucked them in the saddlebags. They rode for nearly an hour without saying anything, yet it was curiously comfortable.

All at once, Mariah pulled in Shadow's reins. "Good boy," she said, rubbing his neck.

"What's up?" Jacob asked.

"Just a broken line." She got down and took a pair of pliers, gloves and other supplies from a saddlebag.

"Wait a minute." Jacob dismounted himself. "Can't you tell one of the wranglers there's a repair needed and send them out?"

Mariah rolled her eyes. "You mean, send a man?"

"I didn't say that. But your hand is still healing. Why do you have pliers anyhow? We went out for a picnic."

"I always have them. That's how we do things here—you have to be prepared."

She put on her leather gloves, and visions of flailing wire, ripping and cutting, ran through Jacob's head. Shocked, he realized he was having the same impulse to protect Mariah that he had for his daughter.

He didn't want her to get injured.

After so many years of guarding his heart from pain, he'd slipped.... Mariah was beginning to matter to him far too much for his peace of mind.

"*Wait,* let me do it," he called as she put her hand on the fence post and reached for the length of wire.

MARIAH LOOKED UP, exasperated. "You don't know how and you don't have work gloves with you."

"I don't care." Jacob stepped close. "And anyway, I can think of much more appealing things to do right now. Can't you?" He ran his thumb across her jaw, his gaze fixed on her lips.

Mariah's pulse quickened. "You're a guest. I don't get involved with guests."

"Whatever you say," he whispered before kissing her.

The same heat streaked through Mariah as it had the previous night. *Drat him,* she thought fuzzily as the pliers fell from her hand. He drew her into his arms and everything spun as he dropped to the ground with her, stroking her hair, her face…her breasts. A faint popping sound came as he opened the buttons on her shirt and unhooked her bra.

Mariah couldn't remember the last time she'd felt warm sunlight on her bare breasts, probably when she had gone skinny-dipping in high school. She certainly hadn't…

Her back arched as Jacob's tongue flicked the tip of her nipple, his thumb teasing the other with expert precision. The thoughts nagging her brain fled, banished by pure sensation.

Mariah yanked the tails of his shirt from his jeans and splayed her hand on Jacob's smooth, hot skin. He groaned and sucked her breast deeply into his mouth as she traced up and down his spine. A thrill of feminine power went through her.

They rolled and Mariah found herself astride his hips, his arousal pressed snugly to her center, separated only by layers of denim. She rocked and Jacob gasped. He opened the snap at her waist and tugged the zipper open. It took some effort, but he eased his fingers inside the opening and slid them beneath the thin protection of her panties.

Then something cold distracted her…. It was his wedding ring.

Mariah returned to her senses and scooted off his thighs, her chest heaving.

"What's wrong?" he groaned.

"You..." It took a moment for her to remember why it was a bad idea to kiss Jacob and what had started the whole thing in the first place. "You're just trying to make me forget working on that fence." Anger replacing desire, she fastened her bra and buttoned her shirt.

"I was trying to keep you from hurting yourself."

"You're a Seattle businessman. What do you know about it? I began mending fences when I was eleven. The ranch and Reid are *my* responsibility and I can handle them just fine."

He sat up and crossed his arms over his chest. "What about your grandparents? Aren't the ranch and Reid a shared responsibility? You may be his legal guardian, but Reid is their grandson. And how about Luke Branson? He must have wanted to be there for you, yet you seem hell-bent on doing most of it yourself."

"That's my business, not yours."

"Maybe somebody should make it their business. You accuse me of being a workaholic, but how many hours do *you* work every week?"

"It isn't the same. Summer is our busy season and we're doing it together as a family."

Jacob snorted. "Except you think it's all on your shoulders. And I'm betting you didn't share any of it with your fiancé. If I'm right, then Luke has more fortitude than most men if he had to stand by, prevented from truly being included in your life. He must have wanted to chew nails."

A sick feeling hit Mariah's stomach. She had never, *ever* intended to hurt Luke. Jacob was partly right, but she'd had her reasons for trying to manage things on her own. "It wouldn't have been fair to ask him to take on more when we weren't married yet."

Jacob raised one eyebrow. "So why *didn't* you get married? Maybe I'm not the only one concerned about losing someone special—is that why you got engaged to a man you didn't really love? No one could blame you after the way your mother and father died. Especially your dad, giving up like that."

Mariah hadn't ever slapped a man, but she was within inches now. Jacob didn't have any place questioning her relationship with Luke or bringing up her parents. She hadn't told Jacob about their accident or her father's despair in the hospital so it could be used as a point in an argument.

"For your information, we were talking marriage *before* I lost my mom and dad." Mariah grabbed her gloves and hunted through the grass for the pliers. "So back off," she ordered furiously, not letting Jacob say another word.

The repair took less than five minutes and she efficiently replaced the tools in Shadow's saddlebag.

"We're done," she said shortly.

"No 'we' about it. You wouldn't let me help."

"Don't push me, Jacob," she warned. "I may not have liked the city, but I took self-defense classes when I lived there and you wouldn't like being on the receiving end of what they taught me."

To her utter aggravation, he just laughed.

MARIAH RACED THROUGH her work the next few days, staying away from Jacob as much as she could manage. She wanted to outrun the things he'd said, but it was impossible.

Again and again, Luke had wanted to help her and she wouldn't let him. And what about the times she didn't even tell him about something bothering her? She'd let Luke help with a sick animal or other small task, but never with anything essential.

It didn't matter how often she told herself it was the Weston way—that ranchers were supposed to be strong and self-reliant. She'd also wanted a husband who was a partner, with shared values and interests. However much Luke had wanted to be a partner, she hadn't let him be one.

Though Mariah wasn't ready to talk with Luke about things until she'd sorted out her feelings, she spotted a faint hesitation in Moonfire's gait that Wednesday. Her examination suggested a sensitive area on the mare's right foreleg. While it didn't appear serious, she was Luke's horse, and Mariah wanted him to check for himself.

So Luke came over that evening and Mariah walked to Moonfire's stall with him.

"What would have made a difference for us?" she murmured after a long moment.

He had crouched and was running his hand over the mare's legs. "That's easy—loving me enough."

"Maybe I *can't* love anyone enough."

Luke shook his head. "I don't believe that. The timing was just bad. We were shifting from friends to lovers and your folks' accident happened in the middle. You had so much to deal with, and we never got back to the right place."

He probed Moonfire's right fetlock again.

"Mind if I take her out and see how she moves?" he asked, standing. "I don't think it's anything, but I want her in top form when she goes to California."

"Why should I mind? She's your horse. I'll lead her so you can watch."

Mariah led Moonfire from the barn and walked her up and down under Luke's attentive gaze. From the corner of her eye she saw Jacob leave the mess tent and quickly looked away. She'd already discussed more intimate things with him than she ever had with Luke and it made her feel worse.

After a couple of minutes, Luke patted the horse's shoulder. "I think you're right. It's nothing. She must have gotten hit with a rock or thrown her leg against the stable door and has a bruise. No big deal, at any rate. There's no need to get Doc Crandall. Just keep an eye on her. I trust you the same as him anyhow."

Oh, wonderful. He *trusted* her. He might as well pour hot

coals on her head. She hadn't cheated on him, but it felt that way with Jacob consuming more and more of her attention. And what would happen when Jacob was gone? It was remotely conceivable she'd come to her senses and realize she'd blown the greatest thing in her life.

"Luke, I've been thinking about us. What if—"

"No," he interrupted. "Not if you're thinking we could try again. It's over and we both know it, but it means a lot that you're concerned. I'd better get back to my spread. See you Saturday at the dance."

JACOB SAW LUKE BRANSON drive away and, from the man's bleak expression, guessed the final coffin nail had been driven into his relationship with Mariah. Jacob knew it was selfish to be pleased about it, particularly since he still wasn't certain what he wanted from her. He was experienced with city women, not down-to-earth female ranchers. The decision he'd made to stay single had seemed best, but now he wasn't so sure—Mariah made him feel things he'd forgotten were possible.

"Dad, come play Monopoly with us," Kittie called.

Lately it had been a seesaw with his daughter—one minute pleasant, the next angry defiance. But, thanks to Mariah, he was recognizing that some of Kittie's problems could have been caused by the way he'd tried to protect her. Was she improving simply because he'd let go a little?

It was hard for him. He wanted to keep her safe, but he might have gone overboard.

"I want to be the race car," Jacob said, joining the Monopoly players in a corner of the mess tent. "'Cause I'm going to speed around the board buying up property."

"Watch out for my dad," Kittie told Shayla conspiratorially. "He's a tycoon or something. He…uh…makes stuff."

Jacob frowned thoughtfully, realizing Kittie didn't actually know what O'Donnell International did. Of course, it would be hard to define his company, a conglomerate with multiple manufacturing and other business interests. Still, he'd rarely brought Kittie to the office, even on the annual national Bring Your Daughter to Work Day.

It was another opportunity he'd missed to spend time with her. Jacob knew he'd be awake that night, worrying that Kittie thought she was less important than his company. She wasn't, but he might have given her that impression…he might have even buried himself in work instead of dealing with his life and the loss of his wife.

As for Mariah…they would have to talk. If nothing else, he owed her an apology.

CHAPTER THIRTEEN

"MARIAH, I NEED to speak with you privately," Jacob said the next evening.

She sighed. He'd planted himself squarely in her path so she couldn't ignore him. You could only avoid people for so long on a ranch.

"Where's Kittie?"

"She's in the kitchen, working cleanup with the McFees. The girls prefer doing things together, but I asked Reggie if it would be all right first. Shayla will also take a turn on our night to wash up."

Interesting. Mariah didn't know if he was learning to be more considerate or just learning to play the game.

She'd wanted time to sort out the changes in her world, but maybe taking time meant missing opportunities. She had spent the past four years trying to get her life sorted out, and look what had happened—she wasn't married to Luke and she didn't have a clue about the future except that she'd begun to care too much for a different man.

"Come on, let's take a walk," Jacob urged.

They walked out to her favorite hill and sat watching the sun setting low on the horizon. The silence was oddly comfortable, though she wondered what he wanted.

"I'm sorry I interfered with your repairs on the fence," Jacob said finally.

Mariah stared. She hadn't expected an apology. "You… are?"

"Believe it or not, I can sometimes figure out when I'm wrong. The problem is, I can't promise I won't do it again. I'll try to be reasonable, but protecting you was an instinctive reaction."

An illogical thrill went through Mariah, as well as alarm. Jacob might mean nothing by his statements, yet the intensity in his eyes told her there was more to it.

"Yeah?"

"Yeah."

The long, golden rays of sunlight chiseled his features with shadow and light, and if she hadn't known better, she would have thought he was a cowboy of old. It was so much simpler a hundred years ago: you fell in love and followed your heart, the way Catherine Heider had followed hers.

"This hill," Mariah murmured, "is where Catherine and Timothy Weston knew they had gone far enough and were home. They camped here the first night, and the next day they found a shallow valley to start building their ranch."

"How do you know it's the right hill?"

"It's marked on the old family maps, but mostly because they brought their children and grandchildren here and told them the story."

"And their grandchildren brought *their* children."

"Yes. Catherine and Timothy originally wanted to be buried here, but they decided it should be a place of hopeful memories, not a cemetery."

Jacob looked out across the landscape, yet Mariah couldn't tell if he felt the tug of the land or was simply admiring the setting sun. "It took courage to come the way they did."

"You have no idea. Catherine was eight months pregnant when they arrived. Timothy delivered their first son himself, though he was able to get a midwife for the other children."

"God in heaven." Jacob sounded appalled. "If he loved her so much, how could he risk taking her into the territories?"

"Actually, they adored each other. Timothy was the middle

son of a mill owner. He wasn't going to inherit, though he was left some money through his maternal grandfather. He and Catherine wanted to build something together, and this was their best chance." Mariah had read both her ancestors' diaries, and their passionate love came through on every page.

"Why didn't he just use his grandfather's bequest to buy property in the East where it was civilized?"

"It would have taken a lot more than he'd received. But by homesteading and purchasing and trading for cheaper land in the Montana Territory, they ended up with a large ranch."

Jacob glanced at the ponderosa pine cresting the rise. She doubted he was listening to the ancient echoes of the people who'd found and settled the ranch—he was far too pragmatic. But she could hear them whispering each time she visited the hill that Catherine and Timothy had loved.

"You make me wish I knew more about my ancestors," Jacob said after a minute. "You even know your great-great-grandmother was considered fey."

Mariah smiled. "I should show you a picture of Grandmother Aileen. She left Ireland to escape a marriage her parents were pressuring her to accept. It must have taken guts to leave everything behind that way. According to family stories, she was feisty, filled with laughter and a daring horsewoman, though she'd never ridden before immigrating. And she sang beautiful, lilting Irish songs."

"See what I mean? I don't even know my great-grandparents' names, much less what they were like."

Mariah lay back on the grass. Overhead she saw three stars, glinting palely in the evening sky. Day still hadn't surrendered fully to night and there was a kind of hushed waiting in the air.

Jacob leaned on his elbow. "You have your grandmother Aileen's auburn hair, don't you?"

"So I'm told."

"I can't imagine having your roots." For a moment, in the

light from the setting sun, he looked both sad and envious. "Do you ever want to escape the weight of expectation from all those ancestors?"

"It's part of who I am. I don't know anything else."

Jacob traced the outline of her mouth with the tip of his finger. "I suppose we should be getting back."

Mariah didn't move. "I suppose we should."

"Except I don't want to…not yet." He bent over her, his kiss tasting of mint and need.

She put an arm around his neck so it wouldn't end too soon. The reasons for stopping and using good sense flitted through her mind, yet they seemed unimportant, swept away by her quickening pulse and the insistent pull in her abdomen. It wasn't until she felt Jacob's fingers on her breasts that she realized he'd managed to unfasten both her shirt and bra.

"That was slick," she breathed. She was having trouble concentrating.

"What?"

His thumb rubbed her nipple and it tightened into a taut crown while he sucked on the other, teasing her with his tongue. Heat surged through Mariah and she returned the favor, exploring his chest and then lower, finding the hot, demanding arousal straining the fly of his jeans.

"What was slick, Mariah?" Jacob groaned harshly as she eased his zipper open and slipped her hand inside.

"Uh…what do you think? Unhooking my bra one-handed."

"I'll bet cowboys are just as slick." His palms ran down her legs.

"Well, they're definitely better with boots," she said as he worked to remove her footwear. He'd gotten the first one off quickly; the second was more stubborn

"I'm used to pumps and hosiery, not Levi's and Stetsons." He sounded breathless.

"Stetson makes both hats and boots."

"See what I mean?" Jacob managed to pull off the second

boot and tossed it to one side. Mariah knew she might have been more help, but his technique was interesting. The cut on her jeans was snug to protect her legs when she was riding, but they didn't slow him as much as the boots.

The Levi's landed on top of her boots.

He kissed her thighs and teased her aching center with his fingers, pressing in and withdrawing with expert skill that nearly sent her over the top. One long, drugging kiss later, Jacob rocked back on his heels, his intense gaze fixed on her face. With deliberate movements, he took a condom from his wallet and put it in her hand.

Deep down Mariah was annoyed. He was making sure she knew what she was doing, that the choice was hers. But it wasn't enough to stop her. She rolled it over him and he thrust inside her, hard and fast, sensation exploding beyond anything she'd ever experienced, spinning her out of control.

IT WASN'T UNTIL they'd dressed and were walking back to the ranch that Mariah mentally slapped herself on the forehead.

What happened to her restraint?

Hell, what had happened to her *sanity?*

She didn't engage in casual sex. It didn't fix anything and sometimes made things worse. From now on the best thing she could do was stay away from Jacob. She didn't want to think about the mistakes she'd made since his arrival.

How did things get messed up so fast?

AS THE DAYS PASSED, Jacob grew increasingly frustrated with the way Mariah kept ducking him. Like it or not, he was no longer just a guest at the U-2, and she wasn't just the owner and manager of a vacation business.

He couldn't even force the issue on the biological question—he'd been quite responsible with protection and checking to be sure the condom hadn't broken. He didn't know how he would have reacted if it had torn, though the thought of having a child with Mariah didn't alarm him as much as it should have. And the fact he was thinking that way ought to send him running for the hills.

The weekly barn dance came and went, with Kittie once more the belle of the ball, though she shared the spotlight with Shayla. She'd glowed when the teenage boys asked her to dance, and while Jacob loved seeing her so happy, it was no easier for him than the week before. How could she be interested in boys? She was only fourteen.

After Jacob's fifth attempt to engage Mariah in a conversation about what was going on between them—which required a degree of privacy—he decided he needed to change his approach.

Maybe she'd talk about the ranch. Plainly, the U-2 wasn't as profitable as he'd assumed, but they could be more viable if they expanded and made it a real resort, maintaining a limited herd of cows for tourist appeal. He'd considered investing in small businesses; perhaps he could start in Montana.

On Tuesday morning Jacob approached Benjamin Weston in the mess tent. "I wondered if I might get together with you and Mariah today. I have a business proposition to put to you both."

"Business? That's mostly Mariah's bailiwick," Benjamin said. He munched a slice of bacon from the food table. "As my wife is quick to remind me, I didn't want to start this ranch vacation business in the first place, figuring we'd lose our shirts."

"It seems to have turned out well."

"Indeed." Benjamin's blue eyes twinkled. He was a good match for his wife; both of them seemed to possess an inner calm that was immensely appealing.

"I would still like to speak with you both," Jacob said. "It shouldn't take long."

"After breakfast, then? The mess tent will clear out and be fairly quiet. I'll tell Mariah."

"Great." Jacob hid a triumphant smile—Mariah wouldn't refuse her grandfather.

MARIAH WASN'T HAPPY when Granddad told her they had an "appointment" with Jacob to talk business.

"What could he have to discuss with us?"

Granddad shrugged. "Mayhap he wants to buy a ranch and needs our advice. His daughter has certainly caught the horse bug. She's a delightful child," he said reflectively. "I rather miss her black clothes and lipstick. They weren't so startling once you got used to them, and they *were* unique."

Mariah couldn't help laughing. "Yes, they were. Nevertheless, while Caitlin might be horse crazy, I can't see Jacob living on a ranch, even part-time."

"It's possible. He's stayed here over three weeks without going off his rocker, and he doesn't seem to be working as much at night. Whatever it is, we'll have to meet with him to find out."

"Okay, *fine.* We'll talk." She pressed her lips together irritably. She felt cornered, which undoubtedly was Jacob's intent. He'd tried to get her alone without success and was adopting another strategy.

"It'll get better," Granddad said, squeezing her hand. But unless he'd read her mind, Mariah knew he wasn't talking about Jacob—he was talking about Luke. She'd told her grandparents a few days ago that she'd ended her engagement, and while they were disappointed, they supported her decision. They were so much in love themselves, they didn't want her to get married unless she wasn't utterly committed in her heart.

Jacob was waiting in the mess tent when they got there. He actually had his computer out and a notepad in front of him as if it was a genuine business meeting.

"Hello, Mariah," he said, standing courteously. "You're difficult to…uh, connect with lately."

She glared. They'd connected, all right. She'd gone off like a firecracker out on the hill. Thank goodness it was almost dark by the time they'd made love or they could have been visible to anyone taking a walk in their direction. Ranching might intimately bond someone to life and death and birth, but that didn't mean she was an exhibitionist.

"If you're thinking of buying a ranch for yourself, I know of a nice spread near Bozeman that's up for sale," Granddad volunteered. "It's a beauty, small and well kept. A friend has owned it for three decades, but he's getting on in years and wants to take it easy."

"That's not exactly what I had in mind." Jacob twisted his computer so they could see the screen; an impressive graph was displayed. "I've been thinking about your vacation business."

"What of it?" Mariah asked suspiciously.

"It could be more profitable if you made a few changes. For example, building permanent accommodations with private baths. Visitors could come earlier in the spring and later in the fall, and would be willing to pay a higher daily rate for the visit if it was more of a real resort. And you wouldn't have to keep your large herds, just enough for tourist appeal."

Granddad inclined his head noncommittally as Mariah glowered.

"This way there would be even greater employment opportunities for the people around here," Jacob continued. "I realize how important the U-2 is to the local economy—this would be a way for me to invest in a worthwhile business outside my own company. Which brings me to the other side of my proposal—I provide the investment funds. You can see from the graph that the projected income from—"

Mariah stood up, interrupting him. "Please excuse us, Granddad. I'd like to speak with Mr. O'Donnell. *Privately.*"

"Fine. I'll leave it in your hands." Granddad looked concerned rather than offended, and she winced. He might have realized there was more going on with Jacob than she'd told the family.

Trying not to go ballistic, Mariah dragged Jacob to the farthest barn, where nobody was around. His "proposal" was just one more piece of proof that he didn't understand her. *Big whoop.* She shouldn't get upset. Yet it had dawned on her as he was showing them his graph that she was disappointed. *Really* disappointed, the same as when he'd let Caitlin go off with the McFees so he could work on a business deal. She hadn't wanted to think of it that way, yet it was true. Disappointment implied higher expectations, and she knew better than to expect anything from Jacob.

"You don't like my idea?" Jacob asked.

"Were you serious?"

"Absolutely. You could make a lot more money."

"You really don't get it, do you?" Mariah demanded incredulously. "Ranching *is* our business. It's a way of life we love. The vacation business just keeps us going when raising cattle doesn't pay the bills. What's more, the U-2 is popular because people want to experience the romance of the West. A fancy resort wouldn't cut it. Or haven't you paid any attention to what people like the Sallengers or Susan and Chad have said?"

Jacob frowned. "I know the Sallengers are moving to Buckeye."

She waved her hand. "I doubt they'll do it. They'll get home and decide they can't leave the city. It happens all the time with our guests, thinking they're going to move here. But that's beside the point. They loved their visit to the U-2 because they got a taste of real ranching and a chance to connect with nature. Anyway, money can't buy everything. It couldn't save your wife and it hasn't solved Caitlin's problems, so why do you think it's so important?"

He stiffened. "Money *is* important. Kittie wasn't insurable for health care after her heart defect was repaired. I had to have money, and lots of it, to take care of her properly."

"But how much is enough?"

Jacob gave her a hard look and strode out as Mariah sank onto a bale of hay.

She was furious, yet his motivations weren't as simple as she'd thought. *Nothing* was as simple as she'd thought. Jacob worked long hours, but during the summer season she worked just as many…as he'd been happy to point out during one of their arguments. It was an inescapable fact of ranching and the U-2's vacation business. Her advantage was that since the ranch was a family business, she spent a lot of those hours with her brother and grandparents.

Still, she hadn't let *Luke* share the responsibilities she'd taken on with her parents' deaths, or told him of her pain and uncertainties, no matter how much he'd tried to be a partner. Would things have turned out better for them if she'd confided in him more? Maybe. Things might also be better with Reid if the family wasn't so closemouthed about everything.

Mariah stood up resolutely.

At least that was one thing she could try to fix. She'd have to find the right time, a time Reid couldn't easily duck out of, and talk about what was really bothering him.

JACOB RETURNED HIS LAPTOP to his tent and joined Kittie and Burt in the front barn where they were cleaning and oiling saddles and other leather goods.

He was torn between anger and chagrin. His great idea to force Mariah to talk to him had gone down like the *Titanic*. He ought to have known the Weston family wouldn't be interested in transforming their ranch into a resort, and it was entirely possible their regular clientele wouldn't be interested in coming to one, either. That was something else he hadn't taken into account. What was wrong with him? Once, he wouldn't have made such mistakes—he didn't build a large conglomerate by missing key details.

"What's that?" he said, realizing Kittie had asked him something.

"*Dad.* Reid wants to take me into town this afternoon to have a chocolate ice-cream soda. He says the drugstore has an old soda fountain, whatever that is, with marble counters and a pressed tin ceiling from a long time ago."

"A soda fountain is a place where they serve cold drinks and sandwiches and such. They were in drugstores and five-and-dimes," Jacob explained, his brain working furiously.

His daughter had been asked out on a date? The fear that he'd missed Kittie's childhood came back with tidal force.

She wanted to go on a date.

A date.

He was being rushed into a strange new world that he didn't like in the least. She would be eighteen in four years, attending college, getting married…*driving.* His heart began pounding in his chest.

Kittie seemed puzzled. "What's a five-and-dime?"

Jacob felt very old and curiously nostalgic at the same time. How many kids today had ever heard of a five-and-dime store? The old Woolworths store in his hometown had closed when he was a boy, but he still remembered the variety of goods it had carried—things a kid could afford on a modest allowance. Not that *everything* cost five cents or a dime back then—*that* had changed decades before he was born.

"They were stores where everything was priced either five or ten cents," he said.

"There's a shop or two in Billings where everything is a buck," Burt said. "Closest thing we got now to a five-and-dime."

"Oh, well, can I go, Dad? Reid is celebrating because his finals are over at school and he got straight A-pluses. He's supersmart, you know."

Jacob wanted to refuse more than anything. But of all the young men who could take Kittie on her first date, Reid Weston was the most trustworthy. He was intelligent, respectful, worked hard and couldn't possibly be a member of a street gang—the nearest gang had to be a hundred miles away. Or more.

"Uh, okay...unless Burt has an assignment for us that would interfere." He gave the wrangler a hopeful glance.

"Naw." Burt rubbed some oil into his saddle. "Matter of fact, I'm pickin' up a load of feed grain in town later. Was thinking of havin' a soda myself. 'Course, I prefer strawberry over chocolate. Y'er welcome to come with me."

"Sounds good." Jacob could have kissed the old guy.

Kittie didn't seem as pleased, but she didn't throw a fit.

Burt unwrapped a stick of mint gum and stuck it in his mouth. "Glad to have you along, young man. Three o'clock, then."

KITTIE RUSHED to the tent at two-thirty and grabbed one of her new dresses so she could be ready whenever Reid wanted to go.

She could hardly believe it—he was taking her for an ice-cream soda. Not that you always got kissed on a date, especially the first one, according to Shayla. It probably couldn't happen anyhow, not if her dad and Burt were going to show up in the middle to have ice cream, too. She wished she could tell Shayla that her dad had actually given her permission, but the McFees were out for the day, moving a couple of herds to fresh pasture with their wrangler.

Kittie also wished she could ask Mariah what to wear and stuff, but she hadn't seen her, so she had to guess.

At the last minute she changed back into jeans, but picked out a prettier top than the ones for every day. That, with her cowgirl boots, didn't seem as if she was making a big deal of Reid's invitation.

While Kittie was waiting in the mess tent, she put her finger over the scar on her chest, some of her excitement fading. She couldn't talk to her dad about it, even if things weren't so awful with him right now. It just made her so mad that sometimes she wanted to bust out screaming.

Maybe she'd get used to knowing her heart was bad and that her mom had lied to her dad, but she doubted it.

ON WEDNESDAY NIGHT Mariah stayed in the barn with Knicker, one of the horses they assigned to the guests. A wrangler had told her that he'd caught a visitor feeding grain to the five-year-old, *lots* of it. Too much grain could cause colic, and the friendly horse was already in a fair amount of pain. Knicker's only vice was greed; otherwise he was a fine, gentle mount with an inquisitive nature.

"Okay, boy, you'll be all right," she soothed, noting he'd started sweating on his flanks and kept turning his head to peer at the side of his body. She'd been walking him steadily to insure he didn't lie down and roll. "Doc Crandall is coming."

"He's here," a familiar deep voice said. The veterinarian smiled kindly. "I don't get many calls for colic at the U-2."

"Unfortunately, one of our guests thought Knicker should have extra grain as a reward. Two days on the ranch and Mr. J. J. Scullin fancies himself an expert horseman."

"Tenderfeet and lazy-assed cowboys cause a lot of problems," Doc complained without rancor. He checked Knicker carefully and opened his bag. "I don't think he's too bad, but we'll take measures to be sure."

They worked with the sick animal until the symptoms subsided. But it was when Knicker playfully caught Mariah's sleeve in his teeth and tugged it that she relaxed. Colic could be serious in a horse. "Good boy," she said, patting his neck.

"He'll be fine," Doc Crandall assured, packing up his medical bag. “Just keep an eye on him. You know, if all my clients were like you, I wouldn’t have much of a practice.”

She grimaced at the compliment. “I could’ve prevented him from getting too much grain. I’ll have to put locks on the feed.”

“Don’t beat yourself up. You can’t take care of the entire world, Mariah.”

It was eerily similar to what Jacob had said about her thinking everything was on her shoulders. She wished she could get him out of her head—even if she had feelings for him, nothing could come of it.

“Uh…you know me,” she said.

The veterinarian nodded wryly. “I do indeed.”

When she was alone, Mariah resumed walking Knicker up the long barn as a precaution and saw Reid at the door as she turned thc horse.

“What’s up, sis?”

“Colic. Doc Crandall was just here.”

“I saw him leave. You should have called me or Granddad to help. Have a seat and I’ll take over. You look bushed.”

Reluctantly, Mariah surrendered Knicker’s lead and sat on a hay bale, then realized it was the kind of opening she’d been hoping for. When it came to horses, neither one of them would go to bed unless everything was all right, whatever the provocation.

“Reid, I found those college applications in the trash.”

His eyes went blank. “I don’t walk to talk about it.”

“I do,” she said quietly. “I don’t want to fight. I only want to find out what’s going on. And I’m not dropping it, so you might as well talk to me.”

He didn’t say anything for a long moment. The only sound was the clomp of hooves on the wood barn floor and the distant call of a coyote. “No point in fooling with them. That’s all there is to it, so there’s nothing to talk about,” he finally muttered.

"Come on, Reid. That isn't true. You can study something else if you don't want to be a veterinarian, but you should experience life away from the ranch to be sure of what you want. At the very least, you can go the State University in Billings and come home on weekends if you want."

"Or I could just stay here."

"Reid, talk to me," Mariah insisted. She'd meant it when she had said she wasn't dropping the subject—this was a critical time for Reid and she couldn't live with herself if she blew it. "*Are* you worried you'll be homesick? You probably will be, but that's not a reason to stay. The U-2 will be here when you're ready to come back."

"I'm not… It isn't that exact…" His voice trailed off miserably. "How can I go away and leave you with everything? You gave up being a vet because of me."

Mariah sighed. "Reid, that isn't your responsibility. Maybe you don't understand because we've never really talked about the accident and what it meant."

"It sucked like the worst thing ever. That's what it meant."

A ghost of a smile curved her lips. Yup, her brother had summed it up nicely. "I agree."

"I wish…I wish they hadn't told Dad that Mom was dead," Reid burst out. "Why couldn't they have waited until he was better? He'd be here now, wouldn't he?"

Mariah felt as if the ground was being shaken beneath her feet. She would have sworn her brother didn't know what had happened in the hospital with their father.

"Oh, Reid, I don't know. Dad was badly hurt, and it's impossible to say how it would have turned out if they'd waited to tell him. He kept asking to see her and became more and more agitated when the doctors put him off. We could do the what-if question forever and still not get an answer."

His young face worked furiously. He came from a world

where "men" weren't supposed to cry, and it must have made things harder for him. Hell, *she* thought she shouldn't cry, that she had to be strong and keep emotion from consuming her.

"I really loved them, sis. But sometimes…sometimes I'm afraid that if I talk about them, it'll upset everybody."

Mariah got up and gave him a hug. Obviously the "Weston way" of keeping things bottled up needed to change. "You can talk to me about whatever you want."

"Whatever I want?" He gave her a sideways look. "What about Luke? You'd be married to him if it wasn't for me. It's my fault it got screwed up."

Well…she *had* invited him to ask anything he wanted.

"No, Reid. None of it is your fault. It turns out that Luke and I weren't enough in love to get married. And as for school, there were a whole lot of reasons I left. For one thing, I couldn't let the ranch go further into debt for my education. But that was my decision—do you really think Granddad and Grams didn't try to convince me not to quit?"

"But it'll cost money if I go to school."

"I'm not claiming it's going to be easy, but we're out of debt. I've saved money toward your college fund and we've still managed to make improvements like the new guest bathrooms and the power station. You know all that, so why are you making excuses?"

Her brother shifted from one foot to the other while Knicker nuzzled his arm. "I…I do want to be a vet…only I want to be as good as you," he confessed in a rush. "I don't have your way with animals. You can't get that out of a book."

Ah, *damn.*

"You can't compare yourself to me or to anyone. You'd be a great vet. But it's your turn to choose what *you* want."

"You didn't."

Mariah hesitated, searching for the right words. Her reasons were more complex than she'd ever acknowledged, even to herself.

"Reid, it's complicated. I *wanted* to be here for you and the rest of the family, but I also felt guilty for being so far from home when the accident occurred. I used to tell myself that if I'd only been home, Mom and Dad might not have gone to Billings that day. I'm sure I would have made the same choice to leave school, but I would have handled it better if I hadn't felt so guilty."

THE WEIGHT IN REID'S CHEST began to ease. He couldn't believe that his sister felt guilty, too. Not Mariah. She was the one everybody admired.

"That's stupid," he said.

"I know. The accident was horrible and senseless and we may always be angry about it, but Mom and Dad would want us to be happy and stop wasting energy with irrational feelings. We don't have any cause to feel guilty—either one of us."

Reid stepped out again, tugging on Knicker's lead. He loved the ranch; it was home. But he *really* wanted to be a veterinarian. He'd have to rely more on science than instinct, but was that such a bad thing? And he did know a bunch about animals—he'd grown up with them.

"So, what do you think?" Mariah asked after several minutes.

"I'll take another look at the applications," he said slowly. "There's time—they aren't due for a while."

"Right. And if you send them in and get accepted to more than one school, you could visit the different campuses to see which one you prefer."

"Yeah. Maybe."

Of course, he already had an idea of where he'd like to go. It would save money to attend the State-U in Billings, but he might have an easier time getting into veterinary school if he was in a high-profile pre-vet program attached to a veterinary college.

"Then we have a plan?" Mariah prompted.

"Yeah, I guess we do."

CHAPTER FOURTEEN

"THIS DOESN'T LOOK too bad," Grams said, inspecting a red, swollen lump on Delores Wheeler's arm. She nodded approval at Mariah over the older woman's shoulder.

Dolores hadn't wanted to visit the dispensary after being stung by a wasp, but it was the U-2's policy to have all stings checked to insure there weren't any unpleasant consequences. The dispensary was more than what it sounded like. It was a mini medical station where Grams could treat a variety of health emergencies.

Mariah remained near the door in case she was needed, but her mind drifted. She was still in a quandary over Jacob, though she felt better about things with Reid. He was poring over his college applications as if they were due in days, and was far more cheerful.

She wasn't fooling herself; it would take more than a single talk to resolve everything, but they'd made a start. In a way she understood why Jacob didn't want to have more children—there were so many ways to screw up and worry yourself to death.

"Have you ever had an allergic reaction to an insect bite?" Grams asked, taking her patient's blood pressure.

"Nope. Though I admit this really itches and burns."

Grams pulled out her stethoscope. "Any trouble breathing?"

"I've never been stung. It scared me at first and I got breathless, but I'm okay now."

Mariah's cell phone rang and she stepped outside after exchanging a look with her grandmother. "Yes?"

"Reid and me are ridin' toward some smoke we spotted," Ray Cassidy told her. "Seems to be a half mile northeast of the house. Thought you should know."

"I'm coming." Mariah's pulse shot upward. They'd already had one fire from a dry lightning strike and she hoped the reports predicting rain by the end of the week were accurate. "Do you need me, Grams?" she called.

"No, we're fine."

Mariah made another call, alerting Granddad, then ran to the corral, whistling for Shadow. She'd saddled him earlier, but hurrying to a possible emergency wasn't the ride she'd planned on. She could see the smudge of smoke on the horizon and urged the stallion forward.

By the time she rode up to the scene, the smoke had lessened, and she found Jacob, Reid and the others putting out smoldering flames in a gully filled with dead brush. Kittie was holding Ray's and Reid's horses a safe distance away and Mariah handed her Shadow's reins.

"Thanks."

She grabbed a collapsible shovel from her saddlebag. All guests and wranglers carried small shovels in their saddlebags. They were a standard piece of U-2 equipment along with the wranglers' cell phones and first-aid kits.

"If you can manage with all three, walk them around to cool them off," Mariah added.

Kittie grasped the reins even tighter. "I can manage," she said firmly, and a corner of Mariah's mind marveled. The teenager was almost unrecognizable from the angry rebel who'd shown up at the U-2 a few weeks ago. Yet it wasn't just her clothing—she was more self-confident.

Burt was in command and he waved his hand in a circle. "Firebreak."

The word meant he wanted her to join the diggers clearing

patches of earth around the area, so she dug into the ground. The blaze wasn't serious, especially since the grass wasn't as dry as it would be later in the season, but they had to make sure it stayed that way.

The brush was tucked into a gully that was too small for the entire crew to work in at one time, and Jacob was doggedly shoveling dirt onto the worst of the flames. Burt signaled to Mariah when Jacob didn't respond to another command to give way and let someone else take his spot.

"Jacob," Mariah said.

"What?" He didn't look at her, instead beating down a smoking branch and covering it with loose earth. His shirt was soaked with perspiration and his breath was coming in deep, hard gasps.

"We do this in relays."

"I'm fine."

"Step out. *Now.*"

He looked at her finally and backed out reluctantly, his face grim beneath a layer of soot and dirt. Ray slid in and took his place. Twenty minutes later there was a ten-foot strip of ground cleared around the gulley. The dead brush had largely burned or was buried, and only coals and wisps of rising smoke remained.

Burt called for a break and they stood back, keeping watch on the site.

"Is anyone hurt?" Mariah asked.

She heard a chorus of "No," and Kittie came closer, leading the horses she was tending. Mariah could see the other mounts a hundred yards away, tethered near a spreading cottonwood tree. From the items scattered nearby on the ground, it was apparent they'd been having lunch when the fire broke out.

Shadow nosed Mariah from head to foot, his nostrils flaring at the scent of smoke.

She stroked his mane. "It's okay, boy."

"He was awful good," Kittie assured her. "He didn't fight one second while I was walking them."

Mariah nodded. "I'm glad you were here to help. There's no telling what an animal will do around a fire."

"I wanted to help more, but Dad said to get back, and then Ray and Reid needed me to hold Buttons and Nappy." Her voice was anxious and a touch indignant.

"Kittie, everyone's job is important. I'd hate to put out a fire and have to go chasing all over creation for my horse when I was done."

JACOB LOOKED at his daughter, his blood still surging with adrenaline. She'd mistakenly begun one fire by smoking—why not another? He should have searched her baggage for cigarettes, he decided bitterly. He'd told Mariah that smoking wasn't going to be a problem, and now they'd suspiciously had a blaze, with Kittie raising the alarm as she came running back from taking a "short walk."

"Kittie, did you have something to do with this?" he asked, trying to stay calm. "I know you resented coming to Montana."

She went pale and he regretted his hasty words.

"I would never do anything to harm the U-2", she said icily. "And maybe I didn't want to come at first, but it's different now."

"Kittie, I—"

"I love it here and I hate Seattle. I want to stay in Montana forever and ever," Kittie declared passionately. "You're the one who really needs fixing, not me."

She stalked to where they'd left the other horses with the same air of chilly dignity.

Reid cleared his throat. "I'll go with her."

As they rode toward the ranch, Kittie's body was ramrod straight on Blue, stiff with wounded outrage.

"She warn't near the gully. You was talking on the phone

and didn't see nothin'," Burt Parsons said in disgust. "It was a lightning strike."

He didn't add *dumbass,* but his tone said it all.

Ray and Burt returned to throwing dirt on the coals and spots where tendrils of smoke still rose. Jacob widened the firebreak, his mind churning. When would he learn? Was he just paranoid after the phone calls and visits with annoyed school officials, or did his suspicion and worry simply feed the cycle? Worse, had he just destroyed the progress Kittie had made while being here in Montana?

Steeling himself, he turned to Burt. "I'm sorry I jumped to conclusions."

"Don't tell me. Tell your young'un."

"I plan to."

Two other wranglers rode up and greeted Mariah, blanket rolls attached to their saddles. Burt and Ray said hello and began packing up their gear.

"You know the drill. Watch to be sure it doesn't flare," she told the newcomers. "We'll send replacements later."

"Yes, ma'am."

Jacob saw her glance at him. He was expecting her to rip into him for overreacting with Kittie again, but she motioned to the slope under the cottonwood tree where they'd stopped for lunch.

"Let's clean that up, too."

They picked up the containers and trash that had been abandoned when Kittie alerted them to the fire. Jacob's sandwich was still in its wrapper, abandoned when he'd taken a phone call immediately after they'd started the meal...another thing to regret. Perhaps that was why he'd wondered if Kittie had defiantly gone off to smoke a cigarette—resentment over his answering his cell.

"I'm trying," he said quietly, tucking the picnic debris into his saddlebag.

"Trying what?"

"Not to handle business matters around Kittie, but I spoke with a business associate from Japan at lunch. It was a mistake. I don't want her to believe she's less important to me than my company. That's what you suggested, isn't it?"

"Jacob…" Mariah made a helpless gesture. "I was upset and said all sorts of things."

"It doesn't mean you were wrong." He rubbed his neck, every muscle in his body aching and tense. "Hell, I have to stop making these mistakes. I love her so much, and I've been scared silly she's going to self-destruct or start drugs… or worse."

"She seems to be doing well."

"Appearances can mean nothing. One of the kids at her school…" Some things were particularly hard to talk about, and he clenched his fingers into a fist. "A sophomore at Garrison committed suicide this winter. At the service I spoke to her father and all he could say, over and over, was 'I thought she was getting better, I really thought she'd be all right.' I can't forget his expression—all the hope was gone. I've been on edge ever since because Kittie was already acting up."

Mariah looked appalled. "It would have scared me, too… even worse now that I…" She hesitated, then plunged ahead. "Four years ago I had a similar situation without knowing it. I told you my dad died in the hospital soon after they told him my mother was gone, even though they thought he'd make it."

He nodded.

"I was so angry." A tear traced its way through the soot on her cheek and she dashed it away. "I thought, why couldn't he want to live for us? Didn't we matter enough? But I also know how terrible it was for him. My mother was the center of his world and his injuries were so severe…"

Jacob didn't know how he would have reacted if he'd been critically injured and had to deal with Anna's death, but he hoped he would have chosen to live for his daughter.

"What I didn't realize," Mariah continued, "was that Reid

knew what had happened with Dad. He's dealt with it for four years without telling any of us. You can never know for sure, yet as far I can tell, he's okay."

Jacob had an idea that Reid wasn't the *only* one who'd dealt with things in silence. The elder Westons had surely confided in each other, but Mariah and Reid seemed to have kept things bottled up. It couldn't have been easy for her, telling him about it, but it was oddly reassuring—hopefully, kids were more resilient than adults gave them credit for being.

"He's a great kid, Mariah. You have a lot to be proud of."

"Thanks, but my parents get the credit. Tell you what. Let's wash up at the creek. You need to think about what to say to Kittie."

They mounted their horses and rode northwest into a low area, cut through by a meandering creek. Cottonwoods sheltered a wide, lazy curve in the waterway, and some of Jacob's tension eased at the sight.

They tied the horses to a tree and took off their boots. Jacob had purchased a pair the previous week in Buckeye when he'd accepted how practical they actually were for ranch work. They provided protection and the heels assisted with keeping his feet in the stirrups. Until then he'd mostly thought cowboy boots were an affectation. He was breaking them in slowly, but he'd been especially grateful for the hardy footwear while fighting the fire.

The creek water was cold and clear, and Jacob splashed it on his face and hands, scrubbing at the grime. After a while he lay on the grass with his bare feet still submerged, water flowing gently around them, soothing his jangled nerves.

A thread of what Mariah loved about the ranch sank deeper into him. The Westons and their neighbors were preserving a life filled with the rhythms of nature. It was tempting. He could see why someone who'd grown up here would be reluctant to leave...and he could even see how someone who'd always lived in the city could learn to love it, the way Kittie seemed to have.

"You don't think the Sallengers will really move to Buckeye?" he asked idly. "They mentioned it several times... supposedly even had return plane tickets to come hunt for property to buy. They seemed serious to me."

Mariah kicked her own boots aside. "It seems unlikely. They're used to the bustle and activity you get in large population centers. Edna is an opera lover and Carl is so addicted to mangoes and fresh bagels, I'm surprised he didn't go into withdrawal while they were here. Those aren't items easily obtained in Buckeye."

Jacob looked at her in wonder. "How do you know so much about everyone?"

"I pay attention. Our guests are like having extended family visiting that you need to get to know."

"You mean, I could do the same if I didn't have a cell phone stuck in my ear all the time?"

Mariah grinned. "I didn't say that, though you gave me the perfect opening. At any rate, it would be difficult for the Sallengers to stay away from Hartford, even for a handful of months each year."

"Then you don't believe people can change."

She didn't say anything for a long minute. "How many people really *want* to change?" she said finally. "I grew up watching guests come and go. This is our world, but for our guests, it's an entertaining break from their lives. Most of them leave here and remember they had fun, and that's all."

Jacob turned on his side and propped his head on his hand. "One of them broke your heart, didn't they?"

"Summer promises get forgotten," she murmured.

"You didn't forget them, but he did," he guessed.

She shrugged. "I was fifteen. It was puppy love. I'm not living with a broken heart, if that's what you think. And I learned a valuable lesson."

"Yeah, not to trust anyone outside a fifty-mile radius of Buckeye."

Mariah made an exasperated sound. "No, to be realistic."

"You're splitting hairs."

"There's a difference. I think most people have good intentions—they just get influenced by the moment and think they can make huge decisions based on a few days."

Her observations were enlightening. No wonder she'd avoided him after they had kissed and later when they'd made love. She didn't want to discuss it, because she didn't believe anything could come of a connection between them. Once he would have said she was right, but now he wasn't as certain—a month ago he wouldn't have gotten involved with a temperamental redhead who expected to marry one day and have children.

More kids meant more teenagers, and Jacob wasn't sure he could survive another Kittie, as much as he loved her. Of course, it would help if he could stop screwing up. He wasn't accustomed to failing to the degree he'd failed with his daughter.

He shook his head and sat up, needing to distract himself.

"Is something wrong?" Mariah dipped her toes in the water, swirling the surface.

God, she was beautiful. And complicated, with a temper to match. She was also mulishly stubborn and didn't mince words when her dander was up. Yet making love to her was as close to heaven as he'd ever gotten. Maybe if things were better with Kittie, he could figure out what he wanted from Mariah…aside from just *wanting* her.

He sighed.

Now he needed a distraction from the distraction.

MARIAH'S THROAT ACHED at the lingering anguish in Jacob's face. He'd mismanaged the situation badly, but it was out of love for his daughter and the fear of what could happen if

Caitlin's troubling behavior continued. She didn't blame him. She was horrified that one of Caitlin's classmates had killed herself—every parent at Garrison Academy was probably running a little scared.

"It's true that this weather makes for a greater fire risk, but there's something else it's good for," she said lightly.

"What's that?"

"Lying on the grass and necking." She leaned forward and deliberately kissed him.

Jacob didn't move for a second and Mariah wondered if she'd misjudged the situation. She thought she had seen a glint of heat in his eyes, but maybe she was wrong.

Suddenly the world spun wildly as Jacob rolled with her. He gazed down with a faint smile.

"Necking, huh?"

"Just necking," she warned. She didn't think having sex again was the wisest idea in the world, but kissing seemed relatively harmless, all things considered.

He dropped a kiss on the side of her mouth. "Hmm, I haven't necked since high school. Not old-fashioned necking anyhow. Any rules I should observe?"

"Are there any rules you didn't break when you were a teenager?" Mariah asked drily.

"Can't think of one."

"That explains why you're worried about Caitlin dating."

Jacob pulled away a few inches, his face resigned. "It's the eternal payback. Now I know what a girlfriend's father meant when he said that he hoped I'd grow up and have nothing but daughters."

Mariah chuckled. "Ooh, vicious."

"You have no idea. At the time I thought he was being chauvinistic, suggesting sons were more valuable than daughters, and felt virtuous for being offended." His lips trailed the curve of her cheek. "Hmm, Eau de Smoke. Curious choice of perfume."

"I was just thinking the same thing of your cologne, Essence of Burned Shrub."

"But I'm smelling something else…." Jacob pressed a string of nibbling kisses down her neck, his fingers threaded through her hair. "Hints of vanilla and spice."

"Real sophisticated, I know. What do your city-slicker lady friends wear?"

"Got me…. Even with the smoke, yours is better." He fanned her hair out on the ground, playing with it before catching her mouth again in a drugging kiss that went on forever. One of his hands crept under her shirt and cupped her breast, his thumb flicking across the sensitive crest.

A piercing need shot down Mariah's body. Necking might not be so harmless after all…not with Jacob O'Donnell. He must have alarmed quite a number of fathers when he was a teenager—they'd probably started cleaning their shotguns the instant they met him.

A moment later Jacob spread the edges of her shirt and bra apart. The sunlight filtering through the trees above was warm on her skin, yet it was the heat in his mouth that burned the hottest.

He tickled her nipples with the tip of his tongue, then drew one into his mouth. Mariah arched, breathing in and out so quickly she was in danger of hyperventilating. So far he hadn't gone near the snap on her jeans, but this was already a lot more than what she'd had in mind.

"Jacob," she said thickly, "I think you should—"

"Should what?" He rolled so she was perched on top of him.

With the small shred of sense left in her head, Mariah scooted away and stepped into the eddying creek. "You should cool off." With one hand she held her shirt together and with the other she scooped a handful of water over him.

Jacob sat up, laughing; he didn't seem the least bit annoyed. "That felt good."

He jumped in himself and she backed up, careful to stay in the extreme shallows of the creek. "Be careful," she warned. "It's one thing to get your cuffs wet, another to ride home in wet jeans."

"How about a wet shirt?" A spray of water went flying as his hand swept the surface and she shrieked, dashing to the opposite bank. Jacob gave chase and tackled her before she'd taken two steps onto the grass. He stripped her Levi's, followed by his own, and carried her into the narrow curve of the creek where it was waist deep.

"Don't you dare," she said without much concern.

"I dare anything."

He dropped low with her in his arms, kissing her mouth as the water closed over their heads. They finally surged upward, gasping for breath.

"I bet cowboys learn quick that getting a girl *out* of wet jeans is practically impossible," he murmured. "Thank you for alerting me that wet denim is a challenge."

"Don't you thrive on challenges?" Mariah undid the buttons on his shirt and rubbed against him.

Jacob groaned and the bulge pressed to her thigh became even more impressive.

Protection, she thought, hoping he had a second condom in his wallet...and that his wallet was in his jeans and not in his tent. She didn't overly mind the thought of getting pregnant, but knew he would profoundly resent it—the last thing Jacob wanted was another child's safety and well-being to worry about.

Jacob lifted her leg over his hip and explored beneath the thin barrier of her panties. He pushed it aside, his blunt end teasing her, dipping in and out a fraction of an inch. But it was when he was half-buried inside of her that she jerked away, falling backward in the water. She nearly screamed with frustration as their bodies separated.

He drew her upright and stared into her eyes. "Is there a problem?" he queried politely.

"Yeah, a little one." Her gaze drifted downward. They were waist deep in the creek, but the crystalline water did nothing to conceal his erection. "Actually, not such a little one. Do you happen to have a condom with you?"

Jacob's strained expression relaxed. "Wise woman. Wait here."

He splashed to the creek edge and fished around in the pocket of his jeans, returning with a plastic-wrapped packet. He sheathed himself and pulled her to him.

"I've never done it this way, upright in a river."

"You still aren't. This is a creek."

"Minor point."

He caressed her breasts for long, fiery minutes as she ran her fingers across his chest, teasing and tickling, then moving lower and holding him in her palm.

"Too much," Jacob growled.

He cupped her bottom and settled her over him. They moved together, Mariah's legs clasped around his hips, clinging to him with internal muscles that felt each tiny pulse.

She felt his release an instant after hers. Then, to her surprise, he held her tight and walked to the grassy bank. He lay with her and began thrusting once more, stoking the lingering pulses in her abdomen. Her blood raced again, impossibly fast, and she shattered, the world tumbling in a kaleidoscope of pure sensation.

AS MARIAH'S BREATHING SLOWED she became aware of a light breeze and the chirping of birds overhead. Jacob held her, stroking her back soothingly. She raised her head and blinked at him.

"Hi," he said.

"Hi." She sat up and began fastening her bra.

"Gee. I thought women enjoyed the afterglow."

Afterglow was one thing; lying nearly naked on the banks of the ranch's swimming hole was another. The guests usually weren't told about the creek, but they could have discovered it on their own. What if some of them decided to take a dip on a hot day?

Thinking of which…Mariah stepped into the creek again and started searching the banks.

"What now?" Jacob complained.

"I'm looking for the packaging from the condom."

"Why?"

"Is that something you want Kittie to find if she comes swimming again with Reid? You can't be sure it was washed away by the current. Besides, it's trash and won't ever degrade."

Jacob vaulted to his feet and searched, as well. Several minutes went by before they located the telltale piece of plastic, and he dealt with it along with the discarded condom.

The silence grew as they got dressed. A part of Mariah regretted the end of their sexy play, but she also knew it had been a mistake to get closer to Jacob—*she* was the one who would be surrounded by reminders long after his vacation was over.

Mariah's mixed feelings were reflected in his eyes as they mounted their horses. Their lives were poles apart, yet he'd captured her heart with his humor and intelligence and his love for Caitlin—even his enduring devotion to Anna's memory was compelling. Surely someone who could care so deeply once was capable of feeling that way again, yet he gave no indication that he had changed his mind about getting remarried or having more children.

Her fingers tightened on Shadow's reins and he tossed his head in protest. Mariah eased her grip and urged him ahead, still lost in thought.

When it got right down to it, the only thing she knew for certain was that Jacob liked having sex with her. And that was hardly enough to reassure a woman in love.

CHAPTER FIFTEEN

KITTIE CLIMBED TO THE HAYLOFT above the orphan calves and blinked furiously, determined not to cry.

Reid sat next to her. He hadn't said anything on the ride to the ranch; he'd just put their mounts in the corral and followed her to the loft.

"Don't Blue and Buttons need to be cooled down?" she asked. It was nice to have Reid there, only she didn't want the horses to get sick.

"We came back at a walk. They're fine."

"Oh." She felt stupid, but it didn't seem important at the moment. How could her dad think she'd do something that would hurt the ranch? She wanted to stay there forever and ever and take care of it.

"Your dad is a jackass," Reid said finally, as if he'd read her mind.

Despite her wounded feelings, Kittie went instantly defensive. "No, he isn't. He's just weird right now."

"He sounded like a jackass to me."

Well, yeah.

Kittie heaved a sigh. "I guess it's kinda my fault. I got into trouble a lot this year and was expelled a few weeks ago. I sort of...*accidentally* started a fire at my school. I didn't mean to, but a sophomore gave me a cigarette and I tried it in the locker room. It was lunchtime and I thought nobody was around."

Reid gave her a sideways look. "Smoking sucks."

"I know," she said, exasperated. "But Dad and me got into

a fight before school that day and I was ticked off about junk. I don't know. I just did it."

"So, what happened?"

"I heard a teacher come into the gym and I threw the butt away so I could hide in the showers. Then she didn't even come into the locker room. After a while I came out and found the trash can and a bench on fire. I tried putting it out with the extinguisher, 'cept I didn't know how to use it very good. Honest, I didn't mean to do it, and I pulled the alarm when the fire got worse."

"Did the sprinklers come on?"

"No, they were upset about that, too. And that part wasn't my fault, though they acted like it was. You'd think they'd be glad to know there was a problem."

"Go figure." Reid stretched out his legs and one of the barn cats jumped onto his lap and began purring.

The pens below were filled with sleeping calves. That morning the wranglers had said they were keeping the doors open so the babies could come in to get shade from the sun. Kittie spotted Emily and stuck her lip out; she didn't want to leave Emily, even though the baby calf was eating good now and Mariah and the other wranglers had stopped worrying about her.

"I'd already decided not to smoke again," she explained. "But I got caught and everything turned into a mess. That's what Dad meant. He thought I'd brought some cigarettes from Seattle and sneaked off to smoke one."

"I tried a wad of chewing tobacco in fifth grade," Reid volunteered. "It was gross and I threw up a bunch of times. Pop was great—he said there were worse things and that I'd learned a lesson."

Kittie thought about the past year. The first few times she'd gotten in trouble, her dad was pretty mellow, but he became more wacko with each dumb thing she'd done. She wasn't even sure why she'd started causing trouble; it wasn't always because she'd *meant* to do something wrong.

Well, that wasn't completely true.

She put a finger over her heart. The scar was just a pale silvery line you could barely see except when her skin got really cold. Her friends had asked about it once or twice, but nobody stared or anything when she went swimming. She'd hardly paid attention to it herself before finding out the truth.

"Reid, did you see my chest when we were over at the swimming hole?"

"No." He looked alarmed. "And you shouldn't ask guys things like that. Not till you're older."

"I don't mean my breasts." Kittie rolled her eyes. "I mean the scar."

"What scar? And don't show it to me," Reid said hastily.

"There's a scar on my chest. I had surgery when I was little. I got born with something wrong with my heart."

"JEEZ."

Spreckles yowled at the loud exclamation, so Reid scratched her neck and she settled down with a grumpy meow.

"Do you remember them doing it?" he asked when Kittie didn't say anything else.

"No. I was two or something. Dad told me a long time ago that my heart was fixed and not to think about it anymore."

"Didn't he tell you anything else?"

"No. He doesn't like talking about it." Kittie wrinkled her nose. "I think it reminds him of my mom—she died on account of *her* heart."

Reid shifted uncomfortably. It stunk that her mother was dead, and it stunk that Kittie had needed an operation when she was only a kid. But if she was fixed and all right, why was she bringing it up?

"You told me your mom got sick in high school," he said.

Kittie bobbed her head and her face got more miserable.

All at once Reid remembered something—they thought they had fixed her mother, but it didn't work, or some such thing. Appalled, his eyes widened. *That* was what was bugging Kitty. She was afraid her operation hadn't worked.

"Then your heart…"

"Could be bum, too," she said gloomily. "And my mom kept all kinds of stuff from my dad. I found her diary when I was staying at Nana Carolyn and Grandfather Barrett's house last fall. The diary was hidden in a secret compartment in a big old piece of furniture."

Reid wondered idly why Kittie had gone hunting through her mom's things.

"I was just exploring," Kittie said, as if she'd read his mind. "And they let me sleep in there, so I kind of had permission. My dad was in college when they got married. Since they lived in a tiny apartment, Mom left lots of junk behind. I used to like staying in her old room until I read her diary."

Personally, Reid thought it was creepy leaving everything that way for years and years. "So she didn't take her diary, either?"

"Nope." Kittie's voice lowered with significance. "She even came back and wrote in it *after* they got married. You know, when she got sick again."

"That doesn't have to mean anything."

"But it did." Kittie sounded quite certain. "Anyhow, one of the things my mom wrote was that Nana Carolyn was my mom's stepmother. Dad doesn't know that *or* that my first grandmother died because of her heart, too."

"But if you *had* the operation, shouldn't your heart be okay?"

"Well…" Kittie reached over and petted Spreckles. "Dad hardly ever lets me do anything like other kids. We stopped going horseback riding ages ago, and he won't let me have a bike or even a pet guinea pig. I've never gone roller-skating or sailing or anything. *Sailing,*" she said indignantly. "We live next to Lake Union and the Puget Sound, and I've never gone sailing."

Neither had Reid, but he didn't live near a lake. "That doesn't mean your heart doesn't work right. And your dad seems real busy. He probably doesn't have time to go sailing."

"Yeah, but he's also dragged me to a ton of doctors. Besides, if everything's okay, why won't he talk about it? I tried after Christmas and he got tense and acted funny. He said not to worry and wouldn't say anything else."

"He brought you to Montana."

"Because of the fire. I heard him on the phone before we left—he thought this was a place where they take care of messed-up kids. And he keeps telling me not to do things, even here."

"I don't think you're messed up."

"Thanks, Reid." She smiled and was awful pretty.

He felt bad for disliking her when she first arrived—when it got down to it, it really *was* dumb to be mad at people from Washington because of a drunk driver from Seattle. His Dad used to say that if you have to point a finger, make sure it's pointed in the right direction. And Reid *was* mad at the driver—the asshole had walked away from the accident with barely a scratch.

"Why don't you tell Grams about the surgery and the rest of it?" he suggested. "She's a doctor and might be able to help."

Kittie shook her head. "No. She'd have to tell my dad since I'm under eighteen—that's the way doctors work—and then he'll only get upset."

Reid tried to think of another solution. Under the circumstances, Kittie might know more about how doctors did things than he did, even if his grandmother and aunt were both M.D.s.

"Then talk to Mariah. She almost graduated from veterinary school, so she knows some medical stuff."

"I don't know. Maybe."

MARIAH EXCUSED HERSELF as soon as they got back to the ranch. The one spot she could be sure of privacy was her bathroom, so she dropped her clothes and stepped into the shower. Her body still hummed from making love with Jacob and a part of her wished they could have stayed at the creek, exploring new ways to satisfy each other.

Idiot, she scolded silently. She was an idiot for falling in love with Jacob in the first place.

What if he decided he wanted something permanent with her? Did she love him enough to give up having a baby? Caitlin was a great kid, but she was nearly grown and Mariah wanted her own kids to raise, though being responsible for her brother had given her a regular diet of sleepless nights and churning stomachs.

Mariah turned off the water and donned a soft satin bathrobe. Reid had given it to her for Christmas and she slid her hands over the sleek fabric. She didn't indulge in that sort of thing often, yet she had a secret love for expensive, frivolously feminine nightclothes and lingerie, just like Grams.

She looked in the mirror, smoothing her damp hair, remembering how Jacob had played with its heavy length. On a ranch, long hair might be as frivolously feminine as a silk negligee or satin robe. That could be why she'd kept it long—she wanted to feel like a woman in the midst of wrangling cattle and repairing fences.

She sat on the bed, fighting a wave of melancholy. It was late afternoon and she ought to be working, but realizing you were in love with a man like Jacob O'Donnell was enough to disturb any woman.

Okay, say they got married.

There wasn't much common ground between a Montana ranch and Seattle. Either she'd have to give up the U-2 for the city, or he'd have to be willing to live in Montana; Mariah didn't know if either one of them could make that choice. And even if they got married and she moved to Seattle, how would she deal with having a workaholic husband she rarely saw? It was hardly the marriage she'd envisioned for herself. Yet she'd shared things with Jacob that she hadn't told anyone—not her grandparents and certainly not Luke. That meant something, didn't it?

She'd always felt she should share the same goals and interests as a potential husband, but the thought of never seeing Jacob again hurt more than she could have imagined a month ago. And she had to wonder, were they *that* different in the things that counted, or was she rationalizing an impossible situation?

Mariah resolutely got up and combed her hair, plaiting it into a French braid.

The debate was academic.

Jacob might have mixed feelings about her, but marriage was less likely than going over Niagara Falls in a teacup. She was silly to even think about it.

REID WALKED OVER the hill, west of the house, and down to the gate of the family cemetery. The prairie grassland outside the fence was long and swaying; inside it was closely mowed around the gravestones.

He swallowed hard and opened the gate.

Grams and Granddad came up here every week, but he hadn't been since the funeral. Even Mariah visited. The flowers on the graves were faded and he cleared them away before laying down the two bunches of wildflowers that he'd picked after talking to Kittie.

It was because of Kittie that he'd come. At least he'd known his parents, while she didn't have any memory of her mom.

That stunk.

He let out a painful breath. The long rays from the sun deepened the shadows in the letters cut into the granite stones for Tamara and Sam Weston. The markers in the small cemetery were all straight and well maintained. Granddad said it was a sign of respect for Weston history and he wouldn't let things get run-down.

"I really miss you guys," Reid said awkwardly. He sat on the grass and tried to picture his mom and dad in his head. For the past four years, no matter how much he tried, all he could see was the funeral when he thought of them.

"Hey, are you all right?"

He peered up at Mariah.

"I guess. How did you know I was here?"

"I saw you walk this way with the flowers." She sat next to him and gazed at the two gravestones. "They were so proud of you. The last time I phoned before the accident, Dad kept telling me how brilliant you were in science and math and other subjects."

Reid squirmed. "That was just him being a dad."

"You *are* brilliant. It's nothing to be embarrassed about."

He shredded a piece of grass. "Can you see their faces? I mean when you think about them and not just when you see a picture." He didn't want her to think he was awful for forgetting, but she had said he could talk about their parents whenever he needed.

"Most of the time. When I do, Mom is usually laughing, and Dad is smiling."

"I can't see their faces.... That is, whenever I try, I just see us standing up here, with the flowers and the preacher and feeling as if the world had ended."

Mariah leaned on one elbow. "For me it used to be the hospital in Billings. But they aren't here, you know, any more than they were at the hospital."

"Sis, do you believe we'll see them again?"

"I'm sure we will," Mariah said quietly. "I even feel Mom and Dad next to me sometimes, especially in the Big Barn."

"I wish I could."

"You will, probably when you least expect it."

"I hope so." He poked at the wildflowers he'd brought. "I should get back to work."

"You're sixteen, Reid. You don't have to work so much."

"You don't, either. You keep talking about Granddad retiring and trying to take over for him, but he doesn't want to retire. That should count, right?"

"Yeah…that counts."

"And Grams wants to get involved with the business end of the ranch," Reid said doggedly. He might as well get it all out. "Aunt Lettie doesn't need her much now that the new school principal's wife turned out to be a nurse and is working at the clinic. Grams wants to feel useful."

"Okay, well, I'll speak to her."

They were both silent for a while, then Mariah got up.

"I'll let you be alone…unless you want me to stay?"

"I just want to think awhile."

She squeezed his shoulder and left. Reid screwed his eyes shut and thought about his parents, letting the memories come, thinking of how Mariah had described her images of them…Mom laughing, Dad smiling.

He saw his mom's blue eyes first.

She'd loved to play word games. He had gotten his dark brown hair from her and his height from his dad. Sam Weston had smiled more than laughed and usually refereed while the rest of them gave each other a hard time.

Mom had loved comedies. Dad had preferred mysteries. They'd done everything together and were the greatest mom and dad in the whole wide world.

Hot moisture leaked from the corners of Reid's eyes and he wiped it away impatiently. He turned his head to read the names on the carved stones, but he didn't see them…. Instead his parents were standing there in shiny Technicolor. Dad was wearing his favorite hat and going-to-church boots, and Mom wore that pretty pink dress she'd gotten the winter they went to Disney World.

They weren't hurting, and they were happy.

That was all he needed to know.

JACOB WENT HUNTING for Kittie before dinner, finding her at the calf barn feeding Emily. She ignored him when he came in, but he could tell that she knew he was there. He climbed into the pen and sat next to her on the hay. He didn't care who else heard him as long as Kittie did.

"I'm sorry," he said.

She cast him a quick glance and pressed her lips together.

"I should have known better—known you better," Jacob continued. "I didn't have any basis for thinking you had something to do with the fire. You've been very responsible while we've been here in Montana."

Her jaw quivered, then stiffened. "Whatever."

Hell.

They were back to *whatever.*

"I also found out that you tried to put out the fire at Garrison and pulled the fire alarm when it kept burning," he said determinedly. "I'm really proud that you tried to make it right."

Emily butted Kittie's arm, demanding her second bottle, and his daughter held it for the calf without a word or look at him.

Crap. He obviously wasn't going to get more from her, so he got up and dusted his jeans. "Anyway, I wanted you to know that. I'll see you at dinner."

She nodded, a slight, almost imperceptible nod, but Jacob saw it and breathed a thankful prayer. Maybe he hadn't entirely blown everything, after all.

THOUGH JACOB HAD BEGUN sleeping better, that night he stared into the darkness for hours, unable to rest. Each sound seemed intensified, from the breeze ruffling the walls of the tent to the distant cry of a wild animal and answering whinny from a horse in the barn.

He twisted the gold band on his left ring finger.

What *did* he want from Mariah?

Nothing would ever be easy with her—she was too outspoken and short-tempered and quick to dive into danger. He had nearly lost it when he'd realized she was fighting the fire as well, though he'd managed to keep his mouth shut. Worse, she didn't believe they were compatible or that city people could adapt to Montana—she didn't even think the Sallengers could make it work here for a few months out of the year.

She could be right.

Still… He inhaled deeply. The scents were varied—fresh air, grass and a faint odor from the canvas tent that reminded him of boyhood and camping with his folks. A light, cooling breeze blew toward the barn, so the aroma from the horses was absent, though he didn't even mind that anymore.

Mariah's conviction that people didn't really change was a valid concern, but it didn't mean it couldn't happen. She'd certainly made him see things he hadn't been willing to admit previously. After Anna's death he'd convinced himself that if he built a big enough fortune, everything would be all right. But regardless of where the funds had come from, there'd been more than enough for Anna's and Kittie's medical care. What was more, he knew full well that money couldn't have saved his wife; her parents would have spent every penny they possessed to help her, the same as him.

Perhaps pride had driven him as much as anything.

As a young man it was hard to take financial support from Anna's parents. The fact that they'd done it quietly and graciously hadn't mattered—he'd felt he ought to be able to take care of his own family. Now he had more money than he could ever use, and he kept trying to make more.

Jacob didn't enjoy admitting it, but his situation wasn't the same as Mariah's. Ranching was her heritage. She'd grown up on the U-2, working side by side with her family and with animals. She wouldn't be Mariah anywhere else; it was a vital part of her, the same as her laughter and quick mind.

A faint sniffling came through the canvas and Jacob got up to peer into the other side of the partition, barely able to make out his daughter's silhouette on the mattress. "Kittie?" he called softly.

The only thing he heard was another sniff.

"Do you want to talk?"

"Go away."

Jacob hesitated. He wanted to comfort her more than anything, but he was likely the cause of her tears. "Let me know if you change your mind."

He lay down again and listened, but there were no more sounds from Kittie. If she was crying, it was silently.

Damn. He might as well accept he could no longer soothe most of her woes with a hug, and it was painfully clear that being a parent didn't get easier as children got older. He'd probably be just as paranoid and worried when she was thirty or forty or fifty.

Jacob pressed the base of his palms to his throbbing forehead. Sure, it was tough being a father, but when Kittie was happy, his whole world lit up. There wasn't any reason to think he'd feel less for another child, so if he and Mariah had a family together…

He bolted to his feet, shocked at the direction of his thoughts. Trying to decide what he wanted from her was one thing; leaping ahead to considering a family was over-the-top.

Frustrated, Jacob stepped outside the tent.

The lights were off in the main horse barn, but he went inside anyhow. He got two apples from the barrel and fed one to Blue.

"You've been a good friend to my daughter, old boy. I appreciate it."

Blue snorted companionably. In the stall next to him,

Moonfire woke and peeked out inquisitively; she got the second apple, taking it with ladylike care. On Blue's opposite side, Shadow pawed the wood floor and made a low, warning noise. He was a stallion from nose to tail, not an easygoing gelding.

"Easy, boy. I'm not a threat."

The black horse peered over the stall door and whinnied sharply, a demon phantom in the filtered light.

"Fine, I get the message."

Jacob returned to the tent and resumed staring at the canvas above his head. Mariah hadn't avoided him that evening, but she hadn't invited conversation, either. He'd made mistakes with her since they'd met, almost as many mistakes as he'd made with Kittie.

Once again he found himself turning the gold band on his finger around and around. He missed Anna; he'd always miss her. Yet the frozen hole in his chest was gone…as if Mariah had filled it.

Slowly, he drew the ring off and put it in his wallet. He'd worn it all these years, holding on to his memories of love as though they'd be lost if he didn't leave the band where Anna had placed it on their wedding day. Yet he'd also held on to the pain.

Maybe it was time to try something new.

KITTIE STOOD AT THE FRONT of the food table and said hello to the people arriving for breakfast. Her dad was at the end, using tongs to serve the pancakes, and the rest of them were spooning out eggs and stuff. The fruit and yogurt were on another table where everyone could help themselves.

She could tell that her dad felt bad about what had happened, and he'd even said he was sorry—and he'd actually *sounded* sorry, too.

"What's that?" asked one of the new guests, pointing to a long pan.

"It's a Reggie special," Kittie said. "Potatoes and cheese and onions—all kinds of things. We usually have country-fried potatoes in the morning, but there were baked spuds left from last night, so he made this. It's awesome. Reggie is the best chuck-wagon cook in the state."

"Well, I'll take some. Wouldn't want to insult the best chuck-wagon cook in Montana, would I?"

"No, ma'am." Kittie gave her a generous scoopful, feeling like a pro…as if she really belonged on the ranch.

Reid came in and tipped his cowboy hat at her. He was so cute and he wanted to take her for ice-cream sodas again. Hopefully Laura Shelton would see them together this time, too. Kittie giggled, remembering Laura's sour-pickle expression when they'd run into her at the soda fountain.

When nearly everyone had gone through the food line, the wranglers took over and the serving crew got to eat. Kittie took her plate and sat with Shayla and her parents. She'd told her friend about the lightning strike hitting the dry brush, but not about her dad thinking it was her fault, mostly because she'd have to explain about smoking and setting fire to a trash can at school.

"We're leaving the day after tomorrow," Shayla reminded her. "Don't forget you promised to write."

"I'll have to send short emails from my smartphone until I get home," Kittie said, hating the hollow drop in her tummy. She didn't want her friend to go anywhere.

"No worries. Same here. We're driving to California before flying home. And when we get to Brisbane, I'm just going to surf until school starts, but I'll write you at night."

Kittie sighed. When they went home to Seattle, it would be boring. She'd never realized *how* boring it was, and now it would be worse than ever.

"You'll visit, won't you?" Shayla asked. "Me mum and dad said you can stay as long as you want, and I'll teach you to surf. I have an extra boogie board you can use."

"I'll try, but it won't be for a while," Kittie said, though she didn't know if she could ever go to Australia.

"It won't be so bad. You girls can call and have a nice chin-wag every now and then," Mr. McFee assured.

Two days later, Kittie hugged Shayla and watched the McFees drive away. She sniffed, trying not to cry as the SUV disappeared.

"Hey, you have Blue and Burt and the rest of us," Mariah said, giving her a hug. "How about digging weeds with me in the vegetable garden? Burt has a doctor's appointment this morning, so you have time. Your dad said it's okay."

Kittie gulped. "Is Burt sick?"

"He's just getting a checkup."

They worked for an hour, tossing the weeds into the compost pile. Mariah explained it had been the family's garden plot ever since her great-great-something-grandmother had brought packets of seeds with her in a covered wagon. The Westons still collected seeds every fall to use the next summer.

"It's a tradition Catherine Weston began a hundred and forty years ago." Mariah rubbed a leaf between her fingers and the air smelled like candy canes. "Some of these flowers and plants are from the original seeds she gathered from her mother's garden before she was married."

"You have seeds for everything?"

"We gather them, but not for everything. Some things come back on their own like this peppermint, and we buy seeds for veggies like zucchini."

Kittie made a face. "Yuck. Zucchini."

"You should try it the way my grandmother makes it—in fritters, with cheese and hot peppers and eggs."

"That sounds okay." She looked at the rows of vegetables, and the flowers that were growing everywhere, tucked in here and there. They had all kinds of neat things like corn and pumpkins and sunflowers. "I wish we had a garden at home."

"You have other things in Seattle, things we don't have here, like museums and department stores and big libraries. We have a bookmobile, but no library."

Kittie hunched her shoulder. "I don't care. I like it here best. I wish Shayla could have stayed."

Mariah sat on the grass and extended her legs. "At the U-2 you have to get used to saying goodbye to people," she said slowly. "And it can be lonely during the winter. But the internet helps and we aren't snowed in all the time the way most people think."

"It gets cold and lonely in Seattle, too."

Kittie tried to swallow the lump in her throat. Was it her heart? Maybe she was having an attack or something. Probably not, but she hated feeling as if everything was coming apart and wondering if she was going to die like her mother and grandmother.

Finding out for sure *had* to be better than worrying without really knowing.

She plopped next to Mariah. "Reid says I should talk to you about…uh…something that's bugging me."

"What's that?"

"I… When I was little I had an operation," she said quickly. "On my heart. Something was wrong with it when I was born."

Mariah didn't seem shocked like Reid had been. "I know—your dad told me, but he didn't think you remembered the surgery."

Kittie bit her lip. "I don't, and I don't know why he told you. He hates talking about it."

MARIAH HAD STRAIGHTENED the minute Caitlin mentioned her childhood surgery. She didn't know why the teen was bringing it up, but it must be important to her.

"We've had several discussions about the U-2's safety procedures," she said carefully. "He mentioned your operation in the middle of one of those talks." She was fudging the truth, yet she could hardly tell Caitlin about the intimate conversations she'd had with Jacob.

Caitlin had a disgusted expression. "I know, he doesn't want me to do anything."

"Some fathers are more protective than others." It was an understatement.

"Ha. He acts like I'm going to get broken. And he's been taking me to doctors ever since I started getting into trouble," Caitlin said resentfully. "They took tons of blood for tests. I think they're vampires."

Mariah tried not to smile. "He was probably trying to find out if there was a reason you were getting into trouble."

"No, it's because I…" Caitlin stopped and chewed her lip again.

"Yes?" Mariah prompted gently.

"I…I visited Nana Carolyn and Grandfather Barrett in September and found out they operated on my mom, too, only she died anyhow. And 'cause Dad won't talk about it, I…I can't stop thinking that…that something is still wrong with me," she burst out in a rush.

Suddenly everything made sense to Mariah. Caitlin had started imagining the worst, and her father's reluctance to talk about the past had magnified her fears. No doubt Jacob had thought he was protecting her; instead, he'd sent the opposite message.

"I doubt your dad would have brought you to Montana if he was concerned about your health," Mariah said. "I've seen how protective he is."

"I don't know. He was real pissed about the fire at Garrison and thought the U-2 could fix me. He doesn't get it," Caitlin muttered.

Mariah searched her mind for something to reassure her. The teenager was obviously strong and active, yet it would be easy to assume the worst in her shoes.

"Caitlin, a lot of kids have operations when they're little and are perfectly healthy afterward, but my grandmother can give you a medical check. Then I'll find your dad and tell him that you need to know more about the surgery. Grams can be there when he explains, and you can ask her anything that's bothering you."

Caitlin shifted nervously. "I don't know.... He got mad when I asked him about it before. Well, not *mad,* but he said it was done with and not to fuss. I could tell he was upset. You know my dad—he gets stiff and his voice is uptight when he isn't happy."

Mariah almost laughed.

Stiff and uptight? That was nothing—plainly she'd seen Jacob a *lot* more upset than Caitlin ever had. Anyway, after getting into so many arguments with Jacob, one more wasn't going to make a difference.

"And it's hard talking to him about my mom," Caitlin added. "It makes him sad. I don't like making him sad."

"I understand, but this is important. I'll make him listen to me," Mariah said. She'd make Jacob listen, all right, even if she had to whack him over the head with one of Reggie's iron skillets. "You can't keep worrying about your heart or worrying about upsetting him."

The teenager didn't seem thrilled with the plan, but she finally agreed. "Okay."

CHAPTER SIXTEEN

CAITLIN WAITED BY THE KITCHEN garden while Mariah went into the house to find her grandmother. Grams was kneading a batch of bread dough. She baked a lot more since giving up her primary role at the health clinic. They'd talked things over at breakfast, and she was going to begin handling the ranch accounting and other paperwork.

Mariah gave her a swift explanation of Caitlin's confession.

Grams looked distressed. "The poor child, worrying about something like that."

"Jacob must have thought he was protecting her."

"He should have realized Caitlin is too intelligent not to begin worrying since her mother was treated for the same condition."

The comment was gently critical and Mariah opened her mouth to defend Jacob but swallowed the words. It would be bad enough when he returned to Seattle; she didn't need her family knowing she'd foolishly fallen in love with the guy.

Grams put the dough in a bowl and covered it with a clean dish towel. "I'll do a general health check on Caitlin, though it won't guarantee there isn't an underlying problem. I'd need more equipment than we have in the dispensary to rule out anything for certain. She *appears* to be in excellent health, though."

"I know, and I can't see Jacob bringing his daughter to Montana or allowing her to get on a horse if she had a heart condition. He hasn't fussed about her being active, just doing anything that might carry a physical risk."

"I agree."

Mariah sighed. "Unfortunately, that kind of logic won't help Caitlin. He's the one who wouldn't talk about it, so he's the only one who can make her understand if there isn't anything wrong. Besides, I have a feeling something else is bothering Caitlin. Whether she'll tell Jacob or not is another matter."

"Perhaps. Adolescence is complicated." Grams washed her hands and took her keys from a pocket. "I'll open up and meet you at the dispensary. If you're not back before we're done, I'll send her to Reggie—he has plenty to keep her occupied."

Mariah went out to the garden.

"What did she say?" Caitlin asked anxiously.

"She thinks you look disgustingly healthy, but is always happy to play doctor."

A weak giggle escaped the teenager. "I like Dr. Weston, and your grandfather is awesome, too."

"Thanks. I'm pretty fond of them."

They arrived as Grams was putting on her white coat. "Hello, Caitlin. Come in while I warm up my stethoscope."

"I thought they were supposed to be cold."

Grams smiled. "Not in Montana."

Mariah went searching for Jacob. He'd offered to move bales of hay to the calf barn, so she checked first at the hay shelter. Nobody was there, though a load of hay had been recently hauled out.

At the barn Mariah found Jacob and Billy lifting the bales from the bed of the truck, their shirts straining tight over the muscles in their arms and shoulders. Jacob was working as hard as the other man, and in his jeans, hat and boots, he could be just another U-2 cowhand.

Yeah, right, she jeered to herself. *Just another cowhand.*

Jacob wasn't "just" anything.

Obscenely wealthy or not, women probably chased him right and left. He'd said he was amazed when his wife had fallen for an ex-jock working his way through college, but Mariah would be willing to bet that Anna had taken one look and known instantly she wanted to marry him.

The final bale was deposited on the stack and Billy thanked Jacob for the help. Billy had largely recovered from his romantic misadventures—his black eye had healed and Grams had taken out the stitches on his scalp. Since most cowboys wore their hats indoors and out, the lingering scar wasn't visible, though Mariah had heard he was still trying to earn Judy's forgiveness.

"What's up, Mariah?" Jacob asked after Billy drove away with the truck.

"I've been chatting with Caitlin."

"That doesn't sound good."

"It depends on your point of view." Mariah perched on the edge of one of the pens. She suspected they'd be talking for a while. Or yelling. "Caitlin is worried the operation on her heart wasn't successful."

"That's absurd."

"Absurd or not, it's what she believes. Apparently she tried to talk to you about it a few months ago and you brushed her off."

"I told her she didn't have to worry. There wasn't anything else to say," Jacob said, slapping dust and bits of hay from his jeans.

"She thinks there is, and because you weren't willing to talk about it, she's convinced you might be hiding something."

"I'm not hiding anything. I want her to have a normal, happy childhood and not have to think about the fact that she had heart surgery when she was two."

Mariah winced. This was the sort of thing she'd wanted to avoid when she'd told Jacob he'd have to deal with Caitlin's issues himself. But now she was too deeply involved with both father and daughter to be neutral.

"Jacob, she's growing up. Surely you can't call the past year normal and happy. Not from what you've told me anyway."

He set his mouth stubbornly.

"She's fourteen, not four," Mariah said, exasperated.

"Growing up is not the issue. We've already had this discussion. Though I see nothing wrong with letting her be a kid for a while longer."

"Except it isn't working. Honestly, her mother died of the same congenital heart defect. Did you really think she wouldn't start putting two and two together?"

"Anna was diagnosed too late to be helped—it was different with Kittie." His stiff face and squared shoulders gave Mariah a new appreciation for Caitlin's reluctance to bring up a painful subject with her father.

"Maybe, but when she visited her maternal grandparents last year, she learned the attempt to correct her mother's heart defect wasn't successful."

Jacob shook his head. "Anna never had surgery on her heart. She had some kind of lung infection when she was a teenager and they had to operate, but that's all. Her condition wasn't diagnosed until there was too much damage."

Mariah frowned. "I remember you said that. But Caitlin is under the impression they tried to treat her mother surgically."

"Just with medication. It was a stopgap while she was on the transplant waiting list. The Barretts must have said something that confused Kittie."

"You still need to talk to her, and you can't try to cut it short and tell her it's nothing. You said yourself that she's imaginative. The more she thinks you're ducking the subject, the more she's going to think something is seriously wrong."

JACOB DIDN'T LIKE what he was hearing, yet it made a crazy kind of sense. Kittie *had* begun acting up after a visit to her maternal grandparents. When her actions became too outrageous, he'd taken her to several doctors to find out if there was a medical reason for her behavior; she could have gotten the idea that it was related to her heart.

"You're right. Where is she?"

"Grams was going to do a quick check to reassure her—blood pressure, pulse, that kind of thing—then send her to work with Reggie. If you want, she can be present when you talk with Caitlin and answer any medical questions she might have."

Why not? Confidentiality had gone out the window the minute Kittie began terrorizing the civilized world.

"I want you to be there, as well," Jacob said slowly. He might not be sure of what he wanted from Mariah, but she had every right to be concerned about his daughter. How he'd come to that conclusion he didn't know, but it was true. "Right now Kittie trusts you more than she trusts me. I can't believe she's been brooding about this."

Mariah jumped down from her perch and put her hand on his arm. "For what it's worth, she didn't want to push talking about her mother because she knows you find it difficult. Strange as it sounds, she was trying to protect you, the way you were trying to protect her."

Jacob pulled her close. "Thank you," he whispered, eyes shut against the rush of emotions in his chest. The things Mariah made him feel scared him. He'd lost so much, and now he'd opened his heart to more potential pain.

Mariah had relaxed against him, only to stiffen and push away when they heard a couple of wranglers outside the barn.

"I'd like to speak with your grandmother first," he said huskily.

"Um...sure."

They found Elizabeth Weston at the dispensary doing an inventory on her supplies.

"How did Kittie seem?" Jacob asked.

"Healthy, but in a state of stress," Dr. Weston replied.

"She's genuinely convinced you may be concealing something about her condition."

"I'm not," he said flatly. "Her cardiologist declared the operation an unqualified success. If it would make things easier, you can consult with him before I talk to Kittie."

Dr. Weston agreed and he put a call through to Seattle, giving verbal permission for the specialist to speak with Dr. Weston. One part of his brain heard Elizabeth Weston's side of the dialogue, while another part questioned if he'd missed something in Kittie's behavior that might have explained why she was acting out. Could it *really* be about her heart? The dark clothing and gloomy music she'd been favoring seemed to fit the scenario.

"Thank you, Doctor, I'm sure Miss O'Donnell will be glad to hear it," Elizabeth Weston said at length. "I'll be in touch if anything else comes up." She disconnected and returned Jacob's cell phone to him. "Mariah, why don't you bring Caitlin up to the house? She deserves privacy to hear all of this. I'll walk up with Mr. O'Donnell."

After Mariah left with obvious reluctance, Dr. Weston fixed him with a stern gaze.

"Jacob, you're a good father," she said surprisingly.

"Uh…thanks." He was certain she planned to ask his intentions toward Mariah, and he didn't know what to say.

"So don't just talk to Caitlin—listen to her. Sometimes the thing we need most is to be heard."

He nodded and waited, but she simply patted his shoulder. "Now, let's go talk to your daughter."

KITTIE GULPED WHEN SHE SAW Dr. Weston and Mariah and her dad in the Westons' living room. Her dad looked solemn and anxious, the way she'd seen him look so often over the past year. It didn't make her feel angry anymore, just guilty.

"Hi," she said in a small voice.

"Hi. I understand you're worried your heart surgery didn't work."

"Um…yeah."

"Come here. You need to understand everything."

They sat on the big, comfortable couch and he put an arm around her.

"Kittie, your condition was diagnosed a few months after you were born, and it was corrected when you were two. It was a long operation, but the specialist was one hundred percent satisfied with the result. The reason I didn't talk about it was because I wanted you to have a carefree childhood."

"But all the doctors and…and everything you dragged me to…they tested me for a gazillion things, poking at me and taking blood."

Her dad sighed. "I was trying to find out if there was a physical cause for your change of behavior. I was concerned something else was wrong, not your heart. That never entered my mind or that you were worried about it—I should have realized."

She hugged her tummy. He sounded awfully sure. "But you won't let me do anything like other kids."

He kissed the top of her head. "Kittie, parents always worry about their kids, but after your mom died, you were all I had left and I wanted to keep you safe. I got carried away, trying to make sure nothing could happen to you—it wasn't because you weren't healthy. It was because I couldn't let go."

Kittie blinked hard. "Are you *sure?*"

"Positive, but if you want to hear it from someone else, Dr. Weston can tell you. She just talked to the cardiologist who did your surgery."

Dr. Weston smiled encouragingly. "It's true, Caitlin. Your heart is entirely normal for a girl your age. Dr. Sandoval receives copies of your medical records whenever you see another physician, and he says everything is fine. He did suggest your father needs to stop being paranoid."

Kittie smiled back, though her throat still felt tight. "I'm really okay?"

"Absolutely."

"What about my mom?"

"She had the same condition, but they didn't find it soon enough," Dr. Weston explained. "With the surgery you had as a toddler, you're perfectly healthy. Your mother wasn't that fortunate. There was too much damage by the time she was diagnosed. I suspect it was partly *because* she was sick that they knew what to look for after you were born."

Kittie scrubbed her face, but she couldn't stop crying. She was going to live? For years and years? It seemed forever that she'd been afraid and now it was okay.

"By the way, I have something for you," her dad said. He reached into his pocket and pulled out a piece of jewelry. "This belonged to your mother when she was a girl, and she wore it at our wedding. Your grandparents sent it, saying I'd know when I should give it to you. I think it should be now."

Kittie's eyes widened as he put the gold locket into her palm. It was pretty, decorated with scrolled flowers and leaves. She dropped her head on her dad's shoulder, the tears falling faster than ever.

It wasn't okay, after all.

She hadn't told him everything.

JACOB HELD HIS DAUGHTER as she sobbed. It hurt knowing that she'd been dealing with her fear in silence, but at least he was finally doing something to help.

Dr. Weston left discreetly and Mariah got up, as well. *Please stay,* he mouthed. Though she seemed uneasy, she sat back down in her chair.

"It's all right now," he assured his daughter, praying she believed him. "You don't have to cry. You're going to be fine. I'll try to give you more freedom and accept that you're growing up—I'll even try to call you Caitlin instead of Kittie if that's what you want."

Finally, sniffing, Kittie looked at him, her breath still coming in shuddering gasps.

"You will?"

"Yes. And I'm sorry I've spent so much time at my company. It's just I thought if I had enough money, it would keep you safe and take care of any problems that might come up. I know I was wrong now. Money isn't enough." His gaze met Mariah's—it was something she'd made him see.

"But you wanted to design airplanes," she said, her eyes filling with tears again.

Crap. What had he said now?

"Kittie, that's not important."

"It is. You went to college to do that. You wanted to work for Boeing or even NASA to design spaceships. You were going to be an astronaut."

"What?" Anna was the only person he'd ever told of his dream to be considered for the space program. "Where did you... Who told you that, Kittie?"

She chewed on her lip. "I...er...I found Mom's diary at Nana Carolyn and Grandfather Barrett's house. She thought it was grand that you wanted to go into space. She said *grand* a lot—it was like when I say awesome, though I don't think..." Her voice trailed off. "Uh, never mind."

The advice Elizabeth Weston had given Jacob rang in his ears...about listening. "I remember she called everything *grand,* but I didn't know she'd kept a diary."

Mariah got up again and determinedly slipped from the room, apparently deciding a father-daughter talk about Kittie's mother was too personal. He heard the door open and close in the rear of the house,and didn't know whether to be relieved or sorry.

Kittie chewed on the edge her fingernail and her breathing became ragged again. "Mom wrote in it a lot, even after you guys got married. And she…she felt real bad about some things she didn't tell you."

"Sweetie, it's all right," Jacob murmured. He couldn't imagine it being worth the stress it was putting Kittie through.

"No. I mean, Nana Carolyn wasn't Mom's biological mother—her first mother died really young from her heart, too. And Mom…well…she had an operation when she was a teenager," Kittie stuttered nervously. "So she knew her heart was bad when you guys met. The doctor said it was a matter of time unless she got a transplant, and she knew it probably wasn't going to happen."

Jacob stared at his daughter. "You must have misunderstood. Your mother didn't find out about her condition until after you were born—she would have told me."

Kittie swung her head frantically. "Uh-uh. She was afraid you wouldn't want her or want to have a baby if you knew. Nana Carolyn and Grandfather Barrett were unhappy when she got pregnant, but they didn't tell, either, because she begged them not to. So it's all our fault you didn't get to be an astronaut or do any of the stuff you wanted," she ended miserably. "Mom felt awful bad that she'd lied."

Jacob tried to keep his face from reflecting his shock. None of this was Kittie's fault. She wasn't responsible for something Anna had done. He'd sort out his feelings later, but right now his daughter needed to know she was loved and wanted without reservation.

"Listen," he said, brushing the wisps of blond hair away from his daughter's forehead. "I could never regret having you, or one minute with your mother."

"But you didn't get to do what you wanted."

"I got to have you as my daughter, and I would choose you over flying to the moon, or anything else."

"But you're so sad about Mom."

He let out a long breath. "You're right, I'm sad that she couldn't be with us and didn't get to see you grow up. I'm sad that you didn't get to know her. But having you is the best thing that ever happened to me. I just wish I hadn't wasted so much time working. Now you're practically grown up and are more interested in boys than spending time with your old dad."

A smile began to replace the tears on Kittie's face. "I still want to spend time with my dad."

"That's a relief. You wouldn't care to wait until you're at least forty to move away from home, would you?"

She giggled. "I could stay for a while, but not forty. That's, like, *old.* I can visit at Christmas and Easter, though."

"No summers?"

"I'm gonna be in Montana during the summer. You can visit me here."

"Ah, I see." Jacob wasn't sure where he was going to be during the summer, or the rest of the year, for that matter.

"Actually, I want to live here all year one day," Kittie added. "Even if Mariah says that sometimes it's cold and lonely in the winter after everybody goes home. Anyway, how can you get lonely when you have horses to keep you company?"

Jacob started to ask how she'd gotten into a chat with Mariah about living in Montana, then guessed it was likely because the McFees had left that morning. She'd known Kittie would be melancholy that her friend was going home.

"Maybe we could visit the McFees over Christmas," he suggested. "December is in the middle of summer down there."

"That would be dope," Kittie exclaimed. "Shayla wants to teach me to surf."

Dope?

Jacob's expression must have mirrored his confusion because his daughter laughed.

"*Dope* means *cool,* Dad. Not drugs or stuff when you say it that way. Don't you ever watch TV?"

"Not often."

"I can go surfing, can't I?" Kittie asked, and he knew it was a test of his promise to stop being so overprotective.

"Yeah, if you're careful," he said. He would have to insure lifeguards were on the beach and hire experienced surfers to teach her…not to mention getting King Kong–size tranquillizers for his nerves, but he couldn't refuse.

She threw her arms around his neck and gave him a smacking kiss. "*Awesome.* I didn't think you'd *ever* let me do that. I'm gonna go help Reggie with lunch. One of the guests who was supposed to help did a backflip off the corral fence and sprained her wrist." She rolled her eyes in a knowing way. "It was dumb—Gillian hasn't done gymnastics in forever."

She dashed out the door as if nothing had ever bothered her, and Jacob breathed a grateful prayer that children were more resilient than most people gave them credit for being. He realized that a single conversation wouldn't resolve everything, but they'd made a start.

Jacob glanced around the Westons' living room. He hadn't taken notice of it before, but now he felt the relaxed solidity of the place. It was big and richly colored and a sharp contrast to the modernized Seattle loft home he shared with Kittie. Country rock formed the fireplace and braided rag rugs were scattered attractively on the polished wood floors. A quilt was draped over a stand, and a huge gray tabby was curled up in a basket; it looked up and yawned as Jacob watched.

"Are you Squash?" he said, recalling Mariah's tale of the feline who'd been her companion since she was a teenager.

The cat yawned again and went back to sleep.

Jacob knew he ought to leave to preserve the Westons' privacy, but he dropped his head on the cushions and thought of the things that Kittie had revealed about her mother.

Why, Anna? Why didn't you tell me?

He still would have loved her if he'd known; she'd captivated him from the beginning. But all these years he'd wondered how things would have turned out if they'd started their family later. Would they have learned about her condition in time to do something about it before pregnancy had strained her heart? It appeared the answer was no, and he didn't have any reason to feel responsible.

Could Kittie have sensed the guilt he'd felt and blamed herself because of it? The one thing he was certain of was how much he loved his daughter. Maybe that was one of the reasons he'd felt guilty…because no matter what, he couldn't be sorry that she'd been born.

He would have to talk to Kittie about her mother, tell her how excited Anna was when she'd given birth…share the things he should have been sharing all along.

With a groan, Jacob got up and walked out of the ranch house. He wanted to be angry with Anna for her deception, yet a thought kept going through his mind—his wife had been more courageous than he'd ever been. She'd faced her options and decided to make their marriage the happiest it could be. While he hadn't been willing to get married again or have more children, because he didn't want to chance losing someone else he loved.

But Mariah was right—he couldn't really live unless he took chances. His daughter was choking in the protective bubble he'd created for her, and his own heart couldn't survive shrouded in painful memories. He should have honored the love he'd shared with Anna, instead of hiding from it.

CHAPTER SEVENTEEN

MARIAH SADDLED SHADOW and rode toward the swimming hole. It wasn't the best place to go under the circumstances—there were too many immediate reminders of Jacob—yet it was quiet and she needed to be alone.

Now that the root of Kittie's problems had been uncovered, Jacob would leave. He'd probably set a speed record getting off the U-2.

Tethering Shadow where he could graze under a shady tree, Mariah sat by the water and blinked back the tears—tears that wouldn't help her or anyone else.

Being in love with a man like Jacob was even harder than she'd thought it would be, yet the depth of her feelings were more proof that she hadn't cared for Luke the way he'd deserved. In the end she had never let herself depend on him, despite Luke being one of the most trustworthy men she'd ever met. It must have been difficult for such a strong man to be sidelined in his fiancée's life.

That was one good thing coming from Jacob's stay at the U-2—she'd let Luke go. She just hoped he would find someone who would love him the way he deserved.

Sometime later, the sound of footsteps made Mariah look up. She gritted her teeth when she saw it was Jacob.

"Yes?"

He seemed taken aback at her sharp tone, but she couldn't afford to invest herself in anything else having to do with the O'Donnells.

Jacob sat next to her. "Does the creek have a name?" he asked after a moment, gesturing to the water.

"Not really. It starts higher up and is fed by even smaller streams." She tossed a bit of grass into the water and watched it drift with the current. As a girl she'd dropped grass or leaves into the water, hoping they might reach the Gulf of Mexico. "If you hiked its length, you'd see it flowing into a larger stream, and so on, until it joins the Yellowstone River."

"Which empties into the Missouri River and beyond?"

"Yup."

"Doesn't it make you feel insignificant, being at the beginning of such a vast system? Not even the beginning, just one of the beginnings."

Mariah shook her head. "A teacher once said that if a drop of rain fell on this side of the Continental Divide, it would eventually make its way to the Atlantic Ocean, but if it fell on the other side, it would go to the Pacific. It seemed magical that the creek water I was swimming in would get to the ocean one day, and maybe even return here when it rained or snowed and I'd swim in it again. That's more significant than someone standing on the banks of the Mississippi in New Orleans, seeing it roll past without a clue of where it came from."

Jacob leaned back on one elbow. "I remember being taught about continental watersheds, but I saw it another way."

"Such as building dams and aqueducts?"

He gave her a chastising look. "I wasn't interested in civil engineering—that's a different field of study than aeronautics. No, when I was a boy, I imagined the water in my glass could have traveled anywhere over the centuries. A molecule of it could have been in a puddle that Benjamin Franklin stepped in, or touched a blue whale, or rained on a shogun in Japan."

"It *could* have been to those places."

"And a few trillion more. I suppose it did seem magical, imagining all the possibilities."

Mariah swallowed a sigh. He'd once sensed some of the mystery she felt in nature, only to lose it over the years.

"Perhaps having an imagination isn't such a bad thing," Jacob added reflectively.

She wiggled her toes inside her boots. Not fancy or decorative, they were practical, the way her hat was practical. Jacob was probably accustomed to women who dressed in designer clothes and wore perfume that cost a thousand bucks an ounce.

Stop, Mariah ordered. She wasn't going to apologize for being a working rancher and dressing as one most of the time.

"Mariah, we need to talk."

"Isn't that what we're doing?" she asked flippantly.

She'd had all the talk she could stand in one day. She hurt for both Caitlin and Jacob, but it wouldn't change a thing.

"You know what I mean."

"I know you must be wondering how soon you can get out of here," she said. "I thought you'd be packing, though I suppose you'd have to stay another night before getting a flight from Billings. You could also check what's available from Bozeman. It's a longer drive, but it could be an option. I'm really not familiar with the commercial schedules and what connections you have to make to get to Seattle."

JACOB'S EYEBROWS SHOT UP. He wanted to kiss Mariah, but she had a hands-off expression he would have been able to read a mile away.

"I hadn't given any thought to flights. We arrived in a company jet. It's based in Seattle and can return whenever needed."

"Oh. That makes sense. Caitlin may give you an argument, but you could promise to take her horseback riding in Seattle."

"Mariah, quit talking about me leaving," he said flatly, though it was his own fault that she was expecting him to vanish now that he'd found some answers with Kittie. She was the reason he'd come in the first place, and his initial contempt for Montana and country living couldn't have helped.

"Then what?"

"I need to thank you for being there and listening when my daughter needed you. I truly didn't know how Kittie... *Caitlin* felt," he corrected himself. "Remind me if I slip and say Kittie instead. It won't be easy remembering."

"I'm sure she'll appreciate it." Mariah's face was still remote. "But I'm also sure you're anxious to get home. Think of it, no more communal showers, no more sleeping outside and no more meals in a mess tent. Home must sound like heaven to you."

Home?

Memories of sterile corporate conference rooms and dull contract negotiations flashed through Jacob's head. The loft he'd converted was spacious and modern, with the popular "industrial" details the architect had raved about, yet it was cold compared to the Weston home. And what about the noise and bustle of the city? A month ago he would have said it was energizing being around so many people; now the inevitable impersonal element of living among hundreds of thousands of strangers seemed a drawback.

Then there were the recent memories—his daughter laughing as she held a bottle of milk to feed an orphan calf and flirting shyly at a square dance, the sweet scent of hay and the more pungent smell of cow manure, the gurgle of creek water...and Mariah, her auburn hair blowing in the wind. She was a temperamental redhead...and vibrant and real and loving. For the first time in more than ten years, he felt alive; he wouldn't give that up for a million cities.

"I love you," he said simply. "Being with you is what sounds like heaven."

Mariah stiffened visibly. "Don't say that. You're caught up in the emotion of what happened. You'll regret—"

"*Don't* say I'll regret it in the morning," he interrupted.

"You will. And it's sexual energy anyway. I'll bet you've been so worried about Caitlin's problems you haven't been with a woman for ages."

He clenched his jaw. "I'm thirty-seven, Mariah, not a boy with hormones raging out of control. I know the difference between real emotion and physical impulses. I think what we have together is worth a shot. Can't you consider giving it a try? Maybe we could have a real future together."

Mariah paled. "Jacob, we're so incompatible. I don't have to tell you that Seattle is a world away from the ranch. We just don't speak the same language."

"I'm not saying it would be a cakewalk. But we're not *that* incompatible—we have things we agree on. Hell, Anna and I had *nothing* in common except being in love."

"You were younger then and less set in your ways." Mariah rubbed her arms as if chilled and Jacob wanted to pull her close. Yet he still didn't know how she felt; he might be making wild assumptions. And even if she was in love with him, it was no guarantee they could sort things out.

He stroked the curve of her jaw and saw her eyes darken and breathing quicken at his touch. Once it would have made him triumphant to know she was so responsive to him; now he only prayed she could believe in the impossible.

"I may be set in my ways, but I've lost too much not to recognize something precious."

She dug her fingers into the grass. "This is a pretty big change. You spent a lot of years devoted to Anna's memory."

"I know. But finding out from Kit...*Caitlin* that Anna knew she was sick before we got married has sort of freed me. Maybe I was stupid not to guess the truth, but for years I blamed myself for Anna's death...thinking maybe if we'd waited to have a baby, she would have been okay."

Jacob stretched, trying to reclaim the peace he'd discovered on the ranch.

"To be honest," he continued, "I was searching for anything to stop feeling responsible. All this time I've thought Anna might be alive if we'd waited, and yet I couldn't be sorry I had Kittie."

Mariah squeezed his hand. "It wouldn't have been your fault, either way."

"I've known that logically, but feelings aren't logical. Now I know there wasn't anything I could have done. I was angry about Anna's deception for a couple of minutes, but then I realized how brave she was—she knew we probably wouldn't have long together and wanted to get everything out of every moment. I'm not saying what she did was right, but I understand her motivations. Especially now, after being here."

MARIAH CLASPED AN ARM over her stomach.

She'd noticed that Jacob wasn't wearing his wedding ring and had struggled not to get her hopes up. Now he wanted them to consider a real relationship and she was still struggling—it wasn't that easy.

"Mariah, please love me," he implored. "I don't want to miss out on what we could have. I want to get everything out of every moment, too."

Jacob's sincerity was inescapable and a tear rolled down her cheek. "I…I do love you, but that…" The rest of her reply was smothered in a kiss.

An endless minute later, she drew back; they were both breathing hard.

"It's decided," he said with a hint of his old arrogance.

She glared, exasperated. "*Nothing* is decided. For one thing, our families don't know we're involved, and it's important that Caitlin doesn't get blindsided right now. Return to Washington and see how you feel once you get there, before we even *begin* to think where this might go."

"Mariah—"

"You may not admit it, but you know I'm right," she said, cutting him off and getting to her feet. "Go home for a while and then we can talk."

"I don't need to go anywhere to know what I want."

She gave him a level look. "Maybe. But *I* need you to."

MARIAH RODE TO THE RANCH by herself, wishing her heart didn't hurt so badly. Jacob might leave and never return… but what would she do if he *did* come back, wanting to give their relationship a chance? How could it work? She thought of her parents, perfectly matched to each other, both from Montana ranching families. They'd understood each other so well they could communicate with a single look and know what the other was thinking.

But that kind of love had its price—her father hadn't been able to face a future alone when her mother died. It was frightening to give that much of herself to another person, yet would anything less be enough?

She reached the barn and dismounted, leading Shadow to his stall. By habit she took off his saddle and began grooming him, the ritual as much a part of her as anything on the ranch. One of her earliest memories was her father standing her on a stool and showing her how to run the curry brush along the flanks of his Appaloosa.

Jacob had suggested they might have a future together. Was he thinking a long-distance arrangement—weekends and holidays and visits to and from? It was remotely possible when he had access to a jet, and he knew how she felt about the ranch; even if her family didn't need her, she was part of the land.

Mariah rested her forehead on Shadow's gleaming neck, thinking of her avowed determination not to get involved with a guest. A faint, rueful smile tugged at her mouth. Not only had she gotten involved with a guest, she'd fallen in love with a wealthy, city-loving tycoon who had business interests everywhere in the world *except* Montana.

When she screwed up, she did it big-time.

JACOB WALKED SLOWLY back to the ranch. Mariah had offered to let him ride Shadow, but he knew the stallion would resent carrying anyone but his favorite human being. Besides, he needed to formulate a plan.

Stubborn redhead.

Saying *I love you* might have been enough for most women, but not Mariah. On the other hand, she'd made a good point; he had to be careful after what Kittie had been through the past year. Of course, his daughter seemed ready to move to the ranch, lock, stock and barrel, so she'd probably approve of anything that could make it happen.

He went into the mess tent and found Kittie sitting with Burt, chattering as she gobbled an enormous piece of cake between gulps of milk.

"Hi, Dad," she greeted him happily. "You missed lunch, but I had Reggie save you a plate. Eat, and then we're going out to move a herd."

Food was the last thing on his mind, but he smiled. "Thanks."

Apparently Kittie and Burt had a busy afternoon planned.

It wasn't until evening that they had some private time, and when Kittie learned he was contemplating a permanent move to Montana, she threw her arms around his neck.

"Omigod, thank you, thank you, *thank you.* I've wished and wished we could live here."

"Yes, but do you understand what it means?"

His daughter rolled her eyes. "Duh. I'm not a baby. I know about sex and stuff."

Heat rose under Jacob's collar. "It's not just… I'm not… I mean, we'd get married. And if we do, Mariah will be your, uh…"

"Mother?" Kittie finished for him matter-of-factly. "Would I get to call her Mom?"

Jacob hadn't thought that far ahead, which made him understand why Mariah might have felt he was rushing things. But he was sure that he loved her and didn't want to waste any more time. He'd lost too much already.

"That would be up to the two of you," he said. "I haven't proposed yet, I just wanted to tell you so it wouldn't be a surprise. Anyway, Mariah might not want to marry me."

Kittie made a face. "Yeah, I know. You piss her off a lot, but I'm pretty sure she thinks you're hot, too. Someday I hope I have boobs like hers."

He winced. Keeping his promise to let Kittie grow up was going to be brutal. Mariah had better marry him and help, or he'd never survive.

"Okay," he said. "Let me explain my plan."

THE NEXT MORNING Mariah discovered the ancient fax machine in the office wasn't printing properly. It had always been a cranky piece of equipment, and after an hour tinkering with the blasted thing, she decided to make a run into Billings to an office supply store.

You're making excuses, her conscience argued. *You just don't want to see Jacob.*

True enough.

The fax printouts were readable...barely, and the machine would likely start working again out of sheer contrariness the minute she left for Billings. But excuse or not, she *was* tired of relying on a piece of equipment that seemed to have a mind of its own.

The trip took longer than expected because Reggie had given her a list at the last minute, figuring if she was going anyway, he might as well get the things he needed rather than waiting for the regular supply run.

On the return drive, Mariah forced herself to think about

Jacob. She still couldn't see how it could work if they got together, but was she simply afraid to love the way her parents had loved…afraid to be hurt? It was possible.

Instead of going directly to the U-2, she headed for Buckeye. Grams was tending the Buckeye Medical clinic for a few days while Aunt Lettie recovered from a sprained ankle. Maybe she was available for a chat.

"Hi, Nan. Is my grandmother available?" Mariah asked when she walked into the clinic.

The nurse nodded. "She's in her office. Go on in."

Grams looked concerned when she saw Mariah. "I thought you would have gotten home hours ago. Is something wrong?"

"No, I just need to talk."

They stepped into the courtyard at the side of the clinic and Mariah saw the garden her aunt had created in the small space. It was lovely, with plants tucked into every corner, trailing over a high brick wall, and fragrant with herbs and flowers. It resembled something that should surround a Victorian cottage.

"What is it, dear?" Grams gently prompted.

Mariah paced across the flagstones. "Jacob O'Donnell and I…we've sort of gotten involved."

Her grandmother sighed. "I suspected something was going on."

"Jacob isn't why I broke up with Luke," Mariah quickly assured her. "We happened afterward. And it's so stupid anyway. Nothing could ever work out between us—we're too different." Yet even as she said the words, she didn't know if she believed them or wanted to be convinced otherwise.

"True. You're a woman and he's a man. Fortunately the parts fit together well."

"Grams, this isn't funny," Mariah said darkly.

Elizabeth smiled, despite her granddaughter's ill humor. "I wasn't trying to be funny…not really. Men and women *are* different, and I don't mean simple biology. We think differently."

"Jacob and I are poles apart in *every* way. He's silk dress shirts and luxury cars, I'm jeans and horses. It wasn't that way for Mom and Dad—they were both from ranching families and had amazing communication. That's the kind of marriage I've always wanted, and now I'm in love with a guy who thinks the U-2 is primitive. What would Mom and Dad think?" As the question left her mouth, Mariah stirred restlessly, realizing she felt some of Reid's reluctance to mention her parents to the rest of family. It would be so much easier now if they hadn't guarded their tongues and dealt with the loss in silence.

Her grandmother lifted an eyebrow. "Your parents would have loved Jacob because you love him. As for the rest...have you forgotten that *I* didn't grow up on a ranch? Your grandfather and I were from different worlds when we fell in love."

The reminder brought Mariah up short. "I hadn't thought of it that way."

"You should. We had our rough patches, but we've had a wonderful marriage. Has Jacob proposed?"

Mariah recalled the discussion at the creek. "No. He said something about the possibility of having a future together, but that could mean anything. I told him to go to Seattle and see how he feels once he's there for a while, but maybe I should talk to him more before he goes."

Grams leaned over and picked a sprig of spearmint without looking at her. "He's not at the ranch. It seems he took your advice. Jacob flew to Washington this morning—drove to the airport not long after you left."

The rolling sensation in Mariah's stomach made her grab one of the patio chairs to steady herself.

"He...did?"

"Yes, he mentioned an urgent situation with his company

and said he would return soon. Caitlin loves it here so much I suggested he let her stay with us, but he took her with him."

Damn it, Jacob, Mariah cursed silently.

At least if he'd allowed Caitlin to remain in Montana, she could be self-righteously upset that he let someone else care for his child, but he had done the responsible thing and taken her home. Which was probably best since Mariah doubted she'd ever see him again.

She swallowed shakily. "I guess that's that—it's up to him now. I'd better go. I've got a new fax machine to unpack and a dozen other things to do."

Mariah left despite Grams urging her to stay. She needed to digest the fact that she might never see Jacob or Caitlin again.

THE NEXT TWO DAYS went by with excruciating slowness, and Mariah had plenty of time to think. It wasn't only Jacob she missed—it was Caitlin, too, with her changeable teenage moods and funny ways. Blue moped in the corral, missing Caitlin as well, and Mariah held off assigning him to a new visitor. She had a wrangler exercise him, along with Jacob's horse, and their tent remained unoccupied.

What kind of life was it without Jacob and Caitlin? Was a *place* more important than what she could have with them? They had become her family as much as Reid and her grandparents and Aunt Lettie.

Yet a future with Jacob meant no children of her own. She would have to accept that. It was incredible enough that he was considering a relationship in view of the pain he'd suffered in the past. It would be hard for her, but wasn't Jacob worth the sacrifice? And Caitlin was a terrific kid who already seemed like a daughter.

On the third morning after Jacob's departure, she glanced at her family around the breakfast table and summoned her resolve. "I'm in love with Jacob O'Donnell," she announced.

"Grams knows, but I thought the rest of you should, too. Mostly because, however unlikely, he might come back."

Reid stared with an appalled expression. "He's a guest, sis. You're the one who told me never to hook up with a guest."

"Yeah, well, it wasn't the brightest thing I've ever done. If we don't see Jacob again, you can gloat for a month. That's when the statute of limitations runs out and you get stuffed in a gopher hole. Besides, you've grown quite fond of Caitlin yourself and have been in a sour mood since she left, so I wouldn't gloat too much."

Reid's ears turned red and he shut up.

"What will you do if Jacob returns?" Granddad asked quietly. He didn't seem surprised, and she guessed Grams had told him.

"Most likely faint in shock," Mariah replied drily.

"After that?"

"I'm not sure.... Discuss ways to make a relationship work. The thing is, those ways would impact the whole family. Jacob hasn't proposed and I don't know if he will, but I wanted you to know and start thinking what it might mean."

"You don't have to stay for me, sis," Reid said.

"We'll manage," Grams and Granddad claimed in unison.

"You would have moved if you'd married Luke," Reid added.

"Next door, not to Seattle," Mariah muttered.

She stirred her bowl of oatmeal and wondered how they'd really feel if she ended up in Washington State for part of the year. The thought of being away from the ranch made her sick...but so did living without Jacob and Caitlin—two days without them and she was miserable.

"Actually, I have an announcement of my own," Granddad said. "Jacob phoned last night."

Mariah tensed. "He didn't want to speak to me?"

"It was late and we just had a brief conversation—he was on his way to a conference call with Japan or something. He and Caitlin are flying in today and he wants to meet with all of us—I suggested four o'clock, here at the house."

Her head reeled, both with the news that Jacob was returning and the fact that he was working at night again. Did he think those ridiculous hours were all right now that he'd learned Caitlin's problems were rooted in worries over her health?

She pressed her lips together. When Jacob showed up, they were going to have a discussion before they did anything else.

CHAPTER EIGHTEEN

MARIAH STAYED NEAR the barns all day, keeping an eye on the guest parking lot. An SUV finally showed up, but it wasn't the Mercedes or other luxury sedan she'd expected Jacob to rent.

Then the door opened and Caitlin jumped out.

"Mariah," she shrieked, racing forward to give her a hug. "I *missed* you. Do you see our new car? Dad bought it and had it waiting for us in Billings. You didn't let anyone have Blue, did you?"

"No, he's in the corral."

Caitlin was already dashing off in search of her horse, and Mariah focused on Jacob. Unlike the first day he'd come to the U-2, he was wearing jeans and cowboy boots and looked so good it turned her inside out.

"*I* missed you, too," he murmured in a low voice.

He swept her close and kissed her as if he'd been gone for a year. Though she was annoyed, the tension in her body eased as passion replaced more confused emotions.

Jacob lifted his head and smiled lazily. "Now, explain that pissed-off face you greeted me with."

"Granddad said you had a conference call last night with Japan. I thought you were going to stop working so much and spend more time with Caitlin."

"Ah." He kissed her again. "It was a special circumstance. You see, I was telling my overseas divisions that they would have to learn to be more independent because I was moving to Montana…where my future wife lives."

Mariah's head reeled. "You aren't serious."

JACOB BRUSHED A STRAND of hair from Mariah's forehead. He didn't blame her for having trouble believing him.

"Completely serious. Mariah, I know you've grown up seeing ranch visitors want to change their lives based on a wonderful few days, then go home and realize it was just a nice dream. But I'm sure some of them *did* follow through. I knew the only way to convince you I'm serious was to put things in motion, so I went to Seattle and began making the arrangements needed to move here."

All at once Mariah's jaw dropped. "Wait a minute. Did you just propose? I mean, that part about your wife, it almost sounded like a proposal."

He threw back his head and laughed. "Caught that, did you? Yes, I'm proposing. I got to Seattle, and it was cold and gray and colorless without you. I couldn't wait to get out of there."

"I thought you'd expect me to move there."

"Good Lord, that's the *last* thing I would ask. You can't leave Montana. You have the other ranchers to consider—they count on the U-2. What I have in mind is running my company from Montana with occasional trips to Seattle."

"But you said you couldn't wait to get to the city as a kid," Mariah argued.

Jacob sighed philosophically. He'd known it would be tough persuading her. "That's true, but maybe if you'd lived in my hometown when I was growing up, I wouldn't have been so determined to get out. Anyhow, I think a slower pace is the right way to start a marriage, don't you? I even asked your grandfather's permission. Do you know what he told me?"

"That a woman doesn't belong to anyone and to ask me yourself," Mariah answered promptly.

He grinned. "How did you know?"

"It's a philosophy he learned from his father. My great-grandfather used to say a woman wasn't a piece of property to be given away. He was quite adamant on the subject."

"You know, I like the Westons more every day."

The comment obviously pleased Mariah, but her expression grew more solemn. "Jacob, a slower pace is one thing, but it can't be entirely my way."

"You're right, it will take compromises from everyone. That's why I want to meet with your family. For one thing, there'll have to be changes at the ranch. Reid and your grandparents won't like it—hell, *you'll* hate it."

"You're still not a rancher," she said.

He kissed the corner of her mouth. "I could be, with your help. What a great new challenge…becoming a rancher and learning how to be a good neighbor. I thrive on challenges. I'll limit the time I spend on my company, giving my top management more authority to act independently, but you'll have to share the ranch and not keep everything to yourself."

Jacob couldn't tell what Mariah was thinking, and it hadn't escaped his notice that she hadn't actually said she'd marry him. He was pretty sure she would, but wanted to hear it for himself

He glanced at his watch and saw it was nearly four o'clock. "Let's find Caitlin and go up to the house. I'm sure everyone is going to have a lot of questions."

JACOB BEGAN THE "MEETING" with the Westons by declaring that he'd proposed to Mariah—though she hadn't given him an answer yet—and that he hoped to move to Montana and run his business long-distance.

"For that to work out, changes would be needed at the U-2. I'm not talking about turning the ranch into a technology zone, but to start, I'd need to build an airfield and put in a better communication system. This is a family ranch, so you would all have to be willing. As an alternative, I could build a home for us that isn't on the U-2, but if Mariah agrees to marry me, I know she'd prefer living here. At least for a while."

Mariah's grandparents, brother and her aunt Lettie watched him in silence. They were nice people, but he was on trial and he couldn't fault them for being cautious.

"So would you like Caitlin and me to step out while you discuss this?"

"You can stay. We've run cattle on this land for over a century, but it isn't a historic site. It's a ranch," Benjamin Weston said. "We've always made changes to meet new needs, and we'll continue to do so."

The others nodded slowly.

"You wouldn't want to tear down the house or anything and put up a new one, would you?" It was Reid who'd posed the question, though everyone in the room was probably wondering the same. Including Caitlin. His daughter loved the old ranch house and was dearly hoping it would become her home.

"No, I'd try to make any changes as unobtrusive as possible. Someday Mariah and I might want a place of our own, but we can cross that bridge when we get to it. I've purchased several pieces of property adjacent to the U-2 and will keep acquiring more, so we'll have options."

Mariah leaned forward. "You've bought land? You just pointed out that I haven't said yes, Jacob."

"Yeah, but Caitlin and I are moving to Montana whether you say yes or not. Though I'm not giving up until you're my wife, however long it takes."

Her lips twitched. "I see."

"I don't have any objections." Lettie Weston spoke up. Mariah's aunt was a beautiful woman, with her mother's eyes and sun-streaked, reddish brown hair.

"Neither do I," said Elizabeth.

"Same here." Benjamin looked at his grandson. "Reid, what do you think?"

"We do whatever we have to do. I don't want Mariah to leave the ranch."

"Then we've made up our minds," Elizabeth said firmly. "Now go on and convince my granddaughter to marry you, Jacob. Caitlin is a wonderful girl, but she needs brothers and sisters to boss around."

"Grams," Mariah said warningly, "don't push about great-grandchildren. Jacob doesn't…uh…want—"

"I'll do my best, Dr. Weston," Jacob interrupted. "Mariah, let's find a private place to talk."

"I'M SORRY," MARIAH SAID as they walked toward the swimming hole by silent accord.

"Sorry?"

"For Grams and the grandchildren routine."

Jacob shrugged, seeming unconcerned. "It's natural. I take it your aunt didn't marry and have kids herself?"

"Aunt Lettie met someone when she was in medical school. They fell in love, but he wasn't interested in a career in Montana. She chose Buckeye. That's all I know, though there was probably more to the story."

The late-afternoon sun was warm and Mariah welcomed the cool shade in the bend of the creek.

"Let's get down to business. How much convincing do you need?" Jacob slid an arm around her waist. "I meant everything I said. We can even discuss babies…who I'm hoping will skip their teenage years."

"You don't have to say that."

"Even if I mean it?" He tugged a strand of her hair. "Come on, marry me. I love you so much…need you so much."

Mariah made an exasperated sound. "You know perfectly well that I'm going to marry you. I'm absurdly crazy about you and Caitlin, and I decided yesterday that—"

Her words were smothered in a kiss spiced with both laughter and passion.

"Thank God," Jacob gasped when he came up for air. "I was prepared to wait forever, but I'd rather not. By the way, I don't believe in long engagements. How does a September wedding sound?"

"I can manage that." Mariah focused on the top button of his shirt, a deep certainty filling her. They'd both suffered terrible losses, but that meant they knew what was important, such as finding a way to be together. "Are you absolutely sure that living in Montana is what you want?"

"More sure than anything else in my life," Jacob said, his voice rough with emotion. "I was desperate when I came to the U-2, hoping for a miracle with Caitlin…not realizing I was the one who needed the miracle. I'm a lucky man."

"Wrong." She flicked the button open, then the next. "We're both lucky."

He opened a button himself. "I suppose we're going to disagree on how much independence Caitlin should get on the ranch."

"I suppose we are."

Jacob ran his fingers down her leg and pulled off her boots. "And we'll fight about you taking too many risks."

"Undoubtedly."

"But I'm not going to win on that issue very often, am I?"

Mariah laughed. "I wouldn't count on it."

"Well, at least it won't be boring."

Three months later

MARIAH SMOOTHED THE FLARED SKIRT of her white satin gown, her pulse racing. In a few minutes she would be marrying Jacob in front of dozens of neighbors and wranglers and his friends and family from Washington.

"You look *awesome,*" Caitlin said, excitedly hopping from one foot to the other.

"Indeed," Grams agreed, gazing fondly at the teenager. She and Granddad had taken Caitlin into their hearts, an instant great-granddaughter they could delight in spoiling.

Big changes had taken place at the U-2, though Jacob had made every effort to keep everything low-key and hidden from view. An airfield large enough for the O'Donnell International company jets had been constructed a half mile away, and a building at the end of the field housed the majority of the satellite equipment needed to run his high-tech office. Granddad had surprised Jacob with his knowledge of communications and they'd had long discussions on how technology had advanced in the past fifty years. Of course, Jacob was frequently surprised these days, discovering that life in Montana didn't have to mean your head was in a hole.

Mariah couldn't comprehend the money he'd poured into the airfield alone—he was a man who committed to a course of action without a backward glance. There was also a new asphalt road into the ranch, and Grams's U-2 medical clinic was considerably expanded, along with Aunt Lettie's clinic in Buckeye. Mariah had tried to be patient, understanding Jacob's instinctive need to protect his family and knowing the community would benefit.

The U-2 would never be the same and it *was* difficult dealing with the changes. The next years were going to be an adjustment in more ways than one.

The most exhilarating difference was the small buffalo herd making a home on some of the land that Jacob had purchased bordering the U-2, higher in the hills. Mariah wasn't sure they were ready to bring buffalo in, but she hadn't objected since it was something he wanted so much. Jacob had hired wildlife experts to advise them and had acted like a kid in a candy store when the massive animals came off the trucks, snorting and stamping. They were fenced separately from the other livestock and would always have a safe haven from two-legged hunters.

Jacob was trying to buy even more adjoining rangeland, and she was convinced he had visions of reestablishing the great bison herds, thundering across the plains.

Mariah sat in front of the bureau and looked at herself in the mirror. She'd chosen a simple, mid-calf-length wedding dress, and around her neck she wore the delicate gold cross that Catherine Heider Weston had worn when she got married, and each of the Weston brides since. She touched the cross and prayed that the happiness that Catherine and Timothy had known would be theirs, as well.

Grams fixed a long lace veil to her hair and arranged it down her back.

"Luke came," she murmured. "He said he couldn't miss seeing his best friend get married."

A shaft of sorrow went through Mariah, but she pushed it away. It wasn't a day for sorrow and regrets; it was a day for the future and remembering absent family with love.

"Uh…when can I start calling you Mom?" Caitlin asked. She was fidgeting with her flower bouquet. She'd spent the summer with them in Montana, though her father had traveled back and forth, making arrangements.

"Whenever you want." Mariah got up and hugged her. It was the first time Caitlin had suggested calling her Mom.

"Awesome…*Mom.*" Caitlin grinned.

Her hair was longer now, curling around her face with a charming pixie quality. She wore a pretty sky-blue dress that accentuated her healthy color, and if it clashed somewhat with her black fingernail polish, nobody cared. Quite solemnly she had explained to Mariah that it was okay to fit in, but she liked the idea of being the only cowgirl in Buckeye with black fingernails. Occasionally she also donned her spiked leather collar, just to mix things up.

"It's time," Granddad said with a knock on the door.

While the Westons didn't believe a woman should be "given away" in the marriage ceremony like a piece of property, they held to the tradition of the bride being walked down the aisle. Granddad would walk with her today, but she knew that both her parents would be there in spirit.

Grams and Caitlin left and Mariah took Granddad's arm.

He put a hand over hers. "Scared?"

"Terrified."

"Yup, so was I. Keeps you on your toes."

The Big Barn was banked with flowers and filled with friends and family. Mariah's nerves settled as she saw the people inside. The Sallengers had come. They'd found a tiny ranch outside of Buckeye and were hosting Chad and Susan and some of the other longtime U-2 guests who'd wanted to attend the wedding. Luke was smiling, and if there was a hint of sadness in his eyes, he hid it well.

Jacob's younger brother and sister were sitting in the front, along with his parents, an easygoing couple who'd accepted their son's move to Montana with bemusement. As for Caitlin's other grandparents, they'd flown in, too. Mariah had met the Barretts earlier in the summer and they'd said they were happy that Jacob was getting remarried.

"You're going to be Kittie's mother. That makes you important to us," Richard Barrett had muttered gruffly, kissing her cheek before getting on the plane in Billings after their first visit. "You're…uh…our family now."

They weren't the most comfortable people, but they were sincere and well-meaning.

Caitlin marched ahead of Mariah down the temporary aisle, and Reid stood with Jacob as his best man. An assortment of chairs had been borrowed from all over Buckeye to accommodate the large number of wedding guests, but Mariah didn't see the mismatches; she only saw Jacob, waiting for her.

Another wedding to add to the barn's memories, she thought,

walking toward him. Another celebration to bridge the past and future.

She and Jacob would always fight, and they'd never see eye to eye on a lot of things…but they would love each other forever.

* * * * *

COMING NEXT MONTH FROM

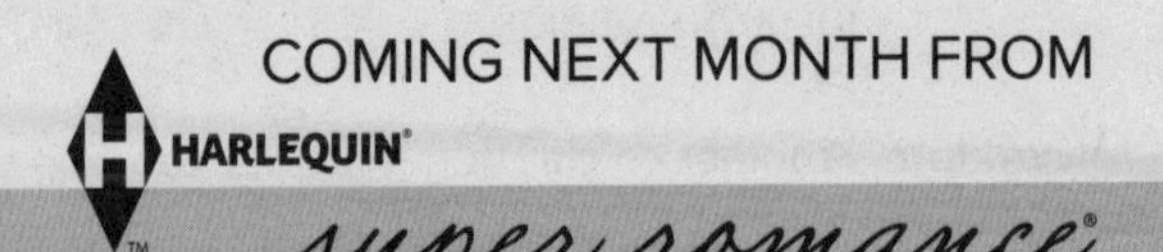

Available August 6, 2013

#1866 WHAT HAPPENS BETWEEN FRIENDS

In Shady Grove • by Beth Andrews

James Montesano has always been Sadie Nixon's soft place to land. Isn't that what friends are for? But something has changed. Instead of helping her pick up the pieces of her life, James is complicating things by confessing his feelings...for her! Suddenly she sees him in a whole *new* way.

#1867 FROM THIS DAY ON

by Janice Kay Johnson

The opening of a college time capsule is supposed to be fun. But for Amy Nilsson, the contents upend her world. In the midst of that chaos, Amy finds comfort in the most unexpected place—Jakob. Once the kid who tormented her, now he's the only one she can trust!

#1868 STAYING AT JOE'S

by Kathy Altman

Joe Gallahan ruined Allison Kincaid's career—and she broke his heart. Now reconnecting a year later, they're each looking for their own form of payback. But revenge would be so much easier if love didn't keep getting in the way!

#1869 A MAN LIKE HIM

by Rachel Brimble

Angela Taylor came to Templeton Cove to start over. But when the press photographs her in Chris Forrester's arms during a flood rescue, it's only a matter of time before her peaceful new life takes a frightening turn....

#1870 HER ROAD HOME

by Laura Drake

Samantha Crozier prefers the temporary. Her life is on the road, stopping long enough to renovate a house, then moving on. But her latest place in California is different. And that might have something to do with Nick Pinelli. As tempting as he is, though, she's not sure she can stay....

#1871 SECOND TIME'S THE CHARM

Shelter Valley Stories • by Tara Taylor Quinn

A single father, Jon Swartz does everything he can to make a good life for his son. That's why he's here in Shelter Valley attending college. When he meets Lillie Henderson, Jon begins to hope that this could be his second chance to have the family he's always wanted.

YOU CAN FIND MORE INFORMATION ON UPCOMING HARLEQUIN® TITLES, FREE EXCERPTS AND MORE AT WWW.HARLEQUIN.COM.

HSRCNM0713

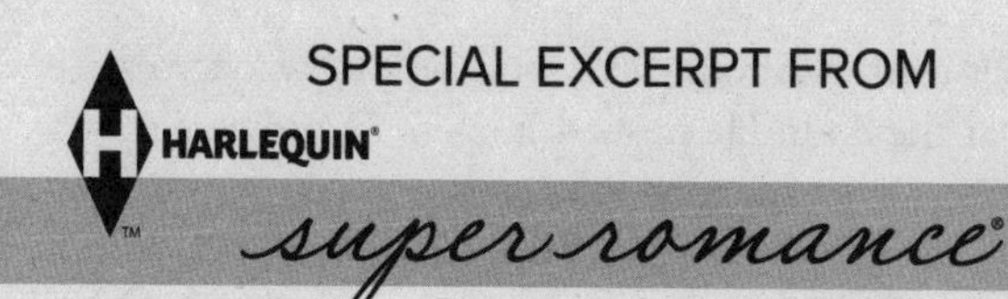

Staying at Joe's

By Kathy Altman

On sale August 6

Allison Kincaid must convince Joe Gallahan to return to the advertising agency he quit a year ago—and to do so, she must overlook their history. But when she tracks him down at the motel he's renovating, he has a few demands of his own.... Read on for an exciting excerpt of STAYING AT JOE'S by Kathy Altman.

Allison tapped her fingers against her upper arm as she turned over his conditions in her mind. No matter how she looked at it, she had zero negotiating room. "So. We're stuck with each other."

"Looks that way." Joe's expression was stony.

"I didn't come prepared to stay, let alone work," she said.

"I can see that." He looked askance at her outfit. "You'll need work boots. I suggest you make a run to the hardware store. Get something sturdy. No hot-pink rubber rain gear."

"I'm assuming you have a separate room for me. One with clean sheets and a working toilet."

"You'll get your own room." In four steps he was across the lobby and at the door. He pushed it open. "Hardware store's on State Street. You can't miss it."

When she made to walk past him, he stopped her with a hand on her arm. His nearness, his scent, the warmth of his fingers and their movement over the silk of her blouse made her shiver. *Damn it.*

Don't look at his mouth, don't look at his mouth, don't look—

Her gaze lowered. His lips formed a smug curve, and for one desperate, self-hating moment she considered running. But she'd be running from the only solution to her problems.

"If I'm going back to the agency and delaying renovations for a month," he said, "then I get two full weeks of labor from you. No complaints, no backtracking, no games. Agreed?"

She shrugged free of his touch. "Don't worry, I'll do my part. Your part is to keep your hands to yourself."

"You might change your mind about that."